After
I'm
Gone

CRA

After I'm Gone

Laura Lippman

ff

FABER & FABER

First published in the United States in 2014
by HarperCollins Publishers
10 East 53rd Street, New York, NY 10022

First published in the United Kingdom in 2014
by Faber and Faber Limited
Bloomsbury House, 74–77 Great Russell Street
London WC1B 3DA

Printed and bound by CPI Group (UK) Ltd, Croydon CR0 4YY

A CIP record for this book
is available from the British Library

ISBN 978–0–571–29966–9

FSC
www.fsc.org
MIX
Paper from
responsible sources
FSC® C101712

10 9 8 7 6 5 4 3 2 1

For David:

To invert Noel Airman's caddish comment to Marjorie Morningstar,
you've had the blame, now take the credit

Where you used to be, there is a hole in the world, which I find myself constantly walking around in the daytime, and falling in at night.

Edna St. Vincent Millay

After
I'm
Gone

Hold
Me

July 4, 1976

They left at dusk, about an hour before the fireworks were scheduled, and by the time they were at the old toll bridge over the Susquehanna, Felix could see glimmers of light through the one tiny window, little celebrations everywhere. He had told Julie to take the old way to Philadelphia, up Route 40. He was being cautious, yet nostalgic, too. He had gotten his start out here, taking action in the bars.

He sneezed. There was hay on the floor and a horse blanket. If they got pulled over, he would arrange the blanket over himself and hope for the best. He had started to do just that when the truck slowed about an hour into the trip, then realized that it was the toll on the bridge across the Susquehanna. Bert and Tubby had said they should put a horse in the trailer because then no one would bother to look inside, but he wasn't going to crouch in a corner for the hundred-mile trip, trying to avoid hooves and shit.

He had said good-bye to Bambi earlier in the day, before she and the girls headed out to the club, where they would stay until well after nightfall. He hadn't told her what was going on, but it was clear she suspected something was up. Bambi was smart, smart enough not to ask questions. When the feds came snooping, she'd be convincing in her ignorance.

The hardest part had been saying good-bye to his unwitting daughters, keeping it casual. They were used to doing things without him; his work had always demanded long and odd hours, then the house arrest had come along, keeping him on a short leash while on appeal. No one would think twice about Felix Brewer not being at the club on the Fourth of July, not this year. The girls had given him perfunctory kisses, so sure of him, and he had not dared to hold them as close and hard as he wanted to. He did give the baby, three-year-old Michelle, an extra-hard squeeze. "Bring me present?" she asked, which startled him for a second. But Michelle got confused, thought she should get a present every time someone left the house, even if she were the one leaving. He pretended to steal her nose, showed her his thumb between his fingers, refused to give it back until she kissed him again. She had a way of cocking her head and looking at him through her lashes. Just like her mother. It slayed him.

As for Bambi, he kissed her as if it were the first time, which had been February 15, 1959, parked in front of her parents' house in the car her parents had given her, a last-ditch bribe to persuade her to return to college. The first kiss was at once passionate and chaste, a kiss that contained everything that was to mark their future together—his aching need for her, the slightest sense of reserve on her part, as if she would always hold back a piece of herself. Their last kiss contained their entire history. A piece of an old song passed through his head, something about flying plates and broken dates, how that was part of being in love. Bambi would never throw a plate. He wouldn't have minded if she had, once or twice.

Bambi wouldn't have liked that Julie was driving him—if

she were ever going to break some crockery, that might be the moment—but Julie was the best person for the job. Her sister actually had horses, or access to them, so it was plausible for the two of them to be hauling a trailer north. Besides, Julie was going to have it hard, once he was gone. Bambi had the girls, friends, family. Julie didn't have anyone except her sister, an odd duck and that was being kind. The puss on that one when she took the wheel. "This better be for forever," she muttered. "You're getting yours," he reminded her. Everybody was getting theirs, one way or another.

"*Forever.*" That was the word that Julie had repeated when he explained things to her last week. It wasn't quite a question, more like a concept she had never heard before. They had been sitting in the little coffee shop, his one legitimate business. The weekly receipts wouldn't have kept his girls in hair ribbons. And his girls actually wore hair ribbons. Bambi dressed them like Towson preppies, all pink and green, taught them how to blow-dry their unruly hair into ponytails. Well, not the baby, but the baby was a dead ringer for Bambi—hair as sleek and dark as a seal's, blue eyes, impossible eyelashes. Linda was the organized one, Rachel was the smart one, and while they were both pretty, Michelle was going to be the beautiful one. They were going to make their mark on the world, each in her own way. And he was going to miss all of it, all of it.

"Forever," Julie repeated, drawing out the syllables, tracing the watery ring left by her Coke. She hardly drank, this one, although she pretended to at night, sipping scotch to keep him company.

"Looks that way. Unless something unexpected happens."

Another long silence. Julie was one of those odd women who was prettier when she didn't smile. Stone-faced, she was a sultry enigma. When she grinned, she still looked like the hick teenager that Tubby scouted in the Rexall four years ago.

"Seven point five percent," she said at last.

"What?"

"The country is two hundred years old this year. They're asking you to give seven point five percent of the country's entire history. That's a lot."

"And you know I don't give points easily."

A quick smile at that. She used to have bad teeth before he fixed them, another reason that she didn't smile much. Julie didn't actually have a great sense of humor, anyway. She was a little literal minded for that, a dollars-and-cents girl, very practical. A practical mistress was a good thing. She had never entertained the thought that he would marry her, for example, although there was that tiny little weirdness last year.

She understood that Bambi was the love of his life. It was Julie, after she started some community college class, who told him F. Scott Fitzgerald said the test of a first-class mind was holding two conflicting ideas in your head without going nuts. Felix was an old hand at that. He loved Bambi, he needed other women. Julie had been with him for a year when Michelle was born, but she didn't act like it was a betrayal, the way some girl-friends might have. Of course he still slept with his wife. She was his wife and very attractive, and he was crazy in love with her. Being with Julie wasn't an expression of dissatisfaction with Bambi. It's just that life was better when you ordered à la carte. There had been girls other than Julie, too, a one-nighter here or there. *Because he could.* Because he needed to. If only Bambi would let go of that piece of her she kept locked away, if only she weren't so goddamn self-sufficient.

Then again, she would need to take care of herself now. He couldn't have left if he wasn't confident that Bambi could manage. Hell, she had always run things. Had run everything except him and the money part. Voluble and flashy as Felix was, he wasn't that removed from the old joke, the one about the kid who came home from Hebrew school and told his mother he had been cast as the husband in the school play. "You go back and ask for a speaking part," the mother instructed. Oh, Felix got to speak. Felix got to talk and talk and talk. But at the end of the day, it was the 110-pound girl with the cerulean eyes who ruled the roost without ever raising her voice.

He was flying from a small airfield outside Philadelphia to Montreal. The Olympics were less than two weeks out, so he figured that was a safe bet, as a starting point. Lots of people were arriving in Montreal right now. From there, he would make his way to Toronto, then to his final location. He had probably overthought it, which was not his usual style. But he had only one shot at this. The main thing was to treat everyone fairly. It was the practical thing to do. Malcontents would rat him out.

He did the math. He had always loved numbers, which had served him well for so long. Fifteen years. Michelle would be eighteen; Rachel, twenty-nine; Linda, almost thirty-one. Bambi would be edging into her fifties. She would probably still be good-looking, too. She was going to age well. Julie—harder to tell. But he wasn't going to last fifteen years with Julie. They had maybe a year or two, tops. She was getting restless. She was ambitious, wanted to move on. Why else would she be taking those college courses? He hoped Bambi wouldn't be too pissed about Julie getting the coffee shop, but it's not like Bambi could run it, and it was the easiest asset to transfer. He would have given Julie the club, too, but she said she didn't want it. Said this was her opportunity to become respectable. He told her respectable was overrated. Besides, if you had enough money, whatever you did was respectable.

Seven point five percent of a nation's history. A young nation to be sure, but still—that was a good way of looking at it. Fifteen percent of his life, *if* he lived to be a hundred. Probably more like 20 percent of his life and not just any 20 percent, but the heart of it, his prime. Even with the legal lottery in place, he was still making good money. Beyond good. The legal lottery seemed to prime the pump in a way he couldn't quite fathom. His old customers played both lotteries now, street and legal. Things had been going so well that he was on the verge of buying Linda and Rachel horses, another one of Bambi's ideas. Good thing he hadn't because those would have been the first things to go. There were going to have to be big changes. He hoped Bambi understood that.

At the airport, he leaned into the car from the passenger side, using his weight to keep the door shut, a barrier between him and Julie. He'd give her a kiss, sure, but not some big *Casablanca* clinch. That would be a betrayal of Bambi.

Yet even their relatively chaste peck left the sister with that same sour expression. "I'm an accessory," she had said when they were loading up. He had wanted to say: *Well, your face looks like leather, so why not be a bag?* He didn't like ugly women. Lord, it had been a relief when Linda had finally grown into the nose he gave her. And even that had needed a little surgical refinement. He made Bambi do it right after his sentence was handed down, and Linda was now the pretty girl she deserved to be.

He handed Julie the briefcase that he had been sitting on throughout the ride and she gave him his valise, which had been riding up in front with her. He didn't want his stuff to smell of manure.

"Don't stop anywhere," he reminded her. "Take it straight to the place, then open it."

"I'll be okay," she said. Meaning, he knew, that she didn't expect or need anything from him. That was part of the reason he had given her as much as he had.

"You'll be with me," he said. "Always."

"Forever," she said, the tiniest wisp of a question mark clinging to it.

On board the small plane, he reached for his new passport and found, nestled next to it, the letters he meant to pack in the briefcase. Damn. What could he do? Julie was on the road, would be for at least two hours. Even if he could call her, would he dare?

Oh well, everyone knew what to do. It was just sad that he would never have the chance to explain himself to Bambi.

He was the only passenger on the plane, an eight-seater. The pilot was a dark-eyed man who didn't want to know him or his story. Smart guy. Felix, who had ceased to be Felix the moment he boarded the plane, looked down at the lights of the city, his real city, which he had left behind years ago. His parents were down there somewhere, as was his sister. They hadn't spoken for almost twenty years. But he didn't want to speak to them. He wanted to talk to Bambi. She'd be back from the club now, and she'd know. She'd know.

Within ten years, a man of means would be able to make a call from his seat on some airlines. Within twenty years, almost everyone would have a cell phone and be able to call anyone, at any time. Within twenty-five years, the Towers would fall and the rules would change and disappearing via Canada, even with access to a private plane, would be much more difficult.

But Felix Brewer was not a man given to imagination, except when it came to ways of getting people to part with their money voluntarily, through a technically criminal enterprise that required neither gun nor force, just a basic understanding of the human weakness for hope and possibility.

Seven point five percent. Talk about the vig. The government had rigged the game until walking away was the only choice. The plane rose in the sky, city lights gave way to vast swaths of dark empty spaces. He was gone.

Kiss Me

March 2, 2012

S andy was at lunch when he got the call that the jury was coming back. They had been out since midday Thursday and it was now early Friday afternoon. Normally, he would be confident with a jury coming in after less than eight hours, but he'd known panels that had been broken down by one adamant member on the grounds of TGIF. These twelve weren't sequestered, but it had been a relatively long trial and they probably yearned to go into the weekend without their civic duty hanging over them. They had been seated last Thursday, then heard four days of testimony. He didn't like the look on number three's face. It didn't help that the defendant appeared so frail. The assistant state's attorney had tried to remind the jury that the crime had taken place thirty years ago, that the defendant had been in his forties then, brawny and vital, his victim seventy-three.

She also was the defendant's mother, for what it was worth. But that could work against them, too. In a group of twelve people, what were the odds that at least two didn't hate their own moms? Sandy had lost his parents young, which haloed their memories, but it was kind of a miracle that he had never lunged at Nabby, the woman who ended up raising him.

Back at the courthouse, Sandy walked through the metal detectors like any civilian, which he now was. No gun, no badge. It bugged him, a little, but only because the absence of those two professional tokens was a reminder that he was on a pension and *still* working at the age of sixty-three. Wasn't supposed to be like that. Working for less than he made when he was full-time, when you calculated the lack of overtime and benefits. Then again, he got to cherry-pick his cases, and he was batting a thousand as a result. Not just in clearances, but in actual convictions. It's not bragging if it's true.

Too bad *his* stats also burnished the reputations of the state's attorney and the chief of police, both of whom he disliked. Big talkers, too slick and glib for his taste.

He took a seat in the back of the courtroom, hunkering down so he could watch the jurors without making actual eye contact. Juror number three looked constipated, bottled up with something. Could be a problem. People didn't usually get that angry over a "guilty." Then again, could be straight-up constipation. The foreman was asked if a verdict had been reached, the piece of paper was passed to the judge, then back to the foreman. Sandy had always wondered at that bit of ceremony, felt it was overdone. If the judge had already read it, why not just have him say it? But, you know, *we the people*. It was their verdict, they got to deliver it. Other than the $20 a day, what else did they get for their service?

"We find Oliver Lansing guilty of murder in the first degree."

Sandy needed a second to absorb it. Even when his hearing was perfect, Sandy had always experienced this weird time shift at the moment the verdict was read, as if he were hung up in time while everyone else went forward. But, no, he wasn't imagining things. *Guilty*. The jury was thanked, and now the process of pro-

cessing began for the defendant, guilty of the first-degree homicide of his own mother. It was a de facto death sentence, given the
guy's age, and Sandy was happy for that. Think of the thirty years
this guy had enjoyed. He was getting off easy, in Sandy's view.

The original detectives on the case had looked at Lansing back
then. Of course they had. Sandy had yet to work a cold case where
the name wasn't in the file. But this guy was so sick that he had
the presence of mind to take his own mother's panties off. Oh, he
knew what he was doing, the sick fuck. No one could imagine
a guy doing that to his mother's body. The other thing was, he
didn't cover up her face, just left her lying on her back in her own
blood, skirt flipped up, naked between the waist and the knee-
high nylons. Who does that? This guy did, and the prosecutor
hadn't been squeamish about hitting that note during testimony
and closing arguments.

But when Sandy decided to work the case, he had focused on
a background detail in the photos from the scene—a cup in the
sink, when all the other dishes were washed and on the drain-
board. It was Sandy's opinion that the victim was not the kind
of woman to leave a cup in the sink for even thirty seconds. Her
house was that neat, based on the photos. Obviously, the cup had
been tested for fingerprints at the time, but it came up clean.

Sandy had studied the cup in the photo, compared it to the
ones on the drying rack. The others were part of a set, dainty
and flower flecked, while this was a mug, solid and sturdy. He'd
bet anything that this mug wasn't chosen because it was at hand,
that someone had reached deep into the shelves for this cup. The
cup wasn't random. It was someone's favorite, the way people get
about mugs. He had the photo blown up, then blown up again, so
he could read the logo. No, it didn't say WORLD'S BEST SON on it or
carry the stamp of the guy's high school, nothing that obvious. It
was a Jiffy Lube mug. But it didn't feel random to Sandy.

So he found the son and talked to him. Lansing didn't confess, but he talked too much, began embroidering the story, then contradicting himself. Sandy reconstructed the time line of that weekend, put the guy in the neighborhood, which didn't jibe with his original statement. He found a relative who was willing to testify that there had been a quarrel about money. Lansing wanted to open a car wash, but his mother wouldn't help him out.

Lansing never did open the car wash, but he sold his mother's house and took an interest in a duckpin lane, only to see it close within five years. Stupid. Not that Sandy sat in judgment of people who made bad financial decisions, but even in the early 1980s, a duckpin lane was a piss-poor investment. There were maybe two left in the city now.

Okay, done. RIP Agnes Lansing. Time to find another case. Given that the city paid him only $35,000 a year, he tried not to start a new file until the last one was done. During the downtime, he continued to organize the files, which had been a mess when he proposed this gig—strewn everywhere, some actually water damaged. He had found some cast-off filing cabinets, wrangled a corner to work in, putting aside cases for future consideration. People left him alone, which was all he could ask for.

He preferred elderly victims. Even if they were shrewish or unkind—and there was evidence that Agnes Lansing was a piece of work, that her son's rage didn't come out of nowhere—they were seldom complicit in their own deaths. Didn't sell drugs or engage in other criminal enterprises. Sandy couldn't help thinking that there was a lack of urgency when the victims were old, that sympathy for them was muted by the fact that they had been playing for small stakes.

He grabbed several folders he had put aside, sat at the empty desk that they let him use. It's not that he was looking for dunkers. If they were dunkers, they would have been solved at some point.

But he wasn't going to assign himself something if he didn't think he had a shot of bringing it home.

A photograph slipped from one of the files. He stooped to pick it up, knees and back protesting. Mary was right. Maintaining the same weight, give or take ten pounds, wasn't enough to be healthy. He needed to exercise, stay flexible. The photograph had landed facedown, and the back said Julie "Juliet Romeo" Saxony. When Sandy flipped it over, he was staring at a stripper, and she was staring back at him. He remembered this one. Except he didn't. Killed by her pimp? Because most of those girls were not much better than whores. No, that wasn't it. But something notable, something notorious.

He opened the file, actually one of several folders, running, he estimated, to almost eight hundred pages. Thick, but not the thickest he had ever seen. Wildly disordered; he had to dig to find the original report, which came out of Harford County. So why was this in the city files? Oh, the body had been discovered in Leakin Park in 2001. *That* was it. Julie Saxony, Felix Brewer's girl. Probably danced under the other name. Brewer disappeared in 1976, and she went missing ten years later. Gossips assumed she had gone to be with Felix. There was a "Missing Person" flyer, circulated by the Havre de Grace Merchants Association, with a black-and-white photocopy of Julie Saxony as she had looked in 1986. Sandy did the math—thirty-three. She wasn't aging well. Too thin, which wasn't good for that kind of heart-shaped face, just left her eyes sunken, her forehead creased. Last seen July 3, 1986, the flyer noted. Reward for any information, etc., etc.

Leakin Park, Baltimore's favorite dumping ground. Although usually not for white ladies from Havre de Grace. How had she ended up there? He reminded himself of his credo: The name is in the file. And the file is eight hundred pages. The obvious thing is to look to Felix Brewer. Maybe Julie knew something. Girlfriends tend to know a lot. More than wives.

Others would call what flashed through Sandy's mind at this moment a hunch, but it wasn't. It was an equation as neat as arithmetic. Or, more accurately, a proof in geometry. You take certain postulates, work toward a theorem. Sandy picked up a phone, dialing—okay, punching buttons, but he liked the word "dialing" and wasn't going to give it up; his English was too hard won to abandon a single word—dialing one of the few reporters he still knew at the *Beacon-Light*, Herman Peters.

"Roberto Sanchez," he said to the voice-mail box. He almost never got a human on the first try anymore. He didn't use his nickname with reporters and got feisty if they tried to appropriate it without his invitation. Sandy was for other cops, friends, although he didn't really have any friends. Mary had called him Roberto most of the time. Peters was okay, though. Might even know the nickname's origins, come to think of it, not that he heard it from Sandy. Whenever anyone asked if he was called Sandy because of his hair, he said: "Yes." And when people asked how a Cuban boy named Sanchez had ended up living in Remington, he said: "Just lucky I guess."

Peters called him back within fifteen minutes. "What's up?" No niceties, no shooting the shit, no parlay. There was no time for that anymore. The reporters, the few who were left at the *Beacon-Light,* were blogging and tweeting, writing more than ever and yet missing more than ever. Reporters used to actually work in the police headquarters, come by, ask about family, make small talk. Sandy had hated that. Then it stopped and he sort of hated that, too. Then Mary died and everything went to shit, and he was glad now that no one ever asked him anything beyond: "What's up?" And didn't really care about the answer, if it came to that.

"You remember Felix Brewer?"

"I know the story," Peters said. "Before my time, but they send me out to his wife's place every now and then, around the anniversary of his disappearance, just to see if she's ready to talk."

"The wife—yeah, what was her name?"

"Bambi Brewer."

"*Bambi?*" Funny, the stripper had the normal name, and the wife had the stripper name.

"That's what everyone calls her. Her given name was something else. I don't remember it off the top of my head."

"She a Baltimore girl?"

"Yeah, Forest Park High School, around the time of Barry Levinson. Married Felix when she was only nineteen. Her family was in the grocery business, success story of sorts, from peddlers to a decent produce wholesaler in one generation."

"Can you find out where she grew up? I mean, what street?"

"Why?"

"A bet with McLarney," he said, referencing one of the few homicide detectives left over from his time. "We got to talking about the case and he thought she was a Pikesville girl, but I said she grew up in the city."

"Bullshit," the reporter said. "You couldn't remember her name five seconds ago, but you were having some random conversation about where she grew up?"

"Look, it's nothing now. If it becomes something, you'll be the first to know."

"Really?"

"Yes." No.

"Does it have something to do with her husband?"

"I don't think so." He didn't think it did and he didn't think it didn't. What was he thinking? He was thinking that Julie Saxony, in her Juliet Romeo incarnation, all but looked him in the eyes and asked him to help her out. And that the older, thinner Julie seemed to need him even more.

He heard a series of clicks on the other end of the line. The world was full of clicks now. At ticket counters, at hotels, all you heard was clicks. At least this one yielded something useful. "She grew up on Talbot Road in Windsor Hills. It would have been nice then, I think. Even into the '60s."

"I've heard." Sandy had spent the 1960s in Remington and didn't think it was possible to go far enough back in time to say Remington was ever nice. Maybe around the time the *Ark* and the *Dove* made land in 1634.

"That meaningful? The address. Did I settle your *bet?*"

"Naw. I thought she was from Butchers Hill. Nobody wins."

"Something going on in Butchers Hill?"

"Always. Gotta go."

He checked the city map, although he already knew what he was going to find. He knew before he picked up the phone. That's how good he was at his job. Talbot Road snaked through Windsor Hills on the southern edge of the neighborhood. It sat on a bluff, high above a deep ravine and Gwynns Falls—and not even a mile from the section of Leakin Park where Julie Saxony's body had been discovered.

February 14, 1959

The dance was an impulse, her date even more so, a barely acceptable young man, a young man who would not have been acceptable a year ago, or even six months ago. For one thing, he was younger than she was, a senior in high school. A very desirable senior, perhaps the most desirable boy in Forest Park High School's Class of '59, but she was the Class of '58. Barry Weinstein was a big wheel in his fraternity, with broad shoulders and a swoop of blond hair that made him look like a Jewish Troy Donahue. But he was a high school senior whereas she was a college freshman.

Or supposed to be. Had been, up until December, and was still pretending to be one. But time was running out. She either had to return to school in the fall or—or what? What else could she do to avoid being disgraced? Thank God no one else from Forest Park had gone to Bryn Mawr. But there was a boy from the Class of '57 at Haverford. So far, she had been able to play off her absence from school as a lark, another thrilling installment in the madcap life of crazy, impulsive Bambi Gottschalk. *Oh, darlings, it was amazing,* she had said to her best friends over the winter break, as they gathered around her bed in her girlhood room, solemn and kind and yet predatory, waiting for her to tumble from the high perch she had occupied her entire life.

The fever—the fever masked everything. I could have died.

But wasn't there pain? Didn't you think to go to the infirmary?

No, no pain at all. That's why I didn't understand what was happening.

No pain, but when my cousin—

I am a medical oddity, dears. It will probably end up in Ripley's Believe It or Not. *I'm surprised they ever let me go. They wanted to make a study of me. As it is, I have to take the entire semester off, worse luck.*

But what would she tell people in the fall? That problem was very much on her mind when she'd run into Barry two weeks ago at Hutzler's downtown. Bambi had been studying silk scarves on the counter as if they were runes that contained her future. Barry, whom she would have cheerfully snubbed a year ago, asked her for help in choosing a gift for his mother. She applied herself to the task with the utmost seriousness. Within an hour, they were eating shrimp salad on cheese bread in the tearoom where Bambi had let it drop that she was just crazy about the Orioles, not that she would *even consider* going to a high school dance, not even one as swanky as the Sigmas' Winter Formal. She was pretty sure Barry already had a date. But he wasn't going steady, which made him fair game, and if he broke a date with some other girl to ask Bambi out—that was on his conscience. And painful for the other girl, not that Bambi had any firsthand experience in being stood up. She supposed it hurt one's pride. Still, some high school girl's pride was of no importance to her. A deadline was fast approaching, and her life was like some tedious board game, Uncle Wiggily or Candy Land. She couldn't linger at the start and hope to rocket to the end in one lucky move. She would have to take small incremental steps, find a way of getting herself back into circulation. Barry was just the first card drawn in a long game.

The problem was, Barry didn't know his place. He was already dropping hints about the senior prom. *The senior prom!* She wanted to weep at the idea, the sheer embarrassment of someone even thinking she could consider such a thing. The Sigma dance was acceptable. Barely. It was exclusive, held in the Lord Baltimore Hotel, with all the trappings. But the prom a year after graduating—she would never live it down. That would be like drawing a card that sent her all the way back to start.

"Do you like the orchid?" Barry asked. "I checked with your mother about the color of your dress because I wanted you to be surprised. I chose a wrist corsage because I hoped you would wear a strapless gown. I remember you at last year's dance."

Bambi's dress, which wasn't strapless but had a very sheer net over the shoulders, appeared white from a distance, although it had a shimmering violet cast up close. The color was a bold choice for a winter dance and her mother had, for the first time ever, argued about the price, the impracticality of it. She thought Bambi should have worn one of the formals she had taken to college last fall. "I've worn them all," Bambi said. "Not in Baltimore," her mother countered. Still, Bambi got her way, as usual.

"It's very nice," said Bambi of Barry's corsage. She had received enough orchids in her life to open her own greenhouse and actually preferred simpler flowers—sweetheart roses, peonies. But orchids were the gold standard, and she would be insulted if a boy had brought her anything less. She realized that it was strange to hide one's desire for something only because the rest of the world felt differently, but she didn't know another way to be. In high school English, the teacher had made a big deal out of *Hamlet*, "To thine own self be true," but Bambi had believed that was an attempt to make the odd kids feel better about themselves. Everyone cared what others thought, even those who were defiantly different. They cared more than anyone.

The trick, Bambi decided, was to care about things while making others care more.

Barry ran his hand up and down her bare arm, ostensibly admiring the flower he had selected. "Now that I think about it, it's the color of your eyes."

"The whites? Yes, I suppose so." Said with a gentle humor, hoping he would drop the subject and avert the faux pas he was about to make.

But, of course, he wouldn't. "The purplish cast of the flower, I mean. Brings out the violet in your eyes. Like Elizabeth Taylor's."

It was not the first time the comparison had been made. It probably would not be the last. Bambi had found it thrilling when she was younger. Then frustrating, because who could win against Elizabeth Taylor? Now, she considered it merely boring. Up until five months ago, she used to contradict the boys who sought to flatter her this way. "My eyes," she would say with flirtatious sternness, as if the fact in dispute were of great importance, "are *cerulean*." This wasn't true at all—cobalt, perhaps, or even ultramarine. But men seldom contradicted Bambi. She was beginning to find this boring, too. She had been dating since she was fourteen. The year she turned fifteen, the book *Marjorie Morningstar* had been published and that was another comparison through which she had suffered. "Oh, it's about you," said her mother's friends. (Her mother, perhaps deducing that this would make her Mama Morningstar, an overweight peasant with a sly wit, was silent on the matter. Ida Gottschalk was thin and quite chic.) Bambi always replied: "No, it's not. I don't want to be an actress and I can't wait to get married and move to the suburbs and have a huge family."

Everyone laughed, but she was telling the truth. The truth

was handy that way sometimes, the best cover for what one really wanted. The problem was, that truth was now *too* true to work: It had been a wonderful gambit when she was seventeen, then eighteen, then heading off to Bryn Mawr. Now she was nineteen, and while the official story was that she was taking a semester off because of a mysterious malady that might have been an inflamed appendix or walking pneumonia or mononucleosis or possibly all three, that story was going to be exposed eventually. So here she was, on a date that was just barely acceptable.

Come to think of it, the same thing happened to Marjorie in the book. She went to a dance with a too-young boy and found only humiliation.

Still, Bambi couldn't afford to coast. She snapped to, turned the full force of her not-really-cerulean eyes on her date. "I'm having a marvelous time, Barry." She used to have marvelous times and maybe she would again. Maybe it was only a matter of trying.

Then again, they had said the same thing about college. All she had to do was *try*.

"Some very smart girls simply aren't ready for college emotionally," the dean had told her parents. The school was apologetic, almost embarrassed, because they had not anticipated a student such as Bambi, who went to every class, took notes, earned passing grades on her midterms—then disappeared finals week, forging an overnight permission slip and never returning. By the time it was apparent what was going on, Bambi had been at the Ritz in Philadelphia for three days, having persuaded the people at the front desk to open an account that would be paid, she said, by her father when he arrived.

And he did, and it was, because what could Sy Gottschalk do under the circumstances with his only, beloved, spoiled-to-death daughter. He gathered her and her luggage—all of it, three pieces and a steamer trunk, a high school graduation gift—and drove her home while she sat in a petulant silence, as if he were in the wrong. She never did tell her parents, or anyone, why she had fled Bryn Mawr—and done so in such a way that she risked expulsion. She was still trying to figure that out herself. Being accepted at the school had been thrilling, another crown in a high school life that had included many such honors. She had basked all spring in her classmates' slightly stunned admiration, for Bambi had been clever about hiding her good grades and ambition. Bryn Mawr was like being homecoming queen or a Sigma Sweetheart. All she really wanted to do was brandish her acceptance letter, then put it in a frame, another triumph achieved.

The problem was that college demanded you do more than just show up and wave.

And then what? She didn't know. She didn't want to work, although her mother had begun to make ominous noises about learning basic bookkeeping, in order to help with the family business. She was too short to model except at department-store teas, which didn't pay. There was only one thing to do, only one thing she really wanted to do. She wanted to marry and have children, as soon as possible. She should have let the Bryn Mawr acceptance be enough, gone to the University of Maryland. She would have been engaged by the Christmas break, either to a desirable senior or maybe a junior. Then she could have withdrawn from school and started planning her wedding and her life beyond it. A life with a house full of children, a house that would be the opposite of the one in which she had grown up.

Instead, she had risked her momentum, her aura of perfection. No one really believed that she had withdrawn from the semester because she had walking pneumonia. Or an inflamed appendix or mononucleosis. She had blown all the hard-won capital of her youth in one single bet. It reminded her of her parents' struggles after they expanded and opened a chain of grocery stores, assuming it was the logical move after their success in wholesale produce. They had overextended themselves and been forced to scale back. They had taken a second mortgage on the house, which her parents found immensely shameful. Ultimately, they had surrendered their dreams of genteel shops and shored up the wholesale side, servicing the very ghetto stores they had been trying to escape. But they had survived and even prospered. So Bambi knew one could recover from missteps. She just didn't particularly want to expend the energy. Recouping one's losses took time and patience, not her strong suits. She had been on a very long winning streak—nineteen years, her entire life. She could not bear to be on a losing streak for even nineteen minutes.

Barry brought her punch, inevitably doctored. The too-sweet punch and the cheap alcohol did not bring out the best in each other. It was like eating a flaming wad of cotton candy.

"Delicious," she said.

He smiled, besotted. He probably thought she was fast, being older and all. Well, he was in for a surprise. If she wanted to go that route, she would have engineered a chance meeting with her high school boyfriend, Roger. He was two years older than she was and had developed a very appealing confidence since transferring to the University of Baltimore. He also was dating her friend Irene, one of the girls who had gathered at Bambi's bedside to hear the horrific story of how she almost died from misdiagnosed pneumonia/inflamed appendix/mononucleosis. It would have been tempting to see if she could get him back, but then she would have him back. And she didn't want to return to her sixteen-year-old self, which is what she would be with Roger. Even then, Roger had been too fast for her, pushing her hard to do things she was not ready to do. He was probably faster now. She had asked Irene point-blank if they were doing it and Irene had—"simpered," that was the word. Simpered. So they were. That was dangerous. Not because Bambi was prudish, but because it limited one's options. You really shouldn't have sex unless you were sure this was the right man because you should

marry the first man with whom you had sex. Before marriage
was okay, but only if he was *the* one. It wasn't morality, it was
simply smart. Your first would be your last. Bambi didn't ponder
the why of this, and she certainly didn't want her husband to be
a virgin. Nor did she expend much time thinking about how her
future husband might have gained his sexual experience. Presumably with other girls, not nice girls, why should she care?
Bambi was a prize, and part of the prize was her virginity, much
in the same way new cars were prized for their unblemished
whitewalls and perfect upholstery. Yet their value dropped the
moment they were driven off the lot.

Barry glanced at the door, which gave her a chance to put
down her drink. They would dance soon and she could "forget"
the cup. There was a potted plant nearby, but that was too crude,
pouring out the contents, and he might get her another one. She
would just tuck it on the windowsill—

"Crashers," he said. "They've got some nerve."

There were three men in the door. One was handsome in a
very conventional way, with broad shoulders and lots of dark hair,
medium height. A boy from the neighborhood, Bert Gelman, a
senior, but not a Sigma. One was enormous, a sphere of a man,
and jolly-looking, with pink cheeks and a sheen of sweat despite
the cold night.

The third was on the short side, with very dark skin, a big-
gish nose, and so much energy it seemed to be coming off him
in waves. Older. Older than the kids at the dance, older than his
companions. She put him at twenty-four, twenty-five. His gaze
seemed to say, *Kid stuff,* although the Sigma dance was very sophisticated, as nice as the country club dances her parents attended.

Then the crasher's eyes caught Bambi's, and any flicker of
amused condescension faded. He walked straight toward her as
if—as if she were a landmark, something famous, something he

had been waiting to see all his life. She was the Eiffel Tower, the Empire State Building, the Grand Canyon.

"Felix Brewer," he said. "And this is Bert Gelman and Tubby Schroeder."

"Which is which?" she asked, and the three laughed. They probably would have laughed at anything she said, though.

"Actually, I know Bert," she said, putting out her hand. "You were a year behind me at Forest Park."

"This is a private dance," Barry said.

"Yeah, I'd keep it private, too, a limp affair like this," said the man who had introduced himself as Felix. *Felix the cat,* Bambi thought, but, no, he wasn't catlike. Nor doglike. He was—what was smart and shrewd, a little dangerous, but not a predator? A fox? But a fox would eat chickens, given the chance.

"Limp affair? Do you see who's on the bandstand?"

"Yeah, not bad, but couldn't you get someone like Fats Domino? He's great. We saw him last week on Pennsylvania Avenue."

"You go to Pennsylvania Avenue?" Bambi asked.

"Of course I do. All the best music is there. You scared of Negroes?"

"I'm not scared of anything," Bambi said. "And the Orioles are Negroes, in case you haven't noticed."

Bert smiled at Bambi. Lord, this was the problem with dating Barry; now every high school senior thought her fair game. The age of the fat one was impossible to tell, but he was at least twenty or twenty-one. They seemed an unlikely trio, mismatched in every way.

Felix could read her mind. "This"—he jerked a thumb at Bert—"is my lawyer's son, although I guess he'll be my lawyer one day. And this"—thumb heading the other way, toward the round one—"is my bail bondsman."

She laughed her best laugh, a delighted trill.

"No, seriously, he's a bail bondsman. Not that anyone's had to set bail on me yet, but you never know. So he's not *my* bail bonds-man, I guess, but he is one."

"Someone has to be," Tubby said cheerfully.

"I'm going to have to ask you to leave," Barry said.

"Young man, have you served your country?"

"What?"

"Have you served? I mean, obviously you haven't been over there, but what's keeping you from signing up?"

"I'm not yet eighteen," Barry said. "I'm going to Penn next year."

"Well, I went to war when I was seventeen. But I guess Penn is something, yes, it is. Your parents must be very proud."

Barry now appeared to be about six years old in Bambi's eyes. Which, she realized, was Felix's intent.

"Look, I must ask you—"

"Oh, as long as you're *asking*. And as long as you must. But tell me something, couldn't a serviceman, one who fought to keep this country safe, who skipped college and all it had to offer—would it be too much to let me have one dance with the young lady here? In recognition of my patriotism?"

"Look, this isn't a dance hall; you don't just come in here and ask to dance with girls."

"Oh, Barry," Bambi said. "What's the harm?"

The Orioles began a new set. "'Hold Me,'" Felix said, and she thought it was a request. Then he added: "They had a hit with this in 1953. They're good. For local boys." He led her onto the dance floor, not even bothering to wait for her date's permission. He was not a smooth dancer, but he was a happy one, full of energy. They did not speak at all. He held her gaze, testing her. They were almost at eye level. She calculated the height of her heels, put him at maybe five-seven. She didn't care. He sang along with the song—not in her ear, he wasn't that obvious. He just seemed to like the song.

" 'The last you'll know.' " He tried to harmonize on that line, but fell a little short.

"That's not right," she said. "It's *find*. To rhyme with *mind*."

"I'm the last you'll know," he said, as if she hadn't spoken.

She tried to tell herself that the light-headedness she was feeling was just the inevitable consequence of wearing a merry widow, which constricted her breathing. That would explain the light film of sweat—on Bambi, who never sweated. She concentrated on holding his gaze. It felt shameful, as if she were necking in front of an audience, as if everyone in the ballroom knew what she was feeling.

"What do you do?" she asked, realizing the song was coming to an end.

"Don't worry," he said. "I do very well. I'll be able to take good care of you."

"I didn't mean—"

"Oh, yes, you did. Look, your date, Little Lord Fauntleroy, is going to make a fuss." Barry had gathered a group of Sigmas and they did look as if they were getting ready to bum-rush Felix. "I'm going to go. I'll find you."

"You don't even know my name."

"That just makes it more interesting. Coke bet—I'll find you within twenty-four hours. We'll have a date tomorrow night, a proper one. I'll come to your house and meet your parents and I will take you out for dinner. If I can't do that, I'll owe you a Coke."

"But if you can't do that, how will I find you to collect?"

"Don't worry about it."

She didn't. The next day, she told her parents that a new boy was coming to call. She said *boy* out of habit. The whole point of Felix Brewer was that he was a man. She put on a dress of polished blue cotton and waited, something she had never done for any date. He arrived at 6:00 P.M. with flowers for her mother and a firm handshake for her father. They seemed taken aback, as help-less in the tug of his charm as Bambi had been.

On the fieldstone path outside her home, Felix glanced back at the house where she had grown up, the house where she had been so lonely. For all her social success, Bambi had no real friends. And siblings weren't to be. She had been her parents' mir-acle baby, born quite late after multiple miscarriages.

"It's nice," he said. "I like this style. Understated. A man's home is his castle, but it shouldn't look like a castle. I want some-thing classy and elegant. But not grand. I want a house where a kid can spill something and it won't be the end of the world. A living room where people live. What do you want, Bambi?"

She didn't dare say what she wanted just then. She wasn't that far gone. But she was close.

"I don't care, really. More than one kid. Not that I'm in a rush."

He gave her a look, as if to say: *Who are you kidding?* He knew her. He *knew* her. How was that possible?

But all he said was: "That dress matches your eyes. I'm not sure what you'd call that color. Cobalt? Cerulean? Yeah, cerulean."

They were married ten months later.

March 5, 2012

S andy stood on Talbot Road, trying to decide where best to trespass. He could knock on any door, ask permission to cut through someone's backyard. But then he would have to go through the blah, blah, blah about not being a detective, just a consultant. He'd rather trespass, assuming he could be sure there wasn't a dog lurking.

He tried a side gate. Unlocked. He wouldn't leave his gate unlocked in this neighborhood, not the way it was now. He was humming to himself, he realized, that corny song from *The Sound of Music,* the one about starting at the very beginning. Sandy and Mary had seen that movie on their first date, a date made more memorable by the fact that they left a world of balmy-for-January sunshine and emerged into a raging blizzard. They had taken a bus downtown—he didn't own a car and Nabby sure as hell wasn't going to let him borrow hers—and Mary wasn't dressed to wait outside, much less walk so much as a block. He told her to stand under the marquee, then trudged around the corner and hot-wired a car, telling Mary that he had borrowed it from a friend who lived near the Mayfair. He drove her home, a five-mile journey of slip-and-slides that took an hour. He literally carried her into her parents' house. He then drove the car back to the space he had left, which he had to clear off by hand. It was a snow emergency route, but that worked out well. The car would be towed and the owner could argue with the city impoundment people over who was responsible for the damaged ignition. He then walked home. His shoes fell apart about a mile from the house and Nabby gave him hell, but it was worth it. He was seventeen years old, and he had met the love of his life. Risked everything for her, truth be told. If he had been pulled over in that car, it wouldn't have been juvie, not this time around. Sandy often looked back in wonder at that afternoon, how his entire life turned on that day. He didn't know it, but he was poised, as if on a tightrope, and things were either going to go very wrong or very right, no in-between.

It had never occurred to him that he might come crashing to earth forty-four years later. When destiny wants to fuck with you, it can afford to be patient. Destiny has all the time in the world.

Anyway, it sounded simple, starting at the beginning, but it was often a challenge in a cold case to know just where the beginning was. First, Sandy had to read the file in its entirety, try to put it in some semblance of order. This one was really two files—the original missing person case from Havre de Grace, then the official homicide case from 2001. It was a jumble of witness statements and reports. He couldn't fault anyone on work ethic. They talked to almost too many people—every single employee at the bed-and-breakfast where Julie Saxony had worked, a couple of associates from her time at the Variety, at least one relative. Friends of Felix—his lawyer, his bail bondsman. Whatever the general public thought was going on, the cops pegged her as a homicide pretty early. Her credit cards had never been used again after July 3, 1986, she hadn't pulled a significant amount of money out of checking or savings—$200 on July 2, then another $200 on

July 3. She had told an employee that she was going to Saks, but her car was found at a Giant Foods on Reisterstown, maybe five miles away. She could have been grabbed and made to make that second withdrawal, but there was nothing on the ATM tape to support that.

And then there was the place her body was found all those years later, which had to be a good ten, fifteen miles from her car. Not buried or concealed in any particular way, just left out to rot. It killed civilians to hear that. People in urban areas couldn't believe how long a body could go undetected, but it happened all the time. Leakin Park was twelve hundred acres, much of it heavily wooded, and it wasn't legal to hunt there, so the odds of people walking through the rough, overgrown areas was pretty remote. The city had created a trail that, theoretically, could be followed all the way into the heart of downtown if one was willing to hike or bike through some sketchy areas, but that was on the other side of a stream from where the body was discovered. Julie's remains might not have been found at all if it weren't for a rambunctious dog that led a young couple on a chase.

Sandy couldn't help wondering about *them,* incidental as they were to the story. One of the things he loved about the show *Law & Order*—and he loved almost everything about it, particularly the fakeness—were the discoveries that started every episode. New York City had, in real life, maybe eight hundred homicides a year, which was nothing per capita. Baltimore's rate had fallen back from the almost one-a-day that he had seen in his glory days, but it was still one of the highest in the country. Yet, if you watched *Law & Order*, and he had done quite a bit of that in the four long months that it took Mary to die, it seemed as if everyone in the city must have tripped over a body here and there. He thought those people deserved a show of their own. He wanted to write the producer a letter and suggest that as a spin-off. *Law & Order: The Discoverers.* There was probably a better title, but that was the drift. A young couple out on a date. Was it a first date? Which one owned the dog? Was the dog running away, or was it off-leash in that sneaky way people used so they could avoid cleaning up? (Sandy lived near a small park and he had taken to eye-fucking anyone who looked like they might not clean up after a dog.) Finding a dead body on a date seemed a pretty bad omen, but he and Mary had hit a deer on their second one, and that had turned out great. The date, if not Mary's parents' car.

He started to head down the hill. Damn. It was muddier than he had anticipated, capable of seriously screwing up a man's loafers. He retreated to his car to see if he had anything he could use. Nada, zip, nothing.

The houses here were big and rambling, although most had been cut up for apartments. As the reporter had said, the neighborhood had been something once. The Gottschalk home, per the property tax records, stayed in her family until 1977, when it was sold for $19,000, not much more than they had paid for it in 1947. Sandy wasn't clear if there had been a death or if her parents had downsized. He might need to run them through vital stats at some point. They weren't part of the file, and not even Bambi had been interviewed after Julie's body was discovered.

Yet Julie had ended up a few hundred yards from here, near the house where Bernadette "Bambi" Gottschalk had lived until her marriage on December 31, 1959. It was a date Sandy knew well, for his own reasons. Sandy had arrived in Baltimore a year later, almost to the day. People talk about having nothing but the clothes on their backs, but for Sandy that had been literal. It was part of the reason that he used to be fastidious about his clothes, even by the standards of a murder police, which was a pretty high standard. He looked at his shining loafers. They were old, but extremely well cared for, exhibit A in the wisdom of buying quality. He knew mud wouldn't destroy them, but it seemed unfair to subject such good shoes to a muddy hillside. He looked around.

The sidewalks were littered with newspapers in plastic wrappers, the weekly freebie thrown by the increasingly desperate *Beacon-Light*. He liberated two of the papers and put the bags on his feet, knowing it would wreak havoc with his traction and he might fall on the steep hillside, getting mud on a lot more than his shoes. But it was easier to brush dirt from a suit, if you did it right.

He worked his way down in a zigzag pattern, using branches to keep himself steady. He was in okay shape for a man of his age, although he had a paunch he couldn't seem to shrink. The paunch was noticeable because he was, had always been, a string bean. The belly had come out of nowhere when Mary was sick. It was as if he had his own tumor growing inside him. "Oh, look at you, jealous as ever," Mary teased. "It was just like when I was pregnant with Bobby Junior and you had all the cravings." For every pound Mary lost during her illness, he gained one. It was like he assumed he could give the weight back to her when she got better. Only she never got better, and he was stuck with the weight.

He reached the bottom of the hill without falling, no small thing. Glancing back at the bluff, he realized that returning to his car would be even tougher. But he probably could walk alongside the stream and come out on Windsor Mill Road, get back to his car that way. His time was unmonitored now, except by him. Every night, he wrote down his hours as if he were still on the clock, burning a little at the thought of the overtime he wouldn't be paid, no matter how long he worked.

It wouldn't have been easy, getting a body here in 1986. Four-wheel drives were not as common then. People would have noticed a truck or a Jeep—the people on the bluff above would have heard it; others would have seen the lights, assuming it came in at dark. And if the body had been carried down from Talbot Road—that would have been tough, too. Yet the juxtaposition of Bambi's childhood home and the body of her husband's onetime

girlfriend—hard to chalk that up to coincidence, even in a dumping ground as popular as Leakin Park.

The dog had found little more than bones. Sandy knew that
from the file, the autopsy. Bones, but the cause of death, a bullet
to the head, had been easy to pinpoint. No casing, though. Nothing but a purse, a purse that looked like leather, but wasn't, so it
had held up to the elements. Inside there was a billfold with $385,
her ID, an earring without a mate, a lipstick. Normal lady stuff.

He walked north. At least, he thought it was north. He wasn't
a nature boy, although a lot of people projected that on him,
thought he had arrived here on a raft, paddling himself across the
Keys. He could understand how kids, his term for everyone under
thirty, confused his arrival with the Mariel boat lift, which they
knew from *Scarface,* the Pacino version. But Sandy had no excuse
for people his age, who should know a little history, for Christ's
sake. Yet it was easier, always, to let people think whatever they
wanted to think. He preferred being lumped in with *Scarface* to
the inevitable questions that followed when people heard where
he was from. *You're Cuban? With that hair and those eyes? Is that why
they call you Sandy, because of the hair?*

His hair was blond, for Christ's sake. Who calls a blond Sandy?

He walked for what felt like forever—going slowly, because
someone weighed down with a body wouldn't make good time—
but it was only ten minutes or so by his watch when he found
himself opposite a group of white buildings. Another abandoned
Baltimore mill, this one renovated for business space. Okay, that
was a possible lead. When had it been redone? Did anyone have
offices here in 1986? He took out his pad, wrote a note to cross-
check the history of the site. Still, it was a long way to carry a
body, and it would have meant fording the stream. Man, someone really went to a lot of trouble to make sure that Julie Saxony
wouldn't be found. And *that* was probably the takeaway, more so
than the proximity to the childhood home of Bambi Gottschalk.

Julie wasn't supposed to be found. Definitely not right away, maybe never. Why?

Because the longer she went without being discovered, the more convinced people became that she had gone to join Felix, wherever he was.

People, he thought. People, not cops. No cop, looking at those dormant credit cards, the lack of bank activity in the weeks before she disappeared, would have assumed she was a runaway. He had read the massive file twice and he would have to read it several more times before he could keep it all in his head, but one detail stuck out now: She had her car serviced on July 1. Who has her car serviced on July 1 if she's running away on July 3? Maybe if she had been planning to take the car, part of the way. But her car made it only as far as Pikesville.

He worked his way back to his car, deciding to take the hill, after all. Harder going up a muddy hill, and he did slip once, dropping to one knee. But the mud would dry and brush off. The key was to be patient enough to let it dry, not to worry it and rub it into the fabric. Lift the dirt with a straight edge, let dry, then scrape.

Mary had taught him that.

September 15, 1960

I t's not going to fit in the nursery, not with all the other stuff you have in there."

Ida Gottschalk, hands on hips, had squared off against an almost life-size baby hippo that was standing in the middle of the living room, an awkward guest who didn't realize the party was over. Ida had taken against this hippo, which was really very cute, from the moment it was unwrapped. Bambi assumed that her mother had seen the yellow tag in its ear, Steiff, and deduced it was German made. Her mother hated all things German.

Bambi just hoped her mother never found out that the hippo cost $200, which would be far more damning in her eyes. *Two hundred dollars.* They didn't pay that much in rent. Assuming they paid the rent every month, and Bambi was beginning to suspect that Felix was casual about what he considered the small stuff, which included, alas, their household bills. At least, she hoped that unpaid bills were the source of the strange phone calls that made talky Felix become monosyllabic. "Yes." "No." "Soon." The sales slip for the hippo had been in the bottom of the elaborately wrapped gift box and Bambi had quickly crumpled it, appalled that a clerk from Hutzler's could be so inattentive that she would forget to remove it.

Come to think of it, maybe it wasn't a clerk who had left the slip in the box. Maybe Bambi was meant to see how much Felix had spent. And then what? Was Bambi supposed to brag about it in a mock-exasperated way? *Oh, that crazy doting dad.* Or had Felix assumed someone else would open the gift and that the gossip about his extravagance would spread among Bambi's friends and relatives?

"It's not going to fit into *this* nursery," Bambi told her mother. "But we won't be here forever. Felix is looking for a house."

"You'll be here at least nine more months," her mother said, tying an apron over her dress, which was very stylish, a little too fancy for a party such as this. Bambi's mother, plain and bone thin, had always bought the best she could afford when it came to clothes. "You signed a year's lease in June."

"Leases can be broken."

Her mother rolled her eyes at this sacrilege. Bambi knew what she was thinking: *A lease can be broken at a cost, but what kind of idiot would take on such an unnecessary cost? My son-in-law, the show-off, that's who.*

Ida was proving to be the one woman, the one *person*, Felix could not charm. She may have been nonplussed upon meeting him, but she didn't stay that way long. "I'm not buying what he's selling," Ida liked to say. She said it a lot. She went about saying it at the wedding reception, where everyone thought she was being droll. Even Felix thought so. Only Bambi and perhaps her father understood the stark literalism of her mother's statement. In Ida's view, Felix was after the Gottschalk fortune, a laughable concept. The Gottschalk "fortune" was about as substantial as the add-a-bead necklace that Linda had been given by her father the day she was born. Felix had no interest in his in-laws' wholesale greengrocer. He wasn't even particularly interested in *them,* although he complimented his in-laws lavishly, behaving like a guest in their home even while living there for the first five months of his marriage to Bambi.

Besides, Felix could never keep the hours required by a wholesaler's life. He was nocturnal. And he wanted to be *rich*-rich, as he called it, *no-doubt-about-it rich. Stinking rich. Screw-the-world rich.* How that goal meshed with ignoring the little bills of day-to-day life was a puzzlement to Bambi, but she didn't want to be a dreary nag like her mother, so she let it go.

Felix had first spoken of his desire to be wealthy on their Bermuda honeymoon. They stayed in a pretty pink hotel on a pink sand beach, not that they saw much of the ocean, for they enjoyed the novelty of being in a bed together all night and all morning and into the afternoon, finally free of the fear of discovery that had marked their premarital adventures, as Bambi thought of them. Those had been limited to her car and, just once, the basement rec room in the house on Talbot Road, her parents' heavy tread going back and forth, back and forth in the rooms above them. Bambi had been so nervous that she kept on even more clothes than she had in the car, which they had parked behind the old mansion on the Crimea estate in Leakin Park. Yet the rec room was the first time she had a genuine orgasm, and she wondered if the drama, the suspense, was essential to that experience.

She was very happy to be proven wrong on her honeymoon. It turned out there were quite a lot of ways to have orgasms and Felix wanted to teach her all of them.

"We're going to be rich," Felix told her, promised her. "Rich-rich. But we're not going to play by the rules. The game is rigged, so I'm making my own game. It's the only way to get out in front. But I need you to understand what that means. Late nights, long hours. Mine is a nighttime business."

"What about the risk?" she murmured into the pillow. He was rubbing her back, running his fingers through her hair.

"Virtually none. Oh, I'll get popped now and then, but they'll never make it stick. You understand what I'm saying, Bambi?" He lay down next to her, turning her head so they were eye to eye. "Things will happen. There will be moments—people will gossip. But we'll be so respectable—so *rich*—that no one will be able to afford to look down on us. We're gonna be benefactors. To the synagogue, to the schools our children attend. We'll be envied, which can be dangerous, but we'll also be admired and liked. You're beautiful and I'm smart."

"I'm smart, too," Bambi said, thinking of Bryn Mawr, her failure there, a story she had withheld from Felix. Pretty much the only thing she had withheld from Felix so far. She was shocked at herself, going all the way before they were engaged. But she knew he would propose, in a grand fashion, and he did—the Surrey Inn, the ring winking at her from a raw oyster in the first course, so she wouldn't be on pins and needles all night. She also knew he would make her first time nice. And now it was getting *better*. No one had told her that. The veiled conversation with her mother— and there had been only one—had led her to believe that sex was something one got used to, like shots or other unpleasant but necessary things. Why hadn't someone told her that it was good and got better? Obviously, her mother wasn't going to share such information, but what about Irene? Bambi was sure Irene had done it, maybe with more than one boy. Irene had been maid of honor at Bambi's wedding and then had her own big wedding in late January. No one got married in late January. Why not wait until Valentine's Day? Bambi, who had noticed the way the waist of Irene's bridesmaid dress strained despite the fitting in early December, was pretty sure she knew why Irene's wedding had been scheduled for January.

"You're smart, too," Felix assured her. "You were smart enough to fall in love with me at first sight."

"Did not." She would never admit that.

"Well, I did, so I guess I'm the smarter of the two of us."

"Which synagogue are we going to join?"

"Beth Tfiloh."

"You want to attend an Orthodox shul?" That came as a surprise. Although Bambi had been raised in an Orthodox home and had married in an Orthodox temple, Felix had seemed indifferent to religion. She knew nothing of his family. Whenever she pressed him, he changed the subject, said they were gone. She worried he might have lost them in the Holocaust, but she didn't know how to have that conversation.

"That's the best one, the one with all those old Germans, the ones who act like they're goys. Behind closed doors, I'm going to eat bacon and I don't care if you mix up the plates. But in every part of our life that's not my business, we gotta be respectable. Best synagogue, best country club, best schools. Behind closed doors, we do things our way."

Then, much to her delighted shock, he yanked her up to all fours and showed her something else that a man and a woman could do behind closed doors. She was surprised at how much she liked it, given how unromantic the position was, like two dogs going at it. But she liked almost everything Felix did. When he was home, which wasn't as often as she would have preferred, it turned out. Late nights, he had said. Long hours. Those words had been meaningless in a soft bed in a pink hotel. By the time Linda was born on September 1, they were all too real. The doctor said she could have sex again in two weeks, but Felix was never around. Football season was under way, he explained.

They had honored the Jewish tradition of not having a baby shower or decorating the nursery until after the baby was born, although Felix thought it a silly superstition. He had painted the room shell pink. (Without the landlord's permission, and Ida was mournful about the cost of that as well. "You'll never get the damage deposit back," she said.) The nursery suite was lavish, too lavish for the apartment: matching crib, bureau, changing table, rocking chair, and toy chest, all white with stenciled roses. Felix said the furnishings were a gift from a loyal customer, but Bambi suspected it was a payment against a debt, as it had arrived on a plain truck, carted in by two surly men who grunted when she offered them lemonade on the unseasonably hot day they set it up last week. Once all the furniture was in, there was barely any floor space left. Ida was right: The hippo wouldn't fit. It didn't fit anywhere. It was going to have to stand sentry in the living room until they moved.

As it was, Linda had yet to sleep in her beautiful, crowded nursery. Bambi was breast-feeding and kept her in a Moses basket in their room. Her mother found this appalling as well—the breast-feeding, the little basket by the bed—and added it to the list of things that were Felix's fault. As to Linda's birth date, which came exactly thirty-five weeks after Bambi's wedding day—Ida had no comment, other than the dry observation that nine pounds was an exceptionally good weight for a preemie.

Bambi was perhaps a month pregnant at her wedding, but who cared? The wedding, after all, had been in the planning stages for six months, so no one could ever say it had been forced on them. (Unlike Irene's engagement, which was announced over the winter holidays, a scant month before the ceremony. *Her* son, Benjamin, was born in mid-August.) Bambi had no problem standing before her guests in the whitest of white gowns, perhaps the loveliest dress she would ever wear. Not long, but cocktail length, in keeping with the simple ceremony, much simpler than Felix would have liked. Simple, in part, because her parents were paying, but also because Bambi had urged them to scale back. Felix's yen for extravagance scared her a little. Bambi sensed that this would be a theme for the rest of their lives together: Felix would want to be lavish, and she would pull back. He was the first person in her experience to use "middle class" as a kind of an insult. Her parents considered the life they had crafted for their only daughter to be one of their greatest achievements, but Felix thought them small-timers, she knew. And that was the worst thing Felix would say of anyone. *Small-timer. He thinks small. He settles for scraps.*

Linda, who had gone to sleep in the middle of the party in her honor, stirred in her basket. Bambi could have gone into the bedroom to nurse her, but she felt contrary so she brought the baby out and nursed her in the living room in full view of her mother, who was folding up the wrapping paper and ribbons in order to reuse them. Thank goodness Bambi had thrust that receipt into the pocket of her smock.

"She looks like Edward R. Murrow," Bambi said fondly.

"She looks like her father," Ida said. Less fondly.

It was tacitly understood before Linda was born that no daughter of Bambi's should be held to that standard of beauty, but Linda really did look like her father. Exactly. Bambi's kinder friends said she had striking features and she would grow into them. By which they meant: *Oh, dear God, the nose is ENORMOUS.* Bambi didn't mind. She believed her daughter would blossom. Besides, being beautiful, Bambi didn't overrate its power. She didn't underrate it, but she didn't overrate it. Bambi's beauty had been like a savings bond procured at her birth. A nice investment. But it couldn't, as it turned out, provide her with everything she needed.

For example—a husband who slept in his own bed every night.

"Toys and clothes, clothes and toys," her mother said, taking inventory of the gifts. "Why don't people give useful things?"

"It's more fun to give a little girl dresses and stuffed animals," Bambi said.

"Fun," her mother repeated, as if it were a profanity. "I don't even understand why you had a party at all."

"People like parties."

"People like a lot of things."

Bambi did not ask what her mother meant by this. Although her parents had always struck her as naïve, Bambi had to wonder if her mother had been onto Felix. If she had been right not to buy what he was selling.

To her own horror, she began to cry.

"Is something wrong?" her mother asked.

Bambi wanted to snap at her like a teenager. *Of course something's wrong.* Instead she said: "I'm just so tired."

"Babies are wonderful," her mother said. "But they change everything."

"For the better." It was a question, but she tried to make it sound confident, emphatic.

"Mostly. But fathers get jealous. They can't help it. The world revolved around them. Now it doesn't anymore."

"Did Papa get—jealous?"

"Papa was older. He had been through—a lot." Bambi's parents had an essentially arranged marriage, albeit one sweetened by genuine love and respect, then saddened by the string of miscarriages.

"Felix isn't that young. He's twenty-five, almost twenty-six."

"Twenty-five." Her mother really could cram a lot of meaning into a single word, a number.

"When we were engaged, you said twenty-five was too old. Now it's too young?"

"You'll see," her mother said. Again, Bambi had to wonder just how much her mother knew. Earlier today, she had insisted on helping Bambi by sorting the laundry and taking it down to the basement. "Such dark lipstick you're wearing these days," her mother said, as she made a pile of Felix's handkerchiefs. "I like you in lighter shades."

"It's the style," said Bambi, who had switched to Elizabeth Arden Schoolhouse Red when she married. It was darker—but not quite as dark as the shade on Felix's collar.

Her mother left at last, leaving behind a shining apartment, for which Bambi was grateful. She was tired these days. The hours crawled by. Linda slept, woke, ate, slept, woke, ate. Bambi waited for Felix, putting together funny stories about the party to entertain him. How her mother's friend, Mrs. Minisch, had frowned at the carpet. How Aunt Harriet, who doted on Bambi and thought Felix was wonderful, had *loved* the hippo. How dowdy Irene looked since her marriage.

After Linda's 10:00 P.M. feeding, Bambi changed into a pretty peignoir, figuring she had up to four hours to focus on Felix, assuming he came home. Eleven o'clock, twelve o'clock, one o'clock. He didn't come and Linda cried and Bambi's breasts spurted, ruining the gown. What had Felix said? *It's a nocturnal business, darling. Your father gets up at 4:00 A.M. I'll be lucky to get home by that time. Two sides of the same coin.* She put Linda down and—tenderly, carefully—touched herself as Felix had touched her on their honeymoon. She didn't like to do it by herself, but it was better than nothing and allowed her to see if she was ready, as the doctor had promised. Her gentle touch took her back to the honeymoon, the suite, Felix's hands, his voice, her dreamy assent to everything he said. What had she agreed to as his hands moved through her hair, over her back, between her legs?

Not legal, but not the kind of illegal that anyone cares about. People want to gamble. I'm the bank. What could be more harmless? I collect the money, I give some away, keep the rest. I'm a dream merchant, sweetheart. No one gets hurt. No one is forced to do anything they don't want to do. The cops don't even care. No one cares, as long as you play by certain rules, stay away from certain things. I'll have an office down on Baltimore Street, above the Coffee Pot Spot.

Baltimore Street was the Block, and his office was actually above a strip club, the Variety. A strip club that Felix owned. A strip club where it was rumored that the headliner had to pass a very special kind of audition. Bambi had tried to confront Felix about this but found she could not say the words. She decided it was better never to speak of it, to pretend that she didn't care, to pretend to be asleep when he crept into bed and whispered: "Everything I do, I do for you."

She had thought it was quite the stupidest thing she had ever heard. But Felix never said anything he didn't believe to be true. Which was not to say he didn't lie, only that he never thought of himself as a liar. But how could he say this? Was he saying that he slept with these whores, these *nafkehs*, as her mother would say, for her? Then again—she considered his practiced hands, the pleasure he gave her. Maybe they had taught him that. Okay, but now he knew. He should stop.

Linda stirred, uttered her bleating, lamblike cry, only to settle back to sleep before Bambi could swing her feet over the side of the bed. Too bad. She would have been happy to be up with the baby. She could use the company. Having a family was supposed to end her loneliness. Yet, in some ways, she was lonelier than ever before.

On their second date, Felix had stopped in front of a large gold-flecked mirror in the lobby of the Senator Theater. "Look at us," he said. "We look like a couple."

Bambi couldn't see it, but she nodded, giving him a half smile.

"We'll have the kind of house where there are portraits," he said. "Of you and the kids, not my ugly mug."

It wasn't ugly, though. Not on a man.

True to his word, Felix had already found a house, although it was unclear how they would pay for it. He said he would commission a painting as soon as she was back in fighting shape. Bambi had cried when he said that because she was unused to being found wanting in that way. The women against whom he compared her had long legs and tiny waists. Bambi would never look like that, no matter how hard she tried.

Yet—she knew he loved her best. If he had to choose, he would choose her. But she was too proud to make him choose.

Besides, she had agreed on their honeymoon to do everything his way when it came to the business. *Whatever it takes to make us rich.* Work nights in disreputable places, bring home all that cash. So her husband went off to Baltimore Street in a suit and a hat at two in the afternoon, acting as if he were as normal as apple pie, and Bambi played along. "My husband works in the entertainment business," she told those nosy enough to ask. "I guess you'd call him an impresario. He books the talent."

Oh, yes, he *booked* the talent.

She was finally falling asleep when he slipped into bed at five. He was freshly showered. Why would a man smell of soap at 5:00 A.M.? He gathered Bambi in his arms and inhaled deeply, as if she were a bouquet of roses.

"I love you," he said. "Do you love me?"

She wanted to claw him and cry. Instead she said: "I suppose I do."

"Things are going to be so great when we move into the new house. It will be beautiful. It's beautiful," he said. "You're beautiful. And we have a beautiful daughter. We are going to fill that house with children."

"It has only four bedrooms," she pointed out. It wouldn't be motherly to object to his inaccurate description of wrinkly Linda, all nose, that dark hair creeping so low on her forehead.

"We'll build an addition. We'll do something with that space over the garage. You'll make it beautiful."

Five beautifuls in the space of less than a minute. She knew what Felix valued about her, and it had never been her parents' modest bank account. Beauty and the slightest bit of reserve, as if she didn't need anyone. The key to keeping him was to never let him feel too comfortable, to maintain that cool competence. The other women would come and go, come and go. She was his wife and he would never embarrass her. Or their children. She hoped there would be lots of them, enough to make up for all the brothers and sisters she never had, and the husband who wasn't home as much as he should be.

"It's going to be a great life," he said.

"Isn't it already?"

The question seemed to surprise him. He pulled his face from her neck, didn't answer right away. "Of course. But it can be better. It can always be better. Don't think small."

"How can we afford the house on Sudbrook Road, Felix?"

"Don't worry about it."

"No one we know has a house like that. Not starting out, not in that neighborhood."

"That's 'cause they're all coming slow out of the gate. I run wire to wire, baby. Wire to wire."

"What does that mean?"

"I'm always in the lead. Some horses have to hold back, wait for others to tire, then surge. I'm always out in front. No one can catch me."

"I caught you."

"I caught *you*."

"You wanted me." This was their litany.

"You bet I did. From the moment I saw you in that dress. You thought you were so grown up, with that little boy of yours."

"I was grown up."

"You were born grown up. That's why you were so bored with those little boys. You needed a man. You needed me."

She was drifting off. It was all well and good for him to talk, but she would have to get up with the baby very soon. Felix had a night job. She had an all-day one.

"I love you, Bernadette." He used her real name when he wanted to be serious. When he wanted her to know he was serious. The first time he said it, under the *chuppa*—"I take thee, Bernadette"—she had almost started, wondering why he was saying another woman's name at such a sacred moment. But now she was used to it. Liked it, enjoyed having this private persona with him. In all the world, only Felix called her Bernadette.

"I love you," he repeated more insistently, demanding an answer.

"I know you do."

March 7, 2012

Next of kin. Sandy mused on the phrase as he drove. *Next of kin*. It's one of those expressions that people use every day, then you stop to think about it, wonder what it means. Next of kin. Kin, obvious, but next of? Next to what? Did it imply a hierarchy—there was next of kin, then the next of next of kin?

More than fifty years after arriving in the United States, Sandy still found that English tripped him up at times, brought out these literal turns. When it came down to it, Sandy didn't have much use for words because so many of the ones he had heard over his life had been lies. Words had been the weapons of choice in the interrogation rooms, used by both sides. By the end of the day, he was done with words. Mary seldom complained about anything, but sometimes she admitted that she wished Sandy would talk a little more when he came home. To Sandy, that was like asking the guy who worked in the ice cream parlor to come home and make himself a sundae. Sure, some murder police were big talkers, storytellers. He wasn't one of them. Sandy got more done with a steady stare.

Not that he planned to stare at Julie Saxony's sister. He'd have to talk a lot, probably, prod her to tell the stories she had told so many times before.

Typically in a cold case, Sandy left the relatives alone as long as possible. Didn't want to get people's hopes up. But Andrea Norr was all he had, so he was going to pay her a visit. Not unannounced—he wanted her to be prepared, to have thought quite a bit about things. He had called Monday and now it was Wednesday, one of those gray, drizzly days that feel so much colder than what the thermometer says. As he pulled into the long driveway for the horse farm where she lived, he wondered if she were as pretty as her sister, if she had aged better.

No and no. Or, maybe, no and who knows? The woman who greeted him was short and stocky, with thick gray-blond hair in a no-nonsense cut. Her body was thick, too, but not from inactivity. Sitting still in her own kitchen seemed to make her crazy and she kept jumping up. Brewing tea, putting box cookies on a plate, suddenly washing a dish that had caught her eye.

"So, something new?" she asked after the teakettle sang and she had settled down with a cup. He accepted one, took a sip. Jesus, it was awful. How did someone make bad tea from a bag of Lipton's?

"No, nothing new. But I have a good track record on these cold cases."

"Person who killed her is probably dead."

He was on that like a cat.

"Why do you say that?"

"I don't know why I said it." She was convincing in this, seemed surprised and confused by what she had blurted out. "I mean, it's not like everyone's dead who was alive then. I'm alive. But then—I didn't keep the kind of company that Julie kept."

"I thought she was on the straight and narrow for some time when she disappeared."

"Yeah, she was, but she still had ties to those bums she knew back on the Block."

"You're saying she still had business with Felix's old bookmaking buddies?"

"I'm not saying anything like that. I'm saying that my sister danced on the Block, hung out with crooks. Lay down with dogs, et cetera. She actually used to defend him to me, say it was *only* gambling and that no one got hurt. Lots of people got hurt by Felix Brewer every day. Gambling is a terrible thing."

"Aren't you a trainer?"

"Show horses, not racehorses."

He was curious about what she did, how it worked, if it paid the bills, why she thought it so pure. He had heard there was plenty of fraud in the show horse world, too. Sometimes, it was helpful to give in to his curiosities. Put the person at ease, primed the pump. But Andrea Norr did not seem like a woman who would have much patience for digressions.

"I know you've answered a lot of the same questions before. But it's the first time I've asked them. We're starting over. Assume I know nothing, okay? Because I don't."

"What's to know? Julie got in her car on July third to drive to Baltimore and we never saw her again."

"Yes, that's according to the guy who worked for her."

"The *chef.*" Said with some disdain. Well, given Andrea Norr's tea, she probably didn't put a lot of stock in preparing food.

"But when was the last time *you* saw her before that day?"

She twisted in her chair, like a little kid playing with a swivel seat, although this chair was rigid, with no swing to it. "It had been almost six months."

"Six months? So you weren't close."

"We were. Once."

"What happened?"

"We had . . . words."

There it was again, another strange usage. *We had words.* Everyone has words. Sandy and Andrea Norr were having words right now. What a useless euphemism. The phrases that people used to make things prettier never worked.

"About?"

"I thought she was stupid, expanding the inn, adding a restaurant. I didn't think it was the smart thing to do."

"Did you have an interest in the place? A financial interest?"

"No."

"Was she trying to borrow money from you?"

"No." She clearly knew where he was headed and decided to jump the gun. "We didn't have any money issues between us. I just thought it was a bum idea. The inn was doing fine as a B and B. She was making things unnecessarily complicated for herself. She had always made things unnecessarily complicated for herself, getting into messes and running to me, as if I could help her. I couldn't."

"Messes like what?"

If only people knew how obvious their lies were, at least to him. Maybe then they wouldn't bother with them. "Nothing important," she said, and he knew it was at least somewhat important.

"Messes involving Felix."

She shrugged. "He was married. That's always a mess. A big stupid mess that everyone saw coming but her."

"What do you mean?"

"Same old story. She fell in love with him. He had a wife. He had always had girlfriends at the club, but he wasn't going to leave his wife. He had a wife, a steady girl, and more girls on the side. Julie thought she was so sophisticated, thought she knew what she was doing. Me, I never got the big attraction. He was short, nothing to look at it. Sure, he had money, and he bought her things, but so what?"

"Didn't he set her up, after he left?"

"Who told you that?" Defensive. Okay, it was gossip, pure and simple, but gossip wasn't always wrong. Someone had staked Julie Saxony.

"Did he or didn't he?"

"He gave her this little coffee shop on Baltimore Street. That's all, as far as I knew. But she was good at running things. She parlayed up."

"That's a big parlay, from a coffee shop on Baltimore Street to an inn on the verge of opening a restaurant."

"Look, I know what I know. I can't tell you what I don't. We weren't in each other's pockets. I never asked her for money, she never asked me. We were brought up to take care of ourselves."

"And where was that?"

"Aw, c'mon, you know this stuff. You told me you read the file. You probably know more than I do."

"I have to pretend I don't."

Andrea Norr sighed.

"We were born in West Virginia. Most of our parents' friends had the gumption to leave during World War II, get factory jobs in Baltimore. Ours didn't, which tells you everything about them that you need to know. They've been dead for years, since before Julie disappeared. We left when we were teenagers. Two giddy girls with a VW bus and four suitcases. Three of them Julie's. She was the pretty one. That was okay with me."

Interesting that she provided that detail automatically, as if it were still uppermost in her mind. It wasn't like he was going to ask. Wonder, but not ask.

"We rented a room on Biddle Street and got hired at Rexall Drugs. Clerks. One day, two guys walked in, took one look at Julie and said she should be a dancer. *A dancer.* We may have been hicks from West Virginia, but it was 1972, we knew the score. One of the guys introduced her to his friend Felix and that was that."

"What do you mean?"

"Love at first sight. I guess I should be grateful it was a re-spectable strip joint, where the girls wore pasties and G-strings, because Julie would have done whatever Felix asked her to. She was a goner. I never got it. Then—I never got men."

"You married, though?"

"Why do you say that?"

"Isn't Norr your married name?"

"No, it's our given name. I'm a happy spinster. Saxony was something that Felix hung on her. It wasn't enough to give her that stupid stage name, Juliet Romeo. He had to rechristen her com-pletely. She made it legal, down at the courthouse. Although— well, she was prone to that. Trying to make herself into what she thought Felix wanted."

He was stuck on that tantalizing *although,* wished she had fol-lowed it through. "Yeah? What else did she do for Felix?"

A vague hand, waving at nonexistent flies. "Silly stuff. Not im-portant. You know how women are."

No, he knew how one woman was, Mary. And, he supposed, Nabby, but he didn't think Nabby's behavior reflected on anyone but Nabby.

"Did your sister know where Felix was after he left?"

"No." Fast, emphatic.

"Did she know anything about the circumstances of his flight?"

"No." *Too* fast, too emphatic.

"You know the statute of limitations is long past on that." He should check to see if that was true. Might be important in deal-ing with people as he went forward. "And your sister's dead. She can't get in trouble for something she might have done in 1976."

"Not everyone is dead."

"You know there was always this rumor about Felix, how he escaped in a horse trailer."

"Rumors are just that. Rumors. It's not my fault I work as a trainer, or that my sister dated that crook."

He let it drop. He didn't want her as his antagonist, not at this stage.

"Ever strike you as weird, the timing?"

"Timing?"

"Your sister disappeared almost ten years to the day. You think he came back for her?"

"To kill her? Even I don't hold Felix in such low esteem."

"No. But maybe someone else was looking for Felix. Someone who followed her that day—I mean, in 1986—in hopes of finding him."

"It was the government that wanted Felix. I don't have much affection for the federal government, but I don't think they kill people."

"Other people might have wanted him, too. Like the bail bondsman, for example."

Andrea laughed. "You didn't do all your homework, Mr. Sanchez. Remember those guys who walked into Rexall? One of them was Tubby Schroeder, Felix's best friend. He wrote the bond, he took the loss."

He did know. That is, he knew that Tubby Schroeder was a bail bondsman, a big fat guy, everybody's friend. Sandy knew that Tubby had written the bond for Felix and been awfully philosophical about his best friend skipping out on him. Everyone assumed Felix had made good on the hundred thousand in cash. Sandy had thrown out the fact about the bond to see what *she* knew.

"Thank you for your time," he said. "And the tea."

"You barely touched it."

"I don't eat between meals," he said. "Nothing but water. Doctor's orders."

"Well, why didn't you say something?"

"I forgot."

Fifteen minutes later, Sandy was at Chesapeake House, enjoying an early lunch at Roy Rogers. En route, he had passed the exit to Havre de Grace. The two sisters couldn't have lived more than ten miles apart, yet they hadn't seen each other for six months when Julie disappeared. Interesting. Nothing more at this point. Just another line in the geometry he was building, a distance between two points.

He was even more interested in the fact that Tubby Schroeder had seen her first, brought Julie to Felix. Might be worthwhile to interview him, assuming a guy that fat was still alive at age seventy-five or so. Sandy remembered seeing him once or twice in the courthouse, had to be almost thirty years ago. Always laughing, big as a Macy's Thanksgiving Day balloon, the life of the party. A back slapper, a joke teller.

Everything that Sandy detested in a man.

December 31, 1969

Not the way I'd run a lottery—"

The ambient sound in the country club was odd. Lorraine Gelman was having trouble hearing Bambi, who was right next to her, yet Felix and Bert's conversation on the other side of the table boomed loud and clear. Their heads were bent together as they lighted cigars, an indulgence for the night. Meanwhile, Bambi's soft voice was lost in the weird jangle of noises.

But Lorraine smiled and nodded, sure she would agree with anything Bambi said. Lorraine adored Bambi. *Adored*. It was hard to remember now that she had been a little snobbish about the Brewers when she and Bert started dating six years ago. "Isn't he just a crook?" she had asked Bert. Lorraine's family were German Jews; her great-grandparents had lived on Eutaw Place when Eutaw was nice. Her mother had attended Park School in the early days. Bert, the son of a prominent attorney, had barely met her parents' standards. And when Bert said Felix Brewer would be best man at the wedding, Lorraine's parents had tried to dissuade him, to no avail. "He's my best friend and one of our best clients," Bert had said. "That's never going to change."

We'll see, Lorraine thought.

But her friends' husbands did seem rather drippy alongside Felix. Plus, Bambi turned out to be so nice. In Lorraine's experience, women like Bambi usually weren't nice, not to her.

Yet Bambi had been a good sport from the start, showing up at Lorraine's bridal party, trying hard to enter into the fun, although she was a little older and didn't know the other girls. Lorraine had ended up being embarrassed by her friends, who seemed young and, yes, even a little tacky alongside Bambi, who came from a perfectly nice family, if not as nice as Lorraine's. Even Lorraine's mother thought Bambi was someone special, once she got past the nickname.

So when it became apparent that life with Bert meant life with Felix and Bambi, Lorraine was fine with that. The men talked about the things they found interesting, politics and sports and, more and more these days, Vietnam. For goodness' sake, they were talking about it again, right now, the draft lottery. Who cared? She didn't have children, and the Brewers didn't have sons. It wasn't their problem.

"I can't believe those earrings," she said to Bambi, looking at Felix's anniversary gift. "Aren't you worried they will fall off?"

"I got my ears pierced, see? At a jewelry store on Reisterstown Road." Bambi leaned closer to Lorraine, let her examine the cunning catch. Large diamonds, good ones, set in ovals of gold, a new design from David Webb. Lorraine knew because Felix had consulted her before buying them. His taste was okay, but old-fashioned. Safe. Like a lot of people who didn't come from money, he was almost too cautious. Lorraine had known that Bambi would appreciate this pair, which were trendy, but not so trendy as to go out of style quickly.

"Incredible," she said. Felix caught her eye across the table and winked.

"Put your eyes back in your head, honey," Bert said. "Bambi had to wait ten years for those."

"Ten is tin," Lorraine said, then wished she hadn't. Who would know that except a woman who had looked up the anniversary list as she had earlier this year, when disappointed by Bert's gift of a carved rosewood jewelry box. She had been prepared to argue, but it turned out he was right: Five was wood. And ten was tin. You had to make it to sixty for diamonds. Still, Bert earned as much as Felix, or close. He could afford diamonds, too.

But Bert was handsomer, Lorraine decided, swinging back to her husband's side. And while he might represent criminals, he wasn't one. Lorraine was forever cataloging the differences between Felix and Bert, Bambi and Lorraine, the Brewers and the Gelmans. Bambi was older. She'd be *thirty* next month. Bambi was beautiful, whereas Lorraine was only well put together. Good haircut, perfect clothes, and, most important of all these days, thin, which required living on Tab and carrot sticks and, after a vacation binge, some pills. She had tried the Dr. Stillman diet that so many Pikesville ladies swore by, but it gave her horrible gas. Bambi carried a few extra pounds, but men never seemed to notice.

The two couples did everything together. Vacations—cruises, Ocean City in the summer. The symphony, plays at the Morris Mechanic. Shopping for the women, sporting events for the men, although Felix considered that work. And when their men stayed out late, which they did often, Lorraine went to Bambi's and drank sweet vermouth, gossiping into the night.

And life was fun, wasn't it? Wasn't it? Here they were at the club on New Year's Eve, which also happened to be their dearest friends' wedding anniversary. There was a band, the kind of band that Lorraine preferred. Lorraine liked to be held when dancing.

Besides, musicians were getting so dirty. They looked dirty, they acted dirty. That nasty Jim Morrison, down in Florida. Who does such a thing? A few months ago, at a party, one of Bert's friends had followed Lorraine to the powder room and tried to put her hand on him, through his trousers. She had told Bambi, expecting her to share her shock, but Bambi had just shrugged, said some men were flirts when they drank. Then Lorraine realized that such things must happen to Bambi all the time and she felt bad that it didn't happen to her more often.

Sometimes, with Bert, handsome as he was, she thought about what it would be like to be with someone else. Bert was all she knew. She had asked Bambi one time if Felix was her one and only. "Of course," Bambi said. "I was only nineteen when I married him." "I didn't mean—" "What did you mean?" Bambi had asked, with a hard look, and Lorraine realized Bambi thought she was asking if Bambi had taken a lover to get back at Felix. Lorraine would never suggest such a thing. Out of loyalty to Bambi, she wouldn't even listen to gossip about Felix's girls. When she said to Bert, just the once, that Felix was attractive in a weird way, he had seemed upset: "Watch out for him. He likes women." "Oh, I'm not his type," she had trilled, embarrassed but emboldened, for saying a crush's name out loud is the same as admitting the crush. Then Bert had to go and say, "No, you're not his type." That had kind of ruined it. He added, seeing her face: "You're much too classy for Felix. As is Bambi, if the truth were known. Felix likes a rough girl."

If Bert were to cheat on Lorraine—but, no, Bert would never do that, good-looking as he was, as much female attention as he got. Bert liked being respectable. He had been drawn to Lorraine because her family was good, solid. Not as much money as people thought, but socially on a par with the old families, the Meyerhoffs and the Sonneborns. Lorraine's father was president of the temple board this year, her mother was a former Hadassah president.

Lorraine was optimistic about 1970. Certainly, she would get pregnant this year. Although, like Bambi, she had married at nineteen, *she* had stayed in college and earned a degree. True, she had expected motherhood to interrupt her education—she didn't try to get pregnant, but she didn't try very hard not to—yet there she was three years later, graduating cum laude from Goucher. She wanted three children, spaced out two years apart. If she had the first one by the end of this year, that meant another in '72 and then she would be done by '74. So she would be twenty-nine when her youngest child was born, which meant she would be forty-seven when that child headed off to college. Forty-seven. It sounded so old. Bambi was going to be thirty in the coming year, Felix would be thirty-six, closer to forty than thirty, and Bert was twenty-eight. Lorraine liked being the baby of the group even if they did gang up and tease her sometimes, act as if she didn't know anything about the world before she was born. She had skipped a grade in elementary school. It felt natural to be the youngest in a group.

The band began playing one of Lorraine's favorite songs. "Our song," Felix said with a significant look at Bambi.

"How can that be?" Lorraine asked.

"I slipped the band a twenty."

"No, I mean—this song was on the radio just a few years ago, when Bert and I were living in the apartment near Mount Washington. You were old married folks by then."

"That was the remake. The original was 1952, but it was also recorded by Connie Francis in 1959 and the Orioles had a hit with it as well. It was playing the night Bambi and I met. Remember, Bert?"

"What I remember is that I was left alone with Tubby and a bunch of fraternity punks who wanted to beat us up, so it doesn't have the same romantic associations for me."

But Bert held out his hand and led Lorraine to the dance floor.

He was a very good dancer—better than Felix, who was a little hoppy for Lorraine's taste—but she couldn't help being aware that Bert's eyes were everywhere, surveying the room over her shoulder, keen to know who was here, who they were with. If Bert were a woman, he would be considered a gossip. Meanwhile, Felix held Bambi as if she were the only woman in the world. Yet Felix was the one who cheated and Bert was the trustworthy one. It was confusing. Lorraine wanted the kind of attention that Felix lavished on Bambi, but she could never work out if such intense devotion was the by-product of cheating, in which case wasn't it better not to have the attention?

The music shifted to something a little fast, so Bert and Felix were out. Lorraine sometimes tried the new dances, home alone, watching Kirby Scott. She thought of it as exercise. But the clothes—the truly mod clothes—did not suit her, thin as she was. They made her look old, mutton trying to pass as lamb. The same with the short haircut she had tried with the two side curls, coaxed out at night and held down with Scotch tape. *What are those, payos?* Felix had teased her. Yet Bambi, so much older, looked divine in her Pucci shift tonight.

She and Bambi went to the powder room together, checked their hair and lipstick, taking their time in front of the mirrors. It was a little hard, being side by side in a mirror with Bambi, but Bambi smiled encouragingly at Lorraine as if she understood, as if even she found her beauty burdensome. It was going to be hard for her daughters. Linda and Rachel. Lorraine could imagine boys falling in love with Bambi when the girls began to date. Lord, it was hard enough to be her friend, to notice how men noticed her. Bert, out of courtliness, always insisted Lorraine was prettier.

"It's exciting," she said, "being at the start of a new decade. The last time that happened, I was fourteen years old. I couldn't have begun to imagine where I'd be tonight—married to someone like Bert, getting ready to start a family."

"Ten years ago tonight, I couldn't really imagine my life, either," Bambi said, taking out a cigarette and lighting it. Lorraine looked at it longingly—so much easier to stay thin while smoking—but she had quit the moment the surgeon general's report came out. "I thought I could, but I didn't have a clue."

"Where did you go for your honeymoon?"

"We spent the night at the Emerson Hotel, before going to Bermuda the next day." She exhaled. "The Emerson Hotel was sold at auction this year."

"We got married at the Lord Baltimore," Lorraine said.

"I know. I was there." Bambi was staring into space, not even making contact with her reflection as she usually did in such a space. Bambi liked mirrors.

"Of course. That was a wonderful night. Maybe the best night of my life."

"I hope not," Bambi said with a shudder.

Lorraine was offended. "What do you mean?"

"Because then it would be all downhill from there, no?"

"Well, I mean the best night of my life *so far*. I know there will be better ones to come. Having children." She ran her hand over her flat stomach. There was a slight bulge, probably from the indulgent meal, although wouldn't it be exciting if she were already pregnant. "A year from now, I'll have a baby."

Bambi pointed her cigarette to the ceiling. "Man plans."

"What do you mean?" Lorraine felt as if she were saying that a lot tonight.

"It's an old saying. Man plans, God laughs."

"You've never had any problem getting pregnant." She realized this made it sound as if everything Bambi had, she should have, too, which sounded grudging. Luckily, Bambi didn't seem to notice.

"Very true. But I can't help it, I still have the evil eye thing. I know it's silly, but some of the old folklore—it's there. Felix doesn't have a superstitious bone in his body. Everything is numbers with him, straight math. He laughs at the people—the people who have reasons, as he calls them."

"Reasons?"

"Oh, you know, people who pick a racehorse based on its name, or bet their ages at the roulette tables, or—well, you get the picture. That kind of thing."

Lorraine realized that Bambi had been on the verge of saying that Felix laughed at his own customers, the people who placed dollar bets on sequences of numbers they found intensely meaningful. But Bambi never spoke of her husband's work. No one did. Lorraine supposed Bert and Felix talked about it at times. Bert was Felix's lawyer, after all. But everyone else played along. Here, at the country club, where Felix's gift had meant improvements, and at temple, where he gave generously to the building fund. He would never be president of the temple, but Felix didn't want to be. He spread his money around like a kind of insurance, spending enough so that no one wanted to alienate him or his family. His girls went to Park, and Lorraine, a very involved alum, knew that Felix had been generous with the school, too. Well, when she had children, they would be third generation at Park and that would make them special, more special than money ever could. Some things can't be bought.

Still, she wished Bert weren't so tight. They had almost as much money as the Brewers did, they could cut loose a little more. At least, she thought they could. She didn't actually know how much money he earned or what their debts and investments were. Bert said it was less than she thought, that being a partner in his father's firm wouldn't be really lucrative until his father retired. But that was part of the reason she wanted to get pregnant. She was pretty sure that Bert wouldn't insist on staying in the apartment once there was a child, even with two bedrooms. She wanted something out near Bambi and Felix, of course, but not in the same style. Something modern, preferably with a pool.

She and Bambi returned to the table, continuing to dance the slow numbers with their husbands, sitting for the fast, although a few women did the twist together when their husbands refused. They never changed partners, not with Felix and Bambi, not with anyone. Lorraine was getting tired, but she stifled her yawns, intent on midnight and her plans beyond it. Maybe they would conceive tonight. Then their child would have a birthday close to Linda's.

By 1:30, Lorraine and Bert were in the car, heading home. They would have gotten out faster if he had tipped the valet a little more, as Felix had. Bert's driving seemed weavey to Lorraine, but they didn't have far to go and the roads were dry, free of snow and ice. Once they were home, she changed into a negligee she had bought for this night, lavender so sheer it might as well be see-through. It was, she realized, perfect for Bambi's coloring. But it was fine with her own and she was very thin, which was the fashion. Some women were even going braless now. Lorraine could if she wanted to, but she couldn't imagine why anyone would want to.

Bert looked at her with appreciation, recognizing the significance of the negligee. She wasn't usually insistent on having her turn, as she thought of it, but she pushed for it tonight, believing, even as she knew it made no sense, that conception would be marked by an orgasm. Perhaps she put too much emphasis on it, because it was a little weak and sputtery, not at all what it should have been. *This is it*, she told herself. *We just made a baby*. Then: *Everything's going to be better now*. The second thought, unbidden, scared her. Why did things need to be better? Things were wonderful. She tried to shoo it away. *We just made a baby*.

She remembered Bambi's face in the country-club mirror, sad and resigned. Had Bambi seen the same expression in Lorraine's eyes? Was this what marriage was? Were diamonds the consolation prize for sticking with it for ten, twenty, sixty years? She batted away these melancholic thoughts, blaming Bambi. Bad moods were contagious, like colds. Lorraine's life was wonderful. It was a new year, a new decade. She was going to have a baby and then everything would fall into place. Maybe she would have boys, who could marry the Brewer girls, except—the boys would be so much younger. No, that wouldn't work at all, not at all.

March 9, 2012

Tubby the onetime bail bondsman was in assisted living up at Edenwald, the kind of place that Sandy wouldn't have minded for himself and Mary, if they had had the money. Although he guessed they would have taken her away from him, in the end, put her in a nursing wing, and he wouldn't have had that for anything. Sandy hoped Tubby wasn't in the nursing wing, or on machines that would make it tough for him to talk. Then again, people often gabbed when the end was near. He had closed more than one case on dying declarations.

He checked in at the front desk, explained his mission. It always took longer without a badge, although he had an ID and that helped. *Yes, official business for the Baltimore Police Department. City, not county. Nothing bad has happened, no, but I need to talk to Mr. Schroeder.* The girl was skeptical. He could tell she was very protective of "her" residents, probably worried about scammers, fake stockbrokers, and the like. Sandy wished there had been someone like her looking after his interests when he needed it. If Mary had a flaw, it was that she never questioned anything he did, although maybe it wasn't fair to call that a flaw. Eventually, the girl called up—Tubby was in the regular apartments, not the health-care wing, as it turned out—but she said there was no answer.

"Is today the day that Mr. Schroeder goes to the pool for water aerobics?" she asked another attendant.

Water aerobics. Sandy envisioned a man-manatee crouching in the shallow end of the pool, barely moving. Still, good on him for trying.

"There's a bridge game today, in the library. I'm pretty sure he signed up for that."

The library was well appointed. There were six tables of four-somes, all women except one man, a lean, leathery strip of a guy, deeply tanned and—what do you know—sporting a full Towson in March. White shoes and white belt, paired with lime trousers. The shoes and belt went nicely with his white hair, and his bright sweater complemented his tan. Pink, Sandy would have said, and Mary would have said, No, coral. Or salmon. Sandy said a lot of things just a little wrong for the pleasure of Mary's corrections, of-fered politely and sweetly, usually after a moment of hesitation. He had never met a woman who took less pleasure in contradicting her man. Yeah, that's not a flaw.

Cock of the walk, Sandy thought, looking at the guy in the coral sweater. Cock of the walk. True, being the only rooster in this henhouse was a little like being the one-eyed king in the land of the blind, but it wasn't the worst thing that could happen to a guy. He just hoped the man could direct him to Tubby Schroeder.

"Can I help you?" the man asked when Sandy's alien presence registered in the room.

"Maybe. They told me I could find Tubby Schroeder here."

A confused murmur among the women, but the man laughed heartily. "Tubby Schroeder is long gone, sir. Long gone. But if you want to talk to *Tubman* Schroeder, that could be arranged. After this rubber."

Sandy took a seat in an armchair and waited. The players were intense, possibly because there was a table of prizes for the winners. He didn't know the game, but he picked up on the fact that Tubby was good at it. So good, in fact, that he was holding back a little, making mistakes out of gallantry. He won, anyway, and excused himself.

"Hate to take you away from the game," Sandy apologized.

"Oh, we break for refreshments now. Your timing is good. Let's go down to the pub for a little privacy. Tubby, huh? That will be the talk of Edenwald for weeks now. I buried that nickname a long time ago."

But his tone was good-natured.

"Tubman—I never thought about 'Tubby' being short for something."

"Yes, most people assumed it was about my girth. Tubman Schroeder. Named for Harriet Tubman, or so claimed my crazy lefty mother, who tried to make me into a red diaper baby, but I loved money too much. Still, it's suitable for a bail bondsman. Let my people go. But, please, no runaways on my underground railroad."

He had the kind of patter Sandy had always distrusted, not being capable of it. *The strong, silent type,* Mary had teased him. A man had to play to his strengths.

"How old are you, if you don't mind my asking?"

"Don't mind at all. I'm seventy-six, and I feel better today than I did at thirty-six. Did you come here for my health secrets?" He didn't wait for an answer. He was used to talking to women who found him fascinating, Sandy supposed, accustomed to filling up any gaps in a conversation. "Here's how it worked for me: I had four heart attacks in four years, starting when I was forty-six. The first time, they told me to lose weight and exercise. The second time, they told me to lose weight and exercise. The third time, they told me to lose weight and exercise. The fourth time, they told me to lose weight and exercise. And, for some reason, the advice took on the fourth time. It started with a walk around my dining-room table. I'm not kidding. That's all I could do at first. I weighed 275 pounds and I walked around my table. But then—I had a pretty big dining-room table."

The story had a polish to it, the mark of a tale that had been told many times. Still, it was interesting to Sandy. People never changed. Until they did.

They had reached the pub, an inviting place of leather chairs and dim lights, quite empty at midday.

"So that's all it took?" Sandy asked. "A walk around the dining-room table?"

"That's how it started. And here's where it ends up. A hundred pounds lighter and I have the smallest pillbox of anyone here. That's kind of a brag, you know."

Sandy knew. He already took two pills with his breakfast, one for blood pressure, another for cholesterol. And a baby aspirin.

Tubby's—Tubman's—light tone changed. "So you're a cop?"

"Retired, yes, but I was a police with the city for a long time."

"I think I remember you. Not that we met, but our paths must have crossed, here or there. Across a crowded courtroom, to change the song slightly. But it probably wasn't enchanted."

"No, not a lot of enchantment in my business. I work cold cases now."

"Felix or Julie? Has to be Julie, I'm guessing. I mean, there's probably no statute of limitations for federal flight, but, Jesus, who cares at this point. If Felix is alive, he's older than I am. What would be the point? It's not like a Nazi war criminal, you know."

"Not sure what you mean."

"He's going to be a frail old man. Who wants to be the person who brings him back?"

"You're not frail."

"Felix isn't me. He never learned from his mistakes."

That was interesting. Tubby—Tubman—intended it to be interesting, dropped it with a big thud, all but begging Sandy to jump on it, this observation about Felix and his mistakes. Which, to Sandy's mind, made it like a dollar on a string, a trick for losers and optimists.

"Yeah, I'm here to talk about Julie. Her sister says you're the one who introduced her to Felix."

"Her sister tell you anything else of interest?"

"What do you mean?"

Tubman flagged a waitress. Young, by the standards here, not quite forty and a nice forty, if not a spectacular one. And even she seemed caught in this guy's charm. What was that about? He had very good manners. Not flirtatious, but kind, which probably worked better. He ordered a red wine for himself—"The cab, the one I like"—and asked Sandy if he wanted anything.

"I'm good."

"It's the elixir of life. You'll live forever."

"Doesn't strengthen the case for me."

Tubman laughed, thinking Sandy was making a joke.

"The sister—"

"Ah, you're quite the pointer. Not going to let go of the scent, are you? Look, I don't tell other people's secrets. Let's just say that Andrea Norr wasn't the innocent bystander she'd have you believe."

"In Julie's death?"

"I don't want to play that game because then you'll ask me another question and another question. No, nothing big, nothing to do with Julie's death. But she knows things, more than she's ever told. She may have even forgotten how much she knows."

"About Felix leaving."

"I told you, I'm not playing. For the record, I've never thought the two were connected. Felix leaving, Julie disappearing."

"Will you tell me why?"

Tubman had to think about that. His wine arrived and he cupped the bowl with his hands, inhaled it, but Sandy didn't think such ostentatious enjoyment of wine was his normal style. The guy had been a bail bondsman, a beer-and-a-shot guy who hung out on Baltimore Street back in the day. People don't change that much. He was stalling.

"You know, I don't have any reasons. Just a feeling. In my business, I lived by my hunches, and my hunches served me well. It's about character, my business. The character of people already thought to be criminals. Yet some thieves have honor and some don't."

"Felix Brewer was your best friend. Did you have a hunch he was going to burn you?"

Tubman laughed. "Men don't have best friends. That's a girl thing. We were friends. Felix, me, Bert. He was a man involved in a criminal enterprise. I was a bail bondsman, Bert was a criminal attorney. We liked each other's company, and we were useful to each other. At times."

"Your friend stuck you with a bond of one hundred thousand dollars, no small sum."

"Yes. Yes, he did."

Sandy looked around the pub. "You weathered it, I guess."

Tubman continued to smell his wine. Maybe he was an ostentatious prick, after all. "If Felix Brewer found a way to compensate me for skipping his bail, you realize there would be serious repercussions for me. IRS, being charged as an accessory."

Sometimes, you just had to repeat a thing over and over, not accept the non-replies and the digressions. "Julie Saxony went missing almost ten years from the day that Felix did."

"And she was murdered, it turned out. Do you think Felix was murdered?"

"No, but it's hard to ignore the juxtaposition." He liked the occasional fancy word like that, which proved to him that he had mastered his second language, even if he had lost his first. Spanish was almost like a dream to him now. There had been no one who spoke it in Baltimore when he was growing up. Now, it was everywhere, and when he heard it at bus stops, in restaurants, it was like running into an old friend—and having nothing to say. Plus, the accents were odd to his ear.

"*Julie* was hard to ignore, wasn't she?" Tubman smiled over the rim of his glass as if they shared some secret.

"Not sure what you mean."

"She was gorgeous. God, she was gorgeous."

"You discovered her, as I hear it."

"How—oh, the sister. Right. Yes, Bert and I stumbled on Julie at Rexall. Not quite like finding Lana Turner at Schwab's, but close enough. There was a soda fountain, still. But she was behind it."

"Did it bug you that she ended up being Felix's girlfriend?"

"No. I took her to him. I knew what I was doing. She was a gift."

"Was she yours to give?"

"Who knows? I took her into Felix's club and that was that. I didn't figure her for having such staying power, though. That surprised all of us."

"Us?"

He didn't answer. He was a smart guy. Smart enough not to talk to a cop at all, if it came to that. But something—Sandy's not-quite-cop status, Tubby's own boredom in his plush nest—made him want to play this game. More challenging than bridge with a bunch of wistful ladies.

"How did his wife feel? About Julie?"

"I wasn't Bambi's confidant. Lorraine, maybe, she could tell you, but I can't."

"Lorraine?"

"Bert's wife. Now *they're* best friends. Bambi and Lorraine. Like sisters. What do the kids call it? BFAs? BBFs? Something like that."

Kids. Sandy's mind jumped to kids, kids playing a game of hot potato. Andrea Norr had sent him to Tubby. Now Tubby was sending him to Lorraine.

And everyone kept trying to send him away from Felix, that night ten years before Julie disappeared. *Nothing to see here, keep moving.* Well, the IRS implications could be enough to scare a guy.

He got to his feet, thanking Tubby for his time, releasing him to the henhouse.

"It's impressive," he told Tubman. "The way you changed. As you said, almost no one ever does. Did you ever think about why it took the fourth time, the doctor's advice?"

"A mystery," Tubman said in a self-satisfied way.

"Four heart attacks in four years. You were how old? When the last one happened?"

"Fifty."

"Which would have been, what, 1986?"

"Thereabouts." As if he didn't know the date to the moment of his last heart attack.

"What month?"

"August."

"Right around the time Julie disappeared."

"I don't see what the two things have to do with each other. Oh, wait, I get it—you think I had the last heart attack carrying her body to its resting place in Leakin Park."

"I just think it's an interesting—juxtaposition." He would have used a synonym if he knew one. "A woman disappears, a woman you discovered, for want of a better term. And, maybe whatever happened to her is somehow connected to the life you introduced her to. Maybe that's on you. You have your fourth heart attack and suddenly you're ready to change your life, to do all the things you never could before, as if you suddenly understand what's at stake, what mortality is. You ever consider that those two things were connected?"

Tubman's face lost something then, although Sandy wasn't able to say what. A bit of color, or maybe just the forced bravado that most older men used to conceal their sadness.

"Many times," he said. "Many times."

Sandy walked with Tubman back to the library where the bridge women awaited their king. There was a plate of food by his place. "I thought you might be hungry, missing the snack break," one said. Had women doted on the old Tubby this way? Sandy thought not. The laws of supply and demand, coupled with a hundred-pound weight loss, can work a peculiar kind of magic.

Sandy got into his car, thinking about the most meaningful moment of the whole interview. *You think I had the last heart attack carrying her body to its resting place in Leakin Park.*

That Julie Saxony had been found in Leakin Park was a matter of public record.

That she had been murdered somewhere else? That information had never been revealed anywhere. Sure, one could infer it, especially if one knew the topography of the park, could spot the telling omissions. But a guy would have to be paying very close attention.

Tubman "Tubby" Schroeder had been paying very close attention to the details around Julie's death, the one in the one-two punch that had convinced him to change his life. The question that Sandy couldn't decide was whether he was carrying a torch or trying to bury one.

March 14, 1974

Julie knew how to drive, had picked it up when she was only thirteen, but she had never bothered to get a license. Andrea had driven them to Baltimore and they had only the one car and then Julie fell in love with Felix. And because she didn't have a car, he drove her home one night and came inside the little apartment she shared with Andrea. That led to him finding her a better apartment, in Horizon House, this new high-rise with a rooftop pool, although the view from the pool included the jail, which amused Felix greatly. Of course, getting a license wouldn't keep Felix from driving her home and coming inside her apartment, but if she got a license, Felix might buy her a car. He had said as much. An Alfa Romeo. But Julie knew what the car would be—her going-away gift.

No license, no car.

No car, no going away.

She knew it was silly and yet—sometimes, silliness worked. Look at Susie, propped up on a telephone book in *her* boyfriend's absurdly large Cadillac, piloting them toward Washington, D.C.

She had already made four wrong turns and they weren't even on the Capital Beltway yet. Julie had built in extra time for Susie's waywardness, so she wasn't concerned about being late. She just remained amazed at how well life worked out for Susie, who didn't have a care in the world or a thought in her head.

Perhaps those two things were connected.

"What do they do, again?" Susie asked. The whole thing was really over her head. It was as if the literal overheadedness of life allowed her to let everything else fly by her, too.

"Well, you strip down—"

"Like we do?" Teasing. Susie wasn't stupid, just not willing to make an effort. Thought Julie was crazy, going for her GED and then starting classes at community college.

"No, I get to wear a bathing suit."

"And that's it? You just put on your bathing suit and do, like, a cannonball off the side?"

"There are questions first."

"Like a test."

"Sort of."

"Do I have to be there for that?" Worried, as if she didn't even want to be in the same room as a test.

"No, you don't have to come inside at all."

"I don't want to sit in the car, though. Tubby says it's bad to run the heater and the radio off the battery and I'll go crazy, alone with my own thoughts."

Yes, it would be crazy-making to be alone with Susie's thoughts. Lonely, too.

"There are restaurants nearby. You can go have a cup of coffee or something."

"Okey-dokey." Susie used such phrases with complete ease. She was only four foot eleven, although she claimed five feet, and her popularity as a performer might have been disturbing if it were not for her enormous chest and wasp waist. She was a pocket Venus with a natural tumble of honey-gold curls and saucer eyes, and Julie would have quite disliked her, except for the fact that Felix never looked at her twice. In fact, he called her "my little freak" in private and thought the men who flocked to see her were pervy. But Felix hadn't become a rich man by making judgments on what people wanted. Sure, he had standards. He was strict about drugs at the club, strict about drugs in general, but that's because that enterprise generated more heat from the authorities. He was also rather straitlaced about sex—girls got fired if they got caught doing any kind of play-for-pay. That was the by-product of having two daughters.

Three, Julie reminded herself. He had three now. Michelle had been born almost a year ago, less than ten months after her relationship with Felix began. She still had a hard time believing that Felix had a baby daughter.

She pulled out a compact and studied herself in the mirror, even as Susie made the mistake of taking the Connecticut Avenue exit and had to circle back to the Beltway, saying cheerfully: "Well, I knew I was looking for a state." As if that was a rarity in D.C., a street named after a state. Julie's makeup was conservative for this occasion, her hair pulled back into a smooth ponytail. She was less sure of the outfit. Short—but everything was either short or long these days, and she hated the maxi look. The shift dress barely skimmed her knees, although the sleeves went past the elbows, and she had paired it with boots and a trench coat. She looked—what did she look like? A young mother, someone who played tennis and kept up with fashion. Cool, but conservative.

Not unlike Bambi Brewer, whom Julie had seen shopping at the little grocery store in Cross Keys after a morning at the indoor tennis barn.

Julie pointed out the various places where Susie could wait for her on Wisconsin Avenue, but Susie fretted that she could never parallel park this huge boat of a Cadillac. At almost three hundred pounds, Tubby, Susie's boyfriend, needed a big car. But even with the seat pulled all the way up, Susie could barely see over the wheel. It probably would be hard for her to put the car in reverse, or see out the rear window.

"I'll just go round and round," she decided.

"It might be a while," Julie warned.

"I don't mind." The amazing thing about Susie was that she didn't. Chances were, she would end up getting lost just making a circle. She wouldn't mind that, either. Julie didn't want to look like Susie, but she wouldn't mind *being* like her. Free as the breeze, not a care in the world.

She took a deep breath and walked inside the synagogue, trying not to let it intimidate her. It was just a building, like any other. She had a right to be here. Or would have the right, soon enough.

"Thank you," she said to the one man she knew among the three who sat in judgment of her. "I appreciate you getting this on the schedule so swiftly."

"You were very diligent in your study," he said. "Besides, we needed to get this done before the holiday."

"St. Patrick's Day?" she asked in wonder, then corrected herself. "Oh, Easter, of course."

She wasn't swift enough to cover the second mistake and he winced. "You mean Passover, Julie."

"Sure, right, because the Last Supper was a seder." *See what a good student I am, Rabbi Tasmin?* "I just got confused, because I didn't see how Easter could be a problem, but I thought because we're in D.C. and it's a federal holiday—"

"It's not, actually," said one of the two rabbis she didn't know. She hadn't been able to focus on their names when they were introduced, but maybe she could get by with calling him rabbi, or even rebbe, although it might sound funny, coming from her. Felix laughed whenever she tried to say a Yiddish word.

The rabbi said: "Easter doesn't have to be designated a federal holiday because it always falls on a Sunday. But it's treated like a holiday for all. This is part of the life you are choosing. You're used to being mainstream, of having your ways seen as 'normal.' Are you really ready to have a life that is otherwise? Of having to ask for holidays that your work doesn't grant?"

"Yes," she said, trying not to smile at the idea of asking for Yom Kippur off at the Variety. "This is what I want to do."

"Why do you wish to become a Jew?"

"I'm in love," she said. "The man I love cannot marry me if I don't convert."

"Has he said he will marry you if you do convert?"

Julie had anticipated that question. "We are not officially engaged, no. I'm not the type of person to give ultimatums. And I don't want my conversion to appear to be a condition, or even a ploy. Religion must be deeply felt. My conversion guarantees nothing when it comes to the love of this man. He doesn't even know I'm pursuing it."

"Really?" asked the third rabbi.

"I thought I should want this, for myself, and that would be the proof that I was making the right choice. It doesn't hinge on anything, any man. It's for me."

But, of course, it would make a difference, she thought. How could it not? Felix had entrusted her with a secret, one he had shared with no one. He cared about Judaism, no matter how much he pretended otherwise. So she must care, too.

"So you would want to be a Jew even without this man in your life?"

"Yes," Julie said. "It feels right to me."

"You were raised—?"

"Protestant. Baptist."

"Was your family religious?"

She had to stop and think about this. "My mother went to church and insisted that the kids go, too, but my father didn't. I think my . . . dissatisfaction with religion started there—how could it be meaningful if my father didn't take part?" She was making things up now, trying to say the right things, but suddenly her fibs felt true. There had been a little worm of discontent. Her father had refused to attend church. But then, so had her mother. Also that was good, saying she had been dissatisfied. Made her sound deep.

"What do you do, Miss Saxony?" asked Rabbi Tasmin, the closest thing she had to a friend here.

"I'm a hostess."

"A hostess?"

"In the Coffee Pot Shoppe. I tell people where to go. Where to sit."

"Ah." The second rabbi now. "Like a hostess."

"Yes." Hadn't she said that?

"Have you thought about Christmas?"

She had, in fact. It had occurred to her to keep the secret from Felix until then and present it as a gift, but—oh, no. They were asking her something very different.

"It will no longer be part of my life."

"Are your parents alive?"

They were, but she preferred to close any line of inquiry she could. "No."

"There are siblings?"

"We're not close." They had been once. Two giggling girls, on their own. But Felix didn't want a girl who lived with her sister, so Julie had moved out. She had told Andrea about what she planned today and they had quarreled. They were always quarreling, though, especially about Felix. It wasn't a big deal.

The rabbis did not trust her, she could tell. They did not want

her. But she had put in the time, done what was required. She continued to answer all their questions in a calm, thoughtful manner.
Eventually they led her downstairs to a room that smelled, disap-
pointingly, like the indoor pool at the Y where she had worked at
the front desk one summer.

"Make sure every inch is covered," one rabbi advised, and Julie
had a strange flashback, her first time dancing, the lecture about
the pasties, what the law allowed. A lecture delivered by Felix,
who pretended to be all gruff indifference, but she understood
that the mere fact that he was tutoring her was indicative of his
interest. There had been no jealousy among the other girls. They
assumed she would fade, as they all had. Felix had a wife and two
daughters, and he claimed he wanted a son, although it seemed
to Julie that ship must have sailed. Surely his wife was too old to
have more children? "I can't name him Felix Junior because of
the Jewish tradition," Felix told Julie the second time they slept
together. "But see if I don't. Not that I would do that to a kid, but I
don't like *rules*. Just because my father was a cantor doesn't mean
I have to do everything by the book."

"Your father was Eddie Cantor?"

"Oh, my sweet little shiksa, the things I have to teach you.
That's a secret, between us, by the way. No one knows about my
dad, not even my wife."

That had been two years ago. Two years.

She took a deep breath and submerged. She wasn't scared of
water, but she had never learned to swim properly, just knew a
paddling kind of motion, the better to keep her hair above the
water.

When she came up, she was surprised at how beautiful the
singing was, how it really did make her feel holy and changed.
The rabbis' eyes were on the ceiling, as if they didn't want to
catch a glimpse of her in her bathing suit, modest as it was. *I'm
a Jew,* she thought in the locker room, as she combed her hair

back into its ponytail, changed into her clothes, and went to collect Susie. "Drinks on me," she said. "Gampy's." It was a place all the dancers favored because it stayed open late. Felix came here a lot. She had a cheeseburger, which was pretty funny, not that Susie picked up on the joke. Felix didn't come in, but she didn't really expect him to. She and Susie went to the Hippo and danced until 2:00 A.M. Then she went back to her apartment, which, like the pool, also overlooked the prison, and stared at her phone until 4:00 A.M., wishing she dared to call him at home. She knew the number, of course. Knew the number, knew the house. Back when she was living with Andrea, she would take the VW in the middle of the night and drive by it, risking so much—Andrea's wrath, Felix's discovery. It was a lovely house. Felix had such good taste. That's why he would choose her, eventually.

She had hoped to make a ceremony out of telling him about her conversion, turn it into something special. But it happened that several days went by without her seeing him, and when he stopped by the club in the early evening, the news had been too pent up and she blurted out: "Hey, I'm a Jew!"

He laughed. "You're not a Jew. You order the lean corned beef at Jack's."

"No, seriously," she said, lowering her voice. "I converted. Susie was there and everything. She was, like, a witness."

Not exactly true, but she knew Susie would cheerfully lie for her. Susie believed women had to stick together. Another way in which she was naïve.

"Really," he said, as if she had commented on the weather. A few minutes later, he had gone upstairs to his office. She didn't see him for a week. Oh, she saw him, but there were no late-night coffees at the Coffee Pot Shoppe, no visits to her apartment. Well, it was Passover now. He had to be with his family. After the holidays, they started up again, as if there had never been a break at all.

A few weeks later, she was window-shopping at an antiques store on Howard Street when she saw an interesting plate. She was pretty sure she knew what it was, but she asked the owner to be sure.

"It's an old seder plate, very rare. There's a place for all the things that matter during the ritual—the lamb shank, the bitter herbs."

"I know," she said, although she had not yet sat at anyone's seder table.

"It's made in France," he said, showing her the unmarked back, as if that proved it was made in France.

She knew she was being sold, but that was okay. She was in sales herself, helping to move the weak drinks at the Variety. The plate was $65, no small sum, but she bought it and put it in an old trunk at the foot of her bed. There, the plate joined china and silverware she had begun to assemble, piece by piece. There was a large serving dish that dated to Revolutionary War times, the kind of item one would expect to find in a house such as the Brewer home in Sudbrook Park, although, of course, Julie would never live *there*. Mount Washington, maybe. Guilford if the divorce didn't leave Felix too strapped. But not that house, that neighborhood, through which she had driven far too many times. At any rate her things kept accumulating in this small wooden trunk, eighteenth-century English, also discovered on Howard Street. Julie never called this trunk a hope chest, but that didn't keep it from being one.

One night, in her English class at CCB, she was struck by a particular F. Scott Fitzgerald quote shared by the teacher, about the test of a first-rate intellect being the ability to hold two conflicting thoughts without going insane. She carried it back to Felix, another tribute to drop at his feet, like a house cat with a mouse.

"So you must have a first-rate mind," she said. "If you think you can really love two women at the same time."

She assumed he would at least have the courtesy to say that he loved her best but couldn't leave his wife while the children were young. Or that Bambi wouldn't give him a divorce under any circumstances. Once he had told her he could never marry a shiksa, but she had fixed that problem. So what was holding him up?

"Yes siree," she said, trying to keep her tone light. "You and F. Scott Fitzgerald, two first-rate intellects for the ages."

"Who says I'm not crazy?" Felix said, kissing the top of her head.

March 9, 2012

Sandy decided to call it a day after talking to No-Longer-Tubby Schroeder. One of the perks of being a consultant was making his own hours. The downside was that those hours could never be overtime. Work as much or as little as he wanted. Didn't matter, no one cared. He earned a flat rate, no benefits.

But it filled the evenings, reading the Julie Saxony file, and he found himself gravitating back to it even as the days were growing longer. It was really two stories, parallel universes. A missing woman from Havre de Grace. A dead woman in Leakin Park. Fitting, he thought, for a woman with two lives—Juliet Romeo, Variety headliner. Julie Saxony, respectable business owner, valued member of the Havre de Grace Merchants Association, which had put up a reward when she disappeared.

He rubbed his eyes. Even now, after two years, the house ached with quiet. Not that Mary had been a loud person, quite the opposite. Nor had Bobby Junior been noisy, not by a child's standards. When he was a toddler, Sandy and Mary had called him the colonel, mistaking his silence for dignity. Who knew, back then, what could be going on in a kid's head? Mary knew. She always knew, even before the trouble started. She kept it to herself as long as possible, outright lying to pediatricians and teachers and, eventually, Sandy. So when Bobby's problems started, about age six or so, they seemed to come out of nowhere. But it was just that Mary had papered over them for so long. For someone who usually couldn't tell a mild fib, she had been a disturbingly good liar when it came to Bobby Junior.

Then there were the five hard years, the years when they fought about what to do, only to have the decision made for them: Bobby needed to go away. It was an ugly truth, but a truth nonetheless, that Sandy had been happy to have Mary all to himself again when Bobby was sent to "school." Maybe if Bobby Junior had been different, normal, Sandy wouldn't have felt that way. How could he ever know what he would feel? His kid was born different, not right. The fact that Mary still gloried in Bobby Junior was the essence of Mary, the reason Sandy loved her so much. After all, she had gloried in him, too, despite his flaws, the mistakes that her parents said made him unsuitable as a husband. He was just grateful that the decision about Bobby was taken out of their hands, that they could stop fighting over it.

Mary wasn't. But she rallied because that's what she did and Sandy thought they had a pretty good time after that. Thank God her family had the money to pay for Bobby's care, set up a trust. There wasn't enough cop overtime in the world to pay for that kind of thing.

The Saxony file was open on the dining-room table, all the various pieces spread out. He started gathering them up, not because he was a neat freak, but because he knew the mere act of organizing a set of papers could highlight something he hadn't considered yet. It was as if his fingers knew things, but they couldn't show him unless they were moving, touching. He had to think it was similar for carpenters and writers, and he knew it was the same for chefs. It was a kind of muscle memory, ingrained by years of doing a thing. The body led, the mind followed. He was good at being a murder police and proud of being good at it. But was it so wrong that he had hoped to be good at something else in his lifetime?

Sandy's retirement, almost ten years ago, had been full of promise. He had stayed on the job longer than most, making it to thirty years of service. But he was only fifty-two then and he had no intention of truly retiring. Almost no one who left the department did. They went to other government jobs, or into private security. Some of his older friends were double-dipping now, drawing *two* government pensions and their Social Security. They lived well.

But Sandy had a different idea for his retirement, a dream he had nurtured for years. He had wanted to open a restaurant, an authentic Cuban one that would serve the dishes of his childhood. There was no place in Baltimore that really did it right, and don't even mention the Buena Vista Social Club to him, which was basically a great location that served nachos. *Nachos!* Sandy was going to make arroz con pollo and plantains and real Cuban coffee. People who had eaten in Miami's best-known Cuban restaurants said Sandy's food was as good, better.

And maybe it was, but that didn't change the fact that no one came. If a plantain falls in the forest and no one's there to eat it—he still had nightmares, thinking about the waste, the un-eaten food, the not-special-to-anyone specials.

The location was good, or should have been. Mary—she was always up for whatever he wanted—found a storefront on Hampden's Thirty-sixth Street, not far from their Medfield home. Hampden was gentrifying at a fast clip at the time, although, like most Baltimore neighborhoods, it never turned the corner all the way. But real estate was going up, up, up in a way that had never

happened in Baltimore. It seemed so smart to extend themselves
to buy the building, with a long-term eye toward renovating the
upstairs for apartments. Within six months of the purchase, the
building was worth twice as much as they had paid for it. Except
they hadn't really paid for it. They had put nothing down, borrowed 110 percent. Everyone was doing it.

Seven years later, when he went to sell the building, it was
worth about 60 percent of the debt they were carrying. They
had never established any real equity because they had used a
second mortgage—and a third and a fourth and then cash from
the money that Mary's parents left her when they died, money
outside the trust set up for Bobby Junior—for improvements to
the restaurant. They sold it in a short sale, the most excruciatingly
long process Sandy had ever endured at the time, although Mary's
allegedly fast cancer took half the time and felt longer still. Sometimes, watching television, Sandy came across a rerun of *Seinfeld*
about a Pakistani guy who runs a restaurant that's always empty
and it's played for laughs, being a sitcom and all, and all Sandy
wanted to do was throw a brick at the TV set. Maybe running a
failing business is funny when you're a millionaire comedian, but
when you lived it, the jokes didn't come so fast.

Sandy was that rare person who understood he didn't have
much of a sense of humor. He had faked it well enough at work,
knowing when to laugh, even getting a good line off every now
and then, but he wasn't inclined to see the funny side of things,
and life didn't tempt him to change his point of view.

And that was before Mary got sick. He knew the two things
were not connected, that she didn't get cancer from the heart-
break over the restaurant. He also knew it wasn't the earlier
surgeries, all those years ago, when she lost so much blood and
needed transfusions, but he couldn't shake the notion. She had
allowed him his dream, bankrolled it without a single word of
reproach when all that money went down a rabbit hole lined with

black beans and flan. And then she got pancreatic cancer. Stage IV. Mary never did anything halfway.

His papers gathered, he started making coffee, the good stuff. He still cooked for himself, but there wasn't much joy in it, and he almost never made Cuban food.

He wasn't stupid or naïve. He went in knowing that a restaurant was hard work; he came from restaurant people. He knew that most restaurants didn't make it. But he also knew that he was smart and that his food was good. So why didn't people come? Sometimes, he blamed the low-carb diet fad, which put rice and bread off the menu for so many people. He blamed the lack of Cubans in Baltimore. There had been a big influx of Latinos on the East Side, but they were all from Central America and Mexico. His food did not speak to them. It seemed that his food spoke only to him and a few stubborn regulars. There had been one young man, a guy who looked like an aging skateboarder, but he turned out to be in business himself, running a music venue with his father-in-law. Sandy and the kid talked about the perils of small business sometimes while the boy sat at the counter, wolfing down cappuccinos. But they never spoke about their lives, probably because Sandy kept that door closed to everyone but Mary. He was shocked, a year ago or so, to see the boy, as he still thought of him, pushing a stroller down Thirty-sixth Street, in the company of an attractive woman, although she wasn't Sandy's type. He didn't like sturdy women. He liked the little flowers, the women who needed protection in this world. He had been drawn to Mary's delicacy, only to be amazed by her steel. First with Bobby, then with her own illness.

Cancer. In his lifetime, it had become less of a thing. Everyone was so *cheerful* about it now. They forgot that it could still be pretty awful. Even he had forgotten. He had been stubbornly, stupidly hopeful, asking the doctor about those commercials, the ones for miracle places that cured people everyone had given up on. But Mary had accepted, from the first diagnosis, that she was being given a death sentence. If she had been thinking only of herself, she would have gone home and swallowed rat poison. She was a dignified woman, and there was no dignity in what happened to her over the next four months. "I carried you to your doorstep on our first date," Sandy said. "What's the big deal in my carrying you now?"

But he was carrying her to the toilet, which she found humiliating. Mary had been a woman who, through thirty-plus years of marriage, insisted on decorum, especially about bathroom matters. To have her body assert all its ugly reality in those final months grieved her so. She put on lipstick and beautiful nightgowns until the end. But she no longer wanted fresh-cut flowers in the house. "When they die, they remind me that I'm dying."

Sandy had objected, defending the flower bearers in a way he was not inclined to defend most people. He had a pretty low opinion of people and whether that was because of the job or the job was because of that tendency was a chicken-or-an-egg question at this point. At any rate, he argued for the flowers. "No, they're pretty, they're nice, you're not—"

"I am," Mary said. "I'm dying. And look at those cut stems in water. They're dying the moment they're cut."

The next day, he had brought her an orchid, in a pot. And although he didn't know dick about plants, he learned to tend to it, and then another, and another, until the first floor was a bower, a word that Mary taught him. After she was gone, he thought about letting the orchids go, or giving them away, but Mary would be disappointed in him, giving up on yet another living thing, so he kept the bower, feeling for all the world like Nero Wolfe or goddamn Ray Milland when he played the villain on *Columbo*, complete with ascot. Only an asshole wore an ascot.

Columbo—that was a good show. Utterly ridiculous, but it wasn't trying to be a documentary on police work. At least the writers knew that solving a homicide was more talking than anything else, although some of those confessions—well, Sandy wouldn't want to be the assistant state's attorney who took Columbo's cases to court.

He turned on the television to keep him company while he puttered among the plants. No one would accuse him of having a green thumb, but he saved more than he lost now.

The rowhouse was still set up as it had been in Mary's last months, so she could live on one floor. Now Sandy lived on one floor, using the first-floor bathroom. He went upstairs only to shower and change his clothes. But he slept in the sofa bed where she died, although it bugged his back.

Mary's last word was "Bobby." He tried to tell himself it was for him, that she had reverted, in that final moment, to the given name he no longer used. But Mary had almost always called him Roberto. Her last word was for her son, who loved his mother so much that he had almost killed her.

A few days after she died, Sandy drove out to the group home where Bobby now lived; tamed and dulled by medication, the boy—a thirty-five-year-old man, but always a boy to Sandy—was puzzled by the news. "Where's Mom?" he asked, although he had been told repeatedly she was gravely ill, that this day would come. "Where's Mom? When is Mom coming to see me again?"

Sandy had not visited him since that day. It wasn't a plan. Nobody plans to be that much of a bastard. Mary's illness had disrupted what routine there was and she was the keeper of that flame. He forgot to go, something came up. Then something else came up and before he knew it, six months had gone by and the caretakers, when he called, told him that Bobby was fine. "Does he ask after me?" No, he was told. He asks for his mother, but never his father. Okay, so that was that. He had no relationship with his son. It wasn't his fault that Mary could forgive Bobby Junior for throwing her through a plateglass window, while Sandy never could. It didn't matter to him that Bobby was only eleven at the time, or that he did not understand what he had done, that he cried over his bloodied mother as paramedics tended to her. She had lost so much blood that day, almost enough to kill her. Did the transfusions cause her cancer? Sandy knew that was ridiculous, that he shouldn't blame Bobby for killing his mother—and yet he did. He just did.

At the table, the one where Mary used to insist on taking her meals despite being so weak she could barely sit up, he ate an early supper and watched the news. He missed having an afternoon paper, although it had been almost twenty years now since one was published. Sometimes, he felt that he was born to miss things, to lose things despite his meticulous ways. In Spanish, translated strictly, things lost themselves to you and that had been Sandy's experience. His restaurant. His parents. Mary. The promise of his son—not the boy himself, but the dream of the child who never was, the boy who had seemed so happy and healthy and perfect at birth, straight 10s on his Apgar. Nowadays, you couldn't open a newspaper, turn on the TV, without hearing about autism and Asperger's, and people were always telling you about this book they read or *Rain Man* or how their boss was on the "autism scale." Not that people talked to Sandy about these topics, because there was no one left in his life who knew about Bobby Junior. But he heard things, on TV and out in the world. He heard things.

The local news got silly after the first break, and he opened Julie Saxony's file again. It was the opposite of whatever picking at a scab was. Something was registering every time, even if he didn't know what it was. He was beginning to prefer the more recent photograph, the one where she was too thin. Yes, to be honest, the va-va-voom shot of her in her stripper days had been what first caught his eye. But the 1986 photo, where she was all of thirty-three—she looked so old and sad. This was the woman who had been murdered, he reminded himself. A woman who had achieved a lot, but at some cost. If he were the kind of a guy who talked to photos, he might have asked her: "What made you so sad?"

But Sandy was not that kind of a guy. He didn't talk to photos or even to himself. When he wasn't working, he might go a day or two without speaking to anyone at all. And that suited him just fine.

Thrill
Me

November 2, 1980

W e never got the bounce," Greg said, staring at the television, numb. "We should have gotten such a *bounce.*"

Norman agreed. "We deserved a bounce. We *deserved* a mother-fucking bounce."

Linda nodded, the third member in this mourning party of three. Greg and Norman had seemed old to her a month ago, even two hours ago, but she realized now that they were young, too. Young and preppy and rumpled, men whose clothes were no longer tended by mothers and not yet under the auspices of wives or girlfriends.

"How did we not get a bounce?" Greg asked.

"We never got a bounce," Norman said.

They were a little drunk and this couplet, which they had been reciting in variation since the polls closed almost five hours ago, was coming more quickly now, abetted by drink and shock.

And although this was not a party per se—John B. Anderson's small cadre of Baltimore believers was not that deluded—

the volunteers had expected a slightly cheerier ending to this chapter in their lives when they planned the gathering at the Brass Elephant. But it was one thing to tilt at a windmill, another to feel as if you were pinned beneath it, arms and legs squirming comically.

The bartender, Victor, who had come to know them quite well over the last two months, had allowed them to bring a small black-and-white television and prop it up on the bar. It had been fun in the first hour or so, just because they were *done;* they had seen a hard thing through, unlike several other volunteers who had fled the sinking ship. No, they were jovial at first, not thinking about the big picture. About reality.

They muted the television when the networks began calling the election for Reagan. And now it was 1:00 A.M. and the enormity of the result had left them all a little numb. They hadn't expected Carter to win, they hadn't *wanted* Carter to win, and yet—and yet. The Reagan landslide felt literal to Linda, as if she were caked in mud, as petrified as a citizen of Pompeii.

"At least they can't blame us," she said, a variation on what *she* had been saying all night.

"Not in Maryland," said Norman. "Still reliably Democratic, thank God, and the average Republican pol here is more Mathias than Agnew."

"They can't blame us anywhere," Greg said. "When everything is said and done, there won't be a single state where Anderson siphoned off enough votes to hurt Carter. Anderson wasn't the problem."

"I thought he was supposed to be the solution," Linda said.

But this was too naïve, even for her fellow travelers in idealism, who usually gave Linda extra leeway because of her youth. They had celebrated her twentieth birthday in this same bar, just two months ago.

They had returned three weeks later, the night of the debate,

right here in Baltimore, when Carter had refused to appear and
Anderson had debated Reagan one-on-one. He had done so well.
That night, the young volunteers had come here in a haze of
giddy possibility. It was happening. They were going to make
history. Maryland's best-known connection to third-party presidential politics would no longer be the assassination attempt on
George Wallace, but the glorious ascension of this practical, reasonable man, a man who embodied the word "avuncular" in Linda's mind.

"Are you going to make book on whether he lives or dies?" Uncle Bert,
in their kitchen, joking to her father about the Wallace shooting only
hours after it had happened.

Her father didn't think it was funny. "If he dies, he becomes a martyr.
That's no good."

Bert, quietly: "He's not wrong about some things."

Her father, fiercely: "He's wrong about everything."

Why was she thinking about this now? Anderson, third-party
candidate, Wallace. Avuncular—uncle, Uncle Bert. Her father.
Her father. How she wished she could talk to him tonight. Would
he have been surprised by the result? His business had relied on
him not being surprised about anything that involved numbers,
always knowing the odds. Oh, he was apolitical because no candidate would ever support *him*, not publicly, although they all took
his money, one way or another. But he claimed politics was just
another game, its outcome shaped by probabilities.

Victor knew her father, it turned out. He spoke to Linda of
him that very first night, after checking her ID.

"Class of 1960," he said, handing her license back. "Just in under
the buzzer." The drinking age was going up to twenty-one, a year
at a time, but she was grandfathered in. She would be the only
Brewer girl who could drink before the age of twenty-one. Linda
didn't care about drinking so much. She just wanted to hang out
with the other volunteers, who had claimed this place as their own.

The bar at the Brass Elephant was a little pricey for a group of unpaid volunteers, even those subsidized by their parents, but it was near Norman's apartment on Read Street, and the converted town house's muted elegance gave them a lift at day's end. Plus, Linda enjoyed the cachet of Victor remembering not only her father, but her as well. He used to wait on them at the Emerson Hotel. Shirley Temples, with extra cherries. Linda was not yet eight, Rachel only six, and the hotel was far from its glory days, but the sisters had no yardstick for decline back then, had not yet observed firsthand how quickly elegance can erode. They certainly did not know of the Hattie Carroll incident, or even Bob Dylan, not in 1968. Linda had known only how much she and Rachel loved being with their father, dueling with plastic swords loaded with cherries, while men came and went, crouching next to Felix, whispering in his ear, then disappearing.

"Do you still drink Shirley Temples?" Victor had asked her after establishing she was one of *those* Brewers.

Linda had blushed, then blurted out an order for the most sophisticated drink she could imagine, which happened to be her mother's drink, a vodka and tonic. The joke was on her. She hated vodka tonics. But she stuck to her original order that night and every night after. She'd rather sip slowly and grimly than admit she had been bluffing.

At least she never got drunk, which was a good thing, as she had to drive all the way out to Pikesville, where she was living with her mother and her baby sister, Michelle. Rachel had left for college just a few weeks ago, and it surprised Linda how keenly she felt her absence in the house. Had Linda been missed the same way during her year and a half at Duke? She thought not, somehow. Rachel was the family confidante, the keeper of all secrets, even their mother's. Linda could be trusted to keep secrets, too, but she was bossy, determined to solve problems that no one else wanted solved. *Put Daddy's photos away if they make you feel sad.*

Don't spend money you don't have. If you must have the latest clothes, get a job at a shop where you can buy them at a discount. At least her mother had heeded the last bit of advice.

Tonight, as Greg and Norman drank themselves into deeper and deeper glooms, Linda found the nerve to turn her vodka tonic back to Victor and say: "Maybe a glass of wine?"

He didn't tease or shame her. He didn't even charge her for the half-drunk vodka tonic she pushed back to him. And she was pretty sure that the white wine he poured was not the house brand. It was far better than any glass of white wine she had tasted before. He poured her a glass of ice water, too, then made a quick call. Within fifteen minutes, he was putting appetizers and sides in front of the famished volunteers.

"My contribution to the cause," he said, when Greg stammered that they couldn't afford any food. Greg and Norman fell on the *mozzarella en carrozza* like dogs.

"Do you really remember my father?" Linda asked.

"Of course," Victor said. "We talked about him the first time you came in here."

"I mean—not just as a customer, or—what he became." She never said "fugitive," not out loud. It wasn't really the right word. "Exile," her mother said, when she was feeling magnanimous. "Coward," when she was not. But never fugitive. "Did you have a sense of him?"

"He was a good guy," Victor said. "And you know what? He would have preferred Anderson, too."

"Really?" Linda was doubtful. Her father was so pragmatic. He was not one to pretend that lost causes were anything but lost causes. Wasn't that why he had run? He couldn't win, so he didn't stay around to lose.

"I moved to the Lord Baltimore during the 70s, but your dad still came in, talked politics. He disliked Carter. Not so much the positions, but the man. He was talking up Udall right up—"

He stopped, clearly not wanting to say: *Right up until he left.* "He thought Carter was small-time."

"Really?" If small-time meant not cheating on your wife, then Linda wouldn't have minded a small-time father.

"That's how I remember it."

"What else do you remember?"

"I remember how pretty you girls all were, the three of you."

"The three of us?" Michelle hadn't been born.

"You, the little one, your older sister."

Linda, blunt within her family, was polite in the world at large, so she did not embarrass him by saying: *I don't have an older sister.* And her mother, beautiful as she was, would never pass for Felix's daughter.

But Julie Saxony might.

"He was a good man," Victor said.

"Thank you," she said. It often happened this way. With strangers, friends, even her mother and Rachel. She started down the road toward a memory, toward a vision of her father that she thought would bring her pleasure. Then she would stumble over something unexpected and ugly.

Now her memory was playing with her again, throwing something else in her path. Five-one-five. Five-one-five.

"We're going to say it was a mix-up," her father told Bert. "Five shots on the fifteenth. Five-one-five. Someone got confused, put out the wrong number. And we'll substitute out five-oh-five, say it was a typo."

"People will get pissed. You could have a fucking riot on your hands."

"They can play the state lottery if they don't like how I run my game. Five-one-five will ruin us."

I was sitting at the dining-room table, doing my homework. I would have been eleven, at the end of fifth grade. No, sixth, because Mama sneaked me into school early, the fall I turned four. She wanted Rachel and me to be three grades apart, not two, and with Rachel's spring birthday, she needed to either hold her back or push me forward, and every-

*one saw even then that there would be no holding Rachel back. Mama
had this weird theory that we would be better friends if we had more distance at school. And we are very close, which is wonderful. But we might
have been close anyway. I didn't understand for years what happened,
that Daddy changed the number because too many people had played it
and they couldn't cover the payout.*

So her father's game was rigged, too.

Rachel may have been the family intellect, but Linda was no
slouch. She had gotten into Duke on scholarship, only to find
herself profoundly homesick. She had thought she wanted a new
start, but found it wearying, trying to create a history that didn't
invite questions. She transferred to Goucher in the middle of
her sophomore year. Bambi had been upset about that, far more
upset than Linda could understand, given how much money was
saved. Linda was happier at Goucher, too, where people knew
just enough not to ask too many questions. Her only problem was
that life as a commuter student at an all-girl school didn't make
for the best dating life. She volunteered for the Anderson campaign because some girl said it would be a good way to meet men.

She had met a lot of men, many of them keen to date the
pretty new volunteer, some of them even suitable, if not Greg and
Norman. But Linda, who had come looking for dates, ended up
caring only about the candidate. Not that she ever got to speak to
him or spend time with him. She met him only once, the night
of the debate, when he was introduced to all the local volunteers.
She was not invited to the dinner afterward, nor did she expect
to be. But she was thrilled to wake up the next morning and discover that the received wisdom was that JBA had won the debate.
A giddy day or two had followed before she realized how meaningless that victory was.

She had been so naïve about politics. Lord, she hadn't even understood how the Electoral College worked, and it still made her
angry to see the election called with less than 100 percent of the

vote in. She had thought a presidential race was one in which two men—three in this case—came before a nation and explained their positions and then the best man would win. *The game was rigged.* How could a man like John Anderson not get more votes? Her mother had said Linda was throwing both her vote and her time away, but Linda didn't feel that way. In fact, she had believed so profoundly in the importance of her vote that she had committed a felony this morning in order to cast it.

It happened like this. Linda, usually the most organized of the Brewer girls, had registered to vote in North Carolina when she enrolled there in 1977. She had gone to a school meeting in the fall of her freshman year, in which it was explained that the town-and-gown tension in Durham could be improved if more students registered to vote, demonstrated a commitment to the community. So she meant to register there. When she moved back home a year and a half later, it hadn't been an election year so there was no urgency to register at all. Caught up in the Anderson campaign this summer, she had quite forgotten that she had never registered in her home state. Yes, she saw the irony in forgetting to register when she had been sitting at a card table at the mall, signing up other people.

Embarrassed, she didn't dare confide in anyone on the campaign. Instead she had asked her uncle Bert, who told her that all she had to do was swear on a form that she was a registered voter at her mother's address, that she had sent in the application earlier this fall.

"It is a felony," he said. "But it's not like there's going to be a recount that forces them to go over all the ballots."

"It might be closer than you think," she told Bert. He laughed and ruffled her hair, as if she were still eleven or twelve.

But this morning, only eighteen hours ago, Linda still believed that anything was possible, that improbable victories could be pulled out in the final moment of any contest. During the Nixon years, people had spoken of a Silent Majority. Reagan had invoked the term during this election. But the true silent majority, in Linda's mind, were young people like herself. Oh, they made a lot of noise, but they forgot to follow through with the actions that really counted. It almost didn't seem right for people over the age of sixty-five to vote. They had so little time left. Shouldn't the policies affecting the future be set by candidates chosen by those who had to live in the world longer? If you were going to weight the importance of certain states, why not weight individual votes? When Linda was eleven, a film called *Wild in the Streets* had shown up on a second-run bill at the Pikes Theater and it centered on the nation's first twenty-two-year-old president, made possible when the voting age was lowered to fourteen. Linda had gone to see it three times. (The lead actor was very handsome.) Crazy, yes—but it made more sense to her than the Electoral College. She wanted to pound her fists on the bar, say *It's so unfair.*

Instead, she asked Victor for another white wine.

A man came into the bar. He glanced around in confusion, taking in the barely audible television, Greg and Norman wolfing down appetizers, Linda staring into her wineglass.

"Are you still open?" he asked. "Is this a private party?"

Although the question was addressed to Victor, Linda answered. "It's clearly not a party," she said. "As for *private,* anyone is welcome, but do you really want to be a part of this group?"

"Did someone die?"

The man was in his twenties, Linda guessed, with the most amazing eyelashes. *He has eyes like a giraffe,* she thought. Linda liked giraffes.

"Just my hopes and dreams." She meant to sound blithe, devil may care, but her mouth crumpled, ruining the effect. "We all worked on the Anderson campaign."

"Well—" He cast around for something to say. "Well," he repeated. "Good for you. You did something you believe in."

"But we didn't change anything," she said. "We didn't even *matter.*" While it would have been awful to be the spoiler, to be blamed for Carter's loss, it was worse, she decided now, to have had no effect at all.

"You don't topple giants the first time out, despite what Jack and the Beanstalk, or even David and his Goliath, would have you think. It takes years of work."

His kindness felt patronizing, as kindness often can. Linda drew herself up haughtily. "Really? Have you climbed any beanstalks lately?"

"I'm a public defender," he said. "Which is as close to being Sisyphus as any mortal might ever know." A sweet smile. "Don't be mad at me."

"Who says I was?"

"I can't seem to get on the right foot with you. Should I go out and come back in again?"

And with that, he walked out of the bar, then returned, hopping on one foot.

"I'm a unipod," he said. "I'm here to audition for the role of Tarzan."

"You stole that," Greg said. "Dudley Moore and Peter Cook."

But Linda had to laugh. Her father had tried such stunts when Bambi was stewing. No, not *stewing,* quite the opposite. Bambi had gotten cold when angry with Felix. Very cold and quiet and grim. They called her the Frigidaire when she was angry.

Linda did a swift, familiar calculation—should she sleep with this man tonight? She had slept with exactly four men since she lost her virginity at seventeen, and she liked to think of herself as progressive, the kind of woman who took what she wanted when she wanted it, although it was a lot trickier since she had moved home.

No, not tonight. It might not be love at first sight, but she was in for the long haul if he was, she knew that much. Her next campaign, only with a lot more potential. She wondered how he would feel when he found out she was a college senior, living at home. She wondered what he looked like naked.

"I'm Linda," she said.

"Henry," he said. "Henry Sutton."

By three that morning, they were making out in her car. It was hard to say who pulled back that first night. Both would claim later that they were waiting for a more genteel first time. That opportunity presented itself two weeks later, when Bambi went to New York with Michelle, Lorraine, and Lorraine's daughter, Sydney. It was designed to be a whole Eloise-at-the-Plaza experience for the two girls, although Michelle, at seven, considered herself too sophisticated for both Eloise and five-year-old Sydney. If Linda hadn't been so anxious to have the house to herself, she might have used Michelle's antipathy to dissuade Bambi from such an extravagance. Her mother was good, most of the time. But in New York, with Lorraine, she would buy clothes she couldn't afford, try to keep pace with her old friend, who was privy to Bambi's difficulties. Maybe that was why it was so important to Bambi to try to hold her own with Lorraine.

But, for once, Linda forgot about everyone else—her mother, Michelle, Rachel, John Anderson, all the sad men she had to prop up. She even forgot about the phantom sister who had passed through the Lord Baltimore Hotel and may or may not have been Julie Saxony. For one blissful Saturday evening, she thought only of herself and what she wanted, opening the door to long-lashed Henry Sutton, who actually brought her a bouquet of supermarket daisies. She was mindful, as the door swung open, of the story of her parents' courtship, how they had married less than eleven months after her father had found his way to her mother's door the day after meeting her. And

Linda had long ago deduced that she had attended her parents' marriage in utero, not the cause of the nuptials, but a happy by-product of a progressive courtship.

There are worse ways to begin, she thought, lying beneath Henry in her mother's bed, the only double bed in the house, taking care to cheat her face to the left so she would not be staring into her father's eyes in the framed photograph on the nightstand.

Yes, they were very large and brown. She knew that. *She knew that.* But the man with her—he was gentle, a dreamer and ideal-ist, someone who would never agree that the game was rigged. He probably thought she was a dreamer, too, given the circum-stances of their meeting, but even as Linda was abandoning herself in this moment, she was also giving in to the pragmatic person she was meant to be. She would have to take care of both of them, she thought, circling her legs around his waist. She had to take care of everyone. That was okay; she was used to it. She remembered walking up the front walk, after the fireworks at the club. Her mother knew before they crossed the threshold. How had she known? Bert had taken Bambi to the side at the club, but Bert was forever taking her mother to the side over the last few months, since the indictment, then the trial. Bambi had run up the walk, thrown open the door, run from room to room, calling his name. "Felix? Felix?" There was no note, no reason to believe he was gone, yet Linda slowly began to see the details that made the case—the small gap in the closet so packed with suits, a drawer in his valet, opened and emptied of his best cuff links. Michelle was upset by their mother's tears and shouts, so Linda put her to bed, singing to her as the little one cried, "Tummy hurts, tummy hurts." She had gorged herself on ice cream and cake at the club. Then Linda and Rachel came into this very room and sat on this very bed with their mother's arms around them. "He better be alone," their mother had said, mystifying them. "Will we ever see him again?" Rachel had asked. Linda knew they would not.

"What are you thinking about?" Henry asked, tracing her jawline with his finger.

"The last time I saw fireworks," she said.

And he kissed her, believing himself complimented.

March 13, 2012

Whenever life took him outside the Beltway, Sandy felt as if he were escaping Earth's orbit, breaking free of a particularly harsh gravity. As built up as the suburbs got, as bad as the rush-hour traffic was, a drive west on a bright March day lifted his spirits. Maybe he should go for more drives in the country. Did people still do that? Probably not. Most people spent too much time in their cars to consider driving fun, or recreational.

Sykesville, Andrea Norr had said when she called out of the blue this morning. *Go see this guy in Sykesville.* Despite five decades in Baltimore, Sandy needed a moment to remember where Sykesville was. Those towns between Baltimore and Frederick kind of blended together for him—Sykesville, Westminster, Clarksville. Sykesville was the closest of the three, it turned out, not even twenty minutes from the Beltway, and Sandy took the exit with something akin to regret. He'd like to keep going, driving on this straight, uneventful highway, past Frederick, into the mountains. And he could. No one would notice, no one would care.

But there's no point in running away when no one wants you back, so he might as well go interview Chef Boyardee.

"Bayard," Andrea Norr had said. "Chet Bayard. I was reading Chowhound, and it turns out he has a new place after all these years."

"Reading what?" She had called Sandy at 8:00 A.M., which probably seemed late on a horse farm, but Sandy enjoyed taking his time in the morning, inching into the day. He had worked midnights much of his life and was still barely on speaking terms with the hours between six and ten.

"It's a website for people who are interested in food."

"I know that." He did. He thought about the woman he had met. Short, stocky, but it had seemed like her natural build, not a body nourished on particularly good or bad food. She had made that god-awful tea, too, and gone back for seconds. Someone who ate for fuel, someone who didn't pay attention to restaurants.

"He was on the Eastern Shore ten years ago," he said, the file alive in his mind. "When the body was found. Cops took a statement then."

"Well, he's in Sykesville now, got a new place."

Hadn't Tubman suggested that Andrea Norr had reasons to divert attention away from her? "So you just happened to be reading this website and you just happened to see this guy's name and you just happened to remember he was the last person to talk to your sister that day and, bam, there he was?"

"No, I did a Google search on him and he came up. I'm surprised you haven't done that."

"He was on my list. There are a lot of people in that file. And I thought he was all the way down to Cambridge or something."

And I have better sources than Google, for Christ's sake. Everyone with a computer thinks they're so slick.

"That place in Cambridge closed a few years ago, but he's trying his luck again."

"Poor sap."

"What?"

"Never mind." He would humor her, go out there. He didn't like relatives telling him what to do. Usually, he had already done it. But he wanted to keep Andrea Norr as his ally in this. She knew something. He just wasn't sure what it was, or if she even realized she had something of significance to share. He'd prefer that she be a liar, actually. You could break a liar down.

Poor sap. Sandy couldn't help evaluating Sykesville as a location for what was supposed to be an upscale French restaurant. The heart of the old town was charming, but it wasn't a *destination*. The way Sandy understood it—and he had learned much of what he knew about the restaurant business in hindsight—you really needed an inn to make a go of a place like this, either one that was connected to the restaurant or a place within walking distance. The Inn at Little Washington, or even Volt out in Frederick. That had been Julie Saxony's business plan when she disappeared— add a big-time restaurant to a B and B, then people would have a reason to come to the B and B. But she had been in Havre de Grace, which had the river, things to do. Sykesville struck Sandy as too close in for a weekend getaway, too far for a big night out.

But the place looked nice enough, and the posted menu was promising. Very traditional French, so old-fashioned as to feel new again. Coq au vin, daily fish specials, lentils, cassoulet.

He tried the heavy wooden door, found it unlocked.

"We're closed," a young woman said without looking up. "No lunch during the week."

"I'm not here for a meal. I'm here to talk to"—he squinted at a piece of paper in his hand, although he knew the name—"Chester Bayard."

"Chester—oh, Chet." She called back to the kitchen. "Chet, some guy for you."

The man who came out of the kitchen wore a chef's coat with his full name embroidered on the breast pocket: *Chester Bayard. Cocksman,* Sandy thought. Sandy could always tell. It was in the tilt of the head, the predatory nature of the man's eyes. He was probably sleeping with this girl, who was much too young for him. He probably screwed every attractive woman with whom he worked. He had probably screwed Julie Saxony, or tried. He was one of those guys. It was what he did, automatic as breathing.

"I'm an investigator with the Baltimore City Police Department." When he came in cold like this, he never said *homicide,* not first thing.

"A detective?"

"Once, but I retired. I'm a consultant now. I do cold cases."

"Murders."

Everyone was so goddamn savvy these days. Or thought they were. Yet this guy, this chef, would probably be appalled if Sandy presumed to know *his* trade based on watching a couple of shows on the Food Network.

"Yes, Julie Saxony in this case. I'm going to assume you remember her."

Bayard nodded. "I'm glad you're taking an interest. She was a nice lady, gave me my start as a chef. You want to sit?"

He indicated a table, then picked up a bottle from a pine buffet—Ricard. He poured the yellowish liquid into a small glass, added water from a ceramic pitcher. He was way too into the ritual, which meant he was either a show-off or a boozer. He offered Sandy a glass, but he passed. He drank with friends. Well, he used to. He hadn't really kept up with any of the other detectives after he retired. Bayard then waggled his fingers at the girl, her signal to leave. She flounced out, clearly miffed, although Sandy couldn't tell if it was the fact of being dismissed or the way it had been done.

"Why now?" Bayard asked. "It's been—"

"Twenty-six years since she disappeared, eleven since a homicide was established." Sandy was aware that he was finishing the sentence, but not answering the question.

"Has something happened?"

"Not really. Sometimes cold cases are nudged back into being by new information, but sometimes we just look at the file and decide there are things that were never properly explored."

"Is there new information?"

"I wouldn't tell you if there was."

"The detectives, the first time around. Small-town cops, didn't know what they were doing. They did a shit job, no?"

"No. They did okay. It's hard without a body. Not impossible, but hard. Havre de Grace police don't work a lot of murders, but their file was complete. Woman drove away, was never seen again. They talked to a lot of people, followed every lead they had. They talked to *you*."

"Well, I was the one who reported her missing. They kept asking me about the boyfriend."

"You mean Felix Brewer?"

"Yeah. That guy. Stupid waste of time."

Sandy couldn't help himself. "Everyone thinks everything's a waste of time when it's not the thing that leads to an answer." He paused, taken by his own turn of phrase, considered its larger implications. It could be a philosophy, almost. Then he realized it was a variation on that hippy-dippy shit about life's journeys. Still, it was a good rule in police work. Ruling stuff out was a kind of an answer. "It would have been irresponsible not to consider it, given the world in which he moved."

"She never spoke of him."

"Really?"

"Not to me. Never mentioned him or her past. She was hurt when the business became successful and he was always part of the things that were written."

"Never" was a big word, in Sandy's experience. If love and hate were intertwined, so were never and forever.

The girl came back with a wooden board of cheese and fruit, a long loaf of French bread already sliced.

"Dig in," the chef said. "It's almost noon, no?" It was the second time he had allowed himself that Gallic inflection, but Sandy thought this guy was about as French as French's mustard.

"No, thanks." He noticed that the girl lingered, pretending to be busy in the immaculate dining room. *Ears big as pitchers.* Nabby's expression, a mangling of what other people said about little pitchers and big ears.

"What kind of relationship did you have with Julie?"

"Very good. She was a great boss. And she gave me my start, got me out of the catering business."

"Was the relationship strictly business?" Bayard's girl was so fair that Sandy could see the tips of her ears flame red. *Honey, this guy is in his fifties. Do you think he's never been laid before?*

"We were friends."

"More than that?"

Bayard glanced at the young woman. Her back was still to them, but her posture was so rigid that it seemed as if she were literally holding her breath, waiting for the answer.

"I would have liked that. But she was past having lovers. A young woman, still in her thirties, and she claimed she was 'done with all that.'" He made air quotes with his fingers. "She needed me as a friend and I was that. I was—"

He stopped.

"Go on."

"No place to go. I was her friend."

"A friend with—hope?"

He laughed. "Where there's life, there's hope. Although—not to be cruel—she wasn't aging well. She dieted herself until her figure was very severe—anything to get rid of her curves, to hide her old self. She didn't want people to see the dancer in her."

"Dancer's a nice way to say it."

"Ah. Now see, that was the problem, no? People are so judgmental about strippers. She wasn't a whore. I'm not saying that girls on the Block didn't do tricks back then, but she didn't. She was Felix Brewer's girl within days of starting there."

The details were awfully specific, Sandy thought, given she had never spoken of her old life to Bayard.

"She danced in a G-string and pasties. Girls today, they go to the beach in less clothing." The chef's eyes rested on his girl, now trying to create busywork over at the bus station, unfolding and folding napkins. He was bored with her, Sandy decided. He was a man who got bored quickly.

"Did she carry a torch for Felix?"

Something caught light in Bayard's eyes, and he aimed his forefinger at Sandy's nose. "Do you know you are the first person to ask me the question in that way?"

"I find that hard to believe."

"No insult intended to your brothers in blue, but no one ever asked me what was in Julie's heart. It was always—'Was she in touch with him? Were there mysterious calls?' They checked her phone bills, her bank accounts. I think they even pulled the records on the pay phone a few blocks away. They were very interested to know if there had been contact, if she had any knowledge of him. As far as I know, there wasn't, she didn't. But she *was* still in love with him."

"How could you know that if she never talked about it?"

"I know women."

A smug thing to say, something only an asshole would say. Didn't make it untrue.

"That bug you? Her carrying a torch for this long-gone guy, while there you were, right under her nose?"

The name is always in the file. Always.

Bayard laughed. "I suppose you have to ask that. But I also have to assume that you have reviewed all the information and know that I spent July 3, 1986, prepping for what we expected to be a very big weekend. We were doing—not exactly a soft open, more of a test for friends. The restaurant was months from its official opening, we hadn't even finished the renovation of the dining room. I was pretty much in full view of my staff from the moment she drove away. I asked her to go to a kitchen-supply place for me."

Sandy did know that.

"You reported her missing that very day, right? She tells you she's going to Baltimore to go shop at Saks Fifth Avenue and you make the first call at ten thirty that night. What made you so sure that something had gone wrong? There are all sorts of reasons for people to stay out late. Traffic jams, a breakdown, running into an old friend, having dinner."

"The car had just been serviced two days before. And stores close, you know, around nine, and she had already been gone so long."

"Some women can easily shop that long."

"Not Julie. She was very decisive. And she had a woman who pulled things for her, to make it easier."

"Pulled things?"

"Oh, you know—what do they call it? A personal shopper."

"Did you mention that to the police at the time?"

"I think so. I don't know. They did take it seriously. Her

failure to come home that night, the following day. And the kitchen-supply store was pretty definitive that she had never made it there. But there was the boyfriend, the car—where did they find it?"

"At the Giant Foods on Reisterstown Road, more than a month later."

"Right. So I assumed they were thinking—well, that fits. She met someone, left the car, didn't plan on coming back. The thing is, she made no provision for the business. Once she was gone, it went to shit. I didn't have power of attorney. Neither did her sister. It was a mess, straightening all that out. She had consulted her lawyer a week earlier, but she hadn't *done* anything. This was not a woman planning to leave."

"How did you meet her in the first place?"

"Catering business."

"Yours or someone else's?"

"Someone else's. Julie was looking for a great chef, but she needed someone she could afford. She was very cagey, putting the word out for someone who was good, but not in a position to open his own restaurant. I was practically an indentured servant. I did all the work, the owner reaped the benefits. But I had no name, no backers willing to take a chance on me."

"But how did she find you?"

The chef played with his Ricard, adding water, swirling it, making quite a production. More show-off than drunk, Sandy decided. "That's another question no one thought to ask. It's quite harmless, really, but I didn't want to talk about it at the time. Out of respect to her, because it just loops around again to the same old topic, and I really did think that was a distraction."

"You haven't answered my question."

"I'm aware of that." He tapped a cigarette out of a pack, glanced at it. "I guess I can break the smoking laws in my own damn restaurant when it's closed. It might be closed forever soon enough. I can't seem to catch a break in this business. My food is good, too. But that's never enough."

"I know," Sandy said. The chef shrugged as if he thought Sandy was making polite conversation. How could some cop know anything about how hard it was to run a restaurant? "Anyway, how did you meet her?"

"My boss was the caterer of choice for big events among the rich Jews on the Northwest Side. Weddings, anniversary parties, bar mitzvahs. A woman named Lorraine Gelman hired me to do a big party, then referred me to her friend, Bambi Brewer, and I did her daughter's bat mitzvah. Julie called me a few days before the event, told me she was looking for a chef for a new restaurant, something very ambitious, but she wanted to sample the food, get a sense of what I could do. So she dropped by, hung out in the kitchen during the party."

"Julie Saxony was in the kitchen during this party for Felix's daughter?"

Bayard smiled, as if at a memory. "Yeah. I didn't have all the pieces then. Didn't understand why she was skittish, why she all but ran into the pantry when one of the family members came into the kitchen. I had tried to talk her out of visiting this particular party, asked that she wait for an occasion where I would be doing something more impressive than crepes and *frites*. I realized later that it wasn't entirely accidental, her choosing *that* event to sample my food. Sometimes, I think she hired me just to save face, you know? Plus, I am a great fucking chef. But that's not enough to make it in this business."

"So I've heard."

"Julie disappearing—I never caught a break after that. That restaurant was my big shot. I left Maryland, came back. Tried a superlocal thing on the Eastern Shore, but that was ahead of its time and too far from the Washington money. Now I'm trying to make traditional work. Want my advice? Look at what I'm doing now and do it in five years, and you'll be a rich man."

"What's the old saying? How do you make a million dollars in the restaurant business?"

Bayard smiled, finished his Ricard, then finished the joke. "Start with two million."

April 12, 1986

Rachel washed her hands, taking far more time than necessary, but she was enjoying listening to Michelle's young friends as they ran in and out of the bathroom, puffed up with their intrigues. *Joey says he likes you more than a friend, but not quite as a girlfriend. Michael kissed Sarah even though he's going with Jessica. Baz—Baz?—says you'll be cute after your nose job.* Rachel loved kids, of every age, but you couldn't pay her to be thirteen again, not even a thirteen-year-old beauty such as her sister, who had been pulling a pout all evening over this party, for which their mother had spent thousands, maybe tens of thousands.

"When did bat mitzvahs start having themes?" Linda had asked Rachel rather crankily when they entered the Peabody Hotel's party room, transformed into the Rue Brewer in the Thirteenth Arrondissement. The thirteen was for Michelle's age, of course. The Brewers had no intimate knowledge of Paris.

"They all do now," said Rachel, who had been her mother's confidante throughout the planning, in part because the mere mention of the party triggered Linda's temper. "One boy in her class did baseball—the family created an entire deck of baseball cards, with all the kids and their 'stats'—and another girl did Madonna, if you can believe it. I don't know what her parents were thinking, and I can't imagine what she wore. Then that one girl, Chelsea, whom Michelle dislikes, also decided to do a Paris theme and hers was first, in March. When Michelle got the invitation, she tried to wheedle Mom into changing the whole thing—I think she wanted to do some variation on Hollywood—but Mother was firm with her."

"For once," Linda had said, apparently determined to be in a bad mood all evening. She was seven months pregnant, and the hormones were taking their toll.

Ah, but Michelle deserved her party, Rachel thought, drying her hands and continuing to eavesdrop. (The girl who liked Joey had sent her emissaries back into the party to further parse his feelings. She remained behind with two others. She was pretty and appeared confident, but Rachel, as the older sister to a truly confident girl, recognized fake bravado when she saw it.) And the ballroom was really very charming, with the catering stations set up as pushcarts and sidewalk cafés. Artists sat at easels, drawing caricatures of the guests, and a strolling band of musicians played the kind of music heard on the sound track for *Charade*. Excessive, yes, but the crepes and *pommes frites* and madeleines were outstanding, not always a given at such a large-scale party. Lorraine Gelman had been right to crow about her caterer.

But—ninety-five dollars a head, and that didn't include the open bar—Rachel didn't want to do the math. The per-plate fee also didn't include the cake in the shape of the Eiffel Tower. Figure another five hundred dollars or so. It would probably be tasteless, too; in Rachel's experience, the more elaborate the cake, the less enjoyable it was. She had requested German chocolate cake for her bat mitzvah, which gave her grandmother Ida palpitations. Nana Ida could not stand anything German, although she made an exception for the Singers, the German Jewish family into which Rachel had married two years ago. And an exception for the BMW that Marc's parents had given them as a wedding gift, in which Ida loved to ride. "It's the least we could do," Marc's father said, "given that you kids took us off the hook for a wedding."

Yes, Rachel had wanted to say. *It really is the least you could do. You're very good at figuring out the least expected of you and doing just that, nothing more. Besides, my mother would have paid for the wedding, insisted on it, which is why we had to elope. But for all your alleged class, you have no antennae for the feelings of others.*

While Rachel had eloped, terrified by the unmatchable elegance of the engagement party thrown by Marc's family, Linda had the smallest wedding possible, only family and the Gelmans. A brunch at the Gelmans' house, coconut cake with whipped icing. Now *that* had been a good cake. *My life in cakes,* Rachel thought wryly. An interesting structure for a book of poetry. Except she wasn't a poet. She had tried to be, but it just wasn't in her. Instead, she had settled on a degree in semiotics, a very fashionable thing to study at Brown and an excuse to lose herself in the words that she could not corral on the page, no matter how she tried. There had been two Baltimore boys in the program, one named Ira, whom she never got to know, and Marc, whom she spent three years avoiding because they had been at Park together and she was all too familiar with his rep as a snob and a player.

Then she fell in love with him. Crazy-insane-head-over-heels in love with him. Marc was the best thing that had ever happened to her. And now the worst.

Respect your first instincts about people, her father had told her the day of her bat mitzvah. *People make fun of love at first sight, but it's just good instincts.*

You fell in love with Mama at first sight.

I did. And she with me, although she always pretends she didn't.

Had Rachel fallen in love at first or second sight? Had she loved Marc back in high school, but pretended indifference because he was out of her reach? She could no longer sort it out. She loved him, he loved her—and he had hurt her more than anyone she had ever known.

Sometimes, Rachel wondered if her parents' big romantic story would be less of a burden if Felix had actually *stayed*. Certainly, that charade of perfect love at first sight couldn't have been sustained as his daughters had grown, become more adept at picking up subtle signs that things were far from perfect. And yet—the myth survived, even after the terrible confidences that Bambi had shared with the two older girls not long after their father left. It was Michelle who was growing up with the full fairy tale, with no knowledge of the other woman. *Women*, although Bambi seemed to be bothered only by the last one, Julie Saxony, whom she described in strangely poetic terms. Flaxen hair. Cornflower-blue eyes. Those pretty words were worse, somehow, than the gag-worthy information that their father's girlfriend was a *stripper*.

The girl who pined for Joey suddenly squealed and ran out of the ladies' room, her handmaidens in tow, and Rachel was left alone. She sighed and tried to do something with her hair, finally admitting to herself that her dawdling had as much to do with avoiding Marc as it did with playing Margaret Mead in the ladies' room. She poked at her usually limp brown locks, which had been amplified by Bambi's hairdresser into seriously big hair, with bangs and tendrils that looked sexily spontaneous until one tried to touch a strand. It all but repelled her comb. She then stuck an experimental finger into her outsize skirt, but the dent repaired itself immediately. Bambi had insisted that all three daughters buy their dresses at Barneys New York, and the result was that the Brewer women were so fashion-forward that they looked hilariously out of place at a Baltimore bat mitzvah. Rachel wished she could have had the cash her mother spent on the dress, but then— she would never take money from her mother. Like Linda, she was terribly worried about the cost of this event. She just wasn't in a dull fury about it. Besides, Bambi *swore* that it was okay, that she had found a way to get the money without putting too much of a strain on the household. Which probably meant she had gone to Bert.

Rachel needed money, too. What a joke, being married to a rich man and being so poor. It would be one thing if Marc's family were cheap across the board. But Marc's parents were exceedingly generous with themselves and their children. They were stingy only with those who had the bad judgment to marry into the family. Sometimes, Rachel would find herself staring mutely, pleadingly, at her brother-in-law, wishing he were the kind of person who would go outside and smoke a cigarette with her so they could share their mutual pain. But that tall drink of water, that stupid *shaygetz,* was so naïve he didn't even know they called him the stupid *shaygetz* behind his back. Which was odd, because the Singers pretended they didn't know Yiddish most of the time. They were too grand, too many generations removed. Oh, how Rachel wished her father had been there the night of the engagement dinner, if only for his commentary on the finger bowls. At least Bambi had been able to humble them a little, through her sheer beauty and poise. But the money in that house—that evening, Rachel had watched her mother's hand go to her necklace, her favorite diamond earrings. A stranger couldn't tell, but Rachel knew that Bambi was unnerved by her new in-laws.

She wouldn't have been if Felix were still around.

Ten years. Ten years. Rachel missed her father every day. Not consciously, but his absence was a part of her, like a vine that wraps around a structure, sustains it even as it weakens it. She assumed Linda and her mother felt the same way, but they seldom spoke of him. They allowed themselves a handful of nice stories—"Remember the time at Gino's?" "Remember the bumper cars?" "Remember the time at the Prime Rib?"— and that was all.

Rachel had avoided Marc at Brown because he knew her story. Rachel had fallen so hard for him because she didn't have to tell him her story. Upon arriving at college, she was determined not to lie about her father, yet also intent on avoiding the emotional promiscuity that dorm life seemed to bring out in people. Sex was one thing, but why were girls so slutty with their life stories? But Marc knew. Knew her and didn't pity her.

"So here you are," Linda said, coming through the swinging door. "Marc looks unhappy."

"It's a pose he affects," Rachel said. "He's more handsome when he's brooding."

"What's going on with you two?"

"We had a fight." Not quite true, but they were going to have one, tomorrow.

"Oh, you two are always fighting."

"Not always. But it's normal to fight sometimes," Rachel said, hoping this was true. "You just think everyone should be like you and Henry in the Peaceable Kingdom."

"We fight," Linda said with a self-satisfaction that belied her words. She sat down carefully on one of the tufted stools. Although hugely pregnant, Linda moved with her usual grace.

"You yell at Henry as though he were a bad dog and he hangs his head and asks for your forgiveness. Or laughs at you. Either way, it's not real fighting."

"We happen to agree on most things. What do you and Marc have to fight about, anyway? Everything is going great for you."

Did it really look like that? Even to her sister? Rachel tried to stand outside her own life and see what others saw. The nice town house, a gift from Marc's parents, although in a rather sterile development. She would have liked to live in one of the old neighborhoods near downtown, but when someone else is paying, choice is curtailed. Marc worked for his family's real estate company, on the commercial side. Big deals, big money, he liked to say. Marc would rather sell one warehouse than five homes, whereas Rachel thought the only lure in real estate was the opportunity to make people happy. Rachel was a copywriter at a Baltimore ad agency, but the job was a favor called in by her father-in-law, and she wrote about things so boring that she literally fell asleep at her desk, which did not impress her boss or coworkers.

"Marc's parents couldn't even be bothered to attend the service this morning. Didn't you notice? His father claimed he had an important golf game. There has never, in the history of time, been a truly important golf game."

"The only thing I noticed was how everyone turned around when the door slammed at the exact moment Michelle got up to give her *haftorah*. But I'm looking at the bright side—now everyone will think she was rattled, and that's why she did such a shitty job."

"Linda!" But she was right about Michelle's abominable Hebrew.

"Is it too much to ask that she make even a halfhearted attempt to do a good job after all the expense and time Mother put in? She had her own tutor, Rachel, spent countless hours with him. And it wasn't just the Hebrew. Her speech was ridiculous."

"I didn't think it was that bad."

"Rachel—she incorporated the lyrics of a Wham! song into the story of the Exodus. It was borderline sacrilegious. Make the bread before you go-go?"

" 'Lose the yeast or it will be too slow-slow.' I thought it was funny."

"Rachel, our semiotician. How's that working out for you as a career?" But Linda, while frequently furious, was not cruel. She put her hand on her sister's arm by way of apology. "I'm sorry, Rachel. I feel like I've been pregnant for three years. And I'm just so pissed that Mother spent all this money she doesn't have."

"She told me it would be okay. She swore. She said she had a little windfall."

"From what? Aunt Harriet is still alive and kicking, with no signs of letting go. She's out there right now, stuffing rolls in her purse."

"She wouldn't say. But she said there's even enough left over to give her a little cushion."

But not enough cushion, Rachel thought, to bail Rachel out. If she left Marc, she would have nothing. She had no savings and quite a bit of college debt. The job, provided as a favor to his father, would disappear. The car, too, would be taken back; the title was in his parents' name. And there was the prenup. Technically a postnup, presented to the happy couple when they had returned from their Las Vegas elopement. How Rachel and Marc had laughed at his silly parents. Why not sign a document that had no meaning, they agreed. They would be together forever.

Rachel believed Marc had been sincere in that moment. He loved her and they were kindred spirits. He even wrote poetry and—knife to her heart—his was good. Second knife to her heart, he abandoned it. "I don't want to get an MFA and teach and be poor," he told her. "I grew up with money. I like it." How could Rachel argue? She had known life with and without it, and there was no contest: money was better.

But *if* she had Marc's gift for writing and *if* her father were still around—she didn't doubt that he would encourage her, support her. Your family should be your Medicis. Maybe if she found a real job, on her own—

"Do you believe it?" Linda asked.

"What?" she said, pretending she had been listening all the while, not lost inside herself.

"You know. The story. The door."

"Oh, no. You know how people go in and out throughout the service."

"But the doors usually just creak, not make that hollow booming sound. Everyone turned around—except Mother."

Rachel smiled. The two sisters had an almost twinlike closeness. Nice for them, hard on Michelle.

"You're saying Mom is like the defendant in that old story about the trial where the attorney announces the real killer is about to walk through the door. He doesn't turn around because he knows he's the real killer. So Mom knows that nothing can bring Daddy back, not even Michelle's bat mitzvah."

"If he were to come back, it would be for that, though."

"Really? Not college graduations, not our marriages? Only Michelle's bat mitzvah would bring him back?"

"You didn't go to yours. Graduation, I mean. And I had no interest in mine because I was already planning my marriage to Henry. Did it ever occur to you," Linda said, dropping her crankiness for earnestness, "that we both chose the kind of weddings where an absent father was less noticeable? You in Vegas, me at a brunch in the house."

"We were only trying to save Mother money."

"And save ourselves from disappointment. Think about it, Rachel." Linda rose to her feet, swaying a little, like a balloon on a string, but still very graceful. "There's always been this stupid fiction that he comes back, like some benevolent spirit, standing at the rear of the synagogue, like Elijah on Passover. He's never come back. And he's never coming back."

Linda looked very pale.

"Are you okay?"

"I think I'm going to throw up. Other women have morning sickness during the first trimester. I have evening sickness in the final one."

Linda walked with admirable dignity to the nearest stall. Rachel waited for her, noting that her sister managed to vomit rather quietly. Ah, the powers of the trained PR person, so skilled in papering things over that she knows how to mask the sound of retching. Or maybe she simply hadn't started yet.

A girl entered, rubbing her eyes.

"Sydney." Rachel had known Sydney Gelman, now eleven, all her life. She had been adopted when Bert and Lorraine despaired of having their own children. Less than two years later, Lorraine gave birth to twin boys.

"Oh—hello, Rachel."

"Are you crying?"

"No. I just had an allergic reaction to the shellfish in the crepes, so Mother asked the waiter to take it away and bring me a fruit plate."

Sydney was plump, always had been. It was a sweet, healthy plumpness, the kind that came with lustrous hair and shining eyes. Rachel thought Sydney would be much less pretty if forced to lose weight. But Aunt Lorraine lived off broiled grapefruit and Tab and didn't see why Sydney couldn't as well.

"Did you get to have the crepes suzette at least?"

"I don't think I saw those."

"Why don't you come with me and we'll see if there are some left in the kitchen?"

She started to take Sydney by the hand, something she would have done naturally a few years ago, before she left for college.

But Sydney was only five then. To treat her that way now would be disastrous. Rachel sneaked her into the kitchen and procured a plate of sweets for her, despite the murderous glances from the man in charge of the catering crew. What was the big deal? Perhaps he didn't want anyone eating there, but she and Sydney knew that if they took the plate back into the dining room, Lorraine would find a way to whisk that one away as well. It was a party. No one should have to diet at a party.

"Are you having a good time?"

"It's okay," Sydney said. "I don't know many of these kids because I'm two classes behind them. One girl asked why I was even here and I said Michelle and I were like cousins. And she said I was lying."

"She's probably jealous," Rachel said. "We are like cousins."

"Michelle doesn't speak to me."

"*What?*"

"Don't say anything." Sydney's voice, while pitched low, was panicky. "I don't care. Really."

Sydney was wise in her own way. It would be counterproductive to remonstrate with Michelle, but, oh, Rachel wished her sister weren't cruel. Rachel and Linda had been kind to everyone, at their father's insistence. The practice had served them well after he left because there were no grudges, no girls waiting for them to fall.

The party was wrapping up when Rachel returned Sydney to the ballroom. The fact that Sydney was at Rachel's side softened Bambi's murderous look, but not Marc's hurt one. Rachel followed him to the BMW, resolved not to fight. This would be Michelle's bat mitzvah day, not the day she confronted Marc.

In the car, she realized she had left her wrap behind. He didn't want to go back and they drove another five minutes, which, as she pointed out to him, only added ten minutes to the trip. Said it nicely, still determined not to fight. The shawl was cashmere, a gift from her mother. There was no way she was going to trust it to the hotel's lost-and-found overnight.

When she entered the ballroom, it was almost empty of people, although the fake cafés and shops were still standing. A woman was walking the ersatz French boulevard, taking it all in.

"Oh, I—I'm . . . I'm here to meet the caterer," she said when she noticed Rachel. "About another job."

The woman was dressed like the catering crew, in black slacks and a white shirt. She had blond hair and blue eyes, Rachel noted. One might even say *flaxen* and *cornflower blue*. She was thin, much too thin. She bolted for the kitchen and Rachel was tempted to follow her, but she let it go, let her go. The encounter was so odd that she had an instantaneous desire to speak to Linda about it, followed by an immediate resolve to never speak of this to anyone. *She couldn't be, she just couldn't be.* Even if she was, it was just one of those Baltimore coincidences. She very well could be hiring the same caterer. Maybe she was getting married. Hooray for her. Rachel found her wrap draped over a chair and headed out into the night.

Back in the car, she sat in silence as Marc wondered aloud again why she had abandoned him all night. He was nudging, trying to pick a fight, then backing away as if nervous about what a quarrel might bring.

"I mean, it's okay, I can handle talking to Lorraine Gelman, although she bores me silly. She and my mom go all the way back to Park. But why would you do that to me, Rachel? You looked so pretty tonight. I just wanted to be with you. Why did you disappear?"

I don't know. Because I was having more fun in the bathroom. Because I missed my father so much tonight. Because you have a girlfriend. Some stupid piece on the side who actually sends you notes at our house.

"There were just so many people to talk to," she said.

Was it really only yesterday that she had opened the hand-lettered note to Marc? She wasn't a snoop by nature. She had picked it up only because it was from Saks and she assumed it was some stupid flyer for a sale and Marc could be needlessly extravagant. She expected to find a notice of a fur sale, given the time of year, or maybe jewelry tied to Mother's Day.

Instead she found the most explicit love letter she had ever read. A sex letter would be a better description. *Your cock here, your cock there, my mouth on your cock.* It seemed as if the letter went on for pages, that it was longer than *Ulysses,* longer than all twelve volumes in *A Dance to the Music of Time,* a work that Rachel and Marc both loved, but it was really only a page and a half, and it wouldn't have been that long if the handwriting had been more controlled. Part of Rachel's mind detached, imagining Marc's horror at such pedestrian language, the sloppy handwriting.

Another part of her mind, even more cool and cruel, chimed in: *Well, look at you. You are truly your mother's daughter now, a woman whose husband loves her so much that he sleeps with other women. Love at first sight, love at second sight—what about love at last sight? Is that too much for a Brewer woman to ask? Or does one have to settle as Linda has, for a man who's sweet but weak and pliable?*

How had Rachel ended up living her mother's life? How could she get out of it with her dignity intact? It was one thing to marry the better poet, but he was supposed to be a better man, too.

"Where are we, Rachel?"

She thought the question existential, but Marc, a suburban boy, had gotten twisted in the city's one-way streets and ended up making a series of squares.

"You're going north on Calvert. You should circle back to the JFX here."

"But I can pick it up in a few blocks, right?" He always asked for her help, always got defensive when she provided it. He couldn't possibly know—or could he?—that his chosen route took them past Horizon House, one of the high-rises thrown up in the 1960s during yet another abortive Baltimore renaissance. It was not quite the spiffy place it had seemed to Rachel ten years ago when her mother had pointed it out to her two oldest daughters, saying in a strangely matter-of-fact voice: "Your father's girlfriend lives here, but I bet she'll be moving now that she has all his money."

March 14, 2012

The day after his meeting with Bayard, Sandy found himself walking down Thirty-sixth Street. The area appeared to be thriving after a few soft years. He stopped tallying up all the restaurants when he got to five. There was home-style stuff, a noodle place, Mexican and the Golden West, with its eclectic mix of Tex-Mex, Thai, and what Sandy thought of as Elvis-Southern. Deep fried, fatty, disgusting, great. A Cuban restaurant would have been a good addition to the current mix. Had he just been ahead of his time? He had used that excuse, but it felt hollow after hearing Bayard invoke it, a loser's defense. "You're an orphan," Nabby would hiss when he disappointed her. "No one wants you and now I'm stuck with you and you're good for *nothing*."

The cost of picking at other people's brains for a living was that Sandy was all too aware of the machinations of his own mind, where ideas pinged around like errant pinballs. He had known all along where he was headed when he went out for this walk today. Now he had reached his old building, currently an antiques store full of things he could never afford. Sandy turned his collar up and put his head down, although the wind wasn't particularly cutting. He felt like a teenager, riding his bike past the home of a crush. *Just passing by. See me. Love me.*

Then he saw the kid, as he always thought of him, one of his few regulars, coming out of some weird bakery that was all muffins and cupcakes, not an honest roll or loaf of rye to be found. The kid was juggling packages while trying to keep a toddler in tow. Sandy had thought the kid had a baby, not a child who was already walking. Then he realized—this was the same baby. Must be two years since he had last seen this guy. Of course the baby had grown. That's what babies do. Normal ones.

"Can I give you a hand?" Sandy offered, catching the bakery bag before it tumbled to the ground, even as the big satchel on the kid's shoulder started to slide.

"Hey, Sandy!" He was impressed at the kid's ability to pull up his name on the spot. For his part, Sandy couldn't have said for the life of him what the kid's name was. And the guy's seeming joy at seeing Sandy, a marginal acquaintance at best, appeared genuine. Sandy couldn't remember the last time someone had been that happy to see him. Only Mary. Never Bobby. That should have been a sign, right? A boy should be excited when his dad comes home.

"What's going on, Sandy? What are you up to since the restaurant closed?"

The kid managed to make it sound positive, as if the restaurant was something Sandy had chosen to leave behind. "I'm a consultant. Doing cold case work for the police department."

"Hey, that's great—" He took a few steps, grabbed his daughter by the back of her coat. "This is Scout. Carla Scout, but we somehow ended up calling her Scout."

"Scout?"

He made a face. "I know. It's so *hipster*. But it's from *To Kill a Mockingbird* and not the least ironic. Besides, I've gone through

life being called Crow by most people, despite having the perfectly respectable name of Edgar, and I'm relatively unscathed."

Now, see, the kid was classy that way. He had managed to
remind Sandy of his name without putting it on Sandy. Sandy now
remembered that he had never called him Crow but had made a
joke out of his real name, dubbing him Fast Eddie. If Sandy were
running a proper restaurant, a white tablecloth place, he would
want this guy for the front of the house.

"Pupcake," the girl said, looking up at Sandy with enormous
blue eyes, but all kids had big eyes. Scout. That was just a crazy
thing to do to any kid, but especially a girl. "More pupcake."

"She's pretty," Sandy said, unsure if she really was, but how
could you go wrong, telling a man his daughter was pretty. The
girl did have amazing coloring—light eyes with dark hair, the
black Irish thing. Like Mary. But her clothing was bizarre—
shorts layered over heavy tights, beneath a sensible duffel coat.
Sandy wasn't exactly up-to-date on what the fashionable two-
year-olds were wearing. Maybe this was—what did the kid call
it?—hipster, too.

"She dresses herself," offered his old customer. "So are you
working on something good?"

Sandy realized he wanted to talk about his case. He suddenly
wanted to *talk,* to have this human moment that so many people
took for granted. *How was work today, dear?*

"It's actually kinda interesting. Julie Saxony, the girlfriend of
Felix Brewer." No look of recognition. "He's a guy who skipped
town back in the '70s rather than do the time on a federal gambling rap. Way before your time, I'm guessing." Details were
coming back to him. The kid had grown up somewhere else, but
his wife was hard-core Baltimore, the kind of local who was said
to be Baltimore born, bred and buttered. "Ten years later, almost
to the day he ran, *she* disappeared. The cops were always pretty
sure it was a murder, but the body didn't surface until 2001."

"Any particular reason you're working it?"

"No." You couldn't tell a guy like this about a sexy photo, the way a dead woman's eyes had pulled you in.

"You know, my wife is a private detective."

"I don't think I did know that." Was Sandy so incurious off the job that he had failed to ask one of his few regular customers what his wife did? Or was he just the kind of man who didn't think about women working in a meaningful way? He had to cop to being both. But the thing about being a murder police is that you spend so much time absorbing other people's lives that you don't solicit people's life stories in your off-hours.

"Anyway, she says money is the thing that drives people. Money and pride."

Sandy wanted to be polite, but he was getting awfully tired of other people telling him his business. A PI wouldn't know that much about homicide. Divorce work, maybe. Where, come to think of it, everything *was* driven by money and pride.

"*Most* murders," Sandy said, "come down to stupidity, impulse, and opportunity."

"Sure, most. But those are—what do you call it? The dunkers?"

Lord, how Sandy wished people would just stop watching cop shows. Only cops should watch cop shows.

The kid continued: "I'm thinking about the cases that go unsolved, which is what cold cases are. The ones where people have done something deliberately, then taken care to cover their tracks."

"Motives," Sandy said, not bothering to suppress his sigh. "Well, no one benefited financially from this lady's death."

Lady. Would he have called her that a week ago? Maybe not. But the more he knew about her, the more he liked Julie Saxony. She was a go-getter.

"I've always been curious—do the police have a lot of access to financial information in a murder? Can you get people's accounts, do a kind of credit report? I mean, my wife—" He suddenly busied himself, wiping "pupcake" from his daughter's face, which hadn't bothered him at all a minute ago. Sandy suspected the kid was about to incriminate his wife, reveal that she had sources that got her information through not exactly legal methods. Must be nice, but she didn't have to stand behind her work in court, delineate every piece of evidence and how it was obtained. Divorce work was like going to war, and all was fair in love and war.

All was fair in love and war. His brain replayed his own thought, telling him to pay attention, not to let go of what might seem like just another cliché passing through.

"Sure, with the proper paperwork I can get what I need. I mean, it's not like the movies where I go click, click, click, and some amazing document opens on the computer. But there's no money to follow here. She had a nice business. Her disappearance didn't benefit anyone, and it screwed up a lot of people—her employees, her sister. In her absence, they couldn't work it out. Business went bust."

"Ah, so what do you think happened? I mean, where do you start?"

"With the original witnesses, every single name in the file—and this file runs to almost eight hundred pages. Of course, I can only get to those who are still around. Twenty-five years, things happen." He considered the youth of the man in front of him, the sunny disposition. "People die."

The kid nodded. "Or disappear, or don't remember. Or they *think* they remember, which is even worse. Did you know the more we tell a story, the more degraded it becomes? Factually, I mean. It's like taking a beloved but fragile object out of a box and turning it over in your hands. You damage it every time."

"That's interesting." Sandy wasn't being polite in this instance. He had begun to pay careful attention to the subject of memory, key in cold cases. He worried that there would be a day when defense attorneys could jettison *all* testimony based on memory. He really thought the United States ought to go the way of the UK, put cameras up everywhere. Oh, all the ACLU types would howl, but if you're not a criminal, why would you care? All was fair in love and war.

Love, he thought. *Love.* It didn't rule out stupidity or impulse. In fact, love tended to run with that crowd.

"Gotta go," he said abruptly, aware he was being rude, unable to stop himself. "She's a cutie."

He went into a diner, an honest one that dated back to the Avenue's pre-chic days, and ordered a cup of coffee. He got out a notepad and began doodling. Sometimes, it was better not to have the file in front of you, just your head and some paper.

He re-created the shapes in his head—the major triangle of Julie, Felix, and his wife, who didn't even show up until the murder file was opened in 2001, and she had been eliminated pretty definitively. Everyone had fixated on Felix when Julie disappeared, but what good does it do to kill your husband's girlfriend ten years after he's gone, having left both of you? But there were other triangles. Felix–Julie–the sister. Julie had kind of dumped Andrea for her boyfriend, hadn't she? Moved out, moved up. He drew another triangle: Felix-Julie-Tubby. The former fat man had met her first, brought her to Felix. Tribute? Or had he wanted her for himself and been surprised when she chose Felix?

Sandy paid for his coffee. A buck twenty-five and this place was cheap by today's standards. Had he really once lived in a world where a cup of coffee cost a quarter, candy bars were a nickel, hamburgers could be had for less than fifty cents? He never flinched at the gas station, no matter how high the prices got, because it made sense to him that something like gas kept going up, up, up, controlled by all those sheiks. It was the small items of his youth that he remembered. And they had seemed expensive then, coming from Cuba. Expensive and bountiful. The first time he had walked into the pharmacy on Twenty-ninth Street, the one with the soda fountain, he had been overwhelmed by the sheer abundance of his new life. It had taken him forty minutes to choose a candy bar. He told that story to Mary, told her it was a Marathon bar. Mary pointed out that Marathons weren't around when he was fourteen.

So the kid, Crow, was right. The things Sandy thought he remembered best were the things he was getting wrong. In which case—what did that say about his memories of Mary? Were they wrong? As long as they were loving, did it matter if they were wrong? He wished, as he wished every day, for her company. True, she could drive him mad with her endless analysis of every single personal interaction, but that was what women did.

He doodled a name on his pad: Lorraine Gelman. Indirectly brought the chef and Julie together. Knew Bambi and Felix, probably knew Tubman through her husband, the criminal attorney. She would be protective of her old friends. Wives side with wives. But she might know stuff, might have spotted the dynamic he suspected. The only worry in Sandy's mind was that a woman married to one of the best criminal attorneys in the city wouldn't talk to him without lawyering up.

Lawyering up. She might even say that. *I'll have to lawyer up.* Jesus. Sometimes, Sandy felt like a magician in a room where even the youngest kid yelled out: "It's a trick box! She's pulled her knees up to her chest!"

June 18, 1991

Michelle was aware of the impression she made as she walked out to the pool in high-heeled sandals and a pink bikini. She strolled the full length slowly, toward the deep end where the adults—her mother, Bert, Lorraine— were seated. She then had to go back and procure one of the chaises at the other end. Again, she made a show of it, letting the wheels clatter, refusing the help of the all-but-panting teenage boys who offered to do it for her. How could her mother possibly think that Michelle—eighteen, a high school graduate—should attend a party of *sixteen-year-olds*. It had been bad enough, having Sydney's company pushed on her all these years, but to attend a Sweet Sixteen on the first beautiful Saturday in June—torture. Especially when her boyfriend had wanted to take her to Philadelphia for dinner, to Le Bec Fin. But her mother couldn't possibly know that, right? She didn't even know about the boyfriend.

Michelle had come up with such a good plan to get away, too. She told her mother that she was going to Philadelphia for the day to visit an art museum with a girl she had met on the College Park visit, a girl who might be her roommate if she proved, on this outing, as collegial as she seemed. This should have been a no-brainer for Bambi—art, a girl, Michelle trying to be sensible and optimistic about the whole College Park thing, which had been a bitter pill to swallow. Not because she was a brainiac like Rachel, or a grind like Linda, but because she had wanted to go someplace *fun*. ASU, Tulane, University of Miami. Only she hadn't got into any of them. Bambi said Maryland was a bargain and if Michelle wanted to go out of state, she should have put more effort into high school, as Linda and Rachel had.

"You might also want to consider if the number of tanning days belongs on a list of things you need in a college," she had added.

Tanning days. Michelle flipped on her stomach, reached behind her and unsnapped her halter top, then slid the top beneath her and onto the table where her Diet Coke was sweating. Her mother and the Gelmans were enjoying Bellinis, although the kids—the kids!—had been promised sips of champagne when the cake came out. Michelle's own sisters—well, Linda at least—had been able to drink at eighteen, but the law had changed. Just another entry on Michelle's List of Everything Unfair.

But now that her top was off, no one would dare approach her. It actually hurt a little, pressing her bare breasts into the Japanese-inspired lounge chair—Lorraine always had the most beautiful things, but she didn't always have the most comfortable things—and it would probably leave marks, but who cared? She wasn't going to see her boyfriend tonight. Her perfect plan had been torpedoed by Bambi, who had blandly told Michelle that she wouldn't cover the cost of the train ticket because Michelle was overdrawn on her allowance by six weeks. And Michelle couldn't have the car because Bambi needed it to go to this party, which Michelle was going to attend, too.

"If it kills you," Bambi had added.

"It just might."

Michelle glanced over her shoulder at the kids in the pool. A few years ago, she might have amused herself by making all the boys focus on her, but it was too easy, not enough of a challenge. The Philadelphia man, as she thought of him, was another story. The Philadelphia Story. That's the kind of joke that Rachel would have made, if Michelle had confided in her, but she wasn't like everyone else, telling Rachel her secrets. The Philadelphia Story was twenty-four, in his second year at Wharton, and Michelle was cock-teasing him within an inch of his life. She loved that men tried to use that term as an insult. She was proud of her technique, as formal and balletic as a matador's. So far, she had slept with him only literally, stripping down to a T-shirt and her underwear, then ordering him out of the bed when she awoke in the middle of the night to find him trying to undress her.

Her mother had thought Michelle was on a school trip to New York City that time. There *was* a Park trip to New York in May. Bambi had given Michelle the money to attend and she had signed up, then gone sorrowfully to the head of school seventy-two hours before departure and explained that there were the "usual issues" at home and she needed a full refund. The head had counted the money out of petty cash and asked Michelle how her senior project was coming along. (Park students did not attend classes in their final semester, but worked on projects that they presented at year's end.) "As well as can be expected," she said, using her brave voice, the voice of The Girl Who Had Seen Too Much, the girl who had been asked to be an adult before her time. The Philadelphia Story, whom she had met in a bar Preakness weekend, was waiting for her outside the school. He drove her straight to a beautiful inn on the Eastern Shore, one that had been in some movie a few years back, and she had tortured him all weekend. She was a virgin, she told him. True. She wasn't ready yet. Also true, although Michelle's not-readiness had nothing to do with fear. Oh, she helped him out, she wasn't heartless. Well, maybe a little heartless, when she crawled into that beautiful bed with him in her panties and T-shirt and told him he could take care of himself while he watched her touch herself. "But use a towel," she added.

They had hit Saks in D.C. before he took her back home. She then hid her purchases at her friend Devorah's, who briefed her on the New York trip so Michelle could provide Bambi with plausible details. The only possible pitfall was that someone would mention to Bambi what a shame it was that Michelle had been forced to cancel, but Michelle was pretty sure that the head would remind everyone to be sensitive about the Poor Brewers. Everyone was so goddamn careful around Michelle. People at school, her mother, her sisters. Just because she used it to her advantage didn't mean it didn't bother her.

Jesus, this chaise was like some kinky bondage chair. She couldn't find a comfortable position on it and she sure as shit couldn't flip over. Lorraine might not know what it was like to try and lie facedown when one had breasts, but Sydney certainly did. Lorraine probably didn't spend much time by the pool, being the kind of woman who never tanned. A shame. The pool was gorgeous. Michelle loved everything about the Gelmans' house, couldn't understand her mother's private disdain for it. When she was younger, she had assumed her mother was pretending to dislike it because she was embarrassed by their own house, but, no, Bambi really seemed to think their old wreck of a place was preferable to this shiny house where everything was so very up to the minute. If this was tacky, then Michelle could only hope to live in such tackiness.

She felt a shadow fall across her back, assumed it was a cloud passing over the sun. When the shadow didn't move, she said: "I'm fine, I don't need anything."

"You need," a man's voice growled, "to put your top on."

Oh, Bert, sent to do Mother's dirty work. Again.

"You have your top off," she said. Bert was very proud of his physique, and Michelle had to admit it was quite good. Slender yet muscled, the right amount of hair. And, like her, he tanned beautifully, quite the opposite of Lorraine with her big hats and moles everywhere.

"You're embarrassing your mother."

And upstaging your daughter, she thought. Michelle actually liked Sydney, who was extremely good-natured about being the overweight redhead in a family of dark-haired, good-looking people. Her twin brothers, Adam and Alec, born less than two years after Sydney was adopted, had the kind of eyes and lips that people said were wasted on boys. They were certainly wasted on those two. Nasty jocks, very competitive. They would have been asked to leave Park School if Lorraine wasn't such a big deal there.

"Okay, I'll just sit up and put my top on," she bluffed.

"You will cover yourself with a towel and go into the house to make sure you're decent."

She started to argue, but something in Bert's tone would not be denied. She did as instructed, thinking about the alternate reality of Philadelphia, the place she should be right now. They might have gone to an art museum for real. Then Le Bec Fin—not that Michelle could eat that much and still wear bikinis, but she liked the idea of expensive restaurants and wine and champagne. She still wasn't ready to have sex with him, though. She might never be. She wanted to be in love the first time and she hadn't been, not even close. She barely *liked* most of the boys and men she knew. She assumed the Philadelphia Story would get mad with her eventually, really mad. That was part of the thrill, testing how far she could push men. No, she did *not* want to be raped, and she felt she had excellent instincts for picking men who would not go that far. Look at Philadelphia Story, making his stealth move in the middle of the night, then skulking off to sleep in a chair when she called him out. No, she was very clear that she wasn't caught up in some moral dilemma, as Rachel would probably have it, in which she wanted a man to take her virginity because she was too guilt-ridden to give it away freely.

It was just so *exciting*, knowing that she had something men wanted, that anyone wanted. Not only did her boyfriends not take advantage of her, they allowed her to boss them around, demand favors. She supposed she would still be able to do that after she lost her virginity, but she wasn't in a rush to find out. Her mother, as far as Michelle knew, hadn't had sex for fifteen years and men were crazy for her. Look at Bert, doing whatever she wanted, without Bambi even having to ask. Yet her sisters had fallen crazy in love and where had that gotten them? Linda was always yelling at Henry, and Marc had divorced Rachel before their second anniversary, leaving her without a penny. Rachel had signed a postnup, the sap. You'd never catch Michelle making that kind of mistake.

Michelle had first discovered her power while working with her Hebrew tutor, a young man who had bought her clothes. Shoplifted them, actually, although she didn't know that at the time. She could imagine Rachel saying, "Do the math, stupe. He was helping you with Hebrew for ten bucks an hour. Do you think he could afford those things he gave you?" But it never occurred to Michelle to worry about how he afforded the items until he was arrested, a month after her bat mitzvah. He was picked up at the Woodies in Columbia with a pair of Guess jeans. Michelle's first thought was: *Wait—he steals for other girls, too?* She had assumed she was special and was irritated to learn that he had made similar arrangements with other female students.

He had been a little pervy. It was funny, how the ones who touched you the least were often pervier than the ones who really did stuff. But weak, so weak. Once, when he tried to get her to model one of the outfits, she had looked at him and said:

"It's not really my style. But thank you." Bambi had been out of the house that day. Who wouldn't trust her twelve-year-old daughter with her Hebrew tutor? He had tried to kiss her once, only once. Michelle had drawn a hand across her mouth and said: "No, thank you." The next week, he brought her three dresses, better ones.

Towel wrapped to ensure modesty, she walked back the length of the pool, still aware of the boys' glances. She did not use the bathroom in the cabana/changing room at poolside, nor did she use the powder room off the kitchen. Michelle, who knew the Gelmans' home as well as her own, climbed the stairs to the master bedroom, where the enormous en suite marble bath had lighted mirrors, heated towel racks, a bidet, even a heated floor, not that it was turned on in June.

The bathroom opened into a dressing room the size of Michelle's oh-so-stingy bedroom. Even as Linda and Rachel decamped, Bambi would not allow Michelle to move into their rooms. Michelle suspected this was because she would then want to redecorate, make the new room hers. Why shouldn't she? Her room was childish. Sophisticated for a thirteen-year-old—she had been allowed to use her bat mitzvah money to redo it. But now the color palette, peach and pale green, bored her. So fussy, so Laura Ashley, which it happened to be.

Her top back on, she sat on the long, upholstered stool in the center of Lorraine's closet and considered its perfection. The problem, as Michelle saw it, was that money came too late. You had to be old, in your forties, before you had the money to have the best clothes, furnishings, jewels. Even if Lorraine had been as beautiful as Bambi, these things would still be wasted on her. Michelle wished she had known her mother in her twenties, when the money flowed and no expense was spared. The photos of this time, in black and white, looked fake to her, props from a film. And by the time Michelle was born in 1973, the clothing was hor-

ribly tacky. Thank God Bambi had made them dress like the preppies they weren't.

She barely remembered her father and worried sometimes
that the memories she did have weren't even hers, just stories
planted by her mother and sisters. But there was a smell, a couple
of them. Cigar stores, anything leathery. And a certain aftershave
that she sometimes picked up in department stores. No one could
have made her remember smells that weren't hers to remember.

If her father had served his sentence, he would be free by now.
Would it really have been that hard? She once overheard Linda
telling Rachel that he might have been out in ten years, according
to Henry. Ten years. He would be here and this would be their
house and she would be allowed to borrow her mother's clothes
and jewels. Because, yes, Bambi was the same size as Michelle.
When Michelle was younger, the boys who came to the house
had gotten crushes on her.

Maybe that was part of the reason that Michelle now preferred
men, men she never allowed to come to her house.

But even if her father had returned, would they have been rich
again? Michelle could never work out that part of the fantasy, and
Michelle was very pragmatic about her fantasies. What would he
do? Could he earn as much in a legal enterprise as he had in his
old business? These were not questions she could put to Bambi,
or even her sisters. So much of what she knew about her father
had been learned from eavesdropping. Michelle was less resentful
than the others thought about being cut off from the family's days
of ease and money. But she hated not being privy to the secrets
that her sisters shared. The stories about the mistress. Did they
really think that Michelle, incurious as she was at thirteen, hadn't
seen the article in the *Star* when Julie Saxony disappeared almost
ten years to the day after her father did? It had been only a matter
of time before someone at school had told her that everyone believed that her father had finally sent for Julie Saxony—and all

the money he had put away, money that was supposed to go to Bambi.

Much to her surprise, Michelle started to cry. And everything around her was so beautiful, silken and pristine, that she wasn't sure where to dry her tears, which were clotted with mascara. She padded back to the bathroom, picked up the towel she had left on the floor.

"What are you doing here?"

It was Sydney, the birthday girl, the girl to whom all this belonged, not that she would ever fit into skinny Lorraine's dresses, no matter how her mother tried to starve her. Sydney was wearing a two-piece, which Michelle found absolutely shocking. She would live in a caftan if she had a body like Sydney's.

"Your father told me to go put my top back on. I was lying on my stomach, just trying to avoid tan lines. But, you know."

"His ideas about femininity basically align with Sir Walter Scott. He's a prude, my dad." A shrug.

Michelle envied Sydney those casual words even more than she envied her these beautiful things. To be able to say that one's father was this or that.

To be able to say: "My dad." *My dad, my dad, my dad.*

"Anyway, we're about to have cake. Don't you want cake?"

Sydney's tone implied that everyone must want cake all the time. Michelle wished she did, that the pleasures of chocolate and frosting could still be meaningful to her. Then again, what did she find pleasurable? She enjoyed things mainly in the planning. If she had gone to Philadelphia today, the thrill would have been in the subterfuge and the escape. And then the night, the hours of denying someone else pleasure. That was what made her happiest, or at least close to something that others might recognize as happiness.

"Oh, I don't know," she said. "I'm not hungry."

"I guess that's why you have the body you have," said Sydney.

Cheerful, not begrudging. "Mom tries to make me live on lettuce and carrots, hoping I'll look like you—or at least like her. But it's just never going to happen."

Michelle couldn't help being impressed by Sydney's matter-of-fact acceptance of herself. "How do you manage that?"

"Manage what?"

This was tricky to word. "Not minding. I mean, you know, being cool with how things are."

Sydney smiled. Half smiled, really, using only the left corner of her mouth. "I've got my stuff. Believe me, I've got stuff that bugs me. Stuff that's bigger than my weight."

"Like what?" Michelle really could not imagine what could bother someone if she had money and didn't care about her appearance.

"I was asked to leave camp last summer."

"That's it? You got kicked out of sleep-away camp?"

Sydney studied her, as if judging Michelle's worthiness as a confidante. "Yes, that's it. But it bugs me. I loved that camp. I loved—well, I wish I could go back. I would have been a junior counselor this year. But I can't go back. They made that clear."

Some boring kid spat, Michelle decided. She wouldn't press further. She tried to ignore the fact that Sydney clearly wasn't allowing her to press further.

"Look, even if you don't want cake, won't you please come back to the party? I know you don't want to be here, with my friends, but I'm so happy you came."

"You are?"

"I am. I don't have any real cousins. You and Linda and Rachel are the closest thing I have. And my brothers are such assholes."

"Sydney!" Michelle didn't disagree. She was just shocked that Sydney was so candid.

"Everyone knows. Except Mom, which I guess is how it's supposed to be. Look, I don't mind that I was adopted, I really don't, and that my brothers were born eighteen months later and everyone's like, 'Oh, that's what happens when people adopt, they relax and have their *own* children.' My parents have never made me feel second-rate. We're all three spoiled, but the twins are extra spoiled. Did you notice they're not here today? They're out with Uncle Tubby playing miniature golf because I knew they would ruin everything. I asked Dad to get rid of them. They're psychopaths."

"Do you ever think about your natural parents?"

"Mom and Dad are my natural parents," Sydney said. Then, after a pause: "I do wonder about my biological parents, though. I mean, I'm curious. How could I not be? And my folks won't tell me much about my adoption. They say it was done through the Associated."

"That makes sense."

"Yes, but there should be a story, right? And the only thing I know is that it happened really fast, that they got a call and they picked me up and they didn't have anything ready. Twenty-four hours after I was born. I don't know. It doesn't make sense."

Michelle thought it made as much sense as anything did. She also realized she better start thinking about birth control. Eventually. The women in her family were fertile. Linda had four kids and was talking about getting her tubes tied. Michelle had been not quite an accident, a by-product of too much revelry, her father trying one more time for a boy, although her mother insisted he had preferred being the only man in a household of women. "He liked women," she said, oh so dryly.

"Anyway," Sydney said, "*I* want cake. And it's my birthday. For one day I get to call the shots around here. Then it will be Heckle and Jeckle's world all over again. Sometimes, I feel like Ferris Bueller's sister. You know, there's probably a reason she was such a freaking bitch."

"Well, if you're Jennifer Grey, you get to end up dancing with Patrick Swayze, so it's not all bad."

Sydney's face was a study. "Yeah, no one puts Baby in the corner, right? Only I spend a lot of time in corners. Well, maybe not so many corners, but watching stupid TV, like *Blossom*. Everyone else in this family is so jocky. Even Mom plays golf." She shuddered.

"So why did you want a pool party for your Sweet Sixteen?"

"I didn't. I didn't even want a party. I wanted to go to a nice restaurant, just Mom and Dad and me. They didn't think that was special enough."

"I'm sorry," Michelle said. She wasn't. It angered her that Sydney had parents who worried about what was special enough for her. Her family was always trying to knock down Michelle's ideas about what she deserved, said she was grandiose.

"That's okay. In two years, I'll go away to college. My mom thinks I should go to one of the Seven Sisters, but I want to live in New York. Columbia, Barnard, NYU—whatever it takes, I'll get into at least one of them, I think."

"I wish I were going away to school. I'm just going to College Park."

"College Park is away."

"Not really."

"Well, then kick ass your freshman year and transfer somewhere you'd rather be."

"You make it sound so easy."

"Not easy," said Sydney. "But possible. You're smart, Michelle. You're just lazy."

The words were specific—thrillingly, awfully specific. Michelle knew they had been snatched from some adult conversation. Lorraine and Bert, most likely, but maybe her own mother. "Smart"—a flicker of warmth because no one ever said Michelle was smart. But "lazy" and this brought a more familiar slap of shame because she knew she was exactly that. Michelle, who didn't panic when she awoke in a strange bed as a man tried to undress her, felt nervous and ashamed that Sydney should have heard grown-ups say these things about her.

"You don't know what it's like to be me."

"No one," Sydney said, "knows what it's like to be anyone. Let's go have cake. Happy birthday to me."

Michelle followed her, wondering how this plump sixteen-year-old had gotten so wise. *No one knows what it's like to be anyone.* Oh, she wasn't so smart. She had probably overheard that, too. A line from a movie or a sitcom, maybe even *Blossom*.

March 16, 2012

I f Sandy had been pressed to put a description to the Gelmans'
house in Garrison Forest, he might have said "fancy" or "interesting." He readied those precise words because the lady
of the house, who was leading him to the living room, struck
him as someone who might solicit compliments, even from a
stranger. The house wasn't really to his taste, but he thought it
was probably in good taste, although maybe not. Mainly, it had
a decorated quality to it, a ruthless perfection that felt cold and
off-putting. Even the one overtly personal touch, an enormous
oil painting of a family that hung over the fireplace, seemed a
little generic to him.

"Nice portrait," he guessed.

"Thank you," Lorraine Gelman said. "It makes me smile,
every day. A lovely time in our lives. The boys were turning
thirteen, Sydney was fifteen. I hate to say it because it sounds so
proud-motherish, but I don't think my sons ever had an awkward
age."

Awkward age. Sandy noticed that Lorraine did not say the same

of her daughter, who was plump and not quite pretty, even as ren-
dered by brush-for-hire.

"How long ago was that?" Making conversation, trying to put
her at ease. And maybe himself. Although Lorraine had agreed to
talk to him alone, he was unclear if she had asked her husband's
advice about this meeting. And she kept stressing that she had
never met Julie Saxony. Not even one time, she said, and she said it
more than once, often the sign of a big whopping lie.

"Almost twenty-five years ago. My daughter is a lawyer in
New York now, and the boys are in Chicago. All settled with
children—well, Sydney has a partner, but we *adore* her. Adriana is
the best daughter-in-law in the bunch."

Sandy couldn't help thinking, as he often did, about the things
this woman took for granted—her home, her healthy children,
now grandchildren. If Bobby had been normal, could Sandy have
accepted a *partner* with this woman's easy grace? He yearned to
think so.

"Well," he said, taking out his pad, signaling the beginning of
the interview. "Julie Saxony."

"As I told you, I never met her."

"No, but you knew Felix."

"Of course. He was my husband's closest friend; I am Bambi's best friend to this day. We were sort of forced on each other,
through our husbands, but we've ended up being as close as the
men, maybe closer. You know how that goes."

Sandy didn't, but he nodded. He and Mary hadn't done that
couple-dating-couple thing. They had socialized with people from
his work and hers, but they hadn't created that dynamic where the
men talk about sports and the women talk about kids. That was
Mary's decision as much as his, another legacy from Bobby. Mary
could deal with a lot, but she learned quickly that people didn't want
her to contribute to their happy chatter about their sons and daughters. When she talked about Bobby, it was almost as if she was one

of those people who offered pet stories as a counterpoint to kid stories. Other people thought Bobby was a tragedy, that it was in bad taste to mention him in a discussion about normal kids. Mary, so naturally sociable, had pulled away from the world when she realized no one wanted her to talk about Bobby. Not even Sandy.

"Felix's relationship with Julie was a pretty open secret, though?"

"I think it appears that way in hindsight." Okay, that answer was as prepared as precut lumber. But then, she had known why he was coming to talk to her. "Felix was circumspect, all things considered. He always had girlfriends, from the first. I asked Bert never to speak of it to me because I didn't want to feel as if I were keeping secrets from Bambi. And Felix managed to keep his worlds very separate—until he disappeared. Only then was he so uncharacteristically inconsiderate."

"How so?"

"He put his coffee shop in Julie's name. That made it public, created a record, something for the newspapers to chew on. And there was Bambi, left with nothing."

"I know that's the official story."

"It's the *true* story. Bambi has been living by hook or crook ever since Felix left. We all thought he would provide for her. But no arrangements were made. Or, if they were, the person he trusted was unscrupulous."

"Who was that? The person he trusted, I mean."

A flicker of the lawyer's wife in her eyes, a pause to consider the words that followed. "I didn't mean to imply that there was anyone. I can only tell you that *if* Felix did make plans for Bambi, he didn't do a very good job of it. Bert and I have done what we can. Bambi and her girls are like family to us. There was a time when I hoped Michelle might even marry one of my boys, but she's almost four years older than they are and that is an insurmountable gap when one is young."

"You say Felix didn't make any arrangements for his wife, but he made sure his bail bondsman wasn't hurting."

"Do you know that for a fact?" she countered. "Or is it more gossip, like the gossip that Felix found a way to provide for Bambi?"

He gave her his best grin. "You got me there. But, come on, Tubman's awfully good-natured for someone who ate a one-hundred-thousand-dollar bond."

"Good-natured now. Time heals even financial wounds. Did you enjoy your visit with him?"

"Ah, so you guys still talk?"

"He and Bert do. Tubman was not someone to whom I was close." She appeared to suppress a shudder, which seemed a little melodramatic to Sandy. The guy had seemed nice enough to him. He sensed some snobbery at work. Funny to him because he wouldn't wipe his ass with a defense attorney, but bail bondsmen were doing honest work, by and large, just cogs in the system.

"So he told your husband that I came by?"

"Yes, and Bert tells me everything." There was an odd emphasis in that sentence, a stress on "me." "They were so close, once. The three men. Felix's disappearance—that was the beginning of the end. Then Tubman got married, and his wife made him drop all his old friends. She was never comfortable with our crowd. Churchy. Maybe a little anti-Semitic, to tell the truth, although I suppose I shouldn't speak ill of the dead. Anyway, I know when Julie Saxony disappeared, Bert and Tubman couldn't help thinking she had gone to Felix. Then, when her body was found—I don't know how to explain this, but it made them terribly sad."

"Sad?"

"They had this fantasy, see, Felix was with his lady friend, enjoying life. They thought *that* would be a happy ending."

"For Felix."

She favored him with a smile. "Whereas—I won't say I was

glad that Julie was dead, but I felt better for Bambi when the body was found. Because it was really hurtful to her, having people think that Felix had chosen Julie over her. Hard enough to have no money, but if Felix had sent for Julie—that would have been a betrayal."

"Not the affair, during the marriage?"

She nodded as if to concede a point. "A different kind of betrayal, then. Look, lots of men do what Felix did."

"Including your husband?"

"Oh, no. Not Bert. Do you know Bert doesn't even really understand how good-looking he is? Women are forever throwing themselves at him and he doesn't even realize it."

I bet, Sandy thought. Although, come to think of it, there had never been a lot of gossip about Bert Gelman, and that courthouse crowd gossiped like old biddies.

"What about Tubby?"

"What about him?"

"Was he, well, envious of Felix? For the relationship with Julie? I can't help thinking he might have had a little thing for her."

"Tubman. *Tubman*." Lorraine Gelman had clearly never considered this idea before. But she was willing to consider it now, which was part of the reason that Sandy had wanted to talk to a woman. Women were natural-born murder police in some ways, at least if a case turned on love shit.

"I mean, he found her, right? Spotted her in a drugstore, took her to his friend's place."

"I guess so. But Tubman had a girl at the time."

"I thought you said that was later?"

"No, he *married* later. After Felix disappeared." *Disappeared*. She kept using that word. As if it weren't quite Felix's fault that he ran away while appealing his conviction. "Before, he dated a girl. A friend of Julie Saxony's. Susie something."

"A friend. You mean another stripper?"

"Yes. We did not socialize—I'm sorry if that sounds snobbish." Why was she apologizing to him? Did she equate strippers with cops? "But even if I had been comfortable, Felix would never have stood for Bert and me to spend time with one of Julie's friends. No overlap between the two worlds. Someone who knew Julie could never be around Bambi."

"But Tubby knew her. And probably your husband, Bert. Right?"

"Men are different. It was the women who had to be kept separate. The worlds. Felix's daughters, to this day—they don't really understand that he actually owned the Variety. They think he had an office there, nothing more. It's a selective bit of revisionism, and I think Bambi's entitled to it."

"So how did *you* know about the girlfriend? If you never socialized, I mean."

Lorraine's smile was polite and practiced, social but not exactly fake. Not exactly. "Tubman threw a party, sort of a holiday open house, and she presided over it, playing the part of hostess. Felix refused to go, even alone—Felix was smart that way. Whereas Bert is naïve in some things. He didn't realize the girlfriend would be there. She was so tiny—I don't think she was five feet tall. The two of them together—I'm sorry, but everyone wondered how he didn't crush her. Anyway, I was trapped talking to her for what seemed like hours. She wore a green velvet floor-length gown. I'll never forget that. She looked like a teeny-tiny Christmas tree. She even wore red ornament earrings."

Lorraine shook her head at the memory, clearly still appalled by Tubman's girlfriend.

"But just because he had a girl—does that mean he didn't have a thing for Julie? He discovered her, right?"

"Discovered. You make her sound like a starlet. He saw a pretty girl in a drugstore and told her that she could make more money. You know, most women wouldn't have done that. That tells you a lot about Julie Saxony's character right there. She wasn't going to work at a drugstore if she could make more money dancing naked. And she wasn't going to settle for dancing naked if she could get the boss."

Sandy couldn't help thinking about the chef, who had defended Julie for dancing in an outfit not much different from a modern bathing suit. Men and women saw some stuff differently.

"Are you saying she expected Felix to marry her?"

"Expected? I don't know if she was that stupid, but it was what she wanted."

"How can you say that with such certitude if you didn't know her?"

"Because Tubman's little girl, the one in the hostess gown, told me so. She told me that Julie was so determined to marry Felix that she had converted. Can you imagine? I almost felt sorry for her when I heard that. She was really very naïve."

"Naïve." Lorraine had used that word before. Yes, about her husband. Sandy always paid attention to the words people repeated. Lorraine Gelman thought being naïve was one of the worst things a person could be.

"When was this?"

"Let's see—Felix hadn't left yet, so . . . '74? '75? I remember I wore a Diane von Furstenberg wrap dress."

Big help that.

"Do you remember her name?"

"Oh, dear—well, Tubman would, you should really ask him. I mean, we spoke for only a little bit."

"You said it was hours."

"I said it *seemed* like hours. In terms of the toll it took, the boredom. But it was just the one time. Susie—*Susie*—I can't summon a last name. I'm sorry, I don't feel I've been any help at all."

"Oh, no, you have." At least she hadn't shot his idea down.

Tubman had dated another stripper, a friend of Julie's. Tubby had married a woman who took him away from the old gang—but not until after Felix disappeared. Had he made a play for Julie? Had he been entrusted to take care of Bambi, then given the money to Julie in hopes that she would reward him by loving him back? Going from the manager of the Coffee Pot Shoppe to an up-scale B and B seemed like an unlikely journey, even over a decade.

He thanked Lorraine for her time, searched for a compliment for her house, feeling himself somewhat lacking in this department. "Your home is really impressive," he said at last. Not a lie, it definitely made an impression.

If you knew Susie—the line stuck in his head on the drive home, like a hamster going around and around in a wheel. Sandy was pretty sure he did know Susie. He walked through the door of his house, not even bothering to hang up his coat and hat, niceties that he observed as a tribute to Mary, who cared so about niceties, who argued every day that the little things mattered. Hanging up coats, making beds, cleaning the kitchen at night. Everything had to be perfect, because of their son who could never be perfect, not even close.

He looked back through the original file. Yes, there it was: Susan Borden had been the housekeeper at Julie's B and B, but she had been on vacation the week that Julie disappeared. The Havre de Grace police had interviewed her, but it was a pretty say-nothing witness sheet, and the Baltimore detectives hadn't even bothered with her fifteen years later.

Could be a coincidence, this Susan Borden and Lorraine Gelman's Susie. Common as a name could be and it wasn't even the same name, not precisely. But Sandy knew they were one and the same. *Not* a hunch. Not a feeling. Knowledge, honed by practice. Sandy had failed as a restaurateur. He had failed as a father. He had failed his wife when he failed as a father, although she had never called him on it, to her dying day. Literally, to her dying day. Not a word of reproach, not a hint of resentment, but he was less in her eyes for his weakness. The man who had swept her off her feet on their first date, carried her home, promised in word and deed to take care of her always, had failed. He wanted to be larger than life to her, wanted her to look at him as she had that day, eyes shining with excitement. That man died when Bobby was diagnosed. He just didn't know how to be a father to a kid like that. Truth is, maybe he wouldn't have known how to be a father to any kid.

But this, this job? This he could do, better than almost anyone.

January 5, 1996

S habbat dinner, although a relatively new ritual in the Brewer-Sutton household, was already a smooth-running routine, a testament to Linda's organizational skills and her determination to see a thing through once her mind was made up. Linda had decided last fall, when Noah entered fourth grade, that Judaism was due for a comeback in her household. True, the winter sunset was long past by the time she got home from work, but her timing was otherwise impeccable. The tenderloin was resting on a cutting board, the rösti potatoes were minutes away from crisp hot perfection. Two loaves of challah waited in the center of the table, wrapped in a green linen napkin. The candlesticks and kiddush cup had been polished to a high shine, thanks to the cleaning woman who now came twice a week. She also baked the challah, but Linda made and braided the loaves in the morning, before leaving for work.

The only thing missing were Linda's sisters and her mother, who had promised to make it tonight for the first time in weeks. Not that Linda cared—she had started observing the Sabbath for her kids, determined to ground them in something, anything—but Rachel had been unusually adamant that the entire family should gather. Strange, because they had seen one another only three weeks ago, for a perfunctory Hanukkah at Bambi's house. It had been a lackluster affair, not so much Hanukkah as Christmas Eve with potato pancakes to Linda's now critical eye. Too much emphasis on the gifts, almost no ritual. Bambi hadn't even bothered to dig out the dreidel, much less buy gelt for the children, and they couldn't light the menorah properly because it turned out the shamas had broken off and never been resoldered.

But Rachel said she was feeling stir-crazy in advance. A blizzard was predicted for Sunday, a big one, and Linda would be on-call once the storm hit, giving interviews about outages and power lines. Linda thought this part of her job a bizarre custom. The people without power couldn't hear or see her confident predictions about the crews working to restore electricity, and those with power didn't really care about those without. They just wanted to know when their streets would be plowed.

Her boss had already told her to pack a bag and check into a centrally located hotel tomorrow and to be prepared to work around the clock through Monday morning. Linda never minded long days or hard work; she was the family breadwinner. And her being on-call didn't upset the family's various child-care arrangements because Henry had left his public defender's job a few years ago and was now teaching science at City College, one of Baltimore's best high schools. His newfound professional contentment was like the little woodstove in the corner of their great room—it didn't really contribute much to the bottom line, but it made everyone feel a little cozier.

And, oh, how Linda envied him at times. *I never get snow days,* she thought self-pityingly, removing the string from the tenderloin and starting to slice. The warm meat almost sighed at the knife's touch. Linda was the only decent cook among the Brewer women, and she recognized her own smugness on this topic. Linda knew all her faults. The more honest you were with yourself, the less you had to worry about the world's opinion. She was always trying to persuade her bosses of this approach. Tell the truth, whenever possible, and start with yourself.

"Hey, sis." Rachel came in the side door, hung her coat and scarf in the alcove of cubbyholes and hooks that Linda's family used as a de facto mudroom. Seeing the ready platter of tenderloin, she took it from Linda and placed it on the table. "Are you making a béarnaise? Go ahead, and I'll do whatever else needs to be done." She waved her arms around theatrically.

Her boyfriend, Joshua, waited in his coat until Rachel pointed him to an empty hook. He then stood in the center of the kitchen, pretty much in Linda's path, until Rachel indicated that he could take a seat in the corner of the large space off the kitchen that served as a family room. Linda liked Joshua. He was a mensch, a word no one would ever use in connection with Rachel's ex-husband, Marc. But he was so passive, one of those people who never take the initiative in *anything*.

"The good silver?" Rachel asked, still making those weird gestures.

"Sure. Oh, fuck—my carrots," Linda said, rushing to the stove before the steamer went dry.

"The carrots are fine," Rachel said.

"The *carrots* are fine."

Still nothing. Rachel had thought it a good bit of wordplay, but no one else noticed, not even Joshua, who was in on the joke, or should have been. She began collecting crystal stemware, continuing to flutter her fingers. She wasn't crazy about religion, but she approved of Linda's dinners. She was going to do something

similar when she had children. Maybe not a Shabbat dinner, but
something regular, ritualistic.

With Joshua parked on the sofa by himself—Henry was upstairs, doing something with the kids, no doubt—Rachel continued to set the table, wiggling her fingers at Linda every chance
she got, but her sister remained distracted, probably by the
weather news. What a horrible job Linda had. She was important
only when things went wrong and then she became the face of
the public utility, the messenger that everyone wanted to kill.

"Everyone is coming tonight, right?" Rachel asked, putting
out the silverware. The good stuff, which had belonged to their
great-grandmother. She was surprised Bambi hadn't pawned it at
some point and wondered at her decision to give it to Linda. Had
she despaired of Rachel ever having a family? Rachel and Marc
had owned nice china and silver, but it had come from his family
and gone back to them. She wondered if he and his second wife,
a pretty, pliable girl whom he had married in an insultingly short
time—and most definitely not the woman he had cheated with—
were putting out the silver tonight. No, she would be forced,
as Rachel had been forced, to eat in the Singers' claustrophobic
dining room, the cold and formal antithesis to this lively hodge-
podge.

Bambi and Michelle arrived. Somehow, it was still a surprise
to Rachel how much Michelle resembled their mother now that
she was in her twenties. And yet Bambi retained some indefinable
edge, even at fifty-five going on fifty-six. Her beauty was more
profound, while Michelle's felt flashy and fleshy, a little too carnal.

The meal ready, the prayers recited, Rachel took the seat to
her mother's right and plopped her hand between their plates.
Still, no awareness. Was she going to have to send up a flare? It
was Michelle, down the table, who finally noticed. Magpie Michelle never missed anything shiny.

"Is that a *yellow* diamond?"

"It was my grandmother's," Joshua said quickly, more or less as they had planned. "We got married this week."

Rachel and Joshua had *not* planned on the long silence that fell. A grave, judging silence.

"Congratulations," Henry said when it became clear that the other three women were not going to speak. "It takes a tough man to marry a Brewer woman."

"Oh, hush," Linda said. "That's hardly the right thing to say."

"And I've never thought of you as particularly tough, Henry," Michelle said.

"I'm the only son-in-law," Henry said, unperturbed by Linda's corrections or Michelle's insults. "I'm thrilled to have the company."

"You weren't always the—" Michelle began. It was hard to say if she stopped speaking of her own accord or because of the look that Linda shot her.

"When?" Bambi asked, slicing her tenderloin into very tiny pieces.

"Two days ago," Rachel said. "At the courthouse."

"Smart," Henry said. "No tax implications for 1995."

"I mean, we're very happy for you—we all love Joshua," Bambi said. "Only—why that way? You could have had a small wedding."

"I don't like weddings," Rachel said. "I never have."

"Yes, we all remember your Vegas elopement," Michelle put in, earning another glare from Linda. It didn't intimidate her. "You could have had a judge just come to a party and marry you."

She was enjoying this, Rachel realized. Michelle was usually the one who disappointed the others. Taking an extra semester to get her degree, then moving back home because she had done absolutely nothing about finding a job, threatening to answer those "live model" ads in the back of the *City Paper* if her mother and sisters didn't get off her back. She would, too. Michelle was never lazy when it came to vindictiveness.

"No, you can't," Joshua put in. "If you get married anywhere but the courthouse, it has to be someone religious."

"Okay, so a rabbi, then."

"I don't like rabbis." True. Very true.

"Then a Unitarian minister or a Wiccan priestess or whatever," Michelle continued. "It's only a ceremony. What's the big deal?"

"I just—I was embarrassed," Rachel said. "It is a second marriage for me."

"But it's Joshua's first," Bambi said. "At least—I think it is." A gentle yet pointed barb. Joshua had been accompanying Rachel to family gatherings for more than a year now, but he never offered much information about himself.

"It is," Joshua assured Bambi. "And although it was hard to let go of that vision I've carried of my wedding day, I found I didn't mind."

Joshua's joke fell flat. Even Rachel found it wanting, and Joshua's sense of humor was a large part of his appeal. But she wouldn't glare at him or correct him. She didn't want a Henry, who loved to be nagged so he could play the henpecked spouse, straight out of a sitcom. Linda and Henry's marriage worked for them, but it wasn't right for her. And Bambi's way hadn't worked for her, either. Rachel was going to find her own way of being married this time.

"May I throw you a party?" Bambi asked. "A small one, for family and friends?"

"No," Rachel said quickly, too quickly, but she had to shut that down. Why did Bambi always want to spend money she didn't have? Good Lord, couldn't she remember what *parties* had cost her? But, no, she never remembered because she had been bailed out time and time again. And whose fault was that? Mostly Rachel's.

Linda's oldest, Noah, bored by talk of weddings, begged to be excused and allowed to eat his food in front of the television. The three younger girls—"Linda breeds like an Orthodox," Bambi had once noted in an unguarded moment, exhibiting that weird anti-Semitism that only Jews could carry—understood enough to realize they had been gypped out of being flower girls. Their voices rose, cascading over one another's until Linda silenced them with a few well-chosen threats, softened by a promise of dessert if they behaved. Rachel looked forward to the day when her children would join them, hoped the cousins would be close.

"So," Henry said, "Linda tells me this blizzard is going to be the real deal. The big one. Is everyone prepared?"

Rachel smiled at Henry, grateful that he had managed to divert everyone from the topic of her marriage—although Michelle left her place for a better look at the ring, which even she couldn't help admiring. The talk ebbed and flowed away from Rachel. Henry had a gift for public relations, too, Rachel realized. Or maybe he just had a lot of experience at soothing angry Brewer women.

Linda brought out the dessert, Berger cookies and ice cream. Linda was very canny about knowing when to do things herself and when to delegate, Rachel thought, where effort made a difference and where it didn't. Rachel sipped her coffee. The evening hadn't been as she had hoped, but it was behind her now. The announcement had been made.

Then Bambi asked out of the blue: "Have you told Joshua's parents?"

"We had dinner with them last night," Rachel said.

"That's not a yes or no," Michelle said. *Jesus, Michelle, go to law school already.*

"We did the same thing," Rachel said. "As I did with you. I waved my hand around a lot, trying to catch the light. His mother noticed—but it's her mother's ring; she gave it to Joshua."

"So you told them last night," Bambi said.

"They happened to guess," Rachel said. "When they saw the ring."

"But they knew *first*."

"We had to reschedule our Sunday night dinner with them because of the blizzard, just in case." She had known this would be a sensitive point, but there was no way to tell Joshua that Bambi must be first. She would sulk for days now.

"We could have had a wedding party in conjunction with my birthday," her mother said. "That's only three weeks away."

"But that wouldn't have been fair to you, stealing your thunder that way."

"I don't care about my birthday," her mother said. "I'm going to be fifty-six. It's a nothing age."

"We'll have a huge blowout when you're sixty," Linda said.

"Please—I'll want to celebrate that even less." A pause. "I got pregnant on my twentieth birthday. January 30, 1960."

The sisters looked at one another.

"Mother," Linda said. "Don't be silly. I was born September first, and I weighed nine pounds. That would make me the world's largest preemie."

Rachel assumed—and assumed her sisters were assuming—that her mother had tripped up on the oft-told lie about Linda being conceived on her parents' wedding night. December 31, 1959. The girls had long ago figured out that their parents had sex before their wedding night. They rather liked them for it. They also liked their mother for her polite fictions about it, her old-fashioned decorum. But now she was taking it too far, telling such an obvious lie. Even Noah could see through it, if his attention weren't consumed by the weird soup he was making from his ice cream and cookies.

Her mother stood. "Michelle, we really should go. I have to get home before the blizzard."

"It won't even start snowing until Sunday," Linda said.

"I want to make sure I have what I need. Maybe I'll drive to the Giant and buy all the clichéd things. Milk, toilet paper, bread. You know our driveway: If it's as bad as they say it's going to be, I won't get out for days."

"I'm not ready to go," Michelle protested.

"I'll take her home," Rachel promised. "It's not that far out of my way."

"Or I could spend the night at your apartment," Michelle said. Rachel could see the wheels turning. Michelle would get to her place—now hers and Joshua's—in Fells Point and propose going out. She assumed Rachel would beg off—she always did—and Michelle could then head out on her own. She would show up late the next morning, clutching a huge coffee from the Daily Grind. It would never occur to her to bring one to Rachel or to divulge anything about how she had spent the evening. She might not even come back for days, blithely lying to her mother via phone that she was stranded at Rachel's because of the blizzard. *Michelle, ma belle,* their father had sung to her when she was a baby. *I love you, I love you, I love you.* Had any other man told Michelle that he loved her? Admired her, wanted her, made love to her, yes. But had she been loved?

Bambi left, clearly affronted. Rachel wanted to believe it was because Michelle was staying behind, or even that all three daughters had ganged up on her over the lie about Linda's conception.

But Rachel knew the real slight was her secret marriage to Joshua. Bambi had to know things *first.* Rachel had disappointed her mother. It was unfair. She could—she had—gone to such lengths to protect her mother, and now she would get the Frigidaire treatment, as her father had called it, Bambi's patented deep freeze, all because Joshua's parents knew first.

"She didn't even say 'mazel tov,'" she said to Linda later, cleaning up, trying to make a joke of it.

"Why did you get married in such a rush?" Michelle asked. "Are you knocked up?"

"Michelle!" Spoken in unison, as Linda and Rachel often did.

"Are you knocked up?"

"Michelle!" the terrible twosome gasped, always in each other's pockets.

Michelle was curled into an armchair, watching her sisters clean up. It wouldn't be accurate to say it didn't occur to her to help. It occurred to her and she decided not to. Even in Linda's big kitchen, there was only so much counter space. A third person would just get in the way.

Henry had decided, after Bambi's departure, to make a late-night run to the Giant as well, and the kids had clamored to go with him. Rachel had sent Joshua with them and now it was just the three sisters. *Three Sisters.* Michelle was supposed to have read that for some course at College Park, but she got by with the CliffsNotes. She doubted Chekhov could tell her anything about three sisters that she didn't already know. She sat in the chair, remote in hand, flicking, flicking, flicking through the channels. She hated Linda's decor, the whole Martha Stewart, country-cozy thing. Michelle liked modern things, sleek and minimalist.

"That was weird," Linda said.

"What?" Rachel sounded guilty to Michelle's ears. Oh, this was rich, Rachel being in the doghouse for once. Michelle must remember to stoke her mother's hurt, try to keep this going for a while. Plus, it would take Bambi's mind off the fact that Michelle didn't have a job.

"Mom trying to persuade us I was conceived on her birthday. We've all lived quite happily with the falsehood of the wedding-night conception all these years. Do you think she's getting addled?"

"Fifty-five is young for that," Rachel said, but she sounded worried. Rachel already had a dent between her eyes from her incessant worrying.

"Trust me, she's fine," Michelle said, settling on MTV. It was a rerun of *The Real World*, which she wouldn't mind auditioning for, although she couldn't imagine a *Real World: Baltimore*. Baltimore was way too real for the *Real World*. Still, with her looks and her story, she would easily make it through the preliminary selection rounds.

The problem was, she found the people on the show a little pathetic. She wanted the free rent in a gorgeous apartment, but not if the price was a bunch of petty squabbles and, worse, those terribly earnest conversations. Could be good exposure for an actress, but did she really want to be an actress anyway? It seemed like a monstrous amount of work, and there was seldom any money in it.

"Mom's just upset that you didn't tell her about your wedding before Joshua's folks knew," Linda said.

"She likes Joshua—"

"We all like Joshua," Michelle said. "Although I always thought he was gay. Are you sure he's not gay?"

She thought she'd get another double *Michelle!* But they held their tongues.

"Okay, okay, he's not gay. But I'm sorry, he seems like such a lightweight compared to—"

"You were thirteen," Rachel said, cutting her off. Man, she couldn't even bear to hear Marc's name. Weird. "You don't know anything."

"I know he was rich. And you let him screw you over. Not a penny." She put on an English accent. "Not a penny farthing for you, Rachel." She thought it would make her sister laugh. She was wrong.

"We were married for only two years. It was a mistake. A very young, foolish mistake."

"It will be sixteen years next fall that I met Henry," Linda said, obviously trying to steer them away from a fight. "Together for fifteen years, married for thirteen. Four kids."

"And Mom was nineteen when she met Dad," Rachel put in.

"So stop acting like I'm a baby at twenty-two. The way I see it, I'm not the one in this room with the blemished record."

That hurt Rachel, and Michelle instantly regretted it. She didn't want to hurt Rachel. She looked up to her, truly. Looked up to both her sisters. But she resented them, too. Those photos in their oh-so-proper riding outfits. The years, however brief, of having their father *and* money. But she resented their closeness, most of all. They told each other things that they didn't tell her. So it was only right that she didn't tell them everything. Not that she had any significant secrets. But she was working on a few.

"When are you going to have kids?" Linda asked Rachel.

"Soon," Rachel said. "Really soon."

"I repeat," Michelle said. "Are you knocked up?"

"Who knows?" Rachel said. "But, no, that's not why we got married."

"Don't expect me to babysit," Michelle said. It was surprising how easy it was to watch *The Real World* without sound. She had no problem following it whatsoever. It was basically fight-fight-fight montage fight-fight-fight montage.

"I wouldn't," Rachel said. "But what if you decide you want to? What if you get married young, like all the Brewer women?"

"Oh, I might get married young. But I'm never having kids. Never." Michelle hadn't had her childhood yet. She wanted to find a job or a man that would allow her to live very well. She wasn't naïve. She realized that both required effort. Different kinds of effort, but effort. And while it would probably surprise her sisters, she had decided that a job was better than a man. For one thing, you could move from job to job with much greater ease than you could move from husband to husband. She was going to find whatever job paid the best for the least amount of work, even if it was boring as hell.

She rode down to Fells Point with Rachel and Joshua. She had forgotten that Joshua was part of the equation now, even though he and Rachel had been sharing her apartment for more than six months. Joshua was just that kind of guy, easy to forget. Once in the apartment, he seemed comically out of place in the feminine environment that Rachel had created in the little one-bedroom under the eaves of an eighteenth-century rowhouse. Michelle realized they would probably be moving before long. She wondered if she could take over Rachel's lease. Again, that would require a job.

Rachel and Joshua did not go to bed right away. Michelle had the sense they were waiting her out, trying to keep her entertained so she wouldn't go out, after all. *Good luck,* she thought. Toward midnight, as Rachel struggled to keep her eyes open, Michelle said sweetly, as if conferring a kindness: "I'll let you two go to bed. But I'm restless. I think I'll go get a nightcap over at John Steven's."

"So late?" Joshua said. Already trained to do Rachel's dirty work. *Oh, won't you be a good little Brewer man, following your wife around like a dog.*

"It's not late at all for someone my age. And if that storm comes through as promised, there will be plenty of time to sit indoors."

"It's just not safe," Rachel said. "For someone alone, I mean. I worry."

Michelle laughed as she adjusted her coat and scarf. Their grandmother had given Bambi an old mink and Michelle had taken it over, even had it tailored and repaired at great expense. A boyfriend's expense. She loved it when someone—always a girl, and almost always an unattractive one—said: "Fur is murder."

Michelle would say blithely: "No, it's the *consequence* of murder. As is most of human history, all the way back to Cain and Abel, so get over it."

"I really wish you wouldn't go out," Rachel said. "We have bourbon here, a bottle of Romanian wine, from the cheap barrels at Trinacria—"

"Oh, what's the big deal, Rach? Do you think I'm going to go out the door and never come back?"

"Well," Rachel said, "it wouldn't be unprecedented in our family history."

Michelle wavered for a moment, but she had too much pride not to follow through on her plans. She went out into the night, snug in her coat, giddy with her prospects. Attention, sex, money, love. The first two were almost always available to her and she was after the third now. Love could wait. The sky was clear, and even in the city one could see the stars. It was impossible to imagine a blizzard was coming.

When Rachel and Joshua woke up the next morning, Michelle was sitting in the little kitchen with a cup of coffee from the Daily Grind, reading a *Beacon-Light* she had found on their neighbor's doorstep. Neither Rachel nor Joshua asked her about her evening, and she didn't volunteer any details. She was her father's daughter. Free as the breeze, accountable to no one, hardwired to understand probability, if not possibility.

March 21, 2012

S usan Borden had told the original investigators many
things about herself, as detailed by the witness sheet.
There was her full name (Susan Evelyn Borden). Her date
of birth, February 25, 1956, in Salisbury, Maryland. Social Security number, her address at the time, which turned out to be only
a few blocks from her current home, which had popped out of the
MVA files in a matter of seconds. She had given a detailed history
of her employment at the bed-and-breakfast, said she counted herself a friend of the owners, for whom she had worked about two
years. But she had been away the week that Julie went missing,
down the ocean with a new boyfriend. Total shock, never saw
it coming, didn't have any insight. When Baltimore City cops
picked up the case fifteen years later, they hadn't done much more
than call her and review her statement from '86.

Rereading this file now, Sandy could see the gaps. Susan—
Susie—didn't say how she knew Julie, just left the impression that
the friendship had been subsequent to the work relationship. She

gave up Salisbury, her hometown, but she didn't volunteer where she had been between Salisbury and Havre de Grace. Her work history included: "Hostess, various Baltimore restaurants." Yes, Susan Borden had been very careful to omit any detail that led back to Susie the dancer.

He made a strategic decision to let her stew a little bit before they met. She was a responsible citizen, at the same address for more than twenty years now. She wasn't going to bolt. He called and left a message, asking her to call him back and set up a time to discuss an old case. He said *case* on purpose, leaving it general.

Two days later, he called and left another message. *Detective Sanchez, would like to talk to you about the disappearance of Julie Saxony.*

The next day, he called and repeated the same message, almost word for word.

By the fourth day, he was pretty sure he was being ignored. Okay, she could be out of town, on vacation. She could be one of those people who no longer listen to their messages, just check the caller ID and call back the numbers they know, ignore everyone else. He called a neighbor, using a reverse directory to pinpoint the number. He said he had a delivery for Susan Borden but couldn't get an answer at her house.

"Her husband is always there. He'll sign for it. Assuming he can."

That was interesting on a lot of levels. Husband? Not according to any records he had found. And—*assuming he can.* What was that about?

"Has to be her, nobody else. It's certified."

"Well, she gets home at four. But, seriously, you could leave it on the steps. It's not like people around here steal."

Oh, country people, so smug. Go read a copy of *In Cold Blood,* you all so safe in your houses.

Sandy arrived at 5:45, although he had intended to be there closer to 5:30, figuring that gave a woman enough time to take off her pantyhose and put on comfortable shoes, maybe get a snack, but not start dinner yet. That was what his guardian, Nabby, had done upon her arrival home each day. Mary had changed to flat shoes, but stayed in her work clothes, as pretty and fresh at the end of the day as she was at the beginning.

A man, the alleged husband, answered the door. Sixtyish, Sandy guessed, a true apple shape in a red sweater that made him look even more like an apple, and very high, ruddy color in his cheeks. It wasn't a healthy color, though. His eyes were rheumy, his manner vague. Alcoholic, or maybe one of those big boozers who somehow kept it in check, watering himself all day long, like a plant.

Assuming he can.

"What do you want?" Grumpy. Ill at ease.

"I've been trying to get in touch with Susan Borden. Left her a couple of messages."

"She never checks the landline, and I never answer it."

"Why not?" Sandy was genuinely curious. He couldn't imagine sitting in a house, listening to a phone ring, no matter how swozzled a guy might be.

"It's never for me. And it's never really for Susie. People who know her call her cell."

"It's a business matter," Sandy said. "Not a big deal. I'm"—his instincts told him to lie, or at least obscure the nature of his mission—"I work as a consultant for the Baltimore City Police Department and I'm—I'm closing down a file. There's paperwork that I need permission to shred."

"She should be here any minute. Went to the store for something we didn't have."

And with that the guy left Sandy in the foyer, went back some-where in the house. A television room, based on the sound, the rhythms of people talking in a not-quite-real way. Sandy imag-ined the guy in an otherwise dark room, drinking steadily from something that *looked* like a glass of water.

He was still trying to figure out what to do when a woman came in behind him with a grocery sack. She was startled, but only mildly. He had a feeling it wasn't the first time she'd found some stranger in the foyer.

"What the dickens! Did Doobie leave you here?"

"Doobie?"

"My husband."

Uh-huh, Sandy amended in his head. Not unless you kept your own name, and you're not the type. You *are* the type to call a live-in your husband, though, and he probably is, by the standards of common law. He wondered how long they had been together, if it had ever been good, or if she had almost always been his care-taker, trading her competence for whatever checks he brought to the household. Not unlike Sandy and Nabby, come to think of it, although the scales had balanced in the end. He had taken better care of her than she ever had of him.

"He said you'd be back soon."

"Are you the guy with the mystery package?"

"You got me. Yes, I'm the one who called your neighbor. You didn't answer my messages."

"What messages?"

"On the home phone."

"Oh, God, I never listen to those. They're just solicitations. Anyone who knows me knows to call on my cell."

"Like, say, Tubman Schroeder?"

That got her attention. She was tiny, as Lorraine had men-tioned, and, for fifty-six, incredibly cute. There was no other word for it. She was like a miniature Marilyn Monroe, if you could imagine Monroe living another twenty years, toning down the hair, but still dressing to flatter an hourglass figure. Staggeringly high heels added to her height, yet she was still short of five-five. He felt a pang for the young woman in the inappropriate hostess dress, all those years ago, chattering about her plans to the more sophisticated Lorraine Gelman.

"Who are you?" she asked.

"I told your husband that I'm a consultant from the police department who needs permission to shred certain files. Only the first part is true. I am a consultant. I have been looking at a file, but it's not going to be shredded. We've reopened the Julie Saxony case."

She nodded. She looked frivolous, but she was quick, practical. She walked back into the house. "Doobie?" Her voice was loud, clear, and deliberate. "This man needs to talk to me. We are going to sit in the front room and talk. So dinner might be a little late."

"What are we having?"

"Turkey burgers and a salad."

"And french fries?"

"No, no french fries."

"But a burger."

"Yes. A *turkey* burger. I'll bring you a plate of crackers and carrot sticks for now."

Sandy remembered that he had taken a similar tone with Mary in their final months. But Mary had fought back, lost her temper, said: *Don't treat me like a child.* Mary's mind had been sharp, all the way to the end.

He went into the front room, taking Susie's words to Doobie as an invitation. She returned a few minutes later.

"He doesn't know about Julie, does he?" he asked.

"He knew her, actually."

"But not how you two knew each other."

"Wouldn't matter if he did, not now. He won't remember meeting you tomorrow."

He waited to see if she would fill in the gaps. Alcoholism? Dementia? Both? Maybe she was a woman long practiced at not saying more than was necessary.

"So I've reopened the investigation into Julie Saxony's murder."

"You said. Why?"

"It's my job. I take on cold cases."

"Why Julie? Why now?"

"No reason."

She laughed. It was a delightful sound. Could Tubman really have done better?

"Right. Well, join the club."

"The club?"

"The not very discriminating club of men taken in by Julie Saxony's smoldering gaze. That's what Felix called it. Juliet Romeo's smoldering gaze. Everyone fell for her, until they saw it was impossible."

"Did that include your old boyfriend, Tubman?"

"In the beginning? Sure. But he was practical. He wasn't going to get her, so he took up with me."

"That would bug a lot of women."

"Not me. I'm practical, too. I liked Tubman. He was a good time, very generous. It was never serious between us, though."

"That's interesting," he said. "Because part of the reason I'm here is because Lorraine Gelman told me you spent an entire party acting like Tubman's wife, babbling about Julie and Felix."

She wasn't fazed. "It takes two people to be serious. Tubby wasn't never serious about me. I knew that, and I accepted it. I probably talked too much to Lorraine because she made me so nervous. The Great Lady. I could tell she didn't want to be at the party, that she found everything there tacky—Tubby, his friends, me. Is that why you're here? Because a young woman once said some nonsense at a party? You'll never lack for work if that's the case."

"I think you know why I'm here. You worked at the B and B. You were on the interview list. But nothing in the notes indicates that you told investigators that you and Julie were old friends, back in the day."

"I told them we were friends, that we had met through our work. It's not my fault if no one followed up. Doobie and I had just started dating, and I wasn't keen for that information about my past to get out. I don't think he would have cared about what I did, but it's a small town and I wanted to stay here. I knew that would be easier if people didn't know I danced on the Block twenty million years ago."

Sandy couldn't speak for the original investigators, but he believed they probably had asked how Julie and Susan knew each other. Which meant she had lied. Then and now.

"You know, people always think they're good judges of whether information matters. But that's like a person holding one piece of a puzzle while I'm on the other side of the wall with this whole jigsaw put together. You don't see it, but I do."

"I wasn't there that day," she said, defensive and defiant. "July third, I mean. She had given me a week off. Doobie and I were in Ocean City. It was a last-minute thing."

"You decided to go away for the Fourth of July the last minute?"

"Julie asked if I wanted the week off, so I went."

"Generous of her. Especially with her own big holiday weekend coming up."

"That was Julie. Look, I didn't even have the skills to be a proper housekeeper. But Julie took it in her head that she was going to rescue me, get me away from the Block. She tried me out at the Coffee Pot Shoppe, as a hostess. Like that place needed a hostess. It was four booths and a counter. But she knew I couldn't wait tables. Physically, I mean. I couldn't carry the trays. I was weak and didn't have the wing span."

She spread her arms, as if to demonstrate.

"But Julie's attitude was, 'We are both going to get up and out. Up and out.' No more dancing. No more unavailable boyfriends, whether they were married or just, you know, out for a good time." She looked wistful. "She approved of Doobie. That was another reason she gave me the time off. He was different then, of course. Worked at the marina."

"Going over the notes, I saw you told the detectives at the time that nothing unusual happened that week. But she gave you a week off, out of the blue."

"Like I said, Julie was generous. And she really liked Doobie."

"Man, you are a loyal friend, aren't you?"

That caught her. Good. It was his intention.

"I would hope so, yes."

"I mean, I can see keeping a secret when you thought she might still be alive . . ."

"I never thought she was alive. Never. I agreed with Chet and, trust me, that big-headed *cook*—oh, pardon moi, *chef*—and I did not agree on much. But I suspected she was dead almost as soon as she left. Always."

"So why didn't you tell police everything?"

"What everything?"

He was fishing, sure. But he was fishing in a stocked pond.

"Here's what I think. You didn't hold back the whole story about your relationship with Julie because you were worried about being in the papers. You held it back to protect her. What were you protecting her from?"

"How could I protect someone I thought was dead?"

"I don't know. But she is dead, more than twenty-five years now. Who knows what might have happened if you had been more forthcoming twenty-five years ago?"

Susie let out her breath.

"It was just so unfair."

"What?"

"Everyone thinking that Julie had Felix's money, when she didn't. Julie wasn't a thief. If she kept the money, it was hers. That must have been hard to hear, but it was true. It's not her fault. I'm sure there was some other plan for the family, but it fell through, or there wasn't enough."

"What money, Mrs. Borden?" He knew she wasn't a Mrs., not officially, but he wanted her to feel dignified, respected. He needed to make her feel the exact opposite of whatever she had felt when she babbled to Lorraine Gelman. Safe, trusted, respected. Yet he also needed her to babble just the same.

"It's not just Julie."

"What do you mean?"

"It's not just Julie. There's someone—that's why I never spoke of it. It's what Julie would have wanted."

"Someone else? Her sister?"

Susan nodded.

"I can promise you the statute of limitations has run out on that." He really needed to check that detail. "No one's going to care about Andrea Norr being an accessory to Felix's escape. But that was it, right?"

So the old rumor was true. They drove him out of state in a horse trailer. He couldn't help being a little impressed with himself, ferreting out this fact, confirming an old legend. Too bad that he didn't have anyone in his life to tell the story to.

She gave the tiniest nod.

"And she got paid? The sister?"

"Something. Not a lot. And all Julie got was the coffee shop and a little cash for herself, too. But she didn't believe it, she wouldn't hear of it. She said she knew that Julie must have gotten lots of money, or how else would she have bought the inn, opened the restaurant? She was—kind of crazy. Not yelling, but loud enough that I could hear her. They were in the kitchen and I was in the laundry room off the kitchen. This was about a week before. She asked Julie for money, said it was only fair. And Julie said she just didn't have it."

Susan had made the mistake he had hoped she would make, rushing ahead, babbling, assuming that he knew more than he did. *She?* Who she, what she? Not Andrea Norr.

A silence of a sort. They could hear Doobie's television set, the familiar chime of the *Law & Order* theme. Must be six now.

"Did you see her?"

"No. And if I thought *she* had anything to do with Julie's murder, I would have told. I would have. But she was soft. Julie always said that. Soft, not used to doing things for themselves. The wife and the daughters. All spoiled, the whole lot of them."

"So there was a confrontation, a week before. Where someone accused Julie of taking money and she said she hadn't."

"She *hadn't*. Julie was really shaken up. She worried that the wife knew how to get to Felix, that the wife had told him these lies about her. That's what really bugged her."

"So she didn't know where Felix was?"

"No. And she was okay with that, as long as Bambi didn't, either. The day the daughter came, that was all she wanted to know. *Had anyone spoken to Felix, what was going on with Felix.*"

The day the daughter came. He didn't let on that he had assumed Bambi Brewer was the *she* in Susie's tale. He flipped open a notebook. "Right, that was—Linda, right? The oldest one."

"I don't remember the name. The middle one, I think. The smart one, who went to the fancy college." She looked defensive. "Julie kept tabs, a little. She paid attention to Felix's family. Maybe more than she should. She accused the girl of doing her mother's dirty work. The daughter said her mother didn't know she had come."

"Susan," called Doobie, his voice as querulous as a child's after a nap. "Susan?"

"Yes, Doobie?"

"What are we having for dinner?"

"Turkey burgers and salad."

"And french fries?"

"No french fries." She looked at Sandy. "He's older than me, by a bit. The doctor says something happens to the brain and we become like little kids again. Fewer inhibitions. We want what we want, we don't care as much about saying 'please' and 'thank you.' He's a good guy. We've had a great life together. I'd be a shit to kick him to the curb now. Look, I'm sorry if you think what I did was a big deal. I had to ask myself what Julie would want, what was most important to her. Even if what I knew might have solved her murder—it would have hurt her sister."

"She wasn't known for putting her sister first when she was alive, not according to her sister."

"All the more reason to do it after she died. Julie felt bad about her relationship with Andrea, wanted to make things up to her. She didn't get the chance. I did."

On the drive back to Baltimore, he replayed the conversation with Susan Borden. She was one of the more credible people he had interviewed. Everyone lied, but Susan had been pretty straightforward about her lies of omission and why she had committed them.

And her loyalty to Doobie, the child-man with the childish name and the enormous gut—it spoke well of her. *We've had a great life together.* They weren't now and yet there he was, every day, totally reliant on her. Would Sandy have traded for more time with Mary if it had meant being with someone who wasn't really Mary? Would he have traded Bobby-as-he-was, now in his thirties and lost to him, for a normal Bobby who died at age five?

You can rewrite life all you want, Sandy thought. It's still a play where everyone dies in the end.

Miss
Me

September 23, 2001

I s there room in the refrigerator for another platter?"

Bambi, who had been in a fog all day, glanced distract-edly at the middle-aged woman who had asked the question. Brown hair, dressed in a knit two-piece, which Bambi's expert eye identified as high end, perhaps even St. John's, a few seasons ago, although that was always fine in Baltimore. But the woman was a stranger to her. Why would someone unknown to Bambi be at Aunt Harriet's shivah?

"Thank you—*Naomi.*" The name came to her in the nick of time. Naomi had been Linda's classmate at Park. Bambi kept for-getting that her daughter, forty-one this month, was a middle-aged woman, too.

She walked Naomi's platter back to the Gelmans' kitchen, which had been redone a year ago and now had one of those enor-mous French-door Vikings, wide and deep enough to hold mul-tiple platters from Seven Mile Market, the kosher deli, not that anyone in this crowd kept kosher. Not even Linda had gone that overboard. Bambi hoped Bert and Lorraine, who had been generous to host this shivah, would also allow her to leave much of the food behind. Oh, she would raid the platters for the cold cuts, maybe some of the cheese and fruit, but now that she was alone in the Sudbrook Park house, she had no use for all the cookies and cakes and pies. Neither did Bert nor Lorraine, with Sydney in New York and the twins at law school in Chicago, but they would find it less shameful to toss out the uneaten food. Rich people were allowed to waste things.

Returning to the living room, Bambi still couldn't get over how many people were here. Her mother had been right, after all, to insist that they needed something bigger than her little apartment in Windsor Towers. Bambi had thought no one would come. Harriet had no spouse, no children, and she had outlived the few friends she hadn't alienated. Yet the Gelmans' first floor teemed with people. Bambi's friends, Ida's friends, even the girls' friends had been coming and going all afternoon. Perhaps, Bambi thought, people were simply desperate to gather. But what was the point of being with other people when the conversation immediately turned back to all the horrible topics—the Towers, anthrax, Cipro, the stories of near misses, the personal connections to those who had died. No one in Bambi's circle really knew anyone who had been affected, although Joshua, Rachel's husband, had a college friend who had been on the upper floors of the second tower and gotten out in time.

"The body was found"—Bambi started at that bit of overheard conversation, but surely they were talking about the attacks? She continued to move through the crowd, checking on people. They would have to say a prayer at some point. Thank God they had Linda's oldest to get them through it. Like most of her generation, Bambi read Hebrew only in transliteration and didn't know any prayers by heart. Her family had been conservative when to be conservative was to be rather lax.

But Felix knew Hebrew. She remembered her surprise, early in their marriage, when she realized that Felix had been raised in a relatively devout home. Synagogue was not just a social network for Felix. He relaxed there, took solace in High Holiday services. It was more than a way to burnish his social standing, although he always pretended otherwise.

After he had gone, Bambi sometimes looked at the new bimah, the Chagall-inspired stained glass behind it, and felt as if she could count the Brewer dollars that had gone into it—and wished she could have every one of them back.

"I'm glad she didn't suffer," a woman said, clasping Bambi's hands. Corky Mercer, the absentee owner of the Pikesville boutique where Bambi had worked for twenty years now, all the while pretending it was a lark, something to do after the older girls left home. The job had kept them all in clothes they otherwise never could have afforded.

"She?"

"Your aunt."

Of course. Her aunt, Harriet. They were here for Harriet. "She hadn't been well for two years, but, no, in the end, she didn't suffer," she said, extricating her hands. Corky meant well, but Bambi didn't appreciate any touch that held her in place. She wondered if Corky would have done the same to a lifelong customer, as opposed to a customer who had ended up being a lifelong employee.

Aunt Harriet had died in her sleep at age ninety-five. It had been at once slow and sudden, the end of a gradual decline that began with a fall at age eighty-three. It was only a broken wrist, but it was the beginning. That was when they started hiring the aides—and when Harriet's eccentricities became more pronounced.

Or was it simply that someone was finally there, paying attention? At any rate, the calls began twelve years ago. Even after Bambi's mother moved into Windsor Towers, just down the hall from her older sister, Bambi still got the calls. Sometimes from Harriet, sometimes from the front desk, but mostly from the nursing aides who were subjected to Harriet's verbal abuse. Bambi wouldn't call her aunt racist—

I would, said the Felix who lived in Bambi's head. Still. Still.

But Harriet was misanthropic and suspicious of almost everyone, regardless of race. She also had a bad tendency to cite people's appearance in her tirades. So, yes, when she yelled *frizzy-haired slut* at the Jamaican aide, or *big-mouthed idiot* at the next woman, it probably seemed racist. "If you knew the things she says to my mother, her own baby sister," Bambi said when she tried to appease the women. "I'm the only person she likes."

They were not appeased.

Bambi really was, according to Harriet, the only person she liked. When Bambi was a child, Aunt Harriet had said: "You are my favorite niece."

Bambi, just ten, had said: "But I'm your only niece."

"Exactly," Harriet said with a scary loud laugh, slapping her thigh. "So you're my least favorite, too. When I write you out of the will, it's so I can put *you* in the will."

But as Bambi emerged as a belle, Harriet's teasing evolved into sardonic adulation. Harriet, never married—by choice, she said—took vicarious pleasure in Bambi's social successes. She always wanted to know if the boys were from good families, by which she meant only one thing: Were they rich? She resented Felix at first. "He nipped you in the bud," she said. "He knew a good thing when he saw it."

Yet Linda, Rachel, Michelle—they were of no interest to her. Even as Michelle began to resemble Bambi more and more, Harriet ignored her nieces. "You're my only heir," she said to Bambi time and again.

"What about Mother?"

"She has a husband."

Bambi's father had died less than a year after Felix disappeared, so it seemed to Bambi that she and her mother were in similar situations, even if her mother did have Social Security, life insurance, and savings to draw on. Still, in Harriet's mind, it was different, a disappeared husband apparently being much worse than a dead one. Even as her animosity toward her sister lessened, softened by Ida's decision to follow her to the Windsor Towers, Harriet insisted that Bambi, and Bambi alone, deserved her money.

How much was there? Enough to make a difference? She hated herself for thinking about it—yet it had been her only thought for forty-eight hours, since the last call about Aunt Harriet came, and she wished it could be her only thought now, that it could force other things from her mind.

She caught Lorraine looking at her, eyes full of pity, and she knew it was not for Aunt Harriet. Bambi wouldn't be pitied. She checked her posture, smoothed her hair, and searched the crowd for her daughters. Here was her fortune, achieved against enormous odds. Linda, the family breadwinner and a good mother, with four terrific kids. Rachel, still trying to be a mother, while now enjoying success doing some computer work that Bambi didn't quite understand, but it had grown out of a silly thing she had done, creating a computer program that sent out a poem every day. And Rachel had helped Michelle find a job at a start-up, although its main appeal to Michelle seemed to be the glamorous offices, created out of an old factory in the heart of Canton.

Where was Michelle? She hadn't slipped out before the prayer, had she? That would be in very bad taste on her part. Not that anyone would remember, tomorrow.

Michelle wandered the upstairs, looking for a computer. She wanted to check her e-mail. Since September 11 she had been even more obsessive about going online. She checked her e-mail as often as possible, used random chat rooms. Everyone was checking in on each other. A few girls from Park, even Adam Gelman, who still had a crush on her. Sometimes she thought she should take him in hand and break him, like a horse. A third-year law student, he was still something of a thuggish frat boy. It would be a good deed for all womankind to tame him and put him back in the population, gentled. But he didn't have any money to spend on her, much less time. So—no thank you.

Adam and Alec's room was as it had been when they left for college, only clean. Their mother had tried to impose her will on the room to a certain extent—the sports and music posters were beautifully framed, not tacked up with tape or thumbtacks. The built-in desks, the bright red chairs, even the basketball hoop mounted to the wall—these were not IKEA finds, Michelle knew. She remembered an earlier version of this room, with *two* sets of bunk beds. Because, of course, Adam and Alec must have both options, up and down. They had never wanted to have separate rooms. They had gone to college, shared a dorm room, and now they were at DePaul together. *Weird.* The only profound difference between them, as far as Michelle could see, was that Adam had a crush on her and Alec couldn't stand her.

No computers here, although there was a television set. She thought about turning it on, settling in, but it wasn't TV she longed for. She wanted to talk—only not to the people downstairs. She wanted to talk on the computer, where people were wittier and understood her jokes and it was okay to be a little ADD. To talk past people, as opposed to talk to.

And to try, again and again, to chase her father down the rabbit holes of various search engines. She was still fond of Alta Vista, although curious about Google, which suddenly seemed everywhere. Imagine, she had been at College Park at the same time as Sergey Brin. Now *there* was a lost opportunity.

She checked Bert and Lorraine's room. Lorraine didn't even have a television set in here, much less a computer. Michelle lifted the sheets, looked for labels. Frette. *Not silk,* she decided, rubbing the fabric between her fingers. Cotton that felt like silk. She filed the name away as she often did with the brands she discovered at the Gelman house, adding it to a voluminous wish list.

She had been living in Rachel's old apartment for five years now, but she yearned to move. Everyone said of her new job, "Oh, you can walk to work!" Sure, if she wanted to wear flats or put on sneakers and then change into her heels. Both options struck her as untenable. What she wanted to do was buy a condo across the street from her office, in this gorgeous building called Canton Cove, with harbor views and all sorts of amenities. But even with the new job, she wouldn't qualify for a mortgage. And almost anyone could get a mortgage these days. You could buy a place with no money down and, by the time you signed your loan documents, you'd already have made ten, twenty thousand dollars on paper. But Michelle had credit card debt. It was Rachel's fault, letting her have the apartment, with its relatively low rent. That had lulled Michelle into thinking she had more money than she did. She had spent what she wasn't paying toward her rent, and then some, and now she was in debt.

She left Bert and Lorraine's room and went down the hall to Sydney's room. For a moment, she thought she had gotten confused. Surely, this was the old guest room? But Sydney's room was now a home gym, a proper one—elliptical machine, treadmill, a television mounted to the wall above them. A rack of weights, serious ones. Those must be for Bert. And—wow, a sauna. Michelle opened the door and leaned in, drinking in that lovely dry-wood smell. When had Lorraine done this? After Sydney moved to New York to take a job?

Or after she had announced right before graduation that

she was moving to New York to live with a thirty-five-year-old woman she had been dating secretly for two years?

Lorraine and Bert had taken it very well, everyone kept saying. Michelle and her sisters found that hilarious. As if *Sydney* had shamed them. Sydney was only the most disgustingly perfect person in the world, so perfect that even Rachel didn't seem quite as shiny alongside her. (Truth be told, it pleased Michelle that Rachel was second to someone, brain-wise and perfection-wise.) Sydney was so wonderful that she had called Bambi and Ida to express her sympathy for the loss of Aunt Harriet, then explained that she would miss the funeral because she was volunteering at a soup kitchen that was providing meals for rescue workers.

No, Sydney was not the kid that Lorraine and Bert should be putting on a brave front about. But then Lorraine and Bert somehow didn't know how awful the twins had been as teenagers. Mellowed now, presumably, but there had been the incident with the drunk girl, the video they had made of her. They hadn't touched her. They had just filmed this poor girl stumbling, then throwing up, and then, with the logic of the inebriated, removing her clothes because they were covered with vomit. They filmed every moment, with a droll running commentary, then screened it for their friends in the Gelmans' den. When the prank—Bert's term—caught up with them, the boys insisted they were protecting themselves against what the girl might say later. "We were just documenting it," Alec said. It was her house, her father's liquor, and the twins were sober. But Michelle thought that was the truly creepy part, the twins' self-control, their clear-eyed decision to sit back and record this girl's humiliation.

She closed the sauna, turned, and found Bert at the door of the room. She felt guilty, thinking such mean thoughts about his sons while prowling through his house, cataloging Lorraine's things, learning to want items she hadn't known existed.

"Your mother's looking for you."

"I was hoping to lie down. I have the most ferocious headache."

"The guest room is made up. Or you could use our bed."

His kindness made her feel even guiltier. Too bad Bert's sons weren't more like him. They had his looks, but something was lacking. Bert made her feel safe.

"I'll be okay. I'll just throw some cold water on my face, maybe take some aspirin."

"Okay," he said. "You know, Michelle, for a moment—in this dim light, I thought you were your mother. You may end up being even more beautiful than she was in her prime."

Michelle realized that Bert thought this high praise, but *really*. "Aren't I in my prime right now?" she asked.

"Not quite."

"When, then?" Said with a pretend pout. She looked up at him through her lashes, parted her lips. She suddenly wanted Bert to kiss her. And when Michelle wanted men to kiss her, they did.

But Bert said only: "I think your mother's prime started in her midthirties or so. Maybe even forty. And she's still in it. Find that aspirin, Michelle, then come downstairs, okay?"

He probably didn't realize what she had offered him, old man that he was. Michelle went to the powder room, took a Tylenol she didn't actually need and stared in the mirror, wondering how anyone could be in one's prime at *forty*.

Rachel had noticed Michelle was missing, but not in the way Linda had, which was to say Rachel wasn't furious.

"Michelle won't stay at any party that's not about her," Linda sputtered. "She did the same thing at Rosh Hashanah dinner last week, went into my bedroom and watched television."

"She had a migraine," Rachel said.

"People with migraines need to be in dark, quiet rooms. She was watching *Gilmore Girls*."

"It's a drag for her, being the youngest. She's the odd one out. The rest of us come in pairs."

"Not Mama."

"Doesn't she? I always feel as if Papa is with her, somehow."

"You're such a romantic, Rachel. He's in—Bali, with his girlfriend, the one who lived at Horizon House. I always wanted to get a good look at her, see what the attraction was."

"They're not in Bali."

"Israel, then. Wasn't that always the other rumor? That he bought a new life for himself by investing heavily in Israeli bonds?"

"I think you've confused Papa with Meyer Lansky."

"Oh, Rachel, the great romantic. Do you really think Papa yearns for our mother after all these years?"

"I met her," she said.

"You *saw* her. You told me, back when it happened. And it's not as if she announced her plans to you that night. It was probably already in the works, don't you think? And all that other stuff she did was meant to obscure it."

Nana Ida came over to Linda and Rachel, pushed her way between them and linked arms. The sisters were not particularly tall, but they dwarfed Nana Ida.

"Harriet loved you both so much," she said of her older sister, with whom she had not even been on speaking terms until two years ago.

Linda nodded carefully, while Rachel made a noncommittal noise. They were not fans of Harriet.

"And although she didn't specify, I know she'd want you to have mementos. We'll go through her jewelry box, see what's left."

Rachel hoped her expression stayed neutral. She knew that her mother had—with Harriet's full consent—sold the better pieces. But everything was to be willed to her mother, Harriet's godchild, so what did it matter? Her mother had sold off things precisely to keep the estate below certain levels in order to avoid the inheritance taxes. She wrote checks over the years, too, although never enough to pay a gift tax. Yet Harriet would never let Bambi see her financial accounts, and that was where the real money was.

"She probably would have wanted you to have a little money, too," their grandmother said. "But we'll have to see what's what when the dust has settled."

Even as Rachel was sorting out her grandmother's syntax, Linda said sharply: "You sound as if you're the executor."

"Oh, no," Nana Ida said. "That's the lawyer. But the estate will be split between your mother and me. Well, not fifty-fifty. Your mother will get a cash gift, and I'll get the rest. Harriet changed it six months ago. We became so close, living at the Windsor Towers. She had resented me all our lives because I was the baby, but she finally saw how silly that was. Plus, she knows now how much I helped out—tuition and such. I put you girls through Park."

"We appreciate it," Rachel said, as she always said when this came up, and it came up a lot.

"Does Mama know?" Linda asked.

"I told Harriet she should tell her."

"Does Mama know?" Linda repeated. Rachel realized how quick her sister was to recognize a nonresponsive answer, given that her professional life was based on giving them.

"I couldn't say," Nana Ida said, looking down into her coffee cup. "It's not so very much, I'm sure. Money shouldn't matter in families."

But Linda had already broken away, plunging through knots of people to reach their mother. Rachel watched her go, remembering how it was Linda, all those years ago, who told her that Julie had been just the latest girlfriend, not the only one. Linda had always known how to break bad news.

Linda tried to move quickly, but she couldn't just plow through the well-wishers. *How much money could it be, anyway?* Two hundred thousand, three hundred thousand? Probably not enough to get Bambi's head above water. Did Nana Ida have any idea how close to the bone Bambi lived, how she sweated the property taxes every year, worried over utility bills, and let repairs go as long as possible? The reason Bambi had asked the Gelmans to hold the shivah was because she couldn't bear for people to see the house's condition—the cracking window frames, the patchy roof. She had been able to maintain the "public" rooms, which required little more than regular paint and the occasional reupholstery job, done on the cheap with tacks. But the kitchen was stuck in the seventies, as were the bathrooms. The Sudbrook Park house was frozen in time, like something out of a fairy tale. Her father had paid it off before he left, perhaps the last decent thing he did. Bambi should have sold it immediately, downscaled. Instead, she held on to it, mortgaging it and remortgaging it. Why hadn't she sold it?

Because, Linda knew, she expected him to come back. She still expected him to come up the walk. So she wouldn't petition for his life insurance, or even ask for the modest veterans' pension to which he was entitled.

And her mother had been so good to Aunt Harriet. Linda remembered an incident a few years back, before Harriet had to go to the nursing wing of Windsor Towers. One of the aides had called Bambi in alarm, and, for once, it wasn't because of something hateful that Harriet had said. When Bambi got to the apartment, the aide showed her that the kitchen drawers were stuffed with packets of sugar and artificial sweetener, cellophane packages of soy sauce and plum sauce, mustard and mayonnaise. It boggled the mind, how Harriet had ever gathered all these things. She must have gone into restaurants and shoved them in her pockets willy-nilly. When the aide had tried to throw them away, Harriet had become enraged and thrown a tantrum like a child. Bambi had soothed her and packed up her "treasures" in marked shoeboxes. Where had Ida been then? Maybe they should contest the will. But, no, it would end up in the news. Just this past July, a reporter had called about doing a story tied to the twenty-fifth "anniversary" of Felix's disappearance. No one in the family had cooperated, but that hadn't stopped the reporter from doing a clip job.

Linda found her mother in the kitchen, sitting at the long, padded bench in the breakfast nook. She looked drained. Had someone else already told her about Great-Aunt Harriet's last spiteful act?

"Drink this," Lorraine was saying to Bambi. "It's decaffeinated."

"I thought you said it would be days, maybe even a week or so, Bert. But if a reporter called you here—"

"The reporter was sniffing. He doesn't have anything solid."

"Even if it is her," Lorraine said, "it has nothing to do with you. Nothing."

"But they'll write about it soon enough. Not tomorrow perhaps, but it's going to be written about. They'll dredge everything up again."

"No one's going to pay attention, given what's happening in the world at large," Bert said. "It's a blessing of sorts."

"The attacks?"

"The discovery. Now you know. It has nothing to do with Felix. She never went to him."

"Do I? Is that what I know, Bert? And do you think the newspaper will care about that distinction?"

Linda could hold still no longer. "What's going on? What are you talking about?"

"Tubby got a tip from a detective this morning," Bert told her. "They think they've found Julie Saxony's body. They still have to do an official ID, and there's no immediate determination on cause of death, but apparently some items—her driver's license, I guess, because that would be plastic—survived. I thought the news wouldn't get out until they had matched dental records, done an autopsy—"

"Where?" Linda asked because it was the only thing she could think to ask.

"Leakin Park."

"And no one found her until now?"

"It's a big place," Bert said. "They say a dog found her on the far side, where there's no path to walk. And they still have to make an official ID. All they have for now is a body, maybe a license. She could have left that body there herself. We don't know for certain it's her."

And not even ten minutes ago, Linda thought, *I imagined her in Bali, sitting next to Daddy on matching chaises, a table of drinks between them.* But she didn't want to feel sorry for Julie Saxony. She didn't want to feel anything for her. She didn't want her dead. She just wanted her never to have existed.

I know she's not in Bali, Rachel had said. *I met her.* Linda looked at her mother. She was shaky and pale, upset. But she didn't seem surprised. Then again, she had known about Julie, possibly all day. It was the call from the reporter that had jarred her. Linda would handle the reporter. She always did.

Michelle chose that time to enter the kitchen, oblivious as ever. She didn't look like someone who had just weathered a migraine, or whatever excuse she had used this time.

"Do we have a minyan? Because I really need to get on the road." Then, when everyone glared at her, "What?"

March 22, 2012

Julie's sister, Andrea Norr, did not seem particularly surprised to see Sandy's car bouncing up her driveway. Resigned, perhaps, like someone who knew a mistake had been made in her favor but had always believed it would catch up to her eventually. Maybe even a little relieved. She walked alongside his car the final ten yards or so, invited him in, made him more bad tea.

"So she told Susie, that little bubblehead? I thought Julie was tighter with a secret."

Sandy felt a knee-jerk instinct to defend both women. "I think your sister chose a good confidante. Susan Borden didn't tell the police about the missing money, or even the argument with the daughter. She sat on a significant lead, believing she was honoring Julie's wishes, that she would put your interests ahead of hers when it came down to it."

Andrea made a face, the kind of face Sandy wanted to make with every sip of her tea. "If that's the case, it was out of guilt, not love."

"Guilt over what?"

"She left me, Mr. Sanchez. We ran away from home together. It was an adventure. And she left me—in the Rexall, in our apartment on Biddle. You know what she called me, when I told her I didn't approve of Felix? She called me the little old biddy of Biddle Street. She chose her meal ticket over her sister."

"What I keep hearing is that she really loved him."

"So what?" A flare of temper. "I was *blood*. He was some stupid married man who was never going to marry her, never. Okay—so secrets are coming out, right? Susie told my secret. Now I'll tell Julie's. She thought, sometimes, about going to the cops, saying that Felix didn't run away. That he feared for his life. That Bambi had him taken out, because he was going to leave her and she didn't think she could get by on the alimony."

"That doesn't sound like your sister."

Andrea's laughter wasn't cruel, not exactly, but a laugh at one's expense always feels cruel and she was definitely laughing at Sandy.

"You think you know Julie better than I do? Another man blinded by a pair of big"—she paused in a practiced way—"blue eyes."

"I've learned a lot about her. Other people, her friends, thought well of her."

"Did they? Well, here's my tip. When you want to measure the worth of a person, ask the family first. And don't forget that Felix, the man she loved, didn't care for her at all. He put us both at risk, asking that we get him out of town. Yes, Tubman knew and the lawyer, Bert, he knew, too, that Felix was going. They knew the how, and they probably could guess the when. Before he left, Felix moved money around, he signed a power of attorney. Julie was too stupid to ask for anything."

"But you weren't."

"I literally bought the farm! Oh, hell, not even I find that funny. Anyway, I had the discipline to wait three years before I spent what he gave me. Someone had to."

"Wait?"

"Have discipline. That bail bondsman ran all over town, making wink-wink, nudge-nudge jokes about getting stuck with the bond. Always the jolly fat guy."

"Your sister had discipline. She didn't tell anyone anything for ten years, as far as we know. And Bert Gelman had discipline."

"Well, Bert would have been disbarred, right? If he helped someone flee." She sighed. "There's one more piece of the story. I know you think Julie was protecting me. But it was mutual. Julie was too stupid to *ask* for anything. But she wasn't too stupid not to take what was right in front of her."

"What do you mean?"

"That night, Felix gave her a suitcase. A small one, like a cosmetic bag. He told her to take it to 'the place.' I don't think she ever did. She hated Bambi that much, she wouldn't share whatever Felix left behind."

Sandy was jolted. It was like finding out that a woman you admired had a bad habit, or an ugly laugh, or made fun of cripples. He was disappointed in Julie, and maybe Susie, too, for not telling him this part.

"What was in the suitcase?" he asked. He was pretty sure he knew the answer.

"Money for Felix's family."

"You can't put enough money in a suitcase for a family to live very long."

"No. But I think there was information, too, about accounts, and how to access them. All I remember is that he said it would take care of everything and she should take it to the place, whatever that was. But she didn't. I mean—it's obvious, she didn't, right?"

"Not to me. It's not like your sister lived like someone who had that kind of money." Even as he defended her, he was remembering his own random curiosity about Julie's ability to make the leap from grubby coffee shop to showplace inn.

"No, but neither did Bambi Brewer—I knew the stable owner who got stiffed for the daughters' lessons. And that was only six months or so after Felix disappeared. I mean, Bambi might have been reckless, but she couldn't have run through it that fast. So you have to ask yourself where the money went. My sister didn't care about having the money, or using it. She cared only that Bambi never have it. See, that's my real beef with Felix Brewer. He made my sister mean. He strung her along, used her to get away, left her thinking 'if only.' He was yammering about being with her right up until the moment he left. You want to take someone's life away from them, then put them in the 'if only' camp. My sister pinned all her hopes on Felix Brewer. When he didn't ask her to come with him, he broke her heart. I mean, why not take her with him? All the way to—well, I don't have to tell you that part. Where we took him. But up until the very last moment, when he said good-bye to her, she thought he was going to ask her to come along. She had a passport with her. Got it just in case. She went to Bert, asked him to help her expedite it. I guess he thought, 'What could it hurt?' Well, it hurt a lot. When Felix left—literally left Julie holding the bag—huh, I did it again. Another stupid joke." She broke off, slumped back in her chair as if all that talk had left her winded.

"You were saying?"

"Felix. He broke her heart. So she lashed out. You know, that's another reason, I think, that we ended up on the outs. Because I was there, I *knew*. She had a little overnight bag. On the trip up, she said to me, 'Where do you think we're going? South America? Oh, I hope I can learn Spanish.' My stupid baby sister, may she rest in peace. She had never been on a plane before, either, and she was excited about that. I knew and she couldn't bear it. That was the beginning of the end for us. She tried to play it proud on the drive back, but I wasn't fooled."

"Where was the place?"

"I dropped her at a diner on Route 40, where someone else was to meet her and drive her the rest of the way. That's all I know. Really. Today, I haven't left anything out."

Sandy believed her.

It was a few minutes shy of 11:00 A.M. when Sandy made his way back down Andrea Norr's driveway. He was hungry, although he shouldn't have been. He stopped at the Chesapeake House rest stop and pushed a tray along the metal bars at Roy Rogers, feeling that it was too late for the breakfast sandwiches, which looked pretty old under the heat lamps, yet too early for the fried chicken that was just coming out. In the end, he settled on a holster of fries and a cup of coffee.

Andrea Norr had committed a felony, helping Felix escape, taking money for it. She wasn't pure, and she had reasons to lie. About the suitcase, the money, all that. Problem was, there was a detail that had never been made public, a detail that served her version of things. When Julie Saxony's body was found in Leakin Park, part of the reason that word traveled so fast, in advance of an official autopsy, was because cops had found *two* forms of ID— her driver's license and her passport, which had survived that damp, wild place because it was in a plastic case inside a leatherette purse, the kind of thing that never decays. The passport, good for ten years, had expired on July 1, 1986. It was blank, utterly blank, not a single stamp in its pages.

February 14, 2004

While the rest of her family had been seated at table number 2, Michelle was at number 12, with all the strays. She was outraged on principle, although she planned to sneak away after the entrée was served, table-hop her way right out of the ballroom and upstairs, where she had taken a room in order to meet the man she was seeing for a Valentine's Day tryst. Still, that didn't excuse Lorraine Gelman for sticking her at such a lousy table.

Her lover had been nervous about the meeting, said it was a risky thing to do with so many people around. But it was important to Michelle to see him on Valentine's Day because that would prove his loyalty to her. She had insisted, and she usually got her way with him. Usually. She glanced at her watch—Cartier, a gift from him. As was the BMW she had driven here tonight, the diamond earrings, and the fur coat she had refused to check because she wanted to be wearing it, and nothing else, when he knocked on the door of the room.

She pulled her phone out of her bag and typed: "1212/2030." Room and time. It wasn't the first time they had met in a hotel.

"What are you doing?" asked the man seated next to her. Barry something. Friend of Adam's from Northwestern or maybe law school.

"Texting."

"That's a rip-off on most plans."

"I'm not worried about it," she said loftily. She wasn't. The phone was another gift. She didn't even see the bills. She wasn't sure exactly how things worked, but it was her understanding that the phone, along with the credit card he had given her—they were all assigned to some fictitious employee. It was a little worrisome that there was a practiced slickness to the setup. How long had he been catting around? Yet he swore he had never done anything like this before, that she had pursued him. She remembered a chance encounter, a stolen kiss outside the Red Maple, wasabi and sake on his breath. Had she really initiated it? Probably.

"And it's generally not deductible, a mobile phone plan. People assume it's a deductible business expense, but that's not always true."

"Are you an accountant?"

"Of sorts. I work for the government."

He grinned as if he had made a joke, but Michelle didn't get it.

"You knew Adam at school, right?" She gave him her attention, if not the full wattage of her charm. Back at Park, when they had read the Greek myth about the birth of Dionysus, how his mortal mother had demanded to see Zeus in godlike splendor and he had chosen his smallest lightning bolts hoping in vain not to kill her, Michelle had felt a rare moment of connection with the bookish world in which her sisters excelled. This guy required only her smallest lightning bolts and he, too, was still at risk.

He nodded. "Alec, too, of course. You can't really know one

without the other. I'm surprised Adam isn't taking Alec on the honeymoon. They are thick as thieves."

"Those of us who have known them all their lives are surprised that they didn't turn out to be thieves. Or, you know, serial killers."

He laughed, taking it for a joke, or at least hyperbole.

"No, seriously, they should have been voted most likely to be hit men. They were awful when they were young."

"Maybe," said Barry something. "But they're nice guys now, and isn't that what matters? Not who we were, but who we become?"

"Adam had a crush on me for years."

She hadn't planned on saying that. Why had she said it?

"Oh, I know. He told me he was doing me the enormous favor of making sure I got to sit next to you tonight."

So it wasn't Lorraine's fault that she was at this awful table. Michelle was mollified, although now skeptical of Adam's intentions. Was he punishing her? Or playing a joke on both of them? He couldn't possibly think she would be interested in this Barry guy.

Besides, these days she just wasn't in the market at all. There was no one else for her. But her lover wouldn't leave his wife, and even if he did, there would be such a shit storm. No, they could never be together. This would be the romance that kept her alive, inside, like—oh, Lord, was she really comparing her life to *The Bridges of Madison County*? Or some Nicholas Sparks book?

She picked at her steak, unimpressed. There had been too many filet mignons wrapped in bacon, too many blinis, too many cheese puffs over the last few years as all her friends got married. Food was becoming excitingly expensive, another luxury to pursue, although one had to range beyond Baltimore to get the really good stuff. Just this month, a new restaurant had opened in

New York, Per Se, and it was said to be impossible to get a table. She had told her lover that she wanted to go there for her birthday. It was a test—not of his ability to snag a reservation, but of his commitment to her. If he didn't find a way to be with her on her birthday, she would—what? Her only power over him was her ability to wreck his marriage, and he had to know she would never do that.

"What do you do?" Barry asked, her least favorite question.

"I work for a tech company," she said. "Marketing. I hate it."

"Stock options?"

"Some." Worthless, or soon to be.

"Still, you're doing well." His eyes rested on the watch, the earrings, the fur on the chair, and—oh so inevitably, and oh so boring —the neckline of her dress, which a man would never recognize as expensive, much less Prada. Her mother had, though, reaching out to touch the fabric, torn between approval and suspicion. She knew Michelle couldn't afford a Prada dress, and she sure as hell hadn't procured it through Bambi's discount.

She opened her purse wide, letting him see the tampons inside, then took out a small bottle of ibuprofen, a time-tested conversation ender. "I hope the ladies' room has a place where I can lie down."

"Oh," he stammered. "Well—feel better."

She went up to the room, 1212, and ordered champagne, the best available. It was already 8:30—2030; he insisted on military time for some reason, one of his quirks, he said it was common in the United Kingdom, where he traveled on business—but she understood that he might be in a situation where he couldn't call her. He often was. She treated herself to some TV. He hated her taste in television, said it was base, but so what if she liked *Extreme Makeover: Home Edition*? If she kept the remote close at hand, she could click it off as soon as she heard his knock at the door. She had left it imperceptibly ajar so she could remain on the bed, the beautiful coat pooled around her, its platinum silk lining so close to her skin tone that she all but melted into it. God, she couldn't believe she had ever worn that made-over mink passed down by Bambi—

She awoke to the show where the girl spy always seemed to be wearing wigs and boots and kicking someone in the face. When she got downstairs, the DJ was exhorting people to do the electric slide, but the party was clearly winding down.

He's going to break up with me, she thought. No one had ever broken up with Michelle before. She could beat him to the punch, have her pride, but she didn't want to stop seeing him.

Adam's friend—what was his name?—pulled out her chair and didn't comment on the fact that she had been gone for more than an hour. He continued to chatter to her, and she tried to make appropriate responses, but it was like speaking to someone on a very bad cell connection. His voice seemed to come from so far away that she had to keep asking him to repeat himself. She looked around the room, desperate to find someone better with whom to flirt. Adam? Inappropriate, even for her. Alec? Funny, but he really disliked her to this day. Everyone else, except her mother, was part of a set—including her two sisters, who were keeping tabs on her, as always. *Get a life,* she wanted to say to them. What will you do when you don't have me to gossip about, disapprove of? Linda looked angry, while Rachel just had her usual sympathetic simper on, which was far worse.

"Is the bar still open?" she asked—Barry. That was his name. "Would you get me a vodka martini?"

"She's almost thirty-one," Linda fumed to Rachel. "When is she going to get her act together?"

"She's nervous about her job," Rachel said. "The rumors are they won't make it through the year."

As a website designer, Rachel was plugged into Baltimore's tiny tech community. Everyone knew that Michelle's company, Sinergie, was going to go down; the only question was when and how. Michelle said she was sticking it out to the end in hopes of a severance package, but how could a company pay severance when it was already stiffing vendors and landlords? Linda thought Michelle was lazy, but Rachel knew their baby sister was scared. It wasn't lost on her that Michelle had wandered into a job that combined her sisters' two fields—communications for Linda, tech for Rachel. And neither one suited her. Michelle needed to find her own thing.

"A therapist I know"—Rachel was careful not to say *my* therapist; only Joshua knew she was seeing someone—"says there's a theory that traumas leave us arrested at the age of the trauma."

"Michelle doesn't even remember Daddy. And that would make you forever fourteen, me sixteen. With all due respect, your therapist friend is kind of a quack."

Twenty-four for me, Rachel thought. *That was my traumatic year, although I didn't realize it until recently.* And, no, Linda wasn't frozen at sixteen, that was true. Linda had been earnest and idealistic as a teenager, qualities she had carried into adulthood. But a professional lifetime of choosing her words with care had left her blunt and hard in her most intimate relationships. Henry handled it well, but it grated a little on Rachel, even though she almost never came in for Linda's criticism.

Then again, Rachel was expert at keeping things from Linda. From everyone, when need be. An open, sunny nature is a great cover for secrets, as Rachel discovered long ago. Even now, with the therapist, she couldn't open up completely. She had gone, at Joshua's pleading, to discuss her depression over not being able to conceive, but she wouldn't give the therapist all the pieces needed to understand the bigger picture. She also refused any medication. So what was the point? Rachel knew why she was sad, and she also knew she wasn't going to do anything about it. Maybe her therapist was an idiot not to see through her.

Joshua came up and put his hand at the small of her back. Together nine years now. Eight years ago, even three years ago, he would have pointed to one of the children present and said: "Ours will be cuter." He knew better than to do that now. She was almost forty-two. No one got everything in this life. Her mother had children, but no husband. Linda had a family, but supporting them meant spending much less time with them than she wanted. Michelle didn't have a family or a real career, although she clearly had a boyfriend who was buying her very nice things. Rachel had Joshua—lovely, marvelous, really—and her business, small but successful. Rachel had always thought small. Why was she like that?

These would probably be very good questions to explore with her therapist. If she were inclined to tell her therapist such things.

Bambi was exhausted, but Lorraine and Bert expected her to stay until the end. Well, Lorraine did. That was the price of having friends like family. They treated you like family. Worse, there was the fact of all the money "lent" over the years, although that was more of a Bert thing and he never guilted her. Bambi had a hunch that Lorraine really didn't know the extent, the various subterfuges Bert had used to prop her up. She always insisted she would pay him back one day and he was always gallant enough to pretend he believed her.

She calculated the cost of the event, a habit she would never quite break. Bambi knew the price of everything. But also its worth, she was no fool. Adam's fiancée came from a family of modest means, working-class types from Southwest Chicago, so Bert had insisted on paying for the wedding. "It's not like we're going to have to pay for Sydney's," Lorraine had said, happy to have the control that came with signing the checks. Such a joke showed real progress for Lorraine, who had gone from being Very Brave about Sydney's lifestyle—"As close as Lorraine will ever come to saying 'lesbian,'" Linda had observed—to being almost capable of accepting Sydney's girlfriend as a de facto spouse. And although Lorraine had always favored her boys, she was, with Adam's marriage, coming up against the hard truth that daughters are forever, whereas sons are absorbed into their wives' families more often than not. Adam was staying in Chicago and wherever Adam was, Alec would probably end up.

Plus, it was Sydney who had delivered the first Gelman grandchild, an adoptee from Guatemala. The little boy was gorgeous, although Bambi had to wonder how that worked, a Latino boy named Reuben being raised by two women in Brooklyn. Could that end well?

Probably about as well as a married-in-name-only woman raising three girls in the Baltimore suburbs without any real income.

She pulled a wrap around her shoulders. The ballroom had felt overheated when it was full, but as the last guests lingered, it took on a sad chill. Fifty, sixty thousand she guessed. Maybe as much as a hundred thousand, but Bert was good at negotiating. And for what? A meal, wine, music, flowers. Within forty-eight hours, the only physical remnants of this night would be the boxes of cake slices that no one ever remembered to put in the freezer. The bride's dress would go into a sealed dry cleaner's bag, and the bridesmaids' dresses would go into closets, never to be worn again. At least they were black. The bride, Alina, had been gently dissuaded from her original color scheme, a red-and-white Valentine's Day tribute. She was a sweet girl, though. Lorraine would take her in hand, best she could over a distance of seven hundred miles, and train her, much as Bambi had trained Lorraine back in the day. Who, for all her money and social status, had been very unsure of herself when they first met, in need of a mentor when it came to clothes and style. The student had surpassed the teacher long ago, but Lorraine was gracious enough to still seek Bambi's advice on most matters.

Bert sank into the chair next to her. "One down, one to go. If only Alina could have had a twin. I'm sure Alec would have married her, and that would have saved me a bundle."

"You're a lucky man, Bert. Your kids have turned out beautifully. You should be very proud."

"I am, of course." Funny, he didn't look proud. "Lorraine deserves the credit, though. For the children. For our life, really. It's all been Lorraine. She said our boys would turn out fine and they have. And Sydney—I couldn't ask for a better daughter."

"They say you're only as happy as your least happy child, so you're in good shape."

"I guess I am. I guess I am." But he sounded more game than convinced, someone putting on the happy face expected of him. Probably just tired at the end of what had been an even longer day for him.

"It would have been my forty-fourth wedding anniversary," Bambi said. "I guess it still is."

Linda was at the valet stand, five people behind her own sister. There was a man hovering close to Michelle, but he was a fool if he thought he had a chance with her. The quarter-size bald spot alone would disqualify him.

"Should we keep going?" Henry asked. Their youngest was

thirteen now, and it was still relatively novel for them to be out and not running up against the babysitter's clock.

"And do what?" Linda asked. Not peevishly or meanly, merely curious. What was there left to do? They had gone to a party, eaten a meal, danced, drunk.

She watched the man who was not quite with Michelle lean into the car, argue with her. No, not argue—*entreat*.

"I don't know. Let's just go sit in the hotel bar until this line calms down. It's cold out here."

That seemed reasonable. Pleasant, even. And when they were settled at the bar, drinks in front of them, Linda was reminded how much she enjoyed her husband's company, one-on-one, and how long it had been since she had had it. Soon, in the blink of an eye, it would be just the two of them again, all the time, for the first time in almost twenty years.

"We met in a bar," he said.

"You hopped for me."

"I've been hopping ever since." Said with the easygoing demeanor that she loved, when she didn't find it absolutely infuriating. "I remember thinking, 'Why is that pretty girl so sad?'"

"I remember being sad."

"Over John Anderson, of all things."

"Anderson and—I don't think I ever told you this."

Henry perked up. It was a rare gift, a new story twenty-four years into a relationship.

"The bartender. He knew my father. And he told me that he had seen him with my older sister from time to time."

"You don't have an older sister." A beat. "Oh. Wow. I'm sorry. Did he mean—that one?"

"I think so. I didn't ask any follow-up questions, that was for sure."

The man from the valet line, the one who had been with Michelle, came into the bar, waved at the younger members of the wedding party, and asked the bartender for a beer. But he didn't go over to his friends, not right away, just sat at the bar, shoulders slumped, a picture of dejection and rejection.

"Don't let my sister get to you," Linda said, leaning across Henry. She could imagine Noah being hurt by a girl like Michelle. Just thinking about it made her angry. "She's a diva."

"She shouldn't be driving. She had a lot to drink."

"No, she probably shouldn't, but it's a straight shot down Boston Street, more or less, and she'll never get above twenty-five miles an hour."

"I live thirty minutes from here and I got a room for the night. They have a rate."

It occurred to Linda that she and Henry should have gotten a room, made a little getaway out of it. Why didn't she ever think of such things? Maybe she could start.

"She'll be fine. She always is, Michelle."

"Look, you're her sister—should I call her? Or is she seeing somebody?"

"Call her," Henry said, even as Linda said: "I think she's seeing someone."

"She gave me her card." He pulled it out. Sinergie. Linda still cringed at the name and was still unsure what the company was supposed to do. Something to do with nightlife?

"Well, if you're going to call her on her work number, do it quickly," Linda said, feeling a little loose, not so much from alcohol but just from the unfamiliar sensation of being unfettered, at no one's beck and call, although she was technically always reachable on her BlackBerry.

"Because she'll forget me?" the man asked.

"Because Sinergie is going down the tubes." *And, yes, because she'll forget you. She's already forgotten you. You could carry*

Michelle out of a burning building and she wouldn't remember you.

He tapped the card on the bar, lost in thought, then went back to his friends, looking a little more resolute and confident. She assumed he was going to call Michelle next week and get shot down.

March 25, 2012

S andy didn't work for a couple of days, not on the file. Again, he couldn't fool himself about his own motivations. He was avoiding an unpleasant task, trying to talk to Bert Gelman, by throwing himself into another unpleasant task, cleaning out the house in Remington and preparing it for a new set of tenants.

Not that Bert would be rude or unkind to Sandy. He just wasn't going to tell Sandy anything. One thing to let your wife share some old gossip, quite another to implicate yourself as an accessory to a fugitive's flight. Sandy was stuck. He couldn't figure out where to go next. So he cleaned.

The old Remington rowhouse was in crap shape, trashed. Again. No matter how carefully Sandy chose his tenants, they all went out the same way, as if they had done some sort of cost-benefits analysis and decided that they'd rather forgo the deposit than, say, clean out the vegetable crisper, which was always full of soggy surprises. This batch had had a cat, too, although that wasn't allowed under the terms of the lease. Sandy was going to have to flea-bomb and replace the carpet in the finished basement.

Over the years, Sandy had done everything he could to make Nabby's house bright—painted all the walls eggshell, installed a transom above the front door, switched out the curtains for neutral bamboo blinds chosen by Mary—but it was hard to pull light into a north-facing row house. He was struck anew by the darkness every time he crossed the threshold. Didn't help that the latest tenants had removed all the lightbulbs, even the ones in the overhead fixtures.

But the house was also dark in his memory of his arrival there, a starless December night when he couldn't quite see the woman who inspected him and said, "Oh—I was expecting someone younger."

"Abuelita?" he asked. Little grandmother? He thought he had been going to a relative, at least a distant one.

"No," she said. "No abuela." Then shouting, as if he were deaf. "NO ABUELA. NO ABUELA. NO ABUELITA FOR YOU."

And that was how Hortensia Saldana became Nabby.

Sandy had come to her through a program known as Operation PedroPan. Cuba had fallen, but the Catholic Welfare Bureau persuaded the government to allow kids to enter the United States and stay in foster homes until their parents could join them. At first, almost everyone went to Florida, but eventually other cities offered homes as well. Sandy was one of the last ones placed, convinced by his parents that it would make it easier for them to follow if they had a son in the States.

Hortensia Saldana had no use for Cubanos, but she liked the idea of being paid to care for one. She was a social worker, although years later, when Mary got to know her, she would describe her as the least-socialized social worker she had ever known. The day they came to tell him his parents were dead, killed in a car accident, an improbable catastrophe—they had a car, but seldom the gas to drive it—Nabby had just looked at him blankly, like a bureaucrat refusing to do a job above her pay grade. She wasn't paid to offer him comfort. She received a check to feed him and clothe him. And they both knew there was no way she was going to adopt him, this teenage boy who wasted hot water and left the milk on the counter sometimes. But he could stay on until he was eighteen, she said, as long as he made himself useful—and as long as the checks kept coming.

Sandy stole his first car a week after he received news that his parents had died. He didn't actually know how to drive, but he taught himself, on the fly. He wasn't sure what he planned to do with the car, once he got it going. It wasn't like he could drive back to Cuba, and there was no one there for him, anyway. He was already beginning to lose his Spanish from lack of use. (The relief agency had assumed Hortensia Saldana spoke Spanish, but she didn't know a word. Her Puerto Rican father had abandoned her mother, an African American, when she was a baby. She thought Spanish the language of demons and bad men.)

The cops pulled Sandy over five minutes after he got behind the wheel of his first stolen car. He was going fifteen miles an hour on University Parkway. A motivated young public defender told his whole story—how, Sandy was never sure, as he didn't share it—and he was given a second chance. Hortensia Saldana was furious. She told him if he did such a thing again, he would be out of her house forever.

He stole another car the next day. To his disappointment, he drove for hours and no one pulled him over. Finally, he left the car on the side of the road, its tank empty.

He was content to do that for a while—take cars, drive them until empty, abandon them. Of course, as soon as he no longer wanted to get caught, he was. They sent him to "training school," and, against all the odds, it worked. He got a high school education, found a friend and mentor in one of the teachers. He left and found a part-time job, a little apartment, his first and only girl, Mary. His juvie record sealed, he was accepted into the police academy. Hortensia Saldana, now frail and needy, reached out to him. He wasn't fooled. He told Mary: "She's mended her fences with me so I can mend everything else in that old house." But when she died, she left it to him and he maintained it as a rental. Then he mortgaged it for the restaurant and—well, that was that. Remington was coming back. That was kind of a mantra among those who owned the houses: *The area is coming back!* He would sell it as soon as he was no longer underwater. But selling required more work than maintaining it for tenants, so he kept renting it.

It took him the better part of three days to ready the place, and when he sorted old mail that had accumulated there, he found a four-week-old letter from the city, claiming he was at risk of a lien because he hadn't paid the property taxes. He knew he had paid online last August, but he wasn't going to trust a computer to screw it up again. He headed down to the courthouse, as familiar as his home, assuming it would take all afternoon to straighten it out.

But the glitch was apparently systemwide and the weary-but-kind clerk immediately credited his account. With time left on his parking meter, he decided to stop for lunch, ending up at Subway, which made him sad. There used to be so many good lunch places near the courthouse, old-fashioned diners. Werner's. The Honey-bee. Now it was mainly chains and a few really dingy places. His heart sank at the sight of the menu board—no knock on the sandwiches, which were fine, but this was not how people should eat. Assembly lines were for things made out of metal and plastic, not sandwiches. Why wasn't there a place in Baltimore to buy a simple, classic Cubano?

There had been. It was a restaurant on the Avenue and it

had failed miserably because of its dumb-as-shit owner, Roberto "Sandy" Sanchez.

Then he saw Bert Gelman in the corner, eating alone. Hello, Smalltimore. But Bert was a lawyer and, as Sandy had just been reminded, there were only a handful of places to eat near the courthouse.

"Hey, Bert. Sandy Sanchez." He offered his hand, then had an inspiration. "I appreciate you letting me talk to your wife the other day."

Bert looked up with a ready impersonal smile. Guy had thick hair, broad shoulders—he had to work out to have that physique into his sixties. He was practiced at guarding his emotions. But Sandy had surprised him, he could tell.

"Ah, well, wives. They do what they want to do, one way or another. She didn't even tell me what it was about."

Uh-huh. She didn't tell you at all.

"We're looking at Julie Saxony. As a cold case."

"Making any headway?"

"Some. You know what they say. If the original detectives did their job right, the name's in the file. I tried to go counterintuitive on it, find a way it didn't lead back to Felix Brewer. But you know what? It did. Circled all the way back to a horse trailer and two sisters, driving the guy to some private airfield out of state."

"Interesting."

Sandy's only advantage was to charge ahead with what he knew, try to catch Bert without a story prepared. "Even more interesting is that Andrea Norr says you knew. You and Tubby. Knew Felix was going and when. Helped him get his affairs in order. Even got Julie a passport."

In a case like this, you hope that the fucker starts talking right away. But Bert was a criminal attorney. He didn't speak for a second or two, and Sandy knew he had lost this round.

"Now, Sandy, you know I'm not going to talk about Felix. He

was my client and he remains my client to this day, with all the privileges. But I will tell you this much—the sister's wrong about the passport. I have no idea what she's referring to."

"You could have forgotten. She said you did it as a nice deed, that you knew Felix wasn't going to take her, but you didn't want to be the person to tell her that."

Bert shook his head. "Come on, Sandy. We're not talking about this. I'm sorry, I can't. Even if I could, I don't think it would help you find the person who killed Julie. I've never believed there was a connection to Felix."

"Your wife does, I think."

"My wife is Bambi Brewer's best friend. I think that Lorraine would like there to be—a point, if you will, to Bambi's suffering. Unfortunately, the only point to the story is that Felix was a selfish prick who didn't care about anyone."

"I thought you were friends."

"We were—until the day he left. It was a rotten thing to do. To Bambi, to their daughters. And, yes, to Tubby and me. You know how much time he would have done, in reality? Five, seven tops. Couldn't, wouldn't do it. He was that cowardly, that weak. I've never talked about it, though. No reason to have tension between the two families. Bambi needs Lorraine. Less obviously, Lorraine needs Bambi."

"Julie's sister told me something about a suitcase. That Julie took money meant for Bambi instead of giving it to someone, probably you. That would explain a lot."

"I can't speak to that," Bert said. "I don't have any knowledge of that. Again, I don't have any knowledge about how Felix left. But my opinion? My thoughts based on a hypothetical situation about which I have no knowledge? It explains nothing even if it's true."

"People hold grudges."

"Are you suggesting that Bambi Brewer decided, ten years

after the fact, that she wanted to kill Julie Saxony because of some rumor about a suitcase?"

"Not a rumor. The sister told me."

"The sister says *now*. Not then, right? No reference to it in the file, I'm betting. No, you open the case again, sister finally admits that she played a role in Felix's disappearance, which is a federal crime, and—oh, look, shiny object, Detective. Go follow it. You're smarter than that, Sandy."

"Am I?" He wasn't being self-deprecating. It was his way of saying: *And how would you know?* "One of the Brewer girls confronted Julie a week before she disappeared. Meanwhile, the sister said Julie was obsessed with Bambi, used to go around saying she thought that Bambi had Felix killed."

"So what?"

"So I think maybe it's time I talk to her. Bambi Brewer, her daughters. Maybe revisit what everyone was doing around that time."

"Not without me in the room, Detective."

"Are you their lawyer?"

"I will be before you get back to your car."

Sandy consulted the old ADC map he kept in his car—he preferred the big paper maps, which provided more context than those little Google squares, whether on phones or computers—and drove out to the home of Bambi and Felix Brewer. It was in an older section of Pikesville, probably very grand in its day. He bet, if Felix had stayed, they would have moved farther out, to something bigger, like the Gelman house in Garrison Forest. But it looked good in its own way. Sandy preferred the houses built in the 1950s and 1960s to the new monstrosities.

He wasn't aware how long he just sat there looking at the house, but it was long enough for a woman to come down the walk, arms wrapped around her body to protect from the cool day. The woman was thin, in her thirties, and plain. One of the daughters? A maid?

"May I help you?" she said.

He held up his ID. "Lady of the house in?"

"I am the lady of the house."

"You're Bambi Brewer?"

"No, my husband and I bought this place from her six years ago. I think she moved to a condo downtown."

Feeling sheepish, Sandy tried to pinpoint his mistake. He had just assumed Bambi hadn't moved after all this time.

"She's a nice lady," the woman said. "I wouldn't want anything else bad to happen to her."

"Anything else? You mean, besides her husband leaving?"

"Isn't that enough?"

It was enough. Leaving, leaving you broke. Leaving you, leaving you broke, and doing little to conceal to the world at large that he had another woman. A woman who might have taken your money. It was all enough to make a woman very angry, to send an emissary to ask for her money back.

And a week after that confrontation, Julie drove off on some mystery errand to Saks Fifth Avenue, passport in her purse, and never came back. Passport in her purse. Expired even then. But only by two days. There are places you can go without a passport, or were able to go at the time. Mexico. Canada.

Sandy tried to never lose sight of the fact that we tend to order things according to the reality we know, as we discover it. All life is hindsight, really, stories informed by their endings. A woman disappeared, presumed murdered as she hadn't made the kind of arrangements one would expect of someone who planned to flee. A woman was found, murdered. Her passport was expired. And she was dead, so it wasn't about her leaving because there was no indication that she was going anywhere.

Except maybe she was.

Saks, which didn't even exist anymore, would have been no more than ten miles from here. The grocery store where Julie's car was found, weeks later? Sandy propped his map book on the steering wheel. He ripped out two pages so he could see them relative to each other. Here was another triangle, a physical one. What if Felix Brewer had sent for Julie Saxony after all, telling her to leave no trail, persuading her that he would be safe only if she left everything behind? And what if Julie Saxony had stopped here, incapable of resisting the urge to tell Bambi Brewer: *Guess which one of us he chose.*

He was going to need a warrant. A warrant and some luck. But, no, it wouldn't be luck. It was never luck, no matter what anyone thought. It all went back to the things that Julie Saxony had in her purse that day, those ordinary items that had been dutifully cataloged but never considered.

He was going to need *two* warrants.

May 15, 2006

Rachel made it exactly five minutes into the party before she said something rude to Michelle. "I can't believe you're having a shower." She didn't mean to. She had resolved not to mention the shower issue at all. The words were like toads, hopping out of her mouth in spite of her. She was like someone under a curse; she couldn't stop saying the wrong thing.

Worse, Michelle didn't seem to realize how hateful Rachel was being. "I know we can afford whatever we need," she said. "But Hamish's friends wanted to do something for us."

"Oh, no—that wasn't what I mean. I mean—just the tradition, you know? The evil eye. Which is nonsense, of course, but Linda observed it and I guess I just assumed we—you—would as well."

Once you've said something cruel, why waste it? Might as well make sure that Michelle knows how awful I can be.

Michelle only laughed. Thirty-three years old and thirty-six weeks pregnant, she was more beautiful than ever. Rachel wanted to chalk it up to her sister eating real food for the first time in her adult life, but, no, this was something else, something beyond the clichéd glow of pregnancy. It was as if love, true love, had drained Michelle of all her petulant grudges.

"Hamish may have agreed to raise our children as Jews"— the plural gave Rachel another pang, and she bit back a caution on hubris—"but he's not superstitious. Besides, he didn't want to paint the nursery after we brought the baby home. Even with the new eco-friendly paints, he didn't like the idea of all those fresh chemical smells. And he was keen to do it all himself, which will be harder once the baby is here. Did you see what he did with the closet? And the changing table—he made that, from his own design, so it can be converted to a straightforward chest of drawers once we no longer need a changing table."

Of course he did. Hamish the handy hand doctor. Hamish the perfect. Hamish the wonderful, Rachel thought, feeling very much like the bad fairy at the christening. But maybe the bad fairy had a backstory. Maybe it wasn't just a misplaced invitation that put her in a pique. Maybe the bad fairy had authentic heartache.

"I haven't gone upstairs yet," said Rachel, who had arrived late hoping to miss the obligatory nursery tour. "I haven't even seen Hamish."

"He's in the outdoor kitchen," Michelle said, motioning to the large fieldstone patio off the indoor kitchen, which was positively Brobdingnagian. She wasn't being grand. Now that Michelle was entitled to put on airs, she never did. The patio was better equipped than the kitchen in Rachel's first apartment—a gas-powered grill, an oven with two burners, a refrigerator, an ice-maker, and a wine refrigerator. Hamish presided over the grill, of course, surrounded by the friends he called mates. Rachel couldn't help feeling that the wafting smoke was really just the heat of all that collective testosterone rising into the soft May evening.

Twenty months ago, Michelle had dented Hamish Macalister's Jaguar in a downtown parking garage. Being Michelle, or the Michelle she was then, she had written a note that read only: "Sorry!," a cover for any possible witnesses. She had not counted on the video cameras that captured her license plate or the dogged Scotsman who tracked her down on sheer principle, determined to make the girl glimpsed on the video do the right thing.

The strangest part of the story was not that they married eight months later but that Michelle actually paid for the work on Hamish's car. Not even Michelle took for granted the appearance of a handsome Scottish hand surgeon on her doorstep.

Plus—a *Jaguar*, Rachel thought meanly. Michelle could assume he was rich as well. And he came with a cohort of rich friends, surgeons and entrepreneurs, weekend rugby players who had found one another in a faux Irish pub that broadcast rugby, hurling, and World Cup matches. Their wives were now Michelle's new besties, stay-at-home moms who lived in similarly huge houses and drove similarly enormous SUVs and could afford the similarly outrageous things on Michelle's baby registry. They also were, Rachel was realizing, extremely nice, shockingly nice. Well, why not? They were young, untested by life so far. She could not resent them or their extravagant getups, could not resent Michelle's thirteen-thousand-square-foot house. Could not even resent Hamish, who had seemed to stride out of the pages of a romance novel and make a beeline for—Rachel had to be honest—the least-deserving of the Brewer girls.

But the baby? The baby that Michelle had conceived on her very first try or two? That was something else. When Michelle had announced her pregnancy at Hanukkah, Rachel had excused herself from the table at the first possible moment and locked herself in Linda's bathroom, where she had cried for twenty minutes.

"You look gorgeous," she told her baby sister now, grateful to find an easy compliment. Rachel had never envied Michelle's beauty.

"You know, Bert Gelman once told me that I would come into

my prime in my thirties, as Mama did. I was terribly insulted at the time, but I think he may have been right."

Bambi still looked wonderful, Rachel thought, watching her mother beguile Michelle's new friends. She looked better than she had in years. Leaving the house on Sudbrook Road behind had been good for her, even if she had fought with her daughters over the most random stuff, refusing to downscale as she should. She had a bit of Great-Aunt Harriet's hoarding gene, right down to the random shoeboxes crammed with stuff. Bambi had initially resisted Hamish's invitation to move to a small condo downtown, the "bachelor" apartment that, he insisted gallantly, he didn't want to give up because he would lose money on a sale, virtually impossible in this market. Hamish had even redecorated his condo for Bambi. Or, more precisely, undecorated it, removing anything that was masculine and boysie-boy, leaving a plain and neutral space that Bambi could make her own. And even with all the mortgages she carried and the fact that the Sudbrook Park house had to be sold "as is," she had a nice sum left over, more money than she had had in years, almost $100,000. That should last Bambi several years, in her new circumstances.

And then what? Rachel asked herself, because over thirty years, *and then what* had been her question, hers alone. *Daddy has left, but our house is paid off. And then what? Bubbie and Zadie will help with tuition at Park. And then what? The scholarships will cover almost all the costs.* And then—what? *There's this amazing thing called an adjustable rate mortgage.* AND THEN WHAT?

Only now there was an answer: Hamish. The Brewer family's personal Messiah had finally arrived in the guise of a six-foot-two hand surgeon who loved Michelle with a kind of gusto that the Brewer women had not seen since, well, Felix met Bambi at a high school fraternity dance in 1959. And only Bambi had seen that. Her daughters had to accept this secondhand version of events.

But don't let him be entirely like Papa, Rachel prayed inwardly, then felt better about herself. She did not wish her sister to be—what? A man was cuckolded. What did someone call a woman who was cheated on?

A woman. A man who was betrayed required a special name. A woman cheated on was just a woman.

Linda clapped her hands, summoning everyone to the family room to watch Michelle open her gifts. She handed Rachel a notepad, instructing her to keep a list of each item's giver. *Why not one of her new friends?* Rachel thought grumpily. She couldn't help noticing that neither her husband nor Linda's had bothered to attend, although they were both crazy about Hamish. Yet all of Hamish's friends were here. They took sperm seriously, these men, and celebrated whenever one of their clan's found purchase.

Lord, there seemed to be more gifts than people. Although Rachel had not traveled in the precincts of the rich for a very long time, she remembered how they did gifts. It wasn't enough for a thing to be expensive—it had to be extraordinary, one of a kind. These women spent a lot of time shopping. They had to elevate shopping to an art, or at least a worthy cause.

"Oh, it's adorable," Michelle said, holding up a miniature leather bomber jacket. "Deanna, you have such exquisite taste. Rachel, did you get that? Deanna gave us the bomber jacket."

"Uh-huh," Rachel said, jotting it down. She wondered, as she had wondered with each gift from Hamish's friends, what it cost. She figured the average was slightly less than her monthly car payment.

"And here's Rachel's gift," Linda said now. She had been fired a few months back, right around the time she and Henry were closing on a new house, and it had been a tense time. But she had picked up a paid position on a political campaign, deputy in communications for the Democratic candidate in the governor's race. Rachel fretted that the candidate, the current mayor, would lose and Linda would be looking for a job yet again come this fall, but Linda was surprisingly calm. She seemed to be thriving on the very changes that were supposed to be so stressful—new job, new house—whereas Rachel, whose life had changed hardly at all, was the one on the verge of a nervous breakdown.

Rachel's gift was a selection of onesies that were a little offbeat— she had designed them herself. There was POOH HAPPENS (against the backdrop of a familiar bear shape, she didn't dare use more for fear of copyright infringement); BREWERS ART, a tip to the family, but also a restaurant on which Michelle doted; and I'M SMARTER THAN THE PRESIDENT. The last brought a few gasps in this crowd.

Michelle smiled, but it was a puzzled smile: "I don't remember putting these on the registry. Are they from that little store in your neighborhood?"

"I made them," Rachel said. Her voice cracked hoarsely, like an adolescent boy's. "They're one of a kind. You know I've been dabbling in silk-screening."

The new Michelle rallied beautifully. (The old one would have pouted at the idea of someone ignoring her stated desires.) "Of course they are—just like you! How proud I'll be when Hamish III wears them."

Bambi winced at that. Rachel knew what she was thinking. She could tolerate the nursery, this party—but naming a child after a living relative. That was too far. Not only someone living, but a Hamish yet, a Hamish who would be one-half Russian Jew, one-quarter Scot, and one-quarter Iranian.

And although the odds seemed stacked in favor of a dark-haired, olive-complected child, Rachel couldn't help rooting for a boy who would look like Hamish's father, whom she had met at the wedding last summer. He had pale gingery hair and a face that looked like a certain kind of Keebler cookie—Pecan Sandies—and slightly bowed legs below his kilt. He was a refreshing presence in a wedding party that otherwise ran to intimidating beauty, if one didn't count Linda and Rachel—and Michelle didn't. Bree Deloit, the wife of Hamish's best friend, was Michelle's maid of honor, as if Michelle had known her all her life. "But I couldn't choose between my sisters," Michelle said when Bambi confronted her. "This keeps everyone's feelings from being hurt." At least she seemed to be sincere. The old Michelle would have smiled a little smile, making sure that everyone knew she was stirring the pot.

So why did Rachel miss the old Michelle? Why did she long for the petulant, peevish, nasty sister in place of this sugar-sweet one? It couldn't just be the fact of the baby.

Except it was. Rachel could overlook everything else that had fallen into Michelle's undeserving lap. Her meet-cute moment with Hamish. Hamish's prince charmingness, his willingness to submerge himself into the insanity that was the Brewer family.

But for Michelle to be pregnant at age thirty-three, when Rachel had been trying to have a baby with Joshua for a decade, since she was only thirty-four—that hurt. That hurt quite a bit. And while New Michelle might be a better mother than Old Michelle could ever have been, neither version of Michelle could love a child as Rachel could. No one deserved a child more than Rachel.

She fled to the bathroom, probably not quickly enough. Both Bambi and Linda knew the telltale signs of Rachel on the verge of tears. Michelle didn't notice. She was the center of attention. She hadn't changed *that* much.

Only maybe she had. Ten minutes later, she waddled into the bath—not the downstairs powder room, where most guests would have gone, but the one attached to the master suite, an overly marbled retreat that Rachel secretly thought tacky—and said "Oh!" as if she didn't expect to find Rachel there. Then, sitting on the toilet after yanking down her pants: "I have to pee all the time now. I wet myself at Superfresh yesterday."

"A sneeze?"

"Not even. It just gave way. It was like"—Michelle thought—

"like a flat roof collapsing after water had been pooling on it for a really long time."

"Sounds lovely."

"Oh, it was. I'll probably never shop there again. Actually, I don't. I usually go to Whole Foods, but Hamish went Scottish after he saw the prices last time."

It was one of Hamish's tics that he was wonderfully extravagant—until he wasn't. He himself described his pulling back as "going Scottish." There was not, as far as Rachel knew, a complementary Iranian strain, although it was his mother whom Hamish resembled physically. She was gorgeous, so gorgeous that it seemed as if Hamish Senior couldn't quite believe his good luck. Hamish's mother looked if she couldn't believe it, either.

Or maybe Rachel was just projecting. She had never quite recovered from her first mother-in-law, and Hamish's mother had that same queenly demeanor. She would have been a formidable opponent if they lived close by. But Michelle's luck held—her mother-in-law lived in London.

Michelle pulled up her pants. "I'm sorry. I know this is hard for you."

That was so unexpected that Rachel began to cry in earnest. "I don't envy you anything—"

"No, you don't. And I've envied you so much. You have no idea, Rachel."

"You mean Linda and me."

"Mainly you. Yes, Linda and you knew Daddy, have real memories of him, and enjoyed the princess phase, whereas I only knew the garret part. Lord, how I hated that movie."

Rachel smiled at the reference to Sara Crewe in *The Little Princess*, the Shirley Temple film that Great-Aunt Harriet had thoughtlessly insisted they watch on the old *Picture for a Sunday Afternoon*, saying all children loved Shirley Temple. Aunt Harriet really was a bitch.

"But you're good, Rachel," Michelle continued. "And you're Mother's favorite."

"Oh, no. Mama doesn't have favorites."

"Of course she does. I'm not saying that she doesn't love each of us, and each in a special way. And she's always been good about loving us as we are, not making comparisons. But you're the family star. The good grades, the *niceness*. Wanting to fix everything and everyone. Rachel—would you wait here for me? I'll be right back."

It was such a strange request that Rachel couldn't deny it. But "right back" was a longish span of time, given the size of the house and Michelle's slowed gait. By the time she returned, Rachel had gone through all the cabinets, if only to prove she wasn't the nice one. The contents were uninteresting, although she longed to know what Michelle paid for her face creams, a brand completely unfamiliar to Rachel.

Michelle had a glass of champagne in her hand and a cloth napkin full of cookies.

"Oh, I'm fine," Rachel said with a wave.

"It's for me," Michelle said. "The baby's cooked, after all, one glass won't hurt, but Hamish would freak. You can have a cookie, though."

"Thanks," Rachel said wryly.

"Everyone tells you everything, don't they?"

"Not really."

"Mama does. And Linda. Everyone confides in you."

"I'm a good listener, I guess."

"You scared me. About the evil eye, Rachel. That was a terrible thing to say."

"I'm sorry."

"Thank you." Said formally, in a new tone. The old Michelle had neither given nor accepted apologies. "It's not your fault. I'm scared because—I don't deserve this. I don't deserve any of this." She gestured, careful not to spill a drop of the outlaw champagne.

"Of course you deserve to be happy, Michelle. You've never really been."

"I thought I was. Rachel—I had an affair. With a married man. For a while. I broke it off, about three months before I met Hamish, if you can believe it, but it was a horrible thing to do."

"I know."

"You know? How could you know? Do others know? Who it was, I mean? You don't know that, do you? Because he was—well, he was well known. By Baltimore standards."

"No, no—I didn't know who. And I wasn't sure he was married. But I knew you were having an affair with someone. You were secretive, you claimed not to be dating at all. You haven't been without a boyfriend since you were twelve. I figured it was someone you couldn't talk about."

"Did *you* talk about it? With Mother or Linda?"

"Linda. Not Mother."

"And what did Linda say?"

"She said you had to be free to make your own mistakes."

"Boy, was I. The thing is, Rachel, that's not the only thing. Remember Adam Gelman's wedding?"

"Sure." Rachel was remembering something else, how Michelle had disappeared that night. Was her lover there then? Who could it have been? Oh, Lord, what if she had carried on an affair with Adam? Younger than her by a bit, but he had had a crush on Michelle most of his life. Or maybe Alec, but why be secretive about Alec?

"My lover"—Michelle made a face—"what an icky word. It makes it sound so, I don't know, grand and sordid at the same time. And it was really just sordid. Awful. But he gave me gifts."

"The coat," Rachel said. "The watch."

"And the car, the one I said was part of my package at that tech company. It was a gift, not a lease."

"Wow." Rachel wasn't sure what such a car cost, but she thought it was probably as much as she made some years.

"So, at the wedding, this friend of Adam's tried to ask me out and I turned him down. I wasn't very nice about it, but I was in a bad mood. I was upset, about the relationship I was in; I didn't care about anyone else's feelings."

Rachel couldn't help thinking: *You never cared about anyone else's feelings, not then.*

"So I was kind of rude to him. Anyway, it turned out that he was an IRS agent. And he opened a file on me."

"That *can't* be legal."

"Doesn't matter. He did some research—he found out my salary, found out what things cost. The coat, the car, the watch. He called me and said he believed that there was money, hidden money, from Daddy and he was going to investigate Mama."

"He wouldn't have found anything." Rachel was sure of that, at least.

"No, but he said he would make sure it leaked to the newspapers, that he knew how to do that without leaving a trace. He made me come see him."

"Did you go?"

"Yes, but with Bert Gelman. And—well, he had to know. Bert, I mean. About the lover. Because it turns out that the man I was seeing—some of the things he did were illegal. He should have paid a gift tax on some of the presents he gave me. But there was no way I was going to tell the IRS who he was, no matter how much they threatened me."

"So what happened?"

"They dropped it, quite abruptly. Bert turned it around on the guy, filed a complaint that he was using his office for a private vendetta, and the guy got reassigned. Bert told me it wasn't hard to show there was no money, not from Papa. Barry Speers."

"What?"

"That was the guy's name. I hope he got fired. But it's out there, Rachel. Still. It's like this big cloud, or this thing that's going to fall on me. I can't bear for Hamish to know, even though it was before I met him. I'm so ashamed. I'm ashamed in a way I wasn't when it was going on, and I was plenty ashamed then."

"Bert didn't tell Mama any of this, did he?"

"No. He was my lawyer. He can't tell. I made sure of that."

"Mama's pretty sophisticated in her way, Michelle. She would be okay with it, now that we know the story has a happy ending."

"Does it?"

"It does," she said, putting her hand on her sister's stomach. "Everything will be fine, Michelle."

To her amazement, Michelle burst into tears. "I don't deserve it. I don't deserve any of it. If you knew, Rachel—"

"But I do know, Michelle. You just told me. It will be okay."

And it would be, Rachel thought, putting her arms around her sobbing sister. Everything always worked out for Michelle. No, not *everything*. She had never known their father, not really, and it must have been hard, growing up in that household, to be indentured into the family practice of Keeping Up Appearances. It was funny how things worked out. Linda had become a professional spinner of stories. Rachel had become almost pathologically honest, with one vivid exception. And now Michelle was Bambi Junior, finding a man who promised her the world. Maybe this one could deliver it.

Please, Rachel prayed to the god she didn't believe in. *Please let Michelle have her happy ending.* And she felt better about herself. Bad fairies want to do the right thing. It's just so hard sometimes.

Hamish Macalister III was born four weeks later. When the nurse came out, she handed Rachel a piece of paper with the exact time, 20:02, the numeric rendering of the date, 6-12-6, and his weight, 8-13. "For the lottery," she explained. "A lot of people like to play the time, date, and weight."

Rachel thought that was hilarious, someone instructing Felix Brewer's daughter to play the lottery. Yet the next day she went to a Royal Farms and placed several straight bets: 2002, 6126, 813. *This is what my father did,* she thought, standing in line, waiting for her chance to play, as uncertain and tongue-tied as she might have been ordering a meal in a foreign country. *How do I word this? What is the custom? Am I holding everyone else up?* At the last minute, she added a Powerball ticket and found she enjoyed fantasizing about that big jackpot for a few days. Had her father sold people joy, after all? Was there something noble about the way he made his money? Because while it was disappointing not to win, it wasn't unexpected, and the daydreams had been lovely, worth a few dollars. Where else could you buy a dream for two dollars?

And perhaps it was the haze of her lottery dream that carried her forward, because the next time she visited her new nephew, she asked Hamish Junior for a loan, so she and Joshua could adopt a child from China. It was not the first time that Rachel had asked someone for money. But she was keenly aware that it was the first time she had asked for herself.

The agency told them it would be eighteen months. It was more than five years before they brought home Tatiana, a twenty-month-old girl who required two cleft palate surgeries. On an unseasonably cold March day in 2012, the Brewer family gathered in the hospital to keep Rachel and Joshua company during the second, simpler surgery—Bambi, Michelle, Linda, Hamish, although not Henry, who couldn't get the day off. Linda's girls were in school, but Noah, now twenty-five, skipped work, a testament to all those Friday night suppers, Linda's insistence that family was primary. Michelle and Hamish's two children were there, too; Helena had followed Hamish III by less than three years.

The Brewers took over the waiting room, but it was such a happy scene, compared to much of what happens in hospital waiting rooms, and they were such gracious, lovely people that the hospital staff indulged them, even Michelle's constant use of her cell phone, which wasn't officially permitted. (She said she needed it so Helena could play Monkey Preschool Lunchbox, although Helena was happy moving beads along the wire paths of a children's toy.) It seemed natural when Bert arrived, old family friend that he was, still natural when he took Bambi aside for a hushed conversation. Bert had been taking Bambi aside for hushed conversations as long as her daughters could remember.

It was unnatural, though, when Bambi came back to them, picked up her purse, and said: "I must be going."

Rachel couldn't leave that be. "Is something wrong? Has Nana Ida—" The old woman was still alive at one hundred one, improbably. Or quite probably, given her tendency to hold on to anything she had, whether it was money or years. She likely had her own shoeboxes of condiments.

"No. I mean—it's not for you to worry about."

"*Mother.*" Where once only Linda and Rachel would have spoken in unison, now Michelle added her voice. Marriage, motherhood—she was part of the club.

"Well, it's the strangest thing. But it seems that the police want to talk to me."

"What?" But only Linda and Michelle asked this question.

"It's nothing," Bert said. "They're just spinning their wheels. But if we go now, on our own, it will be over sooner and we can put it behind us."

"*What?*" Linda and Michelle repeated. Rachel tried to make eye contact with her mother, but she wouldn't look at her.

"Oh, don't be so *obscure*, Bert," Bambi said. "Girls, it looks as if I might be arrested."

"For what?" Linda asked.

"The death of Julie Saxony."

"It's bullshit," Bert said quickly. "She's not going to be arrested. They want to ask her a few questions. It won't take long at all."

"Oh, no. It shouldn't take long at all because I'm going to confess. Does Tubby still write bonds, Bert, or is he quite out of the business?"

"Mama." Rachel wrapped her arms around Bambi. It was less a hug than an attempt to hold her in place. Bambi gently removed one arm, then the other, much as she might have peeled a clinging toddler from her. She used to do just that when Linda and Rachel were very young, and Bambi and Felix headed out to the club, over the girls' protests. Their father was home so rarely in the evenings, it was a double blow to watch him come home and head out again, their mother at his side. They would wrap themselves around his legs and their mother would peel them off, one arm, one leg at a time, laughing all the while.

No one was laughing now.

"Tatiana will be fine, Rachel. I'll be fine. I promise you that everything's going to be okay."

And with that, she was gone.

Tell
Me

July 3, 1986

S aks. Why had she said Saks? She was flustered, too flustered to lie. "I'm going to Saks," she told Chet. *Why?* he had asked. In a mild, curious way, but they were fully booked for the holiday weekend and they were doing dinners for the guests, testing out Chet's recipes.

"To buy bras," she blurted out. *Why? Why did she say bras?* Perhaps she thought the very word, *"bra,"* would keep him from following up. But Chet was not a man who was easily embarrassed.

"Is this *urgent?*" Teasing her. "You're dressed to impress, I see."

"It's just that the ones I have are all too big."

"Yes," he said gravely. *"That* is a problem." And then he let it go, although he asked her to make a stop at the restaurant-supply place and she agreed, because what else could she say? They had a teasing rhythm, not quite brother-sister, more like a boy who has a crush on an older girl but knows it won't go anywhere. It had developed very quickly, a by-product of their mutual animosity toward Bambi Brewer, who, Chet reported, had nickel-and-dimed the catering company to death over costs for Michelle's bat mitzvah. Julie, in return, regaled Chet with stories about Bambi's extravagances during the marriage. Not that Felix had ever told her such stories, but he told Tubby, who told Susie.

Michelle. Julie still remembered the shock of her birth thirteen years ago. Julie had been Felix's girl for a little more than a year, and while she assumed he still had sex with his wife, it had never occurred to her that they would have more children. Then, one day, she had come into the office and there they were, the three amigos, puffing on cigars, drinks in hand, and when Julie had asked what was up, they had shared a look among themselves before Felix said: "And, lo, the Lord has delivered unto me another girl. What are the odds? Well, I'll tell you. They were one in two, even after having two girls. That's what a lot of people don't understand. The odds, each time, are one in two, while the odds of getting the same result three times in a row are one in eight. Longer, but not improbable."

That had been a shock. Almost as shocking as the first time she had seen Bambi. She had expected her to be attractive, but not *that* attractive. She was older than Julie, of course. But not as old as Julie would have liked. And so very beautiful. Possibly more beautiful than Julie, an assessment that she was not in the custom of making. Julie had the better figure, though. No contest there.

Then. She had the better figure *then.* Would Felix mind that she was skinny now? Chet had been joking about the bras, but it was a problem. Felix remembered a different body. The weight loss had taken a toll on her face, too. Susie thought it was hilarious that Julie had this hot-shit chef and barely ate anything all day. But food tasted like dust in her mouth.

For ten years, Julie had sleepwalked through her days, yet not slept at all at night. He had promised they would be together, but he didn't say when. She had filled the waking hours—what the rest of the world believed to be waking hours, all her hours were waking ones—with work. First the coffee shop. Walking up and down, back and forth, walking, walking. Clean the counter. Check the inventory. Write the schedule. And as her savings grew, she looked for something else, a business even more demanding. Innkeeper. If she had to take care of others, she wouldn't have time to think about herself. So she bought the house on the water in Havre de Grace and spent her days, most of them, making breakfasts, changing linens, taking calls, overseeing her bookings. And when that became too automatic, she decided to open the restaurant, knowing there was a spectacular failure rate, but that was part of the lure. She wanted to succeed. With everything she did, she imagined Felix's approval and admiration. She was as good at business as he had been. *She* wasn't extravagant. She worked.

And still she mourned, stuck in time, forever trapped in her sister's truck as Felix walked across the tarmac to the little plane that took him away. She couldn't believe he didn't want her to come with him. Bert had thought he would. Bert had made the fantasy possible, getting her a passport so quickly. She had assumed he knew something. But, in the end, Bert had been as in the dark about Felix as everyone else.

Everyone else. Including Bambi.

But now he had sent for her. Ten years later, but he had sent for her and she was still young. Younger than Bambi had been when he left her, and if Julie looked a little harder, a little worse for wear—that would change. She would sit in the sun with him, although perhaps in a hat, and eat whatever they ate there, fish and fruit.

I won. He loves me, he loves me, he sent for me. Not you. Me.

She was honest enough to concede that Bambi could not go, given that Michelle was only thirteen. Plus, she was a grandmother. The oldest girl had to have given birth by now, given her size at the bat mitzvah. Still—Julie had won. He had chosen her.

She wanted Bambi to know. That was mean of her, and Julie was not, by nature, a mean person. But she was meaner than she used to be, hardened by ten years of living with a heart that was not so much broken as shredded.

She was almost to the exit for Saks, near Reisterstown Road, an exit she knew well, for it led to Felix's house, not that she had ever been inside it. How many times had she driven past the house in Sudbrook Park? It had started early in the relationship with Felix, when she still lived with Andrea. She would sneak out in the middle of the night, get in the VW bus despite not having a license. Just seeing the house had stoked her fury— and her longing. It seemed like a castle to her, its circular drive-way a moat. A castle for the queen and the two princesses, then three. Bambi had to share Felix with Julie, but no one could get between Felix and his daughters. It was the daughters that had kept her from him.

Daughters. At least Julie's surveillance had been respectful, un-detectable. When Felix's daughter showed up at the inn last week, she had broken the rules in this game. Calling her a thief, a whore. As if Julie had two hundred thousand dollars, just sitting around. Why had Bambi told her daughters such outrageous lies? Worse, what if Felix heard these stories? She couldn't bear the idea that he would think her so low, so craven. Her only thought was to make sure that Felix didn't believe these stories.

And he didn't. The call had come at last. It's time. Time to dis-appear as he had, traveling light. Had Chet noticed her absurdly large purse? She would pick up a shift and a bathing suit at the mall, if there was time, but right now all she had was a cosmetic bag, the usual things. It had been stressed to her that she must disappear as if nothing had been planned. No trail, she had been warned. Some cash is okay, but it can't appear that you've made any arrangements. People have to believe you're dead.

She had thought: *No, I was dead. Now I'm going to be alive again.*

She had driven swiftly, foot pressed so hard against the accel-erator that she had averaged seventy, seventy-five miles an hour.

She was more than forty-five minutes early and she knew she mustn't linger at the meeting spot, draw any attention to herself. She could run her errands, but that wouldn't take fifteen minutes. Maybe buy a bathing suit, although she didn't want to see her thin, pale self in a three-way mirror, didn't want to think how sad Felix would be to see this wisp that used to be Juliet Romeo. Felix would probably make a joke about it, plying her with piña coladas and—she tried to make the dream specific. Conch? Shrimp?

She would drive by the house one more time, say good-bye to it for Felix, say good-bye to the space it had taken up in her head, all these years. The brick inn by the water was a rambling version of this very house, not that anyone had ever noticed. Maybe she would even stop this time, park in the circular driveway, march up the walk and knock on the door, bold as you please, and announce: *He chose me, Bambi. Me!*

March 26, 2012

2:30 P.M.

Bambi had known she was fibbing when she told the girls she didn't expect to be away long, but even she was surprised to be sitting, three hours later, in an interview room at the downtown police headquarters, having yet to speak to a detective. The man who appeared to be in charge—such sad green eyes—had greeted them and said he was waiting for another detective before he could proceed.

"They're bringing someone in from the county because they think the case will end up there," Bert told Bambi. "Only it won't, because there is no case."

"How many years do you think I'll get, Bert? If I confess and enter a plea?" She could do five, she thought, maybe even ten. Would they actually give a seventy-two-year-old woman more than ten? Especially if she claimed she was provoked, did it in—what was the phrase?—the heat of passion. Say she served ten—

the number stuck in her head because Felix would have done no more than ten, probably less. She would be out at eighty-two and, based on her mother and aunt's longevity, she could expect another decade, maybe more. Crummy for the younger grandkids, humiliating for the older ones, but it might not be too bad. She could be like the woman who killed the Scarsdale Diet doctor, devote herself to good works while inside.

"Stop it, Bambi. You are not going to confess, you are not going to enter a plea. You are going to sit here and let me talk while they do whatever stupid dance they're going to do."

"Bert, I *want* to talk." Could she order him to leave? If she told him everything, would he be obligated to do as she wished? Probably not. She had been impulsive, back at the hospital, but she had no regrets. After thirty-six years of limbo, it felt good to do something, anything.

"Bambi, I know you couldn't have done this."

"Bert, with all due respect, there's a lot you don't know. I appreciate your kindness, but—it's time. It's time to put things to rest."

The door opened.

"Aw shit," Bert muttered.

"What?" Bambi realized there was a young woman behind Sad Green Eyes. Well, youngish, plump and blond, with a big sunny smile.

"Nancy Porter," Bert whispered to her. "I've seen her work before. She's very good."

"They don't need someone good when all you want to do is confess," Bambi whispered back.

She hadn't considered the possibility of a woman detective, though, and it set her back. She had been counting on a man. Someone like Sad Green Eyes there. She could wrap him around her finger forty times and have enough left over to make curtains as Felix used to say. Two men would have been even better.

She would have played them off each other. But not a man and a woman, and definitely not this cheerleader shiksa.

"Hello, Mrs. Brewer," the girl said, as if greeting her home-room teacher on the first day of school. "We really appreciate you coming in today to discuss Julie Saxony with us. There are just a few things we'd like to go over, a few new facts that have come to light, especially since you granted us permission to search your apartment yesterday—"

"You what?" Bert asked. "You let them in with a warrant and you didn't even call me?"

"I didn't see the harm," Bambi said. She hadn't. She still didn't. The shoebox they had carried away might contain evidence of something else she had done, something not quite kosher. But it wasn't enough to leverage a murder charge.

Unless the person were already inclined to confess. And she couldn't see what other choice she had.

Back in the hospital, in the car on her way here, she had thought it would be so easy to say *I did it*. Yet she couldn't, she didn't. For one thing, she couldn't help being curious about what the detectives thought they knew. She would hear them out, al-though not because Bert had told her to. Bert had his agenda, she had hers.

"On July third, Julie Saxony left Havre de Grace, telling her chef that she was going shopping. She was never seen alive again. Well, she might have crossed paths with a gas station attendant or gone through a fast-food drive-through. But the last person who saw her alive was probably her killer."

Bambi couldn't help herself. "In homicides, isn't the killer always the last person to see the victim alive?"

The girl nodded and smiled, pleased with Bambi. Bert glow-ered. "Good point. So let me ask you, did you see Julie Saxony that day?"

"I did." Bert grabbed her arm. She shook him off.

"Where?"

"She came to my home."

"Invited?"

"No. I can assure you of that. No. She showed up, out of the blue."

"And what happened?"

Bambi did not answer right away. "She told me that my husband had arranged for me to have access to a large sum of money after he left, but she had taken it."

"And?"

Bert grabbed her arm again, hissed into her ear: "Bambi—a *word*, please. I need to speak to you privately because if you continue down this road, I am obligated to recuse myself. I cannot allow a client to lie."

3:15 P.M.

Sandy and Nancy retreated to a lunchroom, where they shared coffee from a thermos that Sandy had brought. On a day like today, they would probably end up drinking the house swill, but they didn't have to start with it.

"It's high-octane, the real deal. I make my own at home. I always brought a thermos, all the years I worked here. I could never get used to the crap that machine makes. The other guys laughed at me, said I was prissy. They thought I was prissy about a lot of stuff and busted my balls for it. But once they had my coffee, they would wheedle me for some. By the time I retired, I was carrying the biggest thermos they made."

She widened her eyes. "Wow—it is strong. I'm a wimp. I hope you won't be insulted if I cut it with a little Sweet'N Low."

"Not at all."

He wasn't because he liked her. So far. Nancy Porter had been recommended to him by Harold Lenhardt, who had done his twenty in Baltimore City, then bounced to the county and was half-way to his twenty there. Lenhardt was a good police and he swore by this girl, the daughter and granddaughter of big Polish cops, one of the few youngsters who used the old vernacular, *a police.*

The mere fact that she was willing to help was a big point in her favor: Most detectives would be reluctant to take on a twenty-six-year-old homicide that wasn't their case to begin with. More risk than upside. But Nancy was intrigued by what yesterday's warrants had produced. Not quite the smoking gun—smoking earring—he had hoped for, but as good as. As good as.

"You're lucky she did consignment shops, all nice and legal, as opposed to pawn shops. Probably wouldn't be that much detail on a pawn slip from 1986," Nancy said now. She was struggling with the coffee, he could tell. But she had manners, unlike so many young people today.

"Yeah, and lucky that the match didn't disappear from the evidence room all those years ago. As the slip proves, it was worth quite a bit."

"Probably worth more than she got for it. Jewelry stores, when they buy back diamonds—it's a total rip-off. I had a girlfriend, had a nice ring from that store in Towson, over by Joppa? She and her husband busted up, they paid her, like, twenty cents on the dollar for the same ring, all the time saying: 'You know, we like to say, it's not the ring's fault.' I did some research on that earring online. David Webb was a big deal, back in the day."

Sandy thought suddenly of Mary's jewelry. Not that it was of significant value, not at all. But he had kept her engagement ring and wedding ring, her other good pieces, in part because he could not imagine anything sadder than trying to sell them. Although maybe having no one to give them to was the real sadness.

"Well, the store she went to, back in '86, down on Baltimore Street—it's gone. But the bill of sale matches to a T. One diamond-and-platinum earring was found in Julie Saxony's purse.

We looked past that, all these years." He thought he was being generous with the "we." *He* hadn't looked past it. "You see an earring in a purse, you think, 'Oh, she lost an earring, put the mate in her bag, and forgot about it.' But where are the earrings she was wearing that day? That's the part that was overlooked."

"Killer could have taken the earrings." But Nancy was just being fair, excusing the work of the previous detectives.

"Could've. But one was in her purse—and the other one was sold a week later."

"Do you think she killed her there, at the house?"

"I can't make up my mind on that. Twenty-five years out—it was a lot, hoping to find a casing, anything like that. I almost wish we hadn't searched the house because Gelman will pretend that proves definitively it didn't happen there. And maybe it didn't. I can see it going down lots of ways. I can see her getting angry, taking a swing—that would have knocked the earring loose, maybe, and she finds it later. But you know what? I can also imagine her hiring someone to take Julie out. And maybe they brought the earring back to her as a trophy or, you know, proof." He was thinking of Tubman again. "She might have asked her husband's old friend, the bail bondsman, if he knew some guys who were available for hire. See, I kept thinking he was mooning over Julie, all these years. But maybe he was just guilt-ridden because he helped to kill her. She leaves Bambi's house, some guy follows her—if she's really lying, as her lawyer says, it might be to cover for Tubman."

3:20 P.M.

"Bambi, I'm sure you have a reason for doing this, but you have to understand that I could be disbarred if I permit you to lie."

"I'm not lying." A beat. "Besides, how can you know that? You can't *know* I'm lying."

"We were all in Bethany that week—you drove over to spend time with Lorraine and me, at the beach house."

"Not until the evening. I had all day to myself."

"But you came over on the evening of the second, not the third."

Hell, was that possible?

"I'm pretty sure I drove over on the morning of the third."

"No. *No.* We had a party on the second. It was Lorraine's birthday. It was her forty-first. Remember? She refused to have a party for her fortieth, so we had a surprise party for her at the beach, on the second, which was two weeks late—but what could be more surprising than that. We were all there. You, Michelle, even Linda and Henry made it, although Noah was a newborn. You went home on the fourth, after dropping Michelle at a friend's place in Rehoboth. You said you wanted to be alone."

"Your memory's playing tricks on you. I wasn't there."

"We have photos. I'm almost sure. Jesus, Bambi, I don't know *why* you're lying about this, but you have to stop. You have a perfect alibi, which isn't something I've been able to say to many of my clients over the years. Just say nothing, okay?"

She felt at once deflated and relieved. She had been relishing the idea of confession, accepting guilt, serving the sentence that Felix had failed to serve, showing him how it was done.

"Okay, I won't lie, Bert. But I want to hear what they have to say. They know something, something new. I need to know it, too, Bert. Don't ask why."

She had known Bert for so long—Lord, more than fifty years now. They had long ago reached a point where she didn't treat him as she treated most men. He was Felix's friend, Lorraine's husband. But he was her friend as well, her only true male friend. So she didn't widen her eyes, or smile her little half smile, or do anything flirtatious. She simply held his gaze until he nodded.

"Follow my lead," he said. "Please don't lie."

"I'll try not to," she said, thinking, *No lies that Bert can catch. That's the new rule. It's only a lie when someone knows it's false.*

4:00 P.M.

They brought the shoebox with them on the next trip into the interview room. Brown-and-white-striped Henri Bendel's. Size 7 and a half.

"Fancy," Nancy had said when she saw it. "And look at the price—two hundred and fifty dollars. That was a lot of money for shoes in 1986."

"Isn't that a lot of money now?" Sandy asked, knowing he was making a joke. He had priced Belgian loafers recently and discovered they were over $400. He'd just have to keep taking care of the old ones.

The key receipt was bagged, separated from the others. They wouldn't let her see that right away. First, they were going to talk about the box itself. Sandy would have to take the lead because he had been the one who accompanied the officers with the warrant. He had taken the box with him because he figured that no one moved that kind of stuff from a house to a condo unless it was deeply meaningful. The receipts were old—some went back to the early 1980s, and they continued through the year 2000. But one receipt stood out. All the other stuff that had been sold had been complete, unbroken—and not particularly valuable. And this slip was for a different store from the rest, a not-quite-as-nice jewelry store downtown. The receipt had stood out like, well, a diamond in a dustbin.

"We're curious about these receipts. You sold a lot of stuff over fifteen years. Was it yours?"

"I sold those things at my aunt Harriet's request. She died in September 2001, right after 9/11."

Right after 9/11. Was that gratuitous detail supposed to import some gravitas?

"Yes, but all these things were sold before that date."

"You see, she was in a retirement home for almost the last twenty years of her life. Things were tighter for her than people realized, and I was her favorite niece." A wry smile. "Also her only niece. I was supposed to be her sole heir, so what did it matter if I sold the things before she died. I would sell things for her, and we would split the proceeds."

"Fifty-fifty?"

"Oh, no. Aunt Harriet wasn't that generous. I brought her the money and she decided, based on some internal formula I never understood, how to divvy things up. I sometimes got as little as ten percent, sometimes as much as thirty, but never more than that."

"And you used this place"—he squinted at the slip, as if reading the printed name for the first time, but he knew it by heart—"the Turnover Shop."

"Yes. They were great to work with."

"And you went there every time?"

"I went to several places, but that was my favorite."

"Like jewelry. Did you sell any jewelry?"

"Some."

"But did you sell it to them?"

"No, I went to a Pikesville jeweler for that. Weinstein's. I knew the owner back in high school."

"Yeah, Weinstein's. We saw those receipts, too. But we found one receipt, and it wasn't from there."

"Well, sometimes a piece isn't right for a certain retailer. They don't anticipate demand for an item. That's how consignment works. As you see from the slips, I sold a lot of clothes, too, over the years, but I went down to D.C. for that. People in D.C. are better about the value of clothes. And the clothes were mine, not Aunt Harriet's."

"But for jewelry you went to Weinstein's. Except this once, when you went down to Baltimore Street. Why didn't Weinstein's want this piece?"

"I can't remember."

"Was it because it was just one earring, one without a mate?"

"Could be."

Bert was looking at her, trying to get her to meet his eyes. She couldn't. Her heart was rising like a skyrocket, up, up, up. She saw herself on her hands and knees, dusting. Cleanliness had been Bambi's only weapon against the house's encroaching seediness. Down on all fours, trying to get a dust mop under that long buffet in the living room. It was a beautiful piece. She should have sold it. French, antique, worth a lot. But Felix had loved it so. He was never happier than on a holiday when that buffet was piled high with food. Above it was a family portrait, commissioned pre-Michelle, which always irked her petulant youngest. Once, when Michelle was four, she attempted to add herself to it. Luckily, Bambi had caught her before she had a chance to touch a single crayon to the oil paint.

So there Bambi was, on her hands and knees on a wretchedly hot July morning, air-conditioning off because she had learned to pinch pennies until they bled copper, and there it was, winking at her, the beautiful diamond in the distinctive David Webb setting, her tenth anniversary gift from Felix.

Her first thought was: *I didn't even realize I had lost one of these.*

Her second thought was: *I didn't. I wore them just last week at Lorraine's party.*

Third thought: *Did Felix buy all his women the same earrings?* Now that she had it in her palm, she saw that it was slightly smaller than the ones she wore, but otherwise an exact copy.

Fourth thought: *Oh shit. Oh shit. Oh shit.*

And now, twenty-six years later, she felt again everything she had felt then. Surprise, correction, muted fury, fear. No, something worse than fear, something primal and huge.

Bambi looked at the detective, the male detective, in the eye: "I killed Julie Saxony. She came to my house on July fourth, and I killed her. Not July third, July fourth. And, no, I don't know where she was during the intervening twenty-four hours."

5:00 P.M.

"Mama?"

The word still had the power to shock Rachel. It seemed to surprise Tatiana, too. Even now, eight months after she had joined them, there was a testing quality to it. The question mark at the end seemed to encompass a dozen questions: *Are you there? Still? Will you be there tomorrow? Are you really my mother? Is this really my life?*

Rachel put her hand in her daughter's and said: "Yes, I'm here, Tatala." Rachel had called her daughter Tatiana, a choice that surprised everyone, because she wanted to use the endearment Tatala without confusing a little girl who was already on her second name, possibly her third. True, "tataleh" was meant for boys, but Rachel had always liked the sound of it. She had justified "Tatiana" to Joshua by saying she had found a similar name in one of the Chinese dynasties. She didn't tell him it was the name of a consort.

Tatiana's Hebrew name was Mazal—the equivalent of Felicia. Bambi had raised one careful eyebrow at this, but said nothing. But, yes, Rachel believed her father was dead. She couldn't explain why. It was a feeling that had come over her the day that Tatiana was placed in her arms. Felix was gone, his energy was no longer a part of this world, but there was someone new to fill that void.

Only now she was in danger of losing her mother. What was

her mother saying to detectives? Why was she doing this? It was crazy, it wouldn't stand. Rachel had to assume that Bambi's "confession" would be seen through quickly enough, then the matter would be over. But what if she managed to persuade detectives of this monstrous lie? How much would Rachel have to tell? Did they know that she had gone to see Julie?

It had been such an emotional time. She had left Marc and promptly lost her job, as she had prophesied. No job for the girl who was divorcing the only male Singer. Marc wanted to reconcile, but he continued to lie about his infidelity, deny anything had happened. How could she return to him as long as he was lying? She was living at home with her mother and Michelle, feeling like such a loser. It was in this state that she first read the article about Julie Saxony's "second act" as an innkeeper and soon-to-be restaurateur. The article ran in the *Star*, an afternoon paper that was a little more down-market, and it included a photo of Julie in her glory. "Saxony at the height of her fame as a Block dancer, in 1975, where she performed under the stage name Juliet Romeo. A year later, her boyfriend, Felix Brewer, would disappear, leaving her only the deed to a small coffee shop on Baltimore Street. Saxony used that opportunity to learn the hospitality business."

So much to hate in just a few words. "Her boyfriend"—no mention, not in the caption, of the wife and three children he also left. "Only the deed to a small coffee shop." That was more than he had left his family. "The height of her fame." What was she famous for? Dancing in pasties and a G-string? Sleeping with her boss?

The more Rachel thought about it, the more it made sense: Julie had their money, just as Mother had always said. Even if all she had received was the coffee shop—that should have been theirs. Commercial real estate downtown wasn't exactly moving in 1976, but by 1980, with the opening of Harborplace, the land might have been worth something. Julie had sold it for a profit she "preferred not to disclose." How lazy of the reporter not to find it out, Rachel thought, reading the article in dull fury.

And next thing she knew, she was driving to Havre de Grace.

Julie Saxony led her into a breakfast room, empty at this time of the day, although Rachel could hear someone banging about nearby, possibly in a laundry room of sorts. A dryer was humming, *whump-whump-whump. Whump-whump-whump.*

"You know who I am," she said. Flat, not sinister, but also not a question.

"Yes," Julie Saxony said. She sat in a dining-room chair, but she didn't invite Rachel to sit. Her posture was impeccable, her hands folded in her lap. *Oh, aren't you the lady,* Rachel wanted to sneer. In some part of her mind, she realized she was having the fight with Julie that she couldn't have with Marc, much less his piece on the side. But that was okay, she reasoned. Being angry would help her get what she needed.

"Why were you at my sister's bat mitzvah?" It wasn't where she had planned to begin. She realized she had no plan, not really.

"I told you—I was observing the caterer. I hired him. He's going to be the chef here. He's already trying out menus and we hope to open this fall."

"So it was just a coincidence." Julie Saxony said nothing. "I didn't think so. Did you spy on us a lot?"

She thought of her own mother, taking the older girls by Horizon House, pointing out Julie's apartment. But that was just once. That didn't count as spying.

"Did you?" she repeated. Her words had real authority to her ears. She felt dangerous, and it was thrilling.

"Certainly, I was interested in Felix's family."

"Don't say his name."

"I think," Julie said, "this is going to be a difficult conversation if I'm not allowed to say his name." A pause. "More difficult, I guess I should say."

"You stole my family's money. My mother told me."

"I'm sorry, but that's a lie. If your mother couldn't live on what was provided, then that's probably because she wasn't willing to economize."

"Economize? Economize? You try to economize with three daughters in private school, with college tuitions and a house that's falling apart at the seams. You try to find a job when you dropped out of college at eighteen and became a mother by age twenty."

"I didn't even finish high school," Julie said.

"Yes, but you had an advantage my mother doesn't have. You were willing to sleep with another woman's husband."

Her words hurt, she was sure of it, although Julie's composure did not crack. She said only: "I loved your father very much."

"Then you should honor the woman my father loved and give her the money that is rightfully hers."

"There is no money. What I had, I invested, and it was mine. I'm sorry, but that's true."

"My mother's about to lose her house. She'll be humiliated. Don't you get it? She's not just an ordinary citizen who can be foreclosed on in private. The house will go to auction when her balloon note comes due and the papers will write about it and it will all be dredged up again, just like the stupid article about you dredged it all up. My father loved my mother, above anyone. I don't care what he told you or promised you. He loved my mother. You weren't the first, you know. You wouldn't have been the last."

Julie licked her lips. "I don't have any money. I just don't have it. Not that I would give it to you if I did. I'm sorry if your mother has been improvident—"

"Such big words from the stripper," Rachel said. Who was this person? Who had she become? It was horrible. It was strangely delightful, too, like playing a villain in a play. She was channeling the fury she felt for Marc, for every woman who had been cheated on.

"I'm sorry if your mother has been improvident." That word again. "I really am. But it's not my fault. What's mine is mine."

"If only you had been so clear about ownership when you started sleeping with my father. He loved her, Miss Saxony. Her and his daughters. Not you, never you."

She sensed this was her best weapon, the only way to hurt Julie Saxony. And if Julie Saxony wasn't going to help her, then Rachel wanted to hurt her. Men couldn't cheat without women's cooperation. Sure, there were men who lied, who misled their partners into unwitting adultery. But not her father. And not Marc. Believe someone the first time they tell you who they are. Marc had been a player in high school. He had been famous, Rachel remembered in wretched hindsight, for breaking up with girls by starting new relationships, then waiting for his ex to confront him. Everyone knew what he did, and every girl assumed it would be different for her.

The difference now was that Marc wouldn't admit his behavior. He called her every night, asking her to come back, but he wouldn't confess to his indiscretions, Rachel realized now, because they were going to continue. Just more discreetly. Marc loved her, but he had no intention of changing. Instead, he said: *Have a baby. Please have my baby. If we have a baby, everything will be okay.* The thing was, he thought he was speaking theoretically, about a baby that did not yet exist.

"Rachel—"

"Don't say my name."

There was a spike of fury in Julie's words now. "Don't say your father's name, don't say your name—why are you so proprietary about names? What's the big deal? Brewer probably wasn't even

your father's family's real name, back in Russia or wherever they
came from. I'll tell you this much—if your father had stayed, if he
hadn't been forced to leave, I'd have his name by now. He loved
me. He wanted me."

"Keep telling yourself that," Rachel said. "Tell yourself whatever lies you need to tell to get through." She had an inspiration.
"He knows you stole from us. He couldn't do anything about it,
where he is, but he knows. He never loved you, not really, and
now he hates you. You destroyed the thing he loved most of all,
his family."

Finally, she had gotten a rise out of the woman. She was quite
livid, almost in shock.

"He—he talks to her? To this day?"

"To this day."

She left Julie's inn with that feeble, hollow victory. The situation hadn't changed, despite her triumph over Julie. Her mother
needed money, now, or she was going to lose the house. And
Rachel knew what she would have to do to get it. It took a little
longer than she anticipated, almost a week, but when her mother
returned from the beach, Rachel was able to present her with the
money she needed.

"Where did you get this?" her mother demanded.

"Let's just say that Julie Saxony made good on her debts," Rachel
said. It felt like a safe lie at the time. But Rachel was an inexperienced
liar and did not know all the ways even a safe lie can go wrong.
Maybe she should have asked Marc for some pointers as part of their
settlement, a settlement brokered by her mother-in-law, who was
very happy to void the prenup if it meant Rachel would grant the get
that Mrs. Singer desired, then go away forever—and take the stain of
the Brewer name with her.

5:30 P.M.

The minute she said July 4, Bert had demanded another confer-
ence. Bambi granted his wish out of courtesy, but her mind was
made up.

"Bambi, I may have to withdraw as your counsel," Bert said,
"if you insist on going forward with this."

Was that all he had? "Then withdraw. I'm ready to tell this
story, with or without you. You can't say what happened on July
fourth, can you, Bert? So you'll just have to listen."

A tape recorder was set up. Both detectives made eye contact
in their individual ways. Nancy Porter was bright and focused,
the kind of grade grubber who sat front and center back at Forest
Park High School. The sad-faced one looked as if he knew every
unfortunate thing that had ever happened to Bambi. *Lugubrious,*
Bambi thought. That is the only word for how he looks. She decided to look at neither detective as she spoke, focusing on a point
between their heads. They probably thought she was trying not
to cry. Well, she was trying not to cry.

"She came to my home on July fourth. She brought me money,
quite a bit. I needed it to pay a balloon note on a mortgage. You
see, I was very foolish and these one-year ARMs, they were quite
new then. I didn't understand how it worked. I just knew that
if I took out this mortgage, I would get a very large lump sum.
Enough to pay for Michelle's bat mitzvah, repairs to the house. So
I took out this loan. I didn't realize that I had to pay it back in a
year, that I had to find the cash equivalent in the form of another
mortgage, and I had—well, I had bad credit, I thought it just converted. I . . . I froze. I didn't know what to do. I felt so stupid. I
owed on the mortgage, I had maxed out my credit cards. I needed
money fast."

"Jesus, Bambi," Bert said. "You could have come to me."

"But I was always coming to you. Always. There had been ten
years of coming to you at that point. I tried my mom, my aunt

Harriet—they couldn't help me. But then I saw in the paper how that . . . that Julie Saxony was expanding her bed-and-breakfast into a proper inn with a restaurant, and I thought: She has money. She should give me the money I need. She came to my house that day to give me the money."

Something changed, then, in the detectives' faces. Sad-face scribbled something on a piece of paper and passed it to the girl. She had a poker face. Bambi couldn't discern anything from it. But maybe it was just that she was a woman and Bambi had spent so much of her life trying to understand men and what they wanted. The two got up and went outside.

"Stop lying, Bambi," Bert said in a low tone. "They know you're lying."

"I'm not lying, though. Julie Saxony did provide the money. That's true. You could probably look up the bank records, see when I paid off the note. In cash."

"She didn't come to your house on the fourth. You're saying that because you know you were at the beach until the night of the third. We were all at the beach."

"Yes. We were all at the beach on the third. Agreed. But I met Julie on the fourth. On the tenth anniversary."

"You didn't. Why are you lying about this? What are you trying to prove?"

"Bert, you're fired. Please leave."

"I can't—"

"You will. You are. Go."

He looked lost, confused, two expressions that Bambi had seldom seen pass across Bert's face. Of course he was confused. Because she was lying, but what else could she do? She had run the numbers. Something, someone, had to be sacrificed. It was as if another onerous financial commitment had come due again. But this time *she* was going to take care of it. What a fool she had been, how inept. She had gone from her father's house to her husband's. She had lived in denial for years about what things cost. Thrown away her father's money on a semester at Bryn Mawr. Let Felix throw money around, too, and never asked the price of anything.

About two weeks before he had left, Felix had sat down with her and their checkbook. "Going forward," he said, "you need to write down everything, keep the balance. Because—well, you're just going to have to keep track. Because once I go away, the money, it will come in at a different rate. There will still be money, but it will be different, okay? You've got to learn to budget, Bambi. Can you do that?"

She could have. Only, after he left, there was no money coming in. Twenty thousand dollars. That was what had been in their joint checking account in July 1976. Twenty thousand dollars. It had been gone in less than a year.

Besides, at the time, she thought Felix meant prison when he said he was *going away*. It was not until the night before that she understood he was going somewhere else. She had been putting things away and discovered a pair of cuff links was missing from his drawer. Cuff links she knew well, for she had given them to him for their fifteenth anniversary. Yet there was Felix, in short sleeves—because it was, after all, July. He was packing, she realized. Squirreling things away, getting ready to go. She didn't ask any questions. She didn't want to know. And not because she feared the police and their questions. She could not bear to hear Felix tell her that he was a coward.

Bert left the interrogation room, his broad shoulders slumped. Lord, how she had leaned on him over the years. Lorraine had been kind about it. But then Lorraine pitied Bambi. In the early days, the pity had been a way for her to mitigate all the things she envied about Bambi, and that had been okay. She had pitied Bambi because Felix had other women, then pitied her because he was gone.

Bambi had forgiven Felix his indiscretions. They had been there from the first. The cowardice—that was different. Felix had slept with other women, but that didn't mean he didn't love her. Perhaps the opposite. Sleeping with other women was the only wedge he had against his love for her. Sure, she knew that sounded like a rationalization, but some rationalizations were true. No, it was in his flight that Felix had betrayed her and their children.

The detectives returned.

"For the record—you are speaking to us without a lawyer at your own behest," the girl intoned into the tape recorder.

"Yes, for the record I am."

"Okay," said the sad-eyed detective. "You contacted Julie Saxony—when? How?"

She looked at him long and hard. "I sent my daughter Rachel. On my behalf. She went to speak to her the week before. I'm not sure of the exact date."

"You sent your daughter Rachel, she asked Julie for money, and a week later, Julie brings you money? On the Fourth of July?"

"Yes."

"And how did she get the money? Banks would have been closed. And, as you must know, Julie Saxony's financial life was pored over. There's no record of any big cash transaction in the weeks before she disappeared."

"I haven't a clue. All I know is I got the money I needed."

"We should probably speak to your daughter."

"My daughter's at the hospital."

It was the first sign of genuine emotion in the female detective's face. So she was a mother. "I'm so sorry."

"It's not major. Her child needs cleft palate surgery. She's adopted, from China. It's pretty common now. For the children to need this surgery. If you don't agree to a special-needs child, it's much harder to adopt from there." She found her speech speeding up. She was chattering, as if she was nervous. Why was she nervous? She had already done the hardest part. "It didn't used to be that way. Foreign adoption has changed so much. And Rachel and Joshua, because they live in the city—well, it seemed unlikely that they would get a child domestically, in the city, and they were over forty, which makes them too old for most U.S. adoptions, and then Guatemala closed and Vietnam had problems and—well, China was it."

Nattering, nattering, nattering. Gathering her thoughts even as she appeared to be fraying. Maybe she shouldn't have sent Bert away. What were her rights now? Did she get another phone call, could she demand a new lawyer? How could she get word to Rachel?

"Look, I said I did it. Can't you just arrest me? The sooner you do that, the sooner I can get before a judge, see if bond can be arranged. My granddaughter had surgery today. I can't possibly spend the night here."

But in the end, that's exactly what she did. They took her into custody and drove her out to Towson, locked her up in detention there and told her to be grateful for that. Granted a phone call, she swallowed her pride and called the Gelmans' home, praying Lorraine would answer.

For the first time in a long time, a prayer was answered.

"Bambi—Bert told me what's going on. He's beside himself. What are you thinking? How can you turn your back on his help when he only wants what's best for you? Why—"

"Lorraine, you have to get to Rachel. Tonight. I think I bought her some time, but the police will come for her tomorrow. Whatever happens, she has to insist she was not at my house on July third, or that she didn't see anyone there."

"I don't—"

"Lorraine, she's my daughter. She finally has the only thing she ever wanted, her own child. Her life is worth more than mine, in so many ways. I know that I can't say such things to Bert. He can't allow me to lie, which is why I've had to let him go. But you're my friend and a mother, not a lawyer. You have to let me do this. Whatever Rachel did—she did it for me. Now I have to do this for her."

July 3, 1986

Her room was as she had left it, a scant six years ago. It was not so much tribute as inertia. Her mother was fighting a running battle with Michelle, who wanted to claim one of her sisters' rooms, then begin a costly redecoration. Easier to keep everything as it was.

The thing that bothered Rachel, however, was that she felt younger and stupider than the girl who had left this room to attend Brown. *That* girl had been skeptical of her high school classmate, Marc Singer. *That* girl had high intellectual standards. She read serious books and aspired to be a poet. The "woman" who had replaced her was now spending her afternoons watching *All My Children*, *One Life to Live*, and *General Hospital*. She hadn't washed her hair or taken a shower since Monday. She knew she was being foolish, that she shouldn't be depressed about the decisions she had made. She was right to give up on Marc, to erase everything of their life together. She deserved better. He was never going to be faithful to anyone. She couldn't live her mother's life.

But that thought, which occurred to her as she stared into the refrigerator, despite knowing its contents by heart by now, seemed treasonous. Her mother was such a good person. Who was Rachel to feel superior to her, to demand something better? It was her mother who deserved better, and now Rachel was going to give it to her. Wipe out her debt once and for all.

She found a jar of olives and took it back to the sofa. If she had gone to the shore with her mother and Michelle, there would be crabs and Silver Queen corn and gorgeous tomatoes, hothouse at this time of year, but still good. The Gelmans entertained so well. A little showily, but that was okay. Her father, too, had been extravagant when it came to parties. He believed there was no point in having money if people didn't know you had it.

The corollary, as best Rachel could work out, was that people should never know that you didn't have money. That was how her mother had lived for the past ten years, and that was what had brought her to near ruin this summer. But Rachel had saved her. At some cost to herself, but she believed it wouldn't feel that way in one, two years. She would meet the right man, they would have a family. She was going to get a do-over. Marc was the wrong person for her. He wasn't a good person. Her father broke the law, made his money from the poor and weak, cheated on her mother. Yet, somehow, he was a good person. Marc sold commercial real estate, was at his parents' home every Friday for Shabbat dinner, cheated on his wife—then lied about it. Then acted as if she were the crazy one when she confronted him. That was evil. That was cowardice.

She remembered a year ago, going to see a film purportedly about a group of young friends not much different from herself. Recent grads of a good school, making their way in the world, anchored by a perfect-seeming couple, a pair of college sweethearts. But the man was cheating on the woman. "What about your extracurricular love life," she snapped at him, at last, each syllable as sharp and hard as a little karate chop. A year ago, Rachel had found the whole thing hilarious. There were no such people. Now she was living it. She may have said those very words to Marc: *What about your extracurricular love life?*

Really, one could argue that watching soap operas was downright redundant at this point. But how could she live with a cheater and a liar?

Her parents—that had been different. Her mother never confronted her father, not to Rachel's knowledge. But then, her mother was trapped. Three kids. No work experience, no college degree. She, at least, could have expected alimony. No prenups in her mother's day; wives still got alimony. They didn't have to negotiate for what they deserved—

The doorbell roused her from the couch, from the land of Luke and Laura. She couldn't imagine who would be coming by. Almost everyone she knew was at the ocean, even Linda, with her sweet new baby boy, Noah. Rachel wasn't ready to be a mom, not yet, not given her circumstances. But holding Noah, seeing Linda's love for him—she hoped she wouldn't have to wait too long.

"Hello," said Julie Saxony. "Is your mother at home?"

She was perfectly dressed. At a time when hair was big and skirts voluminous, Julie wore a throwback of an outfit, a pink linen shift with a matching bolero-style jacket over it. The dress looked like one that was stowed in Rachel's memory. *My mother had a dress like that.* Her going-away dress, the night of her wedding, purchased for the trip to Bermuda. There was a photograph of her in it, somewhere in this very house. And, possibly, in her father's office, although her father had never allowed his wife or children into that part of his life.

The only false note was the overlarge purse, which looked cheap and plastic, a very bad imitation of an old-style cosmetic bag.

"She's away," Rachel said, aware of her baggy shorts and stained T-shirt. But at least her T-shirt said BROWN on it.

"Oh. Will she be back soon?"

"She won't be back at all. And if you're here to make good on what I asked last week, it's too late. I took care of it. We don't need your money. Our money, I guess I should say."

Julie pushed past her, as if she didn't take Rachel at her word. She took in the hallway, the living room beyond it. Out of date, but still pretty and comfortable. Bambi had longed for more modern furnishings, but Felix had argued that they wouldn't work. He believed in comfort, anyway, found the seventies-style furniture too low-slung. The living room looked like a lounge in a country club, but an unstuffy one, a place to sit and smoke, although no one had smoked in this house for ten years.

"I always thought it would be . . . nicer," Julie said. "I'm sorry," she added, as if embarrassed by her own rudeness. "It's just that I thought a lot. About where you lived. But I never got to see the inside."

"That's because there was no reason for you to."

"Are you sure your mother won't be back today? It's very urgent that I speak to her."

"No, she won't be back today. And I can't imagine you have anything urgent to discuss with her."

Julie looked disappointed, almost the way a child would. She shifted on her feet, looked around. "I can't stay. But I want her to know—Felix sent for me. For me."

"You're lying."

"No. I'd tell you more—the arrangements made, where I'm going—but, of course, I've been asked not to. He sent for me. He loves me."

"No, he doesn't." Rachel grasped for something to say, something hurtful and scarring. "You're just a whore with no life. A thief, too. When my father finds that out, he won't want anything to do with you."

"You said he already knew. So I guess you're the liar, after all."

Julie lifted her chin, the proper lady, and began to walk out, making a grand gesture. A line from a movie, an old one, popped into Rachel's head: *You're much too short for that gesture.* But it wasn't even true. Julie was tall and slim, five-eight or so, taller than their father. Rachel was the shorter of the two, a twenty-four-year-old woman who had just agreed to divorce a man she still loved because that was the only way to get the money she needed to save her mother. And for what? What had she done? Preserved this stupid life, this frozen life, like something out of a fairy tale, where everyone was suspended, waiting, waiting, waiting for the man who never came, never called, never did anything to prove he truly cared for them.

Rachel had been going into high school the year that Felix disappeared. As a cost-saving measure, her mother had petitioned to enter her in Western High School's A-course that fall by using her parents' city address, assuring Rachel it would be only for one semester, that the financial situation would work out and it wasn't fair to pull out Linda, who was a senior. Rachel's freshman year at Western had actually lasted less than a week. She had been jumped at the bus stop by another girl for reasons that she could never discern. Jumped from behind in a hair-pulling, kicking, scratching melee that had lasted all of a minute but that felt like an eternity. It was the only physical encounter of her life. Until now.

She sprang at Julie Saxony's back as her onetime combatant had pounced on her, swinging wildly at the woman's head, arms flailing, intent on bringing her to the ground. Rachel's only thought was to make sure the other woman didn't look so damn perfect when she got off the plane wherever she was going. To run her hose, to scuff her shoes.

She hadn't planned to actually bloody her, but when that happened—well, it happened.

March 27, 2012

9:00 A.M.

Sandy actually felt bad locking Bambi Brewer up overnight. But what else could he do? She was lying her head off, and if he let her go home, she was going to brief whoever she was protecting. The only choice was to isolate her, lock her up too late to get before a judge—and get to the one daughter as quickly as possible.

And, yeah, he felt like a bum, going to see a woman whose daughter had surgery the day before. But it wasn't life-threatening, according to her mom. The kid had already been discharged.

Rachel Brewer lived maybe a mile, as the crow flies, from where Bambi Brewer had grown up, but a crow would cover a lot of distance in that mile between the once-grand homes of Forest Park and these modest brick rowhouses on Purnell Drive. Sandy found it interesting that she was the kind of person who didn't mind being in the minority. Hard to know, but he would guess that this stretch of houses was mostly African American. Middle-class, solid citizens, but it wasn't a situation that most white people he knew sought out. Not that Sandy could ever decide if he was white. Sure, he looked white and Cubanos were technically Caucasian, but did that make him *white*? Coming up, before there were so many Latinos in Baltimore, the world had basically been black-white-Asian, and Sandy was white. But now, although he had not changed, he would be called "Latino," a word that meant nothing to him.

It was the July fourth thing that had done it. Not impossible. But it made no sense. Where had Julie Saxony been for twenty-four hours in that case? Not driving, based on her car's odometer. Not at home, not checked into any motel or hotel uncovered by detectives, or ferreted out by the reward money dangled by the Havre de Grace Merchants Association. So Bambi was lying about that. But why? And also lying about sending the daughter to do her bidding, based on what Susie recalled of the conversation. The daughter had said explicitly that her mother didn't know she was there. Okay, Susie's memory could be wrong on that point, or the daughter could have been lying to gain some perceived advantage. But the mother was definitely lying, and the daughter was the one person who could contradict her.

The woman who answered the door to Sandy and Nancy was not the beauty her mother was. It was only then, allowing himself that rather ungallant thought, that Sandy realized he did find Bambi Brewer very beautiful for a woman in her seventies. This one was pretty as middle-aged women go, her features roughened by whatever her father had contributed. But likable, younger looking than her age, even with no makeup and those deep circles under her eyes. She hadn't slept last night. Well, she had a sick kid and a mother in lockup. Those dark circles were earned.

They did the little dance of introductions, the pretense of hospitality. They were keen that she not lawyer up, but it was tricky, playing her this way. He hoped she would be looser at home, more relaxed. He hadn't factored in the demands of a toddler.

"Your mother confessed last night to killing Julie Saxony."

"She's lying," Rachel said.

"Why?"

"No idea. But I know it's a lie."

"How?"

"Because I saw Julie Saxony on July third. I was alone at the house. She came by, she wanted to speak to my mother, I sent her away."

"Did she come by with the money? The money you asked her for a week earlier?"

A beat. "Yes, that's exactly what happened. She came by with the money."

"How much was it?"

"Three hundred and fifty thousand."

"That's more than your mother's mortgage and debt. Based on the papers we've seen."

"Really?" She was surprised they knew about the mortgage. "Well, maybe it was the exact amount she stole."

"Have you ever seen three hundred fifty thousand dollars? It's a lot of money to put in a suitcase. Julie Saxony's sister has described the piece of luggage your father handed to Julie that night. She says there couldn't have been that much in there. And no one saw Julie put anything in her car that day. Why are you so convinced that Julie stole it?"

"My mother said she did."

"Your mother told us she killed Julie Saxony, and you have no problem saying that's a lie."

"I told you, I saw Julie on July third. I was at home. No one else was. She left, end of story. I thought—well, it doesn't matter what I thought. She left and someone killed her."

"She could have come back. The next day. I mean, if she really wanted to see your mother—"

"But she didn't."

"Again, how can you be sure?"

The child began chanting then: *miljews, miljews, miljews.* Sandy couldn't begin to make it out, but it apparently referred to milk and juice, as the woman got up and fetched two cups, the kind with lids that don't spill, whatever those are called. Sandy would probably know those kinds of things if he were a grandfather. He could tell the mother was happy for the distraction, because she made a big production out of it, probably using the time to think about what she wanted to say.

Only liars and very polite people need that much time to decide what to say.

"Do I have any—I don't know—I mean, not confidentiality, but can I tell you things that you won't tell my mother?"

"Maybe. It depends."

She sighed. "Julie Saxony came to tell my mother that my father had sent for her. Of course, that wasn't true."

"How do you know?"

"Because she was found dead."

"But that doesn't mean she was lying. You're working backward from a known fact. She might have been going to your father, wherever he was. And someone might have killed her to prevent that from happening. Maybe your dad wanted her dead."

Rachel was clearly having trouble processing all this. Again, it might have been the fatigue, or it might have been that she had held back this piece of the story for so long that she hadn't thought about how others might arrange the same facts. Felix had summoned Julie Saxony, but Julie was found dead. In this woman's mind, those two things weren't connected.

Sandy believed they were.

"But I didn't—" She stopped.

"You didn't kill her? I mean, you hit her hard enough to knock her earring out, the one that your mother found and sold a month later, but you didn't kill her? Your mom thinks you did."

"She didn't tell you that."

"No, she just confessed to a murder she probably didn't commit. Possibly to protect the person who did."

She wasn't having problems focusing anymore.

"I need a lawyer." It was a statement of fact, flat and plain-spoken. By force of habit, Sandy tried to forestall the inevitable.

"Look, we're still just talking here. If you say you didn't kill her, you didn't kill her. Maybe you just, I don't know, knocked her out, called one of your father's old buddies, like Tubman, to help you? And you didn't know what he did or how it ended. That's okay. We're just talking. You bring a lawyer in, we've got to go out to headquarters, you'll want to find a babysitter and here's your kid, just getting over something really major—"

"No, I need a lawyer. We can drop Tatiana at my sister's house. Michelle, the younger one. And I'll call Bert Gelman before we leave. Is that a problem, Bert representing my mother and me? Is he allowed to be my lawyer, too?"

"I have a hunch," Sandy said, "it's what your mother wanted when she fired him last night."

Noon

Michelle had a nanny whom she called a babysitter. She wasn't fooling anyone, including herself. The woman lived in a private apartment above the garage, worked almost sixty hours a week, with Tuesdays and Sundays off. Michelle felt guilty about this. But Hamish wanted her free to go out, to focus on him. She missed the children when she was out, yet she also dreaded Tuesdays and Sundays, which seemed to last forever. It never stopped. Two was so much harder than one, although thank God Hamish III was in school now. Still, that left her with Helena, who was more outrageous than most three-year-olds.

Helena's high-maintenance ways were thrown into sharp

relief by Tatiana's temperament. A by-product of being in an orphanage, Rachel had said once, and Michelle had said: "Do you
think there's an orphanage where I can drop my kids off for a
week or so?" She thought it was funny. Rachel, not so much.

Today was a Tuesday, but she hadn't mentioned that when
Rachel had called. She had said, "Sure, bring her over." And that
had felt good. Until a few years ago, she had so little to offer her
sisters. It was nice to be the generous one, the bountiful one. To
have the biggest house, to hold the family gatherings, to be able
to help out financially. She was especially keen to do anything she
could for Rachel.

Rachel's one was so dainty, alongside Helena. Of course, she
was younger and, well, malnourished. But there was something
in her movements, something delicate and fine. Michelle watched
her examine Helena's cache of toys in the den—and watched
Helena become instantly passionate about any toy that Tatiana
touched. "Mine."

"Be nice," she said. "Share."

Tatiana didn't seem to mind. She just moved on to the next
toy, which Helena promptly took, saying: "Mine."

She was her mother's daughter all right.

Although the house was toasty warm, Michelle pulled her
sweater tighter around her, took another sip from her homemade
cappuccino. *Why are you going to talk to the police now?* she had
asked her sister. *What is going on?*

It's going to be okay. It's just crazy. No one did anything.

Did Mom—

No, no.

Did you—

*No, Michelle. I think Mom thinks she's protecting me or something,
but I didn't do anything. Honest, I didn't. I mean, I didn't do anything
really bad.*

But Michelle had. Michelle had done something very bad. She

had come so close to telling Rachel, the day of the shower, before Hamish III was born. But she had a moment of—what to call it? Clarity. She wanted to confess to Rachel because it would make *her* feel better. She wanted to tell her sister about the worst thing she had ever done, in hopes of forgiveness that she didn't deserve. She still yearned to be forgiven—and still understood that she didn't deserve it. That was the price she had to pay. For six, almost seven years now, she had tried to persuade herself that her life was proof that she had done the right thing. Hamish, the children—a bad person would not be given these things. And a remorseful person was not bad, right? She used to be bad, but she wasn't anymore.

"Mine," Helena said, snatching another toy from Tatiana's hands. Tatiana never countered, never complained, just went searching for something else. Was Michelle supposed to check her bandage soon? She needed to read the sheet Rachel had left for her.

She sipped her cappuccino. She was really enjoying being nice, if not the Nice One, the role that still belonged to Rachel. It had been a revelation, learning that being nice wasn't for suckers, that living a life in which one could like one's self was akin to being softly massaged, all the time. Every "please," every "thank you"—it was like a coin dropped into a bank. No—a coin tossed into a fountain, like the old wishing fountain at the Westview Cinemas. You gave the coin away. It was no longer yours. It had no currency. And yet you still felt rich somehow, in the moment you released it. *I can afford to surrender this quarter. I can afford to say please and thank you and no, you were ahead of me, because I can afford to be nice now because someone finally loves me.* Someone I don't deserve. If Hamish knew—if Rachel knew—if her mother knew—

"Mine," Helena said again. Tatiana moved on, unperturbed.

She probably should call Linda.

1:00 P.M.

Sandy felt as if he had been working with Nancy Porter forever. He had never been partnered with a woman before. There had only been two in homicide, and one of them was a head case. But Nancy Porter was the real deal. He had trouble remembering she was a woman, even though she was pretty girly. She was good police. Even had the old-school Baltimore accent, all those vowels.

Plus, she agreed with him, most of the time. That never hurt.

"How do you want to play this?" she asked now, very deferential, although it seemed increasingly evident that it would be a county case. Later, if it got written up in the papers—and this case was definitely going to get written up in the papers—his decision to execute the search warrant on Bambi Brewer's apartment would be called a hunch. True, he hadn't known what to expect. He just believed that Julie Saxony went to that house on July 3, 1986, and probably died there. He had thought he might find a gun among Bambi's possessions, maybe even a casing in the old house. But it was the oddity of that one shoebox, in what was otherwise a very uncluttered, serene apartment. An accumulation of papers so meaningless that they had to be meaningful.

"She's not an experienced liar, this one," Sandy said. "Her mom's not very good, either, but she's even worse. She's a nice lady, she's used to doing and saying things that people want to hear. I think everything she's told us is the truth. She stopped talking, though, when things got serious. She shut down fast."

"Is it possible that she thinks her mom did it?"

"I think it's more likely that she realizes her mother suspects her and is trying to save her. Mom probably thought it was slick, but it gives us more leverage. This isn't a girl—"

"She's a woman," Nancy said, manner mild. "She's fifty."

Why had he said girl? "But she seems young, doesn't she? Younger and older than she should be."

Nancy thought about this. It was another thing he liked about her, how she wasn't a rat-a-tat, wisecrack person. He had never been good with those types.

"She takes care of others," Nancy said. "Even more than an average mom would. I can see why she wanted to be a mother badly enough to do it so old. I've got two kids now and I can barely keep up with them and I'm only thirty-five. I had this aunt, whose father died when she was really young, eleven or so, and she had to become her mother's mainstay. That was my mom's word— poor Evie, she's the 'mainstay.' If Rachel didn't do this, she knows who did, or thinks she knows. She's still in protection mode. She knows something and she's desperate not to tell us."

"Desperate enough to take a murder charge?"

Nancy smiled. Lenhardt had told Sandy that she particularly loved interrogations, especially with women. It was a specialty of sorts with her. "Let's go find out."

1:00 P.M.
Bert met Rachel at the Baltimore County police headquarters. He looked as exhausted as she felt. They were left alone in a room that was far more like the rooms she had seen on television than Rachel would have thought possible.

"Bert, why is Mother claiming she killed Julie? She couldn't possibly have."

"Of course she didn't do it. But she was clever enough, if you want to call it that, to say she did it on July fourth, not third. She was at the beach until the evening of the third. She couldn't have been home much before eight or nine."

Rachel sighed. "I was there. On the third. Julie Saxony came by and said our father had sent for her. I hit her, Bert. I actually tore an earring out of her ear. I was so mad—first our money, now our father himself. I know it's not her fault that Daddy got arrested, or even that he ran away. But everything else, all the hardships—that was because of her greed. And for Daddy to send for her—"

"She was probably lying, just to hurt you. Your father's women—look, I can't change the fact that they existed, but none were special. The girls were like Cadillacs to him."

"You mean, he drove them for two to three years then traded them in." She was trying to make a joke, but her mouth crumpled and it was all she could do not to cry.

"Yes, pretty much. But—it was changing, Rachel. He was changing. Do you want to know why? It was because of you and Linda. As he saw you come into womanhood—I mean, Julie was what, seven years older than Linda? I think, in some ways, running was part of changing for him. He saw a chance to start over, to be a better person."

"Mother said he was a coward."

"Well, he wasn't brave. But he didn't think he would survive prison. He had some blood pressure stuff, cholesterol. A family history of diabetes. He wasn't built to serve time, Rachel. He knew that about himself. Your dad, whatever his faults—he never had any bullshit about who he was. Your mom is a thousand times braver than he is. That's why she's willing to go to prison for you."

"But I didn't do anything. I mean, okay, yes, I assaulted her. But you know what I did then? I apologized. Yes, I apologized to my father's girlfriend for what I had done. Helped her clean up, offered to take her to an ER. And you know what she said? 'That's okay, I'm headed to Saks. I'll buy something nicer. And I'll be on the Pacific coast of Mexico before the day is through.'"

"She said *that*?"

"Yes. Uncle Bert—for years, for fifteen years, I assumed that she was with Daddy and it broke my heart. Then her body was found and I was, like, 'Oh, so she was lying.' I decided she must have ripped someone else off. I mean, if she stole from us, then she might have stolen from any number of people. I figured she burned someone and finally got what was coming to her. I didn't see how it could be connected to Daddy. But the detective said, 'Why not?' and now I wonder: Why not? Did he set a trap for her? Did she have something on him? Maybe he found out what she did and arranged for her to be killed. He would have been angry, right, if he knew that she had stolen our money?"

"Yes—he would have been very angry about the money. But Rachel, baby, no one has heard from your father, ever. I can guarantee you that. Not me, not your mother. He's gone. He was gone from our lives the day he left."

Rachel allowed herself a smile at the way that Bert, after all these years, would not admit to having any knowledge of her father's planned flight. God, Bert was loyal.

"Rachel, there is one thing I have to ask you. You told your mother and your mother told the police that Julie Saxony gave you money. Is that true?"

"I don't want to tell you, Bert. I know you're my lawyer and you'll be bound by the usual rules, but you're also a family friend. You'll have trouble being just my lawyer. As my uncle, my mother's friend, you'll want to tell her. She must never know, Bert, how I got that money."

"You can't lie to the police."

"Okay, so I'll just tell them I made an arrangement that has nothing to do with this. That's true."

"I can keep secrets," he said. "You'd be surprised at what I can compartmentalize."

Rachel had an image of her younger sister, sitting on a gleaming white toilet, a glass of champagne in her hand, a napkin full of cookies spread on what little lap she had.

"Michelle's problem. With the IRS agent. Did she tell you who her lover was?"

"Just that he was married."

Rachel smiled. "Ah, but, see, you've already told more than

you should. You should have said, 'What problem with the IRS?' You should have feigned shock. *Married lover? Michelle had a married lover?* And you've probably told Mother everything, long ago. I can't afford to tell you this, Bert. I can't. Because if my mother knew how I got that money, the decision I made—she would blame herself. And she shouldn't, she mustn't. It was absolutely the right thing to do and I've never regretted it."

"Rachel, we're talking about murder."

"Yes, but I didn't kill anyone. So I hit her. So what? You think they would go to trial with so little evidence?"

"Yes, they might go to trial. Especially if you don't tell them where you got the money to pay your mother's mortgage. It will be expensive, a trial. And what if they petitioned to lock you up without bond? You'll miss work, too, and I know your household can't afford that. You don't have to tell them everything, but I need you to tell *me* everything. It's the only way I can represent you effectively. Today, they are going to run back and forth between us and your mother, comparing notes, looking for every discrepancy. What if they decide it was a conspiracy, or that your mother is an accessory? She did find the earring, apparently, and she did pawn it. She assumed you had done something to Julie. And when Julie's body was found—that's why it hit her so hard. Not because of the publicity, but because she had worried, all those years, that you had done something awful, and here was the proof."

"Look, Uncle Bert, I'm not scared. I didn't kill anyone. And the money I gave my mom all those years ago—it was legal. Perfectly legitimate. I even paid income tax and gift tax on it, made sure everything was on the up and up. That's why I said a different amount."

"Really, that's interesting because—" Bert stopped himself.

"Because it didn't come up? When that IRS agent decided to go through Michelle's filings, then Mother's? He had the fact that

Mother paid it off, but as the recipient, she wasn't obligated to report anything and he probably didn't think to pull my file, or Linda's. Because he was just some stupid guy, in a snit over being rejected by Michelle. His own bosses saw that much, right?"

"Your sister got lucky. The agent's misuse of his position was more of a problem than some married *ku fartzer* who, unlike you, didn't follow the letter of the law and report a car, a watch, and a fur coat as gifts."

"Ku fartzer." Rachel laughed. "You never speak Yiddish, Uncle Bert, unless you really dislike someone."

The detectives knocked, entered without being asked. It was their room, after all.

"Are we ready to talk?"

"Yes," Rachel said.

They did their stage business with their tape recorder, got out their pads.

"Late in the morning of July 3, 1986, Julie Saxony came to my mother's home, where I was staying alone. She told me she had been summoned by my father and that she was going to him. I got angry, I hit her, I knocked a pierced earring from her lobe—the right, I think." She mimed the fight for herself, the leap from the back, the ineffectual punch, the grab—yes, it had been the right. "I was shocked at myself. I had never drawn blood on another person in my life. The sight of the blood—I went to get a towel. I even offered to try to wash her dress, or pay for the dry cleaning, but—" She stopped. "Am I allowed to ask you questions?"

"You're allowed to *ask*," the male detective said.

"What was she wearing? When she was found? I mean, the clothes were there, right? Even after fifteen years, there would be some trace of the fabric?"

The detectives didn't answer.

"Okay, I'll tell you then. If Julie Saxony was not found in a two-piece pink linen dress, a sheath with a matching bolero-style jacket, then she changed clothes after I saw her. She said my father would buy her a new dress. She probably bought something herself. She wouldn't want to go see him looking less than her best. That's the last thing she said to me. 'I'm headed to Saks. I'll find something nicer.' I'm right, aren't I? She wasn't wearing a pink outfit when she was found."

The detectives looked unimpressed. Then Bert said: "They would rot, Rachel. After all that time. Her clothes would rot."

"But we'll try to match your description against the statements taken at the time," said the male detective. "I think she was wearing a pink outfit, according to her chef."

"What about the purse? I remember—she was all matchy-matchy. Really, a little tacky, like someone's idea of what a lady should look like. I know you found the purse because it was reported, her ID was in it. It was more of a makeup bag, the old-fashioned kind, for traveling. Pink, to match the dress. If she bought a new outfit, she might have bought a new purse, too."

The detective flipped a Polaroid at her. "It was the same purse."

"Well—maybe she just bought a dress, but found one to match the shoes and purse. Maybe—"

"Maybe," the female detective said, "maybe, we should stop playing the home version of *What Not to Wear* and go over this once again. Because the only thing you've managed to get right, for sure, is your description of this purse. That's dead-on perfect. So, congratulations, we're convinced: You saw Julie Saxony the day she was killed. What are you *not* telling us, Ms. Brewer?"

"I've told you everything I know. Julie Saxony came to my mother's house. We had a fight. I never saw her again."

"And a week later"—the male detective consulted his notes—"your mother paid off her mortgage. With money Julie Saxony provided you, before or after you tore out her earring."

"Okay, that was a lie. The money wasn't from Julie. It was mine, but I prefer not to talk about it."

"You taking the Fifth?" Detective Sanchez smiled as if that were hilarious.

"No, not exactly. Exercising my rights to privacy, I guess."

Two pairs of eyebrows shot up at that, almost comically in unison.

"Maybe she did have your father's money," said the woman, Nancy Porter. "Maybe she shows up and she has your father's money and she tells you that she's going to him with his money. Now that's a reason to hit someone, pull out an earring. You were trying to stop her."

"I was very emotional." Rachel paused. "I mean, more than you might realize. I was just . . . emotional."

"Sure." Detective Sanchez jumping in. "Because here's this woman and she's got your family's money and she's come to rub it in your mom's face. Your mom. I mean, I don't know how you grew up, but where I grew up, someone said shit about your mom—*tu madre*—kaboom!" He banged his fist into his palm.

The woman detective nodded. "I know. Same with the Polacks, my people. I mean, it's universal, as far as I know. People can say anything to me they want. But my mom? My mom or my kids. I bet you feel the same way. I mean, you were the one trying to take care of your mom. You put yourself on the line for her, right, going to see Julie Saxony the week before? Bad enough to have this woman say *No, I'm keeping your daddy's cash—*"

"To be fair," Rachel said, "she said she never had it."

"And you care about fairness, don't you, Rachel?" Sanchez now. Rachel felt as if she were in some dizzying dance, an Apache, being tossed back and forth between two partners. "It matters to you. You're a very principled person. Here was this woman who, even if she didn't have your father's money, she slept with him. A married man, with three daughters."

"He didn't have three daughters when it started."

"See, there you go again, being fair. People think empathy is a good thing and it is. But, sometimes, when you're feeling what everyone is feeling—being fair—you lose yourself a little. There you were, in your mom's house—why were you in your mom's house?"

"I had left my husband and lost my job. I didn't have anywhere else to go."

"So that's why you were emotional. I mean, no wonder."

Rachel paused. "Sure," she said. "That's why I was emotional."

"You say 'sure' like you're being polite. Like that's not it, but you just want to make this conversation go away."

"No, you're reading too much into it. Yes, I was emotional. Marc—I had been in love with him since I was sixteen." Rachel had never admitted this to anyone. But here, in this room designed to elicit confessions, it made sense to say the things she had never said to anyone. She had been in love with Marc from the moment she had first seen him. She had not thought herself worthy. Then one day, five years later, he deigned to notice her, to ask her out, even though he was superior in every way. Handsome, the better student, the better poet, from the better family. Marc's only flaw was that he couldn't keep his dick in his pants. Then, faster than seemed possible, she was twenty-four and she had given up the love of her life, and all the dreams that went with it. From a distance of twenty-five years plus, on the other side of what she now knew was her right life, her correct life, she could see the folly of it. But at twenty-four, she was raw and crazy and shortsighted and she jumped on the back of her father's girlfriend and tore an earring from her ear.

Later, in the bathroom, there had been spotting. On her T-shirt, but in her underwear, too, and that had perplexed her. *How could there be blood in her underwear?* And then she remembered—oh, yeah, they said there could be spotting. They also had recommended against vigorous exercise. Did jumping on your father's girlfriend count as vigorous exercise?

"I left my husband because he was unfaithful to me. He

wanted me to stay. But his mother was delighted. She had hated me, hated being associated with my family. When I learned of my mother's financial problems, I went to his mother and said I would leave him, if she would tear up the prenup and give me three hundred and fifty thousand dollars. Most of the money went to my mother, the rest to taxes. I needed some, to tide me over until I found a job. And for other things."

"Other things."

Rachel looked at Bert: "You can't tell." But she didn't wait for him to agree. She took a deep breath and said out loud the thing that no one knew about her. Not her mother, not her sisters, not Joshua. "I was thirteen weeks pregnant. My mother-in-law didn't know. But my husband did. I had an abortion, and I told him. I wanted to hurt him. I wanted to make things final between us, over forever and ever, with no hope of reconciliation. And I did. I had an abortion on July first, then went to my mother's house to recuperate."

She became aware of a strange sound in the room. It was Bert, weeping.

"Florence Singer, my mother-in-law. I'm sure she'll verify my account. About the money. And if you must, ask Marc if I told him I had an abortion, that I wouldn't carry his child. I wonder if he even remembers. He was remarried within six months, a father the year after that. But I saved my mom from losing the house. And if I had to do it all over again, I would, no regrets. But she can't know. She must never know. She carried us for so long. You know what? I almost wish I had killed Julie Saxony. But my mother wouldn't have wanted that. She wanted my dad, and that was the one thing I could never give her. Please—whatever happens, could we not tell her about the abortion or where I got the money? Or that Julie said those things about my dad sending for her? Can't we just leave things as they are? I didn't kill Julie. My mom didn't kill Julie. Can't you just leave my family alone?"

The detectives left, making no promises. Bert, the kind of man to have a silk handkerchief, took it out and wiped his eyes, but otherwise made no acknowledgment of his own tears. Time slowed, but it felt comforting. Rachel thought about her attempts over the years, all failed, at serious yoga practice, at meditation. For the first time in her life, she was living in the moment, but oh, what a moment. She didn't want to leave this room. As long as she was here, none of this had happened. Bert would tell her mother. She knew he would. Bert could never keep anything from Bambi. Or he told Lorraine, who told Bambi. Same difference.

The detectives returned. "We're going to check out what you've told us," the man said. "And, for now, we have no interest in sharing it. But if it comes to a court case, we can't control information. Things will get out. That's not on us. You control what people find out—if you confess."

"Why are we talking about court or confessions?" Bert asked. "Everything Rachel has said has been consistent."

"This final story has been consistent. She changed up several times getting there, didn't she?"

"Are you going to charge her or not?"

"She's free to go. But her mom, down the hall? She's still adamant that she did it. And at this point, we're going to let her have her way and be arrested for it. Nothing this one says negates the possibility that Julie Saxony came back the next day. Hey, maybe she sat in an ER for the next twenty-four hours, got treated under an assumed name." Sandy pushed a piece of paper toward Rachel. "This is the press release we plan to issue later this afternoon. Feel free to scan it for any possible factual errors."

4:30 P.M.

When Linda learned what was up, she couldn't believe she was the last person in the family to know. And she wouldn't even

have found out if she hadn't called Michelle to ask if she had heard
from Rachel about how Tatiana was doing. Linda had been calling Rachel's cell, going straight to voice mail, and sending e-mails
that went unanswered, unusual for Rachel. She wasn't the quick-
est person to respond to things, but she would want her sister to
know that Tatiana was okay. Plus, they had to talk about their
mother, this insanity. Linda thought Bambi might be exhibiting
some kind of dementia. Bert was great, no worries as long as Bert
was in charge, but what if they had to pay bail? With Uncle Tubby
long out of the business and certain legends still vivid in people's
minds, local bail bondsmen might not be inclined to write a
bond for the wife of the man famous for skipping. Or the judge
might deny bond altogether. But they clearly hadn't charged her
yet, which was interesting. There wasn't a whisper of it on television or the *Beacon-Light*'s Twitter account. Of course, the police
reporter was, like, twelve, but 2011 had been the thirty-fifth anniversary of Felix's disappearance, so it wasn't that long ago that
the paper had run something. It had been almost snarky in tone,
ho-ho-ho, whatever happened to Felix Brewer?

"Oh, Tatiana's great," Michelle assured Linda when she called
her. "Rachel dropped her off this morning. But she had to go out
to Baltimore County because of this whole thing with Mom."

"What's she doing that Bert can't do?"

"She said the cops want to talk to her, too."

"*What?* And you didn't call me?"

"Rachel said it was no big deal, that she was just being super-
cautious, making sure she had a lawyer with her, that Dad always
said that, never talk to the cops without a lawyer." A pause. "Did
he really say that, Linda? It seems like such an odd thing to say to
your teenage daughters—"

"Jesus, Michelle, I don't know. I mean—what the fuck? You
just sat there and didn't even think to call me?"

"I," Michelle said with wounded grandeur, "have been watch-

ing Tatiana and Helena all morning. Have you ever tried to get
two wound-up little girls down for a nap?"

Linda hung up and dialed the public information officer at Baltimore County police. They were friendlyish, usually playing on
the same team more or less, even now that she was working for
the governor. Oh God, the governor—that was going to be fun,
explaining to him why her family was in the news.

"Linda Sutton!" the PIO said. "Damnedest thing to hear
from you because I was wondering what you would do in my
situation."

"Don't be cruel, Bill. Just tell me what's going on."

"Detectives have given me two sets of facts to work with and
asked me to write two press releases. In one, I'm to say your sister
killed Julie Saxony. In the other, it's your mother. Any idea which
one is true? You could save me some work here."

"Fuck you, Bill." Maybe they weren't as friendly as she had
thought. She called her boss, pleaded a family emergency, a gutsy
thing to do when the legislature was in its final weeks, then called
Michelle and told her to find someone, anyone, to take the kids.
But she and Michelle needed to go to their mother and sister.

March 27, 2012

Bert and Rachel sat. What else could they do?

"What's going on, Bert?"

"They expect you to confess. They're bullying you. They think if they tell you that they're going to charge your mom, you'll break down."

"Oh, I'm about to break down. But I can't confess. I didn't do it, Bert."

"I know. Neither did your mother. This is the craziest thing I've ever seen. It's a weak case. An earring. The confession of someone who couldn't have possibly done it, an honest and plausible recitation of events that refutes the confession. I do wish you hadn't been there that day, much less admitted to hitting her—"

Rachel smiled. "I thought the truth was supposed to set me free."

"Not in this legal system, honey. The truth just gets in the way sometimes."

"I'm free to go. That's what they said."

"Yes. And when you leave, they will charge your mother. They're waiting to see if you're up for that."

"What can I do?"

"I don't know, Rachel."

A knock, the round face of the female detective. "Your sisters are here. We don't have to let them in to see you, but we're nice that way."

"They're here? Both of them? Who's taking care of Tatiana?"

"I got the nanny to come back early from her day off," Michelle said, pushing her way into the room. "And you're welcome."

"Bert, what's going on?" Linda asked, right behind her. "Why is Mother doing this?"

"I don't know, girls. I just don't know."

Rachel looked at her sisters, at Bert. She wondered if they had ever longed, as she had, to have him for a father. Or, more accurately, to have Felix be like Bert—steady, loyal, *there*. There. She thought about the famous children's book, the one she was reading to Tatiana now, the special pang that only a nonbiological mother can understand. *Are you my mother?* Why can't a bulldozer or an airplane or a frog be a bird's mother? Pretty-but-ordinary Rachel was the mother to beautiful Tatiana, with her silky hair and perfect eyes and her soon-to-be-perfect face, although it was incomparably lovely to Rachel even before the surgeries. She didn't, couldn't, judge the woman who had abandoned her. She owed that woman everything. And her father had abandoned her, so there was that.

Another knock. The male detective this time. "She wants you."

"Me?" the sisters chorused.

"No, *him*, the lawyer. We're going to allow it, although we don't have to. She says she has to speak to him before she signs the confession."

6:45 P.M.

Bambi was exhausted, but it was that weird kind of exhaustion that leaves one wired. Yet she was sad, too. Life was so horribly sad. Didn't anyone get what they wanted? She thought, hoped, her girls had. They had used her as an example, choosing men unlike Felix. Although Marc, Rachel's first husband, had been very much like Felix, too much like him. Worse, actually. Felix never would have done what Marc did. She wished Bert hadn't told her that. But Bert always told her everything he knew about her girls, even when he shouldn't.

"Bert," she said when he came through the door. "Remember the first time we met?"

Clearly not the opening he was expecting. "Of course I do."

"We had grown up in the same neighborhood, only a few blocks apart. Only a year apart at school, although it might as well be ten years when the girl is older. Then, at least. Rachel's Joshua is almost two years younger than she is. You were handsome, too. Yet I looked right through you. I only had eyes for Felix, as the song said."

"That wasn't the song, though. It was 'Hold Me, Thrill Me, Kiss Me, Bill Me.' The lawyers' anthem." Making a small joke, out of bravado.

"So you remember?"

"Well, you and Felix told the story so many times, it's hard to forget."

"You were always there. Always there."

"Yes, I've tried to be there for you and the girls."

"No, I mean before. We went everywhere together. Felix and Bambi, Bert and Lorraine. She's a good person, Felix. She really is. A good mother, a good wife."

"She is."

"And you were there when Felix met Julie, weren't you? You were with Tubby when he 'discovered' Julie, suggested he take her to the club. You knew Felix's type by then. He liked them long and leggy. You know, as a *contrast*. I was many things, but long and leggy isn't one of them."

"Bambi, I didn't condone what Felix did at all. Not at all. I'm not that kind of a guy."

"Really? You never cheated on Lorraine, not even once?"

"No."

"Not even in your head?"

He sighed. "Bambi, what is this about?"

"It's about alibis, Bert. Yours and mine. That was the word you used. *You have a perfect alibi.* I mean, I know it's a legal term, but it just struck me a little while ago. Yes, I did. And so did you. Rachel would have, too, if she could have borne to come to the beach that weekend, but she was moping. We all had such perfect alibis. You saw to that. The elaborate party for Lorraine—a surprise for her forty-first birthday, thrown after the actual date, pulled to-gether in just a matter of days. Because, you said, that's the only way to keep a surprise. I've never seen you do anything like it."

"Oh, I think it had more of a lead time than that."

"Not much. Certainly, the party was planned after Rachel had her grandstanding moment with Julie Saxony. She told me that she went to see her on June twenty-eighth. Of course, she also told me that Julie agreed to pay my debt and the police now tell me that was a lie, that my daughter got the funds from a source she refuses to disclose. Still, I believe the first part. She went to Julie, confronted her about the money. And Julie denied that she had taken it, refused to give it to her. Do you know where Rachel got it?"

Bert nodded but said nothing.

"Are you going to keep my children's confidences *now*? That would be a first. After all, you're the one who told me about Mi-chelle's problems, how we had an IRS agent all over us because he had noticed those things provided by her lover. You never figured out who he was, did you, Bert? Michelle didn't trust you that much. But I know. It was Marc. She had an affair with her sister's ex-husband. She told me, Bert. Me, because I'm her mother. You're a good friend, like family, but you're not Michelle's father."

A pause.

"No matter how much you wanted to be."

He put his hand on hers. How many times, over the years, had Bert touched her this way. A hand on her hand. A hand on her shoulder. Putting on her coat. Patting her back. Hugging her the day Julie's body was found. And how many times had she failed to see him. She had never seen him. That was the problem.

She moved her hand away. "She was supposed to go with him. That's why you got her the passport. Because you hoped she would go with him. The first time. When she didn't—well, I guess you kept the money to see if that would force me to rely on you. You knew I would come to you for help, and I did. But did you really think it would ever be more than that between us, that I would betray Lorraine that way?"

"It was moot," Bert said. "Lorraine became pregnant and—I couldn't. You wouldn't, I knew that. But I also couldn't figure out how to tell you what I had done."

"So you kept Felix's money. And used it, at least some of it, I'm guessing. I mean, you make a good living, but you always seemed to live awfully high to me. The endless renovations on the house in Garrison Forest, an oceanside house in Bethany—I guess my husband bought you that, didn't he? Okay, so you took my money, hoping I would fall in love with you, and you tried to get my husband to take his girlfriend with him, but that failed. Why kill her, Bert?"

"She began to figure it out. After Rachel went to see her. She knew there was money and she had given it to me. I managed to stall her. I told her that Felix made bad investments, that the money was never there. But she didn't believe me. And she cared,

cared terribly because she did believe that Felix had been in touch with you and you had slandered her. It was only a matter of time before she confronted you, told you that she had taken the suitcase to me as instructed, that I knew where he had stashed everything, all the off-shore accounts and safe-deposit boxes. So I called her July first, told her Felix wanted her, and told her where to go."

"And where did she go?"

"Saks Fifth Avenue. That part was always true. She met a man there, a man I knew from my work. She thought he was going to forge a passport for her. He took care of things. And that was that."

"Is that man still alive?"

"No. He died a few years ago. But he never spoke of it. I knew he wouldn't, even if he was arrested, even if he needed the leverage. He was honorable that way. And he knew I would help him out, if he got in trouble. But he never got in trouble."

"Honor among thieves," Bambi said. "As the old saying goes. So how far are you prepared to go, Bert? Are you ready to represent Rachel in a murder trial, knowing she's innocent? Or are you going to sit back and let me enter my confession? I know enough now. I can get it right, I think. I'll tell the cops that I hired the man who met Julie at Saks. After all, my husband was a criminal. I'll take your story and make it mine. All the pieces will fit now. Is that what you want?"

"No—never. What I wanted—" He could not finish.

"You wanted me. Probably because Felix had me. I wanted Felix. Julie wanted Felix. Tubby wanted Julie. Lorraine wanted you. I wonder—" She looked to the ceiling, saw the years, her husband's face, an image that never quite faded. "I wonder what Felix wanted. It would be nice if at least one of us got what we wanted in this world. At least our kids seem to have. There's some comfort in that."

Bert got up to leave. "I'll tell them," he said. "I won't let you do this. I can't. I'll tell them."

"Go home first," Bambi said. "Tell Lorraine. Tell her it was about the money, nothing else. Tell Lorraine, then call your children and tell them the same thing."

"Is that what you would have had Felix do?"

"Yes." She made a shooing motion with her hands. "Tell the detectives something, anything, to stall them. Tell the girls that everything is going to be okay, because it is. Go home, say goodbye to your wife. The woman who loves you and admires you so. Tell her how much you love her. And you would have loved her, Bert, if you hadn't been so very stupid. You would have seen this woman, right in front of you, who loved you, and you would have honored that."

Bert left. For the first time, Bambi noticed the chill in the room, the rankness of clothing worn on the second day. She was thirsty and hungry. Could she ask someone to bring her something? She probably could, yet it was too much of an effort. Of all the things she had learned today, one stood out: Felix had meant to provide for her. He never knew what Bert had done. Julie had not stolen from her—well, not her money, at any rate. Felix had never sent for Julie, but Rachel thought he had, and she had kept that from her mother for almost thirty years.

She saw herself at nineteen, the college dropout with the impossibly tiny waist, heard the Orioles sing, felt Felix's arms, firm but not too tight as he steered her around the ballroom. She tried to remember Bert's face, and she had a vague impression of noticing him that night, the younger, more conventionally handsome man. But, for her, it had been Felix, only Felix. Would things have been different if—

But things could always be different, *if.* It was more important to know what things were. She was a realist.

If only Bert had been one, too.

Never Let Me Go

December 8, 2012

S andy dressed with unusual care, selecting the tie that
Nancy Porter had given him and putting on his best suit.
He was going to meet with two ladies, after all, even if
neither appointment was exactly a date. He wouldn't mind if one
were—but, no, that wasn't to be. Get over it.

It had been a shock, seeing himself on the news earlier in the
year, during the hullabaloo over Bert Gelman's confession. He
had let Nancy take the lead, although the stat was his. At least
Sandy was pretty sure that the murder had taken place in the park.
Behind the old mill. According to Gelman, he had represented
someone who had office space there and was reasonably sure it
would be quiet on July 3. The guy was supposed to give Julie a big
cover story about meeting someone for forged documents before
continuing to the airport. After all, her passport was expired.
Killed her in the parking lot, then either carried her or drove her
across the stream. So that was why they hadn't found casings at
the scene. Just her bones and that sad, indestructible purse, holding a blank passport, a wallet, a lipstick, and an earring. Then the

killer drove back to the mall. Took her car, moved it to the Giant. Probably took the Metro back to his car, which was why Saks had been chosen as the meeting place. Nice and neat.

Sandy would never know what Bambi Brewer said to get Bert to confess, and he didn't much care. It was his case, his stat. He had brought her in, and the daughter. He had played them against each other, sure that one of them would give him a confession he could use, and Bambi had done that, indirectly. Sandy had found the sales slip, matched the description of the earring to the one in Julie's purse. Without those factors, Julie Saxony's death would still be unsolved. Bert's name, true to Sandy's credo, had been in the file.

What did bug him was how bad he looked on television. It wasn't the pounds that TV added, he wasn't that vain. But—was he really that rumpled? Had his once beautiful clothes aged that badly? Mary would be embarrassed. But now, with his consultant's contract almost up, he was going to be making more money, could afford to buy the good stuff again. He hoped.

His first stop was a row house in Butchers Hill. You had to look closely to know it was an office—very discreet sign by the door, with no hint of the business done within Keyes and Associates. He rang the bell, heard the tumblers turn. *Good girl,* he thought. *No unlocked door for you in this neighborhood, not even in the daytime.*

Eddie's girl—the kid had said wife, why did Sandy doubt him?—was as he remembered her from his onetime glimpse. Tall, broad-shouldered, more handsome than pretty, but with the kind of expressive face that grew on you. Firm handshake, clothes that looked nice, if kind of forgettable.

"So Crow said if I'm serious about expanding, I should talk to you," Tess Monaghan said, after bringing him into an office where a neon sign advertised HUMAN HAIR and a neon clock said it was TIME FOR A HAIRCUT. *Her* hair seemed normal enough, though.

"Do you really think you'll like PI work? It's a lot of document stuff, talking to people, sweating the details. Incredible boredom at times."

"Sounds like police work to me."

"Are you comfortable with a little gray area? I sometimes fudge things to get what I want. Is that going to be a problem for ex-po-po?"

She grinned, letting him know that *po-po* was ironic, that she was making fun of herself. He liked that.

"I'm not a police anymore. I work on a contract, no gun, no badge. I could do the same thing for you. Only for more money, I hope."

"Depending on the caseload, there should be more money in it. And the fact is, I need another equity partner. I have a young child, I can't do eighteen-hour days anymore." She smiled with only half her mouth. "What am I saying? I still do eighteen-hour days, I just don't do eighteen hours of PI work. It's hard, finding the balance."

He nodded, as if he knew. Mary had been Bobby's full-time caretaker until he went away. That's how it was, even with normal kids, back then. Sandy had loved his son. He just hadn't known what to do with him when all the little father-son dreams turned out to be beyond his reach. He wasn't going to teach him to play sports or drive a car or how to fix things. They weren't going to have father-son chats. Mary knew how to be Bobby's mother in spite of his limitations. But that was another thing that made Mary special. Maybe instead of thinking what a failure he was, he could just remember how great she was? Problem was, that just made him miss her even more.

He really needed this job. He needed something, anything, to keep him away from his own thoughts.

"I don't get a lot of cold cases here," Tess said. "It's dull, dull, dull most of the time."

"I could do dull. I like dull." He decided to try to make a joke, although it was not his forte. "I am dull."

She laughed. He felt as if he had just scored a goal in a soccer match, even if he hadn't played soccer since he was thirteen.

"Want to start after the holidays?" she asked.

"Christmas, you mean?"

"Why, yes. Christmas, New Year's. It's a slow time of year for me, but it picks up around Valentine's Day. That's a big holiday for this business, I'm sad to say."

"I just wanted to be clear because Hanukkah starts tomorrow."

"I hate to stereotype, but I didn't think that would be something on your radar."

"The next lady I'm going to see—she told me."

"Well, *Baruch atah Adonai*, Sandy."

"What?"

She laughed. "There's a Weinstein lurking under the Monaghan freckles."

That name rang a bell. "Like the jewelry store?"

"The same, although that's my uncle's business."

"This lady I'm going to see—she has a connection to it."

She shrugged. "In Baltimore, you'd be lucky to make it to six degrees of separation. Usually two, tops. Isn't that what brought you here?"

Sandy had not crossed Bambi Brewer's threshold since he searched it almost nine months earlier, and he was not sure how she would feel about his request to see her. He tried to tell himself it wasn't his fault. You couldn't close Julie Saxony's file without dredging up the Felix stuff. Even if he hadn't been connected, it would always be there, a part of Julie's identity. Four years of her life, 1972 to 1976. She had gone on to run a couple of successful businesses. Helped other people—gave the chef a chance to start his own restaurant, pried Susie out of the Variety. But when it came down to it, she was Felix Brewer's girl, and when her murder was solved, the newspaper ran the photo of her in her glory, the same one Sandy had found in the file. Juliet Romeo trumped Julie Saxony every time.

Then again, Julie threw everything away when she got the phone call. *Felix wants me? Screw the restaurant, screw Chet, screw my sister, screw Susie.* Given the choice, she would be Felix's girl.

When Bert had come to Sandy and Nancy with his own lawyer that night, Sandy had gotten angry. He was so sick of this shit. How many people were going to try to cover for Rachel Brewer, who had to be the killer, even if her name wasn't in the file? Opportunity, impulse, and stupidity—she had them all in spades. She and her mother had sat in their respective interview rooms late into the evening. When Bambi reneged on her promise to provide a confession, Sandy had shooed the other daughters away from Rachel, put her back in a room. He felt like a dad in that moment. *No supper for any of you until you stop lying.* Then Bert had returned with a criminal lawyer even better than himself, although Bert probably didn't concede there was a better criminal lawyer than himself. They wanted to bargain, right off, but the state's attorney wasn't having it. Ultimately, Gelman agreed to twenty years, no parole. He was a healthy man, but he was already seventy and prison life was hard. It was unlikely he would ever see the outside again.

And all for money. Your best friend blows town, you short-change his widow, then kill the one person who knows where the suitcase ended up. Didn't some people ever have enough?

Not that Bambi Brewer appeared to be hurting. Her apartment was in a high-rise called HarborView. When it was built, it had seemed ridiculous, this high-rise in low-slung South Baltimore, a sore thumb. A giant's sore thumb. Now there was a Ritz-

Carlton within spitting distance, a Four Seasons across the water. And the place must have views forever, across the harbor, into the mouth of the bay.

Bambi's apartment faced west, though. The view was rooftops and the big green hump of Federal Hill.

"Let's sit in the living room, Detective," she said, gracious in tone but without any of the offers of hospitality that would signal she wanted him to tarry. Ah, well. It was just a little crush. Not even he took it seriously. Plus, she had a few years on him. But what could he say? She was a good-looking woman.

The furniture was a little low for him, almost as if she wanted to make her guests struggle. She watched him ease his way into an armchair. "Felix refused to have furniture like this because he said it was uncomfortable. It's not, but it's hell getting in and out of it at our ages."

"I've lost fifteen pounds," he said. What was it about her that made you want to blurt things out? He wondered if she had unnerved Felix, too.

"How great, to go into the New Year with a jump on self-improvement. I'm afraid I might find those fifteen pounds before the year is up. Latkes for Hanukkah, then my daughter Michelle's husband insists on a traditional Christmas." She made a face. "My family wasn't religious, not at all—my daughter Linda is the only real Jew in the family—but I still don't like to see a tree. Plus, it's confusing for the grandchildren. What are they, those Iranian-Jewish-Scots with a Chinese first cousin?"

"Regular United Nations," he said, knowing it was weak. He never had the patter. And this woman, she liked talkers, he bet. Felix Brewer had been a big talker.

"Yes," she said. "And it's better, having a mix of things. I assume you come from mixed stock, too?"

Why would she assume that? Oh, she was a typical *norteameri-cano*, had no idea how many blond Cubans there were.

"No, straight-up Cuban. It's not uncommon—the blond hair, the light eyes."

"Is that why they call you Sandy?"

"No. I didn't get that nickname until I was a young detective." He couldn't stop, he was that unnerved by her. "It was a practical joke. You see—I bought myself a briefcase. I don't know why. I was just so excited, when I made detective. And I would carry this briefcase to and from work every day. I saw right away that it was stupid, but I was proud, I didn't want to back down. I used it to carry my lunch, a thermos of coffee. But it had all these pockets, pockets I never opened. And yet, every day, it got heavier and heavier. Just a little bit. Turns out some guy was putting sand in the pockets I didn't use. Figured it out when I turned it upside down one day. So—*Sandy*. With everyone but my wife, who called me Roberto."

"I don't like practical jokes."

"Me, either."

An awkward silence, an unfortunate segue, but there was nothing to be done.

"So when we searched your house, back in March. The shoe-box."

"Yes, that was returned to me a while back. This time, I shredded the contents and put the box in a recycling bin." A little sigh. "I miss Bendel's. My son-in-law takes good care of me, but I can't go that deep into his pockets. You know, even if there was any money left over, from what Bert took, I wouldn't be allowed to have it. The federal government wants it for back taxes. But there's not enough money left to make a difference. Or so Bert says."

"Something was missing. From your box."

"Oh, I know. Do you think I would have shredded the contents without going through it? I'm well aware what was missing, Detective."

He handed the envelope to her.

"How did he get it to you?" he asked.

"No idea."

"I'm not going to be a cop anymore. I'm not a cop. I've just come from a job interview, in fact. I think I'm going to be a private investigator."

"Sandy Sanchez, PI. You'll need a fedora."

She wasn't going to tell him how she had gotten the letter. Why should she? It was idle curiosity on his part. Besides, Sandy Sanchez's questions hadn't been particularly good for Bambi Brewer's family. Or maybe they had. He couldn't tell, and she wasn't sharing. She probably assumed he had read it. He had. Read it and put it aside, in the file, but without tagging it as evidence. It wasn't evidence. But it was a peephole onto one of the city's most famous mysteries, and he couldn't help reading. He was only human.

"Well, then," he said, standing to go. "Happy Hanukkah. Do you say 'Happy Hanukkah'?"

"Sure," Bambi said. "Why not?"

Bambi watched the sun set from her living room, another reason she preferred this side to the harbor view. Not that she had a choice when Hamish gave it to her. Beggars can't be choosers. And Bambi knew from beggars. She had been one most of her adult life.

It was getting close to the winter solstice, the shortest day of the year. She never got over how quickly the sun went down, as if late for an appointment on the other side of the world. There was a red disc, then ribbons of orange and, bam, darkness. Still, there was enough light from the city around her to read the letter she knew almost by heart. It had been written on tissuey Airmail stationery. She never knew how he had gotten it to Tubby, and she had certainly never asked.

April 5, 1986
Dear Bambi,

This letter will get to you long after this date, but I am writing it on Michelle's 13th birthday. I know you will see that she has a blowout of a bat mitzvah, with all the trimmings. I wish I could be there. I wish I could tell you where I am, but all I can say is that it's warm and the ocean is nearby, yet I never swim.

I miss you every day. Every hour. Every minute. But at least I have a sense of you. The girls—who are they? How did they turn out? Beautiful, of course, because you are beautiful. But are they nice young women, Rachel and Linda? Do they have steady men? Are they good people, good earners? What is Michelle like as a teenager?

I ran away because I thought I couldn't live in prison. But these rooms, while unlocked, are prisons, too. I have tried to figure out a way to come back, but it can never be.

I'm sorry for the pain I caused. It was wrong. I don't know how to explain it. Perhaps there are no explanations for doing the wrong thing. At any rate, I'm not going to try. I hurt you. But you hurt me, too, by making it seem as if you didn't really need me. There I go again, trying to find an explanation.

You and our daughters were my greatest happiness. And the single best day, best moment of my life was in February 1959 when Bert and Tubby said we should crash that stupid high school dance.

I hope you have been judicious with what I gave you. It should last a long time, but if you ever run into any difficulties, trust Bert.

With love, forever and ever,
Felix

The letter may have been written in April, but it had not arrived until August of that year. There had been a strange comfort, knowing he was alone, but she still had to live with the torment of believing he had sent for Julie, because why else would she have given Rachel all that money and disappeared? Poor Rachel, incapable of asking for a single dime for herself, yet humbling herself before her mother-in-law to bail out her own mother. Bambi had never doubted that leaving Marc was the right thing for Rachel; Joshua was the far better man. That had been evident long before Bambi had learned of Marc's affair with Michelle.

She had told Michelle in no uncertain terms to keep the secret. She did not doubt that Rachel would forgive her sister, but it was too much to ask. And Bambi was an expert at knowing what was too much to ask.

She had kept this letter, surrounded by what she thought were boring receipts, of interest to no one, allowing herself to read it no more than once or twice a year, puzzling over its one clue, the nearby ocean in which he never swam. Mexico, apparently, according to Rachel. But then, that had been what Bert told Julie Saxony. Who knew what was true anymore. Interestingly, of all her daughters, it was Michelle, who knew the least, who had tried hardest to find her father. That was why she had gravitated to the tech industry in the first place, she had confided. But there was no search engine that could find Felix.

No matter how many times she read the letter, Bambi always got stuck on the line about the happiest moment of his life, more than fifty years ago. How sad. It had been a great moment for Bambi, too, but she had had many happy moments since then. Seven grandchildren, the girls' marriages. Seder dinners, birthdays. She was happy right now, alone in her apartment.

She checked her watch. Time to pick up Lorraine. Bambi tried to see her as often as possible, to include her in family gatherings. Remembering how she had seethed under Lorraine's pitying gaze over the years, she did not coddle her old friend or give any indication that she found her pitiable. And, in fact, she didn't. It wasn't pitiable to love someone who didn't love you, or to love someone who didn't love you in the way you chose, or to love someone more than he loved you. One could even argue that it was brave and pure. Besides, Lorraine didn't know that Bert had acted out of anything but greed. Tonight, Bambi and Lorraine would drive to Linda's for Friday night dinner, the youngest grandchildren already humming in excitement for the holidays. For the first time in a long time all the grandchildren would be there, from little Tatiana to twenty-six-year-old Noah and his wife, Amanda, who happened to be pregnant with Bambi Brewer's first great-grandchild.

Life went on, with you or without you, Felix. What else could it do?

December 31, 2012

Manzanillo

The last thing he saw was the ceiling, an expanse of white. He opened his eyes, looked at the ceiling, then closed them and never opened them again. If he said anything, there was no one there to hear it. The maid found him the next morning.

Señor Felipe, as he was known among the small circle of people he had befriended here, was seventy-eight and he had enjoyed robust good health until the past year. There was no single big thing wrong with him, just many little things. But the little things added up and the local health care was not the best. He liked to joke that he had not chosen this place for its health-care system. He had expected to live a very long time. His own parents had lived into their nineties, although he never saw them. They had harbored different hopes for their son, the one who understood numbers as if they were a language, yet also was sensitive to people, capable of eliciting their confidences, their dreams. Once his parents saw the path he had chosen, they no longer spoke to him. It was easier to pretend they were dead than to tell his wife that he had been disowned. He was a self-made man and he would make his own family, a better one.

He did, too. He had lived long enough to see his daughters grow into beautiful and accomplished women, to make mistakes and learn from them, to have children. Except—he had never seen any of those things.

He saw an expanse of white. A ceiling.

The maid was not disturbed by death. She had seen a lot of death. But she was upset when his only real friend, an *abogado,* a lawyer, told her that the body would be cremated. That was what her jefe wanted, the abogado said, but that did not sound right to her. They had talked often about religion, she and the jefe, and Señor Felipe had said he was *un judio,* that his people did not believe in tattoos or cremation. But then—perhaps he was no longer one of his people. There was no evidence of religion in his life, unless women were a kind of a religion. For years, they had come and gone. He preferred European women, for some reason, as long as they spoke English. European, but never from Germany. With most of the wealthy Americanos around here, the women got younger and younger as the men got older, but her jefe liked women in their forties and fifties. True, those women were young enough to be his daughters now, but she liked the fact that he seemed to choose for brains as well as beauty. Plus, he made it clear that they could stay under his roof, but Consuelo ran the house.

The abogado was firm: The body would be cremated, the ashes taken out to sea and flung into the Pacific, which could be glimpsed through this bedroom window. The house would be sold and there would be sums, nice ones, for people such as herself, who had cared for Señor Felipe all these years. Furniture would be sold, everything else was to be given away. If she wanted something, she should ask for it.

"Y las fotografías?" She indicated the set by the bed in heavy

silver frames. But not like the frames the turistas bought, in the Mercado. These were smooth and heavy.

He shrugged. "If you want," he said, mistaking her intent. It occurred to her that he would throw the photos away, which seemed sad to her. So she said she did, and, when he was gone, she slid the photos from the frames, which she would sell. She would give the photographs to the man who came to collect the body, ask that they be burned with el jefe.

There were six. She knew them well, after years of dusting them. One was of a beautiful woman, but very long ago, at a time when waists were cinched and eyebrows dark, arched. *Bambi, 1961,* was written on the back. The same woman, older but still beautiful, posed with three children, clearly her daughters. *Harpers Ferry, 1974.* There was one of each daughter, too. *Linda, 1976. Rachel, 1976. Michelle, 1976.* Pretty, but not as pretty as the mother, although who knows how they turned out, especially the littlest one, still chubby cheeked here.

And then there was the—well, she did not want to say she was a *puta,* but she wore little more than bra and panties and she leaned forward, blowing a kiss. Consuelo did not approve of her. But she was there, on his bedside. Maybe she was a cousin who had made bad decisions. Lord knows, Consuelo had her share of those. Cousins and bad decisions. She put that photograph with the others, too. There was no name or date on this one, just an inscription, beyond Consuelo's limited English, although some words were clearly close to the Spanish versions: *intelligence, ideas, function.* She put all the photographs in the envelope and wrote a note, saying they were to go with the body. They would be a family again, she thought, which helped her accept the ugly fact of the cremation. They would all be together again, in the ashes, in the ocean, in the afterlife.

But Consuelo was wrong. Felix Brewer was alone when he died and he would be alone forever, whether in eternity or the

Pacific, where five days later his ashes were distributed by an agreeable fisherman heading out for a day's work. The fisherman did not make a ceremony out of it, just tipped the container in one swift movement. The dark beige ashes drifted and then sank, mingling with the sand they so closely resembled.

He was gone.

Author's Note

Almost every writer I know dreads the moment when someone tries to give you an idea. It's not that the ideas are bad, just that the relationship between writer and novel is so personal that it's a little like someone trying to play matchmaker for a happily married person.

But my husband, David Simon, was adamant that I should write a novel inspired by Julius Salsbury, the head of a large gambling operation in Baltimore into the 1970s. Convicted of mail fraud and under house arrest while he appealed his sentence, he disappeared never to be seen again. He left behind a wife, three daughters, and a girlfriend.

I think my husband, who is still a journalist at heart, thought a crime writer could solve the mystery of what happened to Salsbury. But I am not particularly interested in real stories. I found myself fascinated by the idea of the five women left behind. What is a wife without her husband, daughters without a father, a mistress without her lover? I turned it into a crime story because that's what I do, but it's important to stress here that there was no murder case in real life. So beyond the setup, the Brewer family has nothing to do with the Salsbury family. It would be unfair to them to infer otherwise—and also unfair to my imagination.

The character of Roberto "Sandy" Sanchez was inspired by Donald Worden. Their personal histories could not be more dissimilar, but Worden is one of the great geniuses of homicide detection and he did return, for a time, to work cold cases for the Baltimore City Police Department. He was generous with his time and information while I worked on this book.

A chance meeting in San Francisco in August 2012 provided me with a lot of information about the social hierarchy at Forest Park High School in the 1950s. Alas, I lost my informant's name, but she was wonderfully helpful.

I would hope that everyone at William Morrow and Harper-Collins knows of my devotion, but just in case—thank you to Carrie Feron, Liate Stehlik, Michael Morrison, Lynn Grady, Sharyn Rosenblum, Tessa Woodward, and, well, everybody. I'd also like to welcome Nicole Fischer and Abigail Tyson to the fold.

Thanks also to Vicky Bijur and A. M. Chaplin. A shout-out to the baristas who keep me caffeinated in two cities, and all my family and friends who are extraordinarily tolerant of the things I don't get done while on deadline. Sara Kiehne and Dana Rashidi do what they can to take the dysfunction out of our household. David, Ethan, and Georgia Rae are responsible for putting the fun in and they all do a great job. Georgia Rae is increasingly tolerant of her mother's work now that she understands the age-old concept: work = money = candy.

Finally, thanks to the FLs of FB. You know who you are. You know what you did. Please keep a leash on those dang squirrels and stop being such instigators.

ff

And When She Was Good

A suburban mother.
A secret life.

Heloise: single mum, runs her own business, avoids attention, keeps her private life to herself

But Heloise's life is also a precarious one – because her business is one that takes place in discreet hotel rooms and, for the right money, she could be the woman of your dreams.

Now her carefully constructed world is under threat – her once-oblivious accountant is asking loaded questions; her long-time protector is hinting at new, mysterious dangers; and, in the next county over, another so-called suburban madam has been found dead in her car.

With nothing quite as it seems, Heloise faces a midlife crisis which threatens the safety of both her and her son.

'When the barrier between Heloise's two lives starts to crumble, the results are mesmerizing. Lippman writes with clarity and power.'
Stephen King

'Exquisite as fine jewellery.' **Lee Child**

Now available in paperback and ebook